Metamorph

Metamorph

by

Stephen M. DeBock

❈ ❈ ❈ ❈

Gypsy Shadow Publishing

Metamorph
by
Stephen M. DeBock

Gypsy Shadow Publishing, LLC.
Lockhart, TX
www.gypsyshadow.com

Library of Congress Control Number: 2014938611

eBook ISBN: 978-1-61950-211-6
Print ISBN: 978-1-61950-219-2

Published in the United States of America

First eBook Edition: April 15, 2014
First Print Edition: April 25, 2014

For John and Ann Elliott

Chapter One
Friday, January 23, 2009
Hyattsville, Maryland

Suri Clarke shivered in the darkness as she carried her shopping bag from the mall to her car. Bitter cold as it was, and with lots of parking spaces since the Christmas exchanges had tapered off, she still parked as far away from the entrance as she could. Her Weight Watchers leader had stressed *walking is good exercise, and you should get as much walking in as you can every day. Keep moving,* she'd said. Suri even wore a pedometer to keep track of her steps.

And the regimen was working. She had lost ten pounds in twelve weeks, and the increasing amount of give in her clothes was a real motivator. Larry had already commented on how good she looked; as for the kids, well . . . even if she grew another head they probably wouldn't notice.

One Friday evening a month, Suri drove in to Hyattsville from Olney to shop. Not that there weren't a plethora of shops mushrooming there, but as a Silver Spring native and a former nurse at Washington Adventist Hospital in Takoma Park, she enjoyed revisiting her old haunts—though, truth to tell, they were barely recognizable anymore. What were once Washington, D.C. suburbs were now cities in their own right. Larry had been smart, she reminded herself, to relocate the family while the Montgomery County landscape was as yet unsullied by condos and cookie cutter communities.

The shopping center is showing its age, she thought, as the headlights from the few remaining hard-core shoppers carved through the darkness, leaving the lot virtually deserted. She knew where her own car was, at the end of this row, empty now except for the oversized van blocking her view of it.

She stopped. *Oh shit,* she thought, *pardon my French. Alone, dark parking lot, strange vehicle . . . no way, José, you're going to do that.*

Suri walked back to the mall. From behind the glass double doors, she could see lights being extinguished, but the entry hall remained lit. When she arrived, she saw a middle-aged man inside, approaching with a key. With her free hand, she waved, and he opened the door.

"Help you?" he asked. The man wore dark blue slacks and a lighter blue long-sleeved shirt, creases ironed in police style. A utility belt supported a pouch of some kind, probably a first aid kit, and a flashlight.

"I'm sorry to bother you," Suri said, "but I wonder if I might ask you to walk me to my car?"

"No problem at all," he replied and stepped out into the cold.

"Shouldn't you get your coat? It's freezing out here," she said, the cloud of her breath punctuating her point.

"Real men don't feel the cold," he joked. "Besides, the jacket's in my office, and that's way inside the mall. This won't take long. Where's your car?"

She pointed. "On the other side of that white van. It wasn't there when I parked."

They began walking. "That's one of those Sprinters," the security cop observed. "So tall you can stand up inside it." He took his flashlight from his belt as they approached, and when they arrived, he shone his light into the passenger's side window, opposite Suri's own car in the space beside it. "Looks empty," he said. "Can't see farther back, there's a curtain behind the driver's seat, and no windows on the side. Back door doesn't have glass in it either." He tried the doors and found them locked. Next he turned his light onto Suri's sedan. "It looks like a commercial van, lots of them around these days. Probably parked here for the night."

"Does that happen?" Suri asked as she pressed the remote twice. With a blink of the parking lights, her doors unlocked.

"Sometimes you'll see an empty car parked here. Like when two folks happen to meet inside the mall and decide to go out for a drink together."

She nodded. "Okay, then." Turning toward the guard, she thanked him and told him to get back inside where it's warm.

"Happy to help," he said as he walked hurriedly back toward the building.

Nice guy, she thought as she opened the rear door and dumped her packages on the seat. Probably retired police or military, picking up some extra bucks . . .

Something clicked behind her, as if a door were being unlocked.

Suri spun around as she saw the side door slide open. A black-clad man leaped out and pushed her against her car, one hand pressed hard against her mouth. A second man followed him and yanked her pocketbook from her shoulder. Then a third man stepped casually from the van. This one carried a pistol.

"Not a word," the gunman said, his voice deep and gravelly. "Or you die here and now."

"Oh God, no," she whispered, and he pressed the pistol to her forehead.

"I said no talking. Do you understand what that means?"

She nodded, hardly daring to move, and he withdrew the pistol but moved its muzzle against her chin, pointing up. He nodded toward the van. "Get in."

Once inside, Suri whispered, "Please, no. Please don't hurt me. I have two sons at home."

One of the other men, silent until now, spoke. "She thinks we're going to rape her. Relax. Not gonna happen."

The third slid the door closed. The weak dome light showed them all dressed in dark clothing, two in insulated jackets, their leader in a black wool overcoat that reeked of cigarette smoke. All of them looked to be somewhere in their forties. Not kids, then. Professionals.

The leader emptied Suri's purse onto the floor. The second man, the one who had pinned her to the car, produced a felt tipped pen and a notebook and handed it to her. "Listen to me, and you won't get hurt," the man in the overcoat said as he removed the cash and cards from her wallet. "I want you to write the PIN for your ATM card." She began to scribble, her hand shaking. "And your social security number. And your email address and password."

Incongruously, she thought: *Not only are they stealing my money, they're stealing my identity, too. My God, why didn't we subscribe to LifeLock?* She finished writing and handed the notebook to the man who'd given it to her.

The leader, still holding her wallet, looked at her driver's license. "Suri," he said, leaning forward so his hawk-billed nose nearly touched hers. "You and I are going to get out of the van, and you are going to climb into your trunk. Tell me you intend to comply." She nodded. "Good. I will be training this pistol on you the whole time. It's a Smith and Wesson Bodyguard 380, which probably means nothing to you, but in a nutshell, it's a semiautomatic with a magazine of six rounds, plus the one already in the chamber. If you attempt something I don't like, I will press the gun into your coat and fire all seven rounds into your body. The fabric of your coat will muffle the sound of the shots. Please understand I mean what I say."

She nodded again. Her mouth was dry; she'd been breathing through it. Her throat was frigid. She wondered if her legs still even worked. What if she stumbled getting out of the van? Would he shoot her if she fell down?

"Once you are in the trunk," the leader said, "my friend here will place a wad of cloth inside your mouth to prevent you from calling for help. Then he will run a length of duct tape across it and around your head. After that, we will take a little drive. If you do exactly as I say, no harm will come to you. Now get out of the van and open your trunk."

Miraculously, Suri's legs held up. She unlocked the trunk and climbed inside. The second man shoved the gag into her mouth and wrapped it in place with duct tape. *Please let me live,* she thought, eyes wide and watery, the tears beginning to crystallize in the cold. She blinked furiously. The man told her to turn over. When she complied, he used a cable tie to link her wrists. Then he had her turn over again, onto her back. When he was satisfied, he backed away, leaving room for their leader. The two accomplices stood just behind him, as if they were a pair of male OR nurses observing over their surgeon's shoulder. The third man smiled and leaned forward, his face nearing her own.

What is this, she thought. *Something isn't right.* She had cooperated, done exactly as commanded, and they had promised she would be unharmed. She saw the glint in the man's eyes, reflecting the dim illumination of the trunk light. He opened his mouth, and she felt a drop of drool on her neck.

Suri's eyes nearly bugged out of her head as the leader's mouth opened wider, his lower jaw extending farther than a human jaw could possibly drop. A pair of needle-sharp fangs swung down from his upper palate, like those of a rattlesnake. She began shaking violently, twisting her head from side to side, struggling with the cable tie that bound her wrists. She screamed, but only a trace mewling escaped around the gag and through the tape. The two acolytes bent down and held her firmly as he lowered his mouth to the side of her neck and pierced it with his fangs.

It didn't hurt as much as she'd thought it would. It occurred to the nurse in her, irrationally in light of her impending death, that there might be a topical anesthetic in the man's saliva. He withdrew his mouth to allow the fangs to pivot back and his jaw to return to normal. He lowered his lips to the raw punctures in her neck.

Suri knew there was no point in struggling further, and she closed her eyes and folded her fingers together behind her back, as if in prayer. She felt the blood being sucked from her, as if by an aspirator, heard the repeated gulps of the man's greedy swallowing, experienced the lethargy of her body's ebbing vitality.

When the leader had drunk his fill, he applied a strip of duct tape over the wounds. The woman was undoubtedly dead, but he was nothing if not careful, and from inside his coat he drew an instrument that looked like an obscenely elongated icepick, inserted it into her nostril, and drove the point into her brain. He withdrew the pick and applied more tape over her nostrils. No coppery scent of blood would reveal the body in the trunk.

"Nice job," said one of the man's companions, and the other agreed. He didn't bother acknowledging them as he stood. His thoughts were of Suri's family, now bereft of their beloved wife and mother. He smiled. They would find themselves even worse off than she. After all, death is final; suffering lasts forever.

It felt good to be active again, and autonomous for the first time, after almost fifteen years of anonymity. This operation, a minor opening gambit, would conclude tomorrow, and then he would leave for home. Winter break was almost over, and he needed to be back by Sunday night at the latest.

Early next morning, the vampire rose—sunlight was never an issue: another silly campfire tale—and using liquid latex and spirit gum applied a mustache and beard, carefully made in advance out of crepe hair. Satisfied with his appearance, he dressed in a white shirt, narrow black tie, and black suit, topping the outfit off with a wide-brimmed black hat, with drooping ringlets sewn just inside the band. He awoke his companions and told them it was time.

A half hour later, he drove Suri's sedan, with her body still inside the trunk—along with a considerable amount of C4—into a shopping center off University Boulevard, across from where he'd picked her up last night. The frigid overnight temperatures ensured that bodily decay, and the stink that accompanied it, would be a non-issue. He'd stopped at a gas station on the way and filled up the tank, paying cash. Then he drove to an ATM kiosk and verified the balance on Suri's account. It wasn't that much. Perhaps her husband didn't trust her with their joint account and set up this one just for her. He withdrew two hundred dollars, leaving fifty in the account so as not to raise any red flags. He knew her husband couldn't file a missing person report until she had been gone a full day, and by the time the police tracked down the transaction, he'd be hundreds of miles away.

The counter man at the Pep Boys auto service center, a small, round Italian whose name patch read VINNIE, was clearly uninterested in cheerful customer service. "C'n I do for ya?" he mumbled, clearly put off by his customer's attire.

He said, "I'd like an oil change and a tire rotation, please."

Vinnie wrote out the work order. The man gave him a false name and Suri's address and her mobile number, which he'd memorized this morning. "Anythin' else?"

"No, thank you, that will be all."

"Be waitin', or should I call when it's done? Busy today, Sa'days always are."

The customer drew a twenty-dollar bill from his pocket and slid it across the counter along with Suri's keys. "If you can expedite my service, I'd very much appreciate it."

Vinnie looked at him from beneath eyelids so thick they could offer shade. "You just moved to the head of the line," he said as he pocketed the twenty.

The man smiled. "Say, ready in about an hour? I plan to do some window shopping in the meantime."

Vinnie glanced at the work order. "You got it, Mr. . . . Levine." He picked up the phone and buzzed the garage. When he hung up, he said, "I'm gonna use this new twenty I, uh, found to buy myself a cup of coffee and some breakfast at the deli over there. I can't tolerate the slop we have here for the customers."

"You do that. Good day, Vinnie. Enjoy your coffee."

Mr. Levine walked across the center's parking lot to where a white Sprinter waited with the engine running. He opened the door and welcomed the heat. "Wait," he said to the driver. "I want to see it go into the garage." The second man, sitting in a jump seat, grinned. All three scanned the building through the passenger's window and waited.

"Okay," said Levine as the mechanic, a skinny black man, climbed into Suri's car and drove it inside the building. He reached into the glove compartment and pushed a button on a small black box. A digital clock began a countdown. "Fifteen minutes. On to Takoma Park."

The driver took him to the library on Philadelphia Avenue, where Levine exited alone and walked inside, his expression one of purpose. He took off his overcoat but left his hat on, as he sat at a public computer. Google took him to the Pep Boys Headquarters site. He clicked on the Contact Us link, and a screen came up asking for the usual particulars. He signed on using Suri's name, address, and email address. He clicked the store locator and specified the one in Hyattsville, Maryland. Below it was a choice bar marked "Category that best describes the reason for your concern." He clicked on "Attitude/Respect." It was as good as any.

Then, in the message blank, he typed ALLAHU AKBAR.

The explosion, distant though it was, shook the library. Everyone inside flew to the doors as Levine pressed the Submit button, deciding that he very much liked that word, *submit.*

Then he cleared the machine's history, put on his coat, and joined the other gawkers as they watched the black smoke's plume roil into the sky. He stood with them until they began to disperse. Then he climbed into the panel truck and nodded to the driver, who smiled back.

"Take me to my car, please," he said. "I've a long drive ahead of me today." As they drove, he ripped off the crepe hair and took off his hat with the ringlets attached and tossed them into the back. His own hair was dark and cut short, with just a touch of gray at the temples. The white shirt and black tie joined them in the back. He reached into a travel bag and pulled out an insulated undershirt, a cable-knit sweater, and a ski jacket with lift tickets attached to the zipper pull. A stocking cap was last, but he didn't put it on. He nodded toward the discarded disguise and then to the man in the jump seat. "Make sure you burn them," he said.

"Will do, boss."

The driver parked outside his small house off Piney Branch Road, and the three stood outside the Sprinter as they made their farewells. Levine tossed his travel bag into the back of his all-wheel-drive SUV sporting New Hampshire plates, and slid in behind the wheel. He started the engine and turned on the heater. "You did well, gentlemen," he said, lowering the window.

The van's driver put his hands on the sill and lowered his head to peer inside. "Boss, about your promise . . ."

The vampire smiled. "Ahmed, I always make good on my promises. I will sire you and Jawdan after we have completed our next project."

"Which is?"

"Ah, all I can tell you now is that it will be during the summer. Now Jawdan, I know summer is your busiest time, and you will not be able to join us. But your expertise will be much needed, and much in evidence."

Ahmed remarked that they weren't getting any younger.

"Gentlemen," Levine said as if placating children, "you are both in your forties, as I was when I was turned. I have found this to be the ideal age. Women are attracted to men in their forties. They see them as mature, experienced, and still virile."

"So why can't you turn us here and now?" asked Jawdan.

"Forgive me," said Levine. "I know it seems cruel. But you have to understand, we've not seen each other since we went to ground in 1995. I believe in your loyalty, but I must be absolutely certain of it before I commit myself to siring you. An American president once said to trust but verify. That's what I'm doing. One more operation, I promise, and you will join me in the blood." Before the other could respond, he changed the subject. "Thank you for providing the explosives and the detonator." He held up the pistol. "And for the toy. Which I think I'll hang onto for awhile."

"It's not what we're used to," observed Ahmed.

"True. The charge isn't strong enough to do anything but sting one of our soldiers."

"But it is concealable."

"Easily, yes. Doesn't even make a bulge in one's pocket."

Jawdan added, "And just seeing a pistol, even a baby like this, is enough to make an American gun control pussy piss his pants."

Their leader put the gun back in the pocket of his ski jacket. He nodded to the men. "Again, you have done well. Continue to keep a low profile, and I'll be in touch soon. Good day, gentlemen."

The two men watched him leave. Neither was satisfied with his answer about having to wait, but what choice did they have, other than to comply? He had been a brilliant commander in the past, and his reputation for rewarding the faithful—while punishing the disloyal—was carved in stone. They could understand and appreciate his concern. And they were eager to reestablish his faith in them, eager to collect their reward. He'd promised it would come soon. They could wait a little longer. And after he sired them, time would no longer be an issue. Ever.

As *Mr. Levine*—a.k.a. Muhammad Al-Jubeir—picked up the Interstate heading north, he lit a cigarette and smiled, while he contemplated the next project and the roles his subordinates would play. The project was not something he could undertake alone, but after that . . .

Idiots, even useful ones like these, did not deserve im-mortality. In fact, they might not even deserve to live out the span of their natural lives.

Chapter Two

Everything about Camp David, the President's retreat located some seventy miles northwest of Washington in the Catoctin Mountains, is classified Top Secret. It occupies the center of a no-fly zone, designated P-40 on every aviation chart, and every pilot, whether private or commercial, whether behind the stick of a puddle jumper or the yoke of a 747, knows to steer clear—unless he wants a fighter jet escort to the nearest airport, and grief beyond imagining after he lands. The camp is officially classified as a Navy base, an Army communications facility, and a Marine training center. This is the truth. It is not the whole truth.

Since the mid-1990s, Camp David—officially Naval Support Facility Thurmont, but unofficially referred to by permanent personnel as the Hill—was home to a small team of covert operatives assigned to investigate anomalies that might threaten national security. They worked independently of domestic and international intelligence and law enforcement agencies, but had credentials that allowed access to and cooperation from all of them. They reported to the base CO, Commander Lauren Bachmann, who served as their liaison to her handler in Washington, who reported to others higher up, who in turn reported to the Commander in Chief.

One of the team members, Joe Whitehead, was a civilian forensics specialist who once served in the Navy under Bachmann. Another, Matthew Collins, an English émigré, was a full time dye chemist who worked part time with the unit as an analyst, as well as being a photographer, videographer, and computer nerd. In addition, he lived aboard a boat.

The other two, Dale Keegan and his wife Claire Delaney Keegan, were metamorphs—werewolves—who had drunk a vampire's blood and become hybridized. There had been one other like them, but she was no longer listed among the living. In fact, Dale and Claire had killed her. The others in the team, knowing what they were, were grateful that the couple had sided with the good guys.

First thing in the morning two days after Suri Clarke's murder, the team met in Commander Bachmann's cottage. Over mugs of steaming tea, they gathered to discuss their future. "Out with the old, in with the new," said Lauren, referring to the recent inauguration. "The new POTUS, FYI, has picked Renegade as his Secret Service handle. He's in office less than a week and doesn't know our unit even exists." She sipped her tea. "Truth is, he doesn't have the need to know just yet. And I hope he won't have the need for awhile." Lauren looked at the newest member of the team. "On another topic: Claire, are congratulations in order?"

By answer, her husband pulled a piece of colored cloth from his back pocket. "Earned her ticket yesterday," he said proudly, as he held up a sheared shirttail with her name and date lettered on it in Sharpie. "Ready for posting on the bulletin board."

Matthew and Joe applauded as Claire blushed. Lauren, whose dress uniform sported the wings of a naval aviator, reached over and shook her hand. "Good show, top gun."

"Yeah, right," laughed Claire. "A Cessna 172 doesn't exactly qualify me for the Blue Angels."

"No, but it does mean that we have two pilots qualified to drive our government-issue puddle jumper. Redundancy isn't a bad thing."

Dale said, "You can say that again," and Claire, who had been employed as a book editor when they met, shot him a look. She wasn't fond of puns . . . unless they came from her.

Lauren put her mug on the coffee table and leaned back in her chair. "Well, as you're all aware, while Sky King and Penny were aviating yesterday the Pep Boys store in Hyattsville was blown up. Not for publication, but at the moment of detonation the company's HQ received an email from the library in Takoma Park. It read, 'Allahu Akbar.'"

"Not a good thing," said Matthew in characteristic British understatement. "Is any group claiming responsibility?"

"No. But we're waiting. Meanwhile, Messrs. Collins and Whitehead, you guys up for a drive to Hyattsville tomorrow?"

Matthew said, "Afraid I've got to get back to Jersey to-night. Tomorrow's blue Monday, you know."

"I hope that wasn't a pun," Claire said, frowning exaggeratedly.

"Don't bite my head off, now, woman."

"I could, you know."

"Don't remind me. I still wake up screaming."

Joe asked when Matthew would decide to join the team full time.

"Well, the natives are getting restless in dear old Ocean County, New Jersey. The dye plant might shut down sooner rather than later."

Lauren shook her head. "*Blue* Monday. Just got it."

"And this woman is our fearless leader," chided Dale.

"Which means you can be the one to join Joe at the blast site," she said.

"I'll go," Claire added. Lauren and Dale both shook their heads. "Come on, I want to do something besides train, train, train."

Lauren said, "Claire, all due respect, you'd stand out like a rose among thorns. Our team benefits from being invisible. Or at least inconspicuous."

"Don't hate me because I'm beautiful." She feigned a pout. "So what am I supposed to do while these guys are on a field trip?"

Dale said, "You might want to take a few days and visit Rowena in Boston."

Claire was about to say something and then stopped. She looked at Lauren, who nodded. "That's great. All right then. Um, can I have the keys to the company plane, Daddy?"

Dale shook his head. "Nope."

"Why not?"

"You don't want to be like the kid who just got his driver's license and wants to show off to his buddies. Besides, the Northeast corridor is one of the busiest in the country. And I'd hate to see you try to navigate your way into Logan."

"Couldn't hurt to ask."

Lauren affirmed Dale's stance. "You want to fly into general aviation airports anyway, if only to keep a low profile."

Matthew said, "Why don't you follow me in the Goose after noon chow? You can sleep over and go on from Jersey tomorrow."

Claire nodded. "Done. I'll call Ro now."

"Just promise me you won't howl at the moon tonight."

Winter in Boston can be brutal. When the wind whips off the bay, the snow drives into one's face like icy needles; the sidewalks are more like skating rinks; and the only people outside seem to be the all-suffering beat cops. From her office window at Jones Publishing, managing editor Rowena Parr looked down at one of those cops, leaning forward just to keep his balance against the wind. She shook her head for him and then turned to the manuscript on her desk.

She didn't like it. No, she hated it. She wanted to wash her hands after touching the pages. But that wasn't the point, was it?

Was it well written? Yes. Was it topical? Yes. Could it be a best seller? Possibly, and the money wouldn't hurt the company's bottom line. But it reeked of chauvinism, anti-Semitism, and class warfare. Chauvin, Hitler, and Marx, all rolled into one author. One of Rowena's junior editors had forwarded it to her, with reservations. Its working title said it all: *Diatribe*. It read like *Mein Kampf* as written by the KKK's David Duke, with a foreword by Mahmoud Ahmadinijad.

To make matters worse, the actual author was a professor at her alma mater, Criterion University in New Hampshire. The same place where Daciana taught, and from which she killed, killed, and killed again, before Dale and Claire finally killed her.

Daciana Moceanu. It had been three years since the hybrid vampire/werewolf had slaughtered Rowena's husband and baby son, and still the nightmares haunted her sleep. Perhaps they always would. Daciana had intended to kill Rowena, too, and it took both Dale and Claire, acting in concert, to put her down. But not before they were so grievously wounded that they had to drink Daciana's blood to avoid bringing death upon themselves.

Thanks to a wood chipper, Daciana's body had been reduced to buckets of chum and given to a New Jersey fishing boat captain who knew better than to ask questions.

14

If anyone wanted to search for her now, Rowena thought, he'd have to start by analyzing the DNA in mackerel poop.

She looked again at the manuscript and flipped the cover shut. Today was Sunday; she shouldn't even have been working. But she didn't fancy returning to her empty home after church either, and Jones Publishing at least gave her some work to do to keep her mind occupied.

Her cell phone rang, indicating a personal rather than a business call. *Well, duh, it's Sunday. Mom or Dad, probably,* she thought, until she saw the 301 area code on the caller ID. *Claire?*

"Ro, hello, remember me? You were matron of honor at my wedding?" Snide as always.

"Claire. Come back to work here. Jones Publishing needs you. And don't call me a matron. Thirty-seven's too young for that."

"That's okay, Ro, you don't look your age. You people never do."

"Oh, baby, *you people?*" Rowena was the product of a marriage between a black Marine and a Vietnamese bride, and her appearance showcased the best features of both. Her skin was coffee and cream and just as smooth, her long black hair free of kinks, her facial features delicate, her figure full, but without a trace of fat. Still no BWA, she'd say to herself on the rare occasions when she looked into the mirror stepping out of the shower.

Claire herself was taller by two inches, standing at five ten, with light Irish skin, pale blue-gray eyes, and hair so fair and fine it looked like spun gold. "How are you doing, and why are you at work when you should be home?"

"How did you know I'm at work?"

"Because I know you. Hey, reason I'm calling, you feel like company?"

"Where are you?"

"On my way to Jersey, staying overnight at my friend Matthew's. I can be in Boston Monday afternoon, if you can stand my company."

"Super. You know where the key is. I can see you after work. How long will you be in town?"

"A couple days, just long enough to wear out my welcome."

"Honey, the mat's always out for you." *Long as you're not in hunt mode,* she said to herself. "I'll see if Bentley can spare me for a few days. Be careful driving. Don't know what the weather's like in the Garbage State"—it had been a long time before she could resume the banter they'd once shared, before she knew that her best friend was a metamorph—"but the roads are slick here, wind's blowing like stink. Still driving the Highlander?"

"I'll never give up the Golden Goose. She was a present from Ray, after all."

Claire's first perk, from their adored former boss, Ray Jones. Another of Daciana's victims.

"Well, take it easy. All wheel drive isn't a panacea for spinouts."

"Ro, you're forgetting what the roads are like where I live these days."

"Oh, right. You're a hillbilly now."

"See you tomorrow. Can't wait."

Rowena put down the phone and hacked out a cough. *Damn winter cold,* she thought.

"You slept *where?*" asked Rowena late the next afternoon as she sat across the kitchen table from a travel-weary Claire. She sipped from a glass of red wine while Claire inhaled the steam from a mug of tea.

"On a boat, you heard right. You remember Matthew, from the wedding?"

"Honey, I hardly remember anyone but you and Dale. That and standing on the same stone patio that every President since FDR has stood on. *Overwhelmed* doesn't begin to describe it. Yes, there were some people on the lower level, what, two, three steps down, but baby, there were patriotic stars in this girl's eyes. I just wished my dad and mom, especially my dad, had been able to see their little girl there at Camp David."

"You know why they couldn't."

Rowena flashed her friend a grin. "Course I do. But Dad's having been a Marine and all, well, it would've rocked his world. So," she continued, "getting back to the subject, what about this boat deal?"

"Matthew's a chemist who works as a consultant to— well, to the team, we really don't have a name."

"Now that's what I call a secret organization, if you don't even know your own name."

"Uh ... huh. So anyway, he's a Brit, and sharp as the proverbial tack."

"Hmf. Put an English accent on a grade school drop-out, and to an American he sounds like Churchill."

"Your boss is British, I'd remind you."

"Case in point." She laughed. "No, belay that. Bentley's brilliant, and her husband Elliott's fantastic, too. I'm sorry you never got to meet him, you'd like him."

"I liked Bentley, from what little time we spent together before ... well, before."

Rowena needed to change the subject. "Yes, well, does your new best friend live up to his accent?"

"Did I mention he's a Ph.D.?"

Rowena laughed. "As your friend Gracie Allen once said, 'There's no need to spell it out, George. If he's a fud, he's a fud.'"

"Very funny. When she said it to George Burns. Matthew's also a computer geek, still photographer, and videographer. Plus, he plays a mean guitar."

"I'm impressed."

"He immigrated a few years ago to work for a dye company at the Jersey shore. Once he got settled, he bought a boat and berthed it at a yard on the Toms River. Or the River Toms, as he calls it. By the way, your dad would like this, the boat's name is *Semper Fidelis*."

Rowena's eyebrows arched. "He was a Marine, too?"

"No, he bought it from a former Marine and refused to change the name. Says he likes the concept of always faithful."

"That I approve of. So what is it, a houseboat?"

Claire swallowed a mouthful of tea. "Don't let him hear you say that. It's a seagoing trawler yacht with all the comforts of home. Including heat in the winter and air in the summer. Two staterooms—one's his office—plus an extra berth in the pilot house—which is where he slept, alone, before you ask."

"Honey, knowing what you are, I figure there's no way he'd try to put the moves on you."

Claire reached across the table and placed her hand over Rowena's. Ro turned palm up and closed her fingers around Claire's. "Thank you for being able to talk about it without jumping out of your skin. Which you did for a long time. And for which I can't blame you."

"Tell me about it. But listen, I read Arthur Ford's autobiography a while ago, and I'll never forget the first line: 'There's nothing so strange as the way the strangeness wears off the strange.' Something like that, anyway."

Claire considered. "All right . . . I think I get it."

"Girl, how strange was it—make that weird—when you got turned? And then got turned again? Werewolf, vampire. But do you think it's strange now?"

"I can live with it." She twisted her mouth. "So who's this Ford guy, anyway?"

Rowena explained that Arthur Ford was the spiritual medium who had allegedly broken the Houdini code, giving the magician's wife Beatrice the secret message that would confirm Houdini's continued life after his untimely death. This was long before Rowena's time, but these days she tended to do a lot of reading on spiritual matters. "Claire, you're my best friend and closest confidant, so I'm going to ask you something I wouldn't ask anyone else, and you've got to promise not to laugh, or smirk, or roll your eyes. Promise?" Claire nodded. "I want really hard to believe in life after death. What's your take on it?"

Claire knew where this was heading. She gave Ro's hand a gentle squeeze. "I was raised Catholic, like all good girls of Irish descent, so based upon that alone I'd have to say yes, life goes on. But that would be regurgitating what my priest and the nuns told me."

"Uh huh."

"I remember in catechism one day, I came across in the Bible where the disciples tell Jesus that according to prophecy Elijah was supposed to come ahead to announce His coming, and Jesus replies that Elijah did just that, and the disciples realized that He was referring to John the Baptist. So I piped up that this must be proof of reincarnation. And then I took it a step further and said it must be what Jesus meant when He said we must be born again."

"Okay . . ."

"And the CCD teacher said no, Jesus was speaking symbolically. And I, smart-ass that I was, said how can you be so sure, did He tell you personally, and by way of answer she sent me to the priest's office, and he, um, straightened me out."

"Did he?"

"To his satisfaction, he did."

"Well, let's hear it for open minds. Arthur Ford wrote he was open to the concept of reincarnation, but my question then would be, if it's real, how come the population of the world is growing by leaps and bounds? Where'd all those extra people come from?"

Claire nodded. "It seems we have a conundrum, doesn't it? Unless . . ."

"Unless what?"

Claire held up her mug, now empty. Rowena stood and got the teapot. Returning to the table, she carried the wine bottle in her other hand.

"All right, girl, unless what?"

"I've heard the same argument before. And I think the flaw is this: it assumes that God created the universe, enjoyed His day of rest, and then kicked back for good, just sat on the porch drinking lemonade. Who says He isn't creating more souls all the time?"

Rowena stopped pouring her wine. "Wait a minute, wait a minute. Old souls, young souls, we hear that all the time. Ho . . . ly . . . crap."

"And now that we've pondered that problem, how about I take you to dinner before you're too sloppy drunk to enjoy the food?"

Rowena laughed and said, "Let's go." She laughed again. "Just thinking. If reincarnation's a fact, do you tell the guy who wants to carve REST IN PEACE on your gravestone to change it to BE RIGHT BACK?"

Chapter Three

That same Monday, as Claire was driving up the Garden State Parkway bound for Boston, Dale and Joe drove to Hyattsville and checked out what was left of the Pep Boys store. The crime scene tape was stretched on pylons around the demolished structure, one that looked like the scorched and smoldering shells of buildings Dale had seen as an Army ranger in the combat zones of Iraq and Afghanistan. He and Joe were dressed in suits and topcoats, with badges clipped to their jacket pockets. Both wore scarves, but neither wore a hat. They introduced themselves to the local investigators and confirmed that they had been expected. Officials from the Pep Boys home office stood nearby, talking with a man in a down jacket and jeans and taking notes.

"That's the manager," the detective said. "He was taking a coffee break when the shop exploded."

"Timing is everything," Joe said. "We'd like to talk to him."

"Sure." He walked over to the group, said a few words, nodded toward the federal agents, and pulled the manager from the huddle. "This is Vincent Carbonari, gentlemen."

"Thanks," said Dale and extended his hand. Carbonari gave him a weak handshake. He was trembling. Dale introduced his partner and asked the manager to tell his story.

"Not much to tell," the man said. "It was a normal day, like any other Sa'd'y. Lots of service work from guys who couldn't bring their cars in during the week, you know? But no more, no less." He shrugged.

"Anything unusual at all? Customer-wise?" asked Joe.

"Nah. Just the usual, some regulars, some new." He looked up and frowned. "Well, there was this Yid."

"Yid?"

"Yeah, you know. Black suit, big hat, with those funny curls?" He made a circular motion in front of his ears.

"Uh huh. An orthodox Jew," said Dale. "What about him?"

"Listen," Carbonari said, nodding toward the small group of men waiting for his return. "Don't tell them home office guys, all right, but the guy slipped me a twenty to put his car at the head of the line."

"That sounds unusual."

"Yeah, I guess. I mean, it ain't normal, now that I think of it."

"Do you remember his name?"

The manager struggled. "Somethin' like Lev, or Levin, or . . . I dunno, maybe Levine, does that sound right?"

"No way to tell," said Joe.

"You guys think he planted the bomb? And maybe it was on a timer, and that's why he wanted it in the shop first?"

"Again, no way to tell. But thanks for your time. Can we get back to you if we have to?"

"Well, I dunno. I mean, I ain't workin' at this store anymore, you know? They could send me anywhere. Or can me. But here's my number." He wrote it on the back of a business card and returned to where the suits were waiting.

Joe turned to Dale. "Aren't Hasidim forbidden from driving and doing business on a Saturday?"

Dale said, "I think so, yes." He walked to where the detective stood, near to where officers patrolled inside the perimeter looking for evidence. "Any idea who the bomb vehicle belonged to?"

The detective pulled out his notebook. "Guy named Clarke, lives in Olney. He reported his wife missing yesterday morning, but it wasn't twenty-four hours yet, so we couldn't activate a file. He insisted we take down the car's particulars, so we did. After the explosion we found lots of car parts all over the place, you can imagine. A couple looked like they could've come from the Clarke car. Then we happened to find a piece with the car's VIN. Checked it against his info, and . . ." He shook his head. "One of the female psych counselors from the precinct and a plainclothes cop went out to break the news. Whole family's a basket case."

"Understandable. May we have Mr. Clarke's address?"

Joe and Dale shook snowflakes off their topcoats and hung them on the coat tree in Lauren Bachmann's cottage. She was waiting for them with mugs of steaming coffee and a platter of cookies. "From the chow hall, naturally. You know I'm not the cookie-baking type."

"That's okay," said Dale, taking a handful of oatmeal cookies and sitting down. "I'm starving."

"You're always starving," Joe added, taking some for himself. "Like you're eating for two. Which I guess isn't so far from the truth, is it? Thanks, Commander."

When they got settled, Lauren asked what they'd found, and the answer wasn't encouraging. "Body parts," said Joe, "both automobile and human. There'll be DNA testing to determine if some of those people parts belonged to the wife of the owner of the car. I suspect they will." He sipped his coffee.

Dale added, "The manager's alive, he was on break when the building blew. He's suggesting that the perpetrator might have been a Hasidic Jew. The guy tipped him a twenty to put his car at the head of the line."

Lauren frowned. "It was the Sabbath, though."

"Which makes us suspect that he was really someone disguised as a Hasid."

Joe said, "Anyone claim responsibility yet?"

Lauren shook her head. "I've had the news on all day, nothing. Nothing from above either."

They discussed their options and came up empty. The Allahu Akbar message suggested that an organized terror group was the perpetrator, but none claimed responsibility. Which left open more possibilities, including a disgruntled former employee or even a hot-tempered consumer who felt he'd been ripped off on a service call and was using the message to slip investigators a red herring.

The possibility that concerned them most strongly was that whoever was responsible had done it not because of allegiance to a religious or political cause . . . but just because he could.

That Monday, all the student chatter in the hallways of Montgomery Blair High School in Silver Spring, Maryland, seemed to be about the bombing.

"So cool."

"People died, you jerk."

"Nobody I knew."

"Asshole."

Ahmed Mansoor, in his dark blue custodian's overalls, sprinkled absorbent flakes on a puddle of vomit on the hallway floor and let them soak up the slop. *Dumb bitch,* he thought. *Couldn't handle dissection in her biology class and couldn't make it to the girls' room; hell, it was only a friggin' frog.*

The puddle happened to be in the schools' Hall of Fame wing, where portraits of MBHS graduates had been etched onto plaques. There was the actress Goldie Hawn, class of 1963, and next to it Connie Chung, TV news icon, class of '64. *Both damn good looking, back in the day. Though it's like kittens: cute, but they grow up to be cats. Same with women,* he thought: *they grow old. Look at those two now on TV, and you have to wonder.* Wonder what, he didn't bother to analyze. Ahmed wasn't that deep. He did know that working in a high school, even as a janitor, provided more than a perfect cover; it also provided the opportunity to see a shitload of pretty girls still in their prime.

He'd never put his faith in the seventy-two virgins awaiting him in the afterlife that his religious trainers had tried to drill into his head. Ahmed was a here-and-now kind of guy, and certain sections of Washington provided the means of slaking his lust without complications. The women were far from virginal, but they were available; and they were ciphers, just as he himself was anonymous.

Ahmed's attention today wasn't on the puke, and it wasn't on the Hall of Fame; it was on the student and faculty comments about the bombing. He wanted to whistle as he swept the detritus into a dustpan and tossed it into a bucket. He wanted to stand on the auditorium stage with a microphone and announce his part in the plot. In his homeland he'd be hailed as a hero.

The bell rang, and as the students walked by, he felt a tap on the shoulder. He'd been expecting it. "Hello, Sophie," he said before turning around.

"Hi, Monsieur," she said brightly. "You busy?"

Sophie was taking—as opposed to studying—French, and when she first saw MR. MANSOOR on Ahmed's ID tag, she'd given him the nickname that everyone called him by today. When they called him anything at all, that is. She was very pretty, but not in a bring-her-home-to-meet-Mother kind of pretty—unless Mother ran a whorehouse. Sophie overdid her makeup; she had color streaks in her long dark hair that changed by the day; and she wore the lowest-cut pullovers that the school—or the law—would allow.

"Follow me," he said, picking up the bucket and walking toward the boiler room, which also housed the custodial office. It was where they would go to share a smoke during her study hall, which she cut regularly.

"The new teacher's a dork," she'd explained to Ahmed when he'd asked her how she managed to cut without getting reported. "So one day after class I whispered in his ear that I would be absent every day from now on, but if he didn't want me crying to the principal that he'd tried to feel me up in the stairwell, he'd simply mark me present."

"You're evil," Ahmed had said. "I admire that in a girl."

So they became co-conspirators, even friends of a sort. And often as not, after the bell rang and Sophie sashayed off to her next class, Ahmed would take a brief bathroom break, with visions of her deep cleavage and her raccoon eyes and her glossy maroon lipstick dancing in his head.

One day, he thought, *one day we're going to get it on.* He even thought of turning her, once he himself had been turned. Then she'd never grow old, just like him.

One day had come the night before for Jawdan El-Sayed. He'd been driving the Sprinter home to his condo in Solomons Island, Maryland, when he decided to stop at a bar in Parole, just outside Annapolis. Parole was far enough from Solomons that no one would know him, yet close enough to be convenient. He rarely visited the same pub twice.

Jawdan, his name anglicized to Jerry by his employer, was an expert in all things mechanical and electrical—and incendiary, which was one reason he'd been chosen for the original mission that had brought him from Iraq nearly two decades earlier. He worked at the Solomons Island Marina as an engine mechanic and jack of all trades. Summer was his busiest time, as the unwritten rule for boat repair was never *if* something will break down but *when*. When a bilge pump failed; when a stuffing box needed tightening; when jellyfish clogged a seawater-fed cooling line, Jerry was the man. Winters kept him only slightly less busy, because that was when boats were hauled for barnacle scraping, power washing, and bottom repainting in the heated Quonset hut-type sheds. Plus, there was occasional re-laminating and rewiring to do, stepping down of sail masts, and refinishing teak for owners who were too busy or too lazy to do it themselves. The pay was decent, he'd occasionally get good tips, and the work itself kept him sharp. The only downside was that he couldn't take vacation time in the summer, when he was most needed at the yard. And the next job, Muhammad had said, would be in the summertime. That would be fine for the boss and Ahmed, as school would be out, but for Jawdan to take off would be next to impossible. The only consolation was, the boss said his expertise would be needed.

"What's your name?" asked the frumpy-looking girl as she thanked him for the beer.

"Jack," he lied. "Short for John. What's yours?"

"Connie," she replied. "Short for cunny."

"You do get down to business quickly, don't you?"

"I just don't believe in screwing around." She eyed him over her glass. "Well, in a manner of speaking."

They agreed upon a price and stepped outside, where Jawdan slipped the cash into Connie's hand. "Where to?" she asked, and he pointed her to the white Sprinter on the outskirts of the parking lot. He assured her there was bedding inside; well, an inflatable mattress anyway.

When their business was completed, Connie sat up and noticed a pile of clothing behind the driver's seat. Before Jawdan could stop her, she'd picked up a black, broad-brimmed hat with ringlets sewn to the inside band. "What's this?" she asked, running the black braids through her fingers. "Halloween already?"

Jawdan didn't answer; he didn't know what to say. She asked again, this time with suspicion in her tone. He knew the police hadn't released details of the Pep Boys blast yet, but if the media happened to mention that a certain orthodox Jew was a person of interest, this girl might tie the disguise to the crime. So he did what he had to do. It was a shame; she'd been a pretty good lay.

Chapter Four

On Tuesday, the first full day of Claire's visit, Rowena insisted that she join her at work, if for no other reason than to say hello to Bentley Williams, for whom Claire had worked briefly after Ray Jones's death. She explained that she'd not told Bentley anything about Claire's new life except that she was working for Uncle Sam in classified documents, and she knew that the new boss of Jones Publishing had liked Claire and would be happy to renew their acquaintance.

Their first stop, though, was Rowena's office, where she sought Claire's opinion on the manuscript. "I hate it," said Rowena as she slid *Diatribe* across the desk to Claire. "And the author teaches at our alma mater, too, which makes me doubly hate it."

Claire thumbed through the manuscript, picking up a phrase here, a sentence there, and fiery rhetoric everywhere. She tossed it back. "You're right. Makes me want to puke," she said.

"Exactly. You have to admit, though, it is well written. And some other publisher will put it out there if we don't."

"Has Bentley seen it?"

"No."

"Then I'd lose it if I were you. Bury it in a drawer somewhere. My opinion, it doesn't even deserve the courtesy of a rejection slip."

"Thanks. I needed that." She slipped the papers into a drawer. "I'd rather burn it, you know."

"Ten-four on that, but you'll need to 'find' it if the author inquires about it and wants it returned. He could make a stink if he thinks you lost it. Negligence on your part."

"Okay. Now let's say hello to Bentley."

They walked down the hall to the corner office, which had no door, a holdover from the days when Ray Jones ran the company. "My door is always open," he used to say, and he meant it. Inside they saw Bentley conversing with a distinguished-looking gentleman.

"We're interrupting," Claire said to Rowena.

"No we're not. Get inside."

"Claire!" cried Bentley. "Claire, it's you! Tell me you're giving up that dull government job and returning to the fold."

Bentley walked over and took Claire's hand, then said, "What the hell," and hugged her. "We English are too reserved for our own good. Truly missed you around here, Claire, and that's a fact."

"I'm not too reserved," said her companion, "in case you'd like another hug."

Claire blinked, the man winked, and Bentley laughed. "Mister tall, gray, and handsome here is my husband, Elliott Tavender. Elliott, you remember my telling you of Claire."

"I do indeed, luv, but you never did her justice." He winked again and held out his hand. "Delighted." They shook.

"Shouldn't you be in school?" asked Rowena, an eyebrow arched.

"Caught me. Actually, I was out yesterday with some bug or other and thought it might be wise to call out sick today. I love my students, but I hate the colds they bring to school in the winter. Right now I feel well enough to come by and take my wife to lunch. May I include you ladies in that invitation?"

"Well," said Claire, glancing at Rowena, who nodded, "Elliott, you're about to live a fantasy: being entertained by three women."

"Three strikingly beautiful women, I might add."

"I just love the English, don't you?" Rowena declared.

As Claire and the others dined at Legal Seafood, some four hundred fifty miles away, Lauren Bachmann joined Joe Whitehead and Dale Keegan in the chow hall at Camp David. Over a utilitarian lunch of ersatz hamburgers—actually venison, from a deer brought down by Dale and Claire the last time they hunted as wolves—and soggy French fries, with a side of what the Navy called salad—two leaves of lettuce, one slice of mushy tomato, one slice of red onion, and a stuffed green olive alongside a pitted black one—they discussed a new incident that Lauren's handler in D.C. had called to her attention.

"It's a simple murder . . . as if any murder can be called simple, but you know what I mean."

"And we need to take a look at it why?" asked Joe.

Lauren sipped from a mug of coffee and held it between her hands for the warmth. The day was brazenly cold, the air clean as newly-washed linens and crisp as a freshly-starched utility uniform—in other words, a typical winter's day in the Catoctin Mountains.

"The victim was a prostitute, which doesn't put her all that high on police priority lists. She was found in the woods of Calvert County, around Long Beach—somewhere between Annapolis and Solomons Island."

"Solomons: that's where the Patuxent empties into Chesapeake Bay," noted Dale. "On the opposite shore from Pax River NAS."

Joe said, "She was dumped there, or was she buried?"

"Dumped," said Lauren. "Some leaves were piled around her. I'd assume the ground's too frozen to dig even a shallow grave." She took another sip as Dale asked how the victim had died. "Strangled and stabbed, both."

Joe knit his brow. "So the perp strangled her first, and then stabbed her to make sure she was dead?"

"I guess. The stab wound was made by a long, thin object, like a carpenter's awl or an icepick. Through an eyeball and into the brain."

Dale stood up and got another glass of milk from the stainless steel refrigeration unit known as a cow. He needed regular infusions of protein, and tea and coffee alone didn't pass muster. "So," he said, looking over his shoulder, "I echo Joe's question. Why should we be involved?"

"Well, it could be nothing, but it bears checking out. In addition to some skin samples from her attacker, the coroner reports fibers in her fingernails that look like hair." She narrowed her eyes exaggeratedly. "But . . . it's not . . . hair."

"Cue up the *Dragnet* theme," Dale said as he sat down.

"Actually, it's crepe hair. What makeup artists use to make phony beards and mustaches."

"And?"

Lauren continued. "When I was in high school I was in the dramatics club. One year we staged *Fiddler on the*

Roof. I was in the makeup crew, and we had to make crepe beards for the boys. Pain in the ass, by the way. So here's what I'm thinking. The manager of the Pep Boys store said there was an orthodox Jew taking his car in for service, but this was on the Sabbath, which could indicate that the guy wasn't really—of course, with the police looking for a Hasid, well . . ."

Dale picked up her train of thought. "I think I see what you're getting at."

Lauren said, "And if that's the scenario, or even if it's close enough, that means our terrorist probably lives somewhere between Silver Spring and Solomons Island."

"I guess," Dale said to Joe, "it's time for another field trip."

Lauren smiled, nodding. "I already called the Calvert County sheriff and told him to expect you tomorrow."

The sheriff proved highly cooperative. Instead of guarded or territorial, he seemed anxious to share his information with the two government investigators, one of them black, the other white. He was old enough to remember when blacks, or Negroes as they were called by polite society at the time, weren't allowed to buy houses in Southern Maryland communities. Before the Civil Rights Act was signed into law, there had been a welcoming sign at the entrance to the residential community of Long Beach, and the last two words on the sign were SENSIBLY RESTRICTED. But things had changed since his cub days in law enforcement, and so had the sheriff, in both attitude and expertise. He offered his visitors coffee and sat down at a table in the conference room, not in his office with a desk separating them. The two men flanked him as he spread out his file.

"I sent the skin samples out for DNA testing, that'll take a few days, and these inside the baggie are the fibers the ME found under her fingernails. But I think you'll be just as interested in this." He pulled out a close-up photograph.

"Fingerprints," said Dale.

"From the dead girl's throat. You can run 'em through your FBI or whatever database you use."

"I thought prints on skin faded after a few minutes," Dale said as Joe cocked his head and stared interestedly at the officer, who didn't seem to live up to the image of the stereotypical rube.

"Well, let me explain," the sheriff said. "Usually they do fade, but last month a study came out that said if you used Swedish Black powder you could pick up prints up to four hours after the skin had been touched. I had some money left in the budget, so I ordered some Swedish Black right away; but frankly, I never thought I'd ever get the chance to use it. The body was found by a hunter long before sunup. He practically tripped over it and called 911 on his cell. We got to the scene real quick."

"And you knew about the Swedish Black," said Joe. "I'm impressed."

"You're aware of the study?" asked the sheriff.

"Matter of fact, I was part of the peer review committee. I trained in forensics."

"Well now," said the sheriff. "Now it's me who's impressed."

Dale thought, *If Claire were here, she'd correct his grammar, not to his face but to me afterward.* "It's *I* who's impressed," she'd say, still the stickler from her days as an editor at Jones. He said, "May I assume that we can take this file with us?"

The sheriff rubbed his palm over his few wisps of gray hair. "Hell, boys, there's no way I could stop you even if I wanted to, which I don't, am I right? But I dearly appreciate your politeness. If you need me for anything else, you might want to call before the weekend. I retire February second. That's Monday."

His visitors rose and shook his hand, thanking him for his cooperation and wishing him all the best in his retirement years. After they left, the sheriff drew himself another cup of coffee and returned to his desk, visions of boating on the Chesapeake and trolling for blues and rockfish dancing inside his head. He glanced again at the tiny article buried in the local section of the Baltimore *Sun* that announced his upcoming retirement. The last paragraph mentioned his replacement, a former Anne Arundel County deputy sheriff named Mike DeMaira. *Nice young fella,* he thought. *County'll be in good hands.* Farther forward in the same section, the sheriff saw the story of the murder of a local prostitute. Not his problem anymore, not since the government boys took over. "Right nice fellas," he said as he leaned back in his worn leather chair. "Both of 'em."

Nineteen miles south of the sheriff's Prince Frederick office, in the Solomons Island Marina, its chief mechanic noticed the same edition of the *Sun* lying on the harbor-master's desk. It was lunchtime, and but for him the office was empty. The short article about the continuing investigation of Connie's murder—her name wasn't Connie at all, he noted, but how many other local hookers got killed last Sunday?—was in the Annapolis section, above the fold.

"Shit," Jawdan said under his breath.

On Sunday, February first, in central New Hampshire, a middle-aged gentleman with a swarthy complexion and a hawks-beak nose knocked on the door of a farmhouse belonging to a family of evangelical Christians who had just returned from Sunday services. "I'm so sorry to bother you," he said. "My car ran out of gas, and I wonder if I might impose upon you for a ride to the nearest station."

The father, a husky young man with prematurely thinning corn silk hair, and still dressed in his Sunday suit, welcomed the man inside and shut the door to the biting cold. His wife, a thin, wholesome-looking woman with curly blond hair, walked into the living room with an apron tied behind her dress. Her smile was as warm as her husband's. Two tow-headed children, somewhere around seven or eight years old, stood by the table in the next room with dishes and bowls in their hands.

The father, who introduced himself as Bertram, helped his visitor out of his ski jacket and draped it over a chair. "You're lucky," he said. "Fifteen minutes earlier, you wouldn't have gotten an answer to your knock. And even with that insulated jacket, you'd still be mighty cold." He gestured toward his wife. "This is Rachel, and these are our twins, Mary Martha and Jacob. Say hello, children." They nodded and turned to set the table. Rachel excused herself to the kitchen.

"Something smells good," said the visitor.

"Oh, that's Rachel's famous crock pot beef stew. Been simmerin' since sunup." He paused. "Listen, Brother—I'm sorry, I didn't get your name."

"I apologize. Zachary Leach."

31

"Well, Brother Leach, unless you're in a hurry to get back on the road, I know there's plenty of stew to share. What do you say? Oh, and you needn't get a ride to the gas station. I've enough in the shed for the generator to get you there just fine."

"That's very kind of you."

"Children? Another setting for Brother Leach here."

During the meal, their guest explained that he had been skiing at Mount Sunapee, as he tried to do every Sunday, so he could worship in the cathedral made by God's own hands—among the white birches and snow-dappled evergreens. He would ski throughout the mornings and drive back to his home at Criterion University, where he taught, in time for evening vespers. Today, he had simply forgotten to check his gas tank before setting out.

The stew was delicious, the apple cobbler a fitting cap to the meal. The family's visitor pushed his chair back and said he wanted to get something from his jacket.

"Now there's no need to pay us for the gas, Brother Leach," said Bertram. "It's our Christian duty and privilege to share our bounty with you."

"I insist," he replied. He picked up the jacket and withdrew his pistol. "I'd like to introduce my friends Mr. Smith and Mr. Wesson," he said and shot Bertram in the head at point blank range. The children were next, too shocked even to move before the bullets drilled through their brains.

Rachel sat paralyzed, mouth open, breathing in. The man they had welcomed into their home put the pistol in his pocket, walked toward her, and smiled. "You are the dessert I really want," he said. "Taking my pleasure from the living is much more—well, pleasurable."

His hands snapped forward and clapped onto the sides of her head, turning it to face him. His mouth opened, his jaw extended, and fangs fell from the roof of his mouth. Rachel's eyes rolled back in her head as his lips locked around her throat and his fangs drove deep inside. He gave a tug, and her throat opened, spraying his face in hot blood.

When the life force was fully drained from her, *Brother Leach* tore out the throats of the others, in the interest of what he called consistency. After taking some blood from each, he returned to Rachel; hers really was sweeter.

He washed the blood from his face in the kitchen sink and wiped down everything he had touched. When he walked out later, casually lighting a cigarette as he drove away in his SUV, he left the words *Allahu Akbar* scrawled on the dining room wall—in blood.

On Monday, the second day of the month and the first day of retirement for the Calvert County Sheriff, DNA results on the skin found under the fingernails of the murdered girl were reported to Commander Lauren Bachmann at Camp David. As with the fingerprints, there was no match in any database. She sent Dale and Joe to canvass the Annapolis area bars, and finally a bartender in Parole recognized the photo of *Connie* in the paper. But all he could tell them was that the girl was a regular. He'd never seen the Arab-looking guy she walked out with before that night.

When they reported back on Thursday, Lauren told them she was sending them out again, along with Claire, to a small farming village in central New Hampshire, not far from the campus of Criterion University.

Chapter Five

Rowena woke up suddenly, startled from sleep by the nightmare that was by now a regular visitor to her dreams. She saw herself, helpless, as Daciana Moceanu leaned toward her, mouth agape, fangs fallen into place. She felt the vampire's hot breath on her neck. Felt the world go black as something struck her head, and when she came to, there were Claire and Dale, wounded nearly unto death, drinking the dead vampire's blood. She watched their fatal wounds heal before her eyes, and she realized that everything Claire had just that day confessed to her was absolutely true.

The legends about werewolves and vampires had been just stories, Claire had said, designed to frighten children and impressionable adults. Werewolves were not bound by the lunar cycle, and silver had no effect upon them. They could change at will, and even in wolf form they were able to control their lupine savagery. As humans, they still had the wolf's strength and enhanced sense of smell and hearing. They also had accelerated metabolisms, as was reflected in their near-voracious appetites. The stories she'd heard as a child, however, never addressed the fact that all other animals saw metamorphs—whether in human or wolf form—as alphas and deferred to them instinctively. They also never mentioned that from the time of their first morphing, the wolf's aging process was at war with the human's, meaning that the metamorph aged some three to four years for every single human year. It was conceivable that a metamorph could die of old age at forty.

Vampires, Rowena learned, had even more misconceptions strewn about the literary landscape. They didn't sleep by day and prowl by night, unless they wanted to. Unlike Bela "I never drink . . . wine" Lugosi's character, they could eat and drink like everyone else, but they did need blood to ensure their immortality. Their rapid healing was no myth, and if someone like Buffy were to stake them they could simply pull out the stake—or leave it in as a fashion statement. Garlic? No effect. The cross? They could even take communion without lightning striking the church. Decapitation, dismemberment, and disemboweling, in addition to the ever-popular incinerating, were about the only ways to kill them for good.

In other words, both species could walk among humans undetected. And, in matters of practicality, they also needed to earn a living. Claire had been an editor at Jones, working under, being mentored by, and becoming the dearest friend of Rowena Parr. Dale Keegan had been a soldier, later a teacher and, after 9/11, a soldier again. Daciana Moceanu had been a professor at Criterion University.

The turning of humans into vampires and werewolves was affected by the exchange of blood. And now that Dale and Claire had been turned twice, the werewolf's aging curse was moot and the vampire's blood lust could be assuaged by devouring wild game. The best of both worlds, Claire once said—except that by human standards, they were still monsters.

The only monster Rowena feared these days was the one who came to her in nightmares, the model-thin beauty of indeterminate age whose face became a mask of horror as her black eyes grew wide, her jaw became distended, and those fangs pivoted into place . . .

She sat up in bed, her pajamas soaked with sweat. She tried to take a deep breath and ended up coughing, as if she were trying to hack a lump of coal from her lungs.

Her cell phone rang.

"Before breakfast?" she moaned. "Someone is about to get an earful of good old Marine Corps invective, thank you, Daddy." She punched the button. "Hello!" she nearly roared.

"Ro, sorry to call this early, but I didn't want to phone you at work. We need to talk."

"Claire?"

"I'm in New Hampshire with Dale and Joe. Can we come by after you get home from work today?"

"Huh? Sure, and you can all crash here overnight if you want. Tomorrow's Saturday, you and I can spend the weekend doing girly stuff."

"That'll be the day when you do girly stuff. But yes, we'll do that. Thanks. Oh, and not a word to anyone, okay?"

"You're starting to sound cryptic."

"You have no idea."

Rowena dragged herself in to work, thinking that if Claire were still working there she'd boomerang the expression on her that Ro had used when Claire was in the first day of her chronically debilitating period: "You look like you've been shot at and missed, and shit at and hit." It was another colorful expression she'd learned as a child from her dad—by overhearing him say it to a fellow Marine about a non-squared-away private during rifle inspection. Her home, though, had been a sanctuary from vulgarity in any form. Even saying *damn* or *hell* could get her an hour's time out. Those were the good old days. And they had been good, she reflected.

But now here she was, sitting at her desk, with manuscripts in her Inbox . . . and one hidden inside a desk drawer. She pulled it out again.

Diatribe. Now there's a working title, Rowena thought. An attack on all things Western, especially the Judeo-Christian ethic. She hated all attacks on religion and ethnicity, but had to catch herself every time she saw the name of the author: Muhammad Al-Jubeir, Professor of Middle Eastern Studies, Criterion University, New Hampshire. Why, she wondered, didn't old Muhammad just take his diatribe to the university press? There's nothing more accommodating than university presses when it comes to trashing America.

When Rowena was a freshman at Criterion, the female students and women on staff welcomed her with open arms: a woman of color, and mixed ethnicity to boot. But when it became apparent that she didn't share their allegiance to Karl Marx and their blind worship of Che Guevara; when she declared Roe v. Wade a sham and said that a woman's *right to choose* meant she could *choose* not to get pregnant; when she replied to the challenge as to why she was anti-abortion but pro death penalty, that it was for the simple reason the baby hadn't killed anyone, duh, she found herself duly ostracized.

She didn't fare any better with her professors either. One kept asserting that in society everything, but *every-*

thing, was relative, and he wasn't talking about Einstein either. One day she'd had enough, and in a sweetly non-challenging tone, she asked the professor if it was really true that everything was relative. He said yes. She then asked him if the corollary was also true, that nothing is absolute. Well, of course. "But," she asked, the picture of innocence, "didn't you just make not one, but two *absolute* statements?"

Rowena was a hell of a writer, but you couldn't tell from her grades. She wrote an essay immediately following the Rodney King incident in 1991 in which she blamed the media for causing the Los Angeles riots, rather than the alleged racism in the police department. It earned an F. She wrote an essay promoting adoption over abortion, citing the creator of her laptop computer as an example of an unwanted baby's being carried to term rather than aborted. "Where would the world be today without Steve Jobs?" her paper concluded. Her professor castigated her in front of the class, challenging her to justify Hitler's not having been aborted. "I don't blame his mother," she shot back. "How could she know? I blame the complacent Germans for letting him come to power as an adult. They had the ability to shut him down, but nobody wanted the responsibility. Nobody owned the problem." The professor returned her essay with a grade of D. A few fellow students defended Rowena's position to her—but they did so privately, where their peers and profs couldn't hear.

In her senior year, when Rowena responded to a posting on the campus bulletin board for a junior editor's position at Jones Publishing in Boston, Ray Jones recognized her talent and her merit and told her she'd have a job waiting upon graduation. She'd been there ever since.

Rowena had to admit there was merit in Al-Jubeir's writing style, but its content was abhorrent. He cited the atrocities of the Crusades, the Spanish Inquisition, and Hitler's *final solution* as evidence of Christianity's intolerance. But, Rowena recalled, Hitler also denounced Christianity, declared Nazism the state religion, and replaced the Bible in schools with *Mein Kampf.* Al-Jubeir had dug up some obscure fact that at Joan of Arc's trial—at the hands of the French themselves, not the British, who today got blamed for it—the only charge the church authorities could make stick was the fact that she wore pants when she went into battle. French women were forbidden to wear pants in those days, so it was for that heretical sin she was burned at the stake. She was even refused her last request, to have a crucifix to hold in her hands and carry into the next life. Today, the descendants of those same countrymen considered her a saint.

Hey, Muhammad, Rowena raged inwardly, *what would happen to a woman in your social milieu who dared to go outside, unchaperoned, without her burka? What happens to someone who draws a picture of your prophet? And what about some of the soldiers in your holy armies who I've read find release with their fellow soldiers after dark? What's the matter? Goats too fast for them?*

Rowena coughed into a tissue. It grew thick with dark phlegm.

That's it, she thought, *God's getting me for slandering another religion. One God, remember that, girl. And Lord, I've got to get back to work. Just not on this.*

She returned the manuscript to the drawer. *Another time,* she said to herself. *Think happy thoughts. Claire just left a few days ago, and today she's coming back, with Dale and that other guy.*

She had the feeling, though, that this visit would be something other than a social call.

The visit started out quite socially. Rowena had dinner prepared by the time Claire, Dale, and Joe arrived. As they ate, Ro silently appraised the third member of the team. Damned good-looking dude. This wouldn't be a setup, would it?

With the main course completed, Joe remarked, "Claire, you never told me your friend's a sister."

With a blank look, Rowena said, "I don't have any siblings; I'm an only—oh, you mean one of *those* sisters."

Joe shook his head. "Got me," he said, looking embarrassed. "Must be going back to my North Philly days with that ethnic bit. Thought I'd outgrown it."

"Philadelphia boy, huh?"

"Born and raised. Rough neighborhood: any cat with a tail was a tourist."

"First time I heard that one," Rowena said, "I laughed so hard I nearly fell out of my highchair."

He returned the grin. "Shall I continue?"

"Please."

"I actually lived with both my parents, which was unusual for the neighborhood. But it'd probably have been better if I hadn't. My dad was a confirmed racist, and I picked up on some of that. He was a private school janitor, and he hated Whitey with every bone in his body."

"Sounds like a non-sequitur to me," Rowena said.

"Yeah. But that shows you how he thought. And having the name Whitehead really pissed him off. Early on, he went to a lawyer to see about changing the family name to Black. When the lawyer told him what it would cost, he called him an Oreo and stormed out of the office. When I was born, he decided to play up our heritage and named me Jomo Kenyatta."

Rowena frowned.

"The first president of Kenya," explained Dale. "Before that, a leader of the Mau Mau revolt. They drove the white farmers out, even those who were born in Africa—which, by the way, made them just as native African as the Kikuyu—and if the farmers resisted, they got hacked to pieces with machetes and pangas."

"Which suited Daddy just fine. If he could get away with it, he'd have formed a North Philadelphia chapter of the Mau Mau."

They smiled, but shook their heads at the same time.

"I got sent to juvey hall when I was fifteen. Yeah, that's right. Shoplifting. The guys would distract the owner of the store and I'd make the snatch and run. But all I had for my feet was a pair of borrowed sneakers. They were too big for me. I was swimming in them, so the cops were able to catch me no problem."

"How about the other guys?" asked Rowena.

"Oh, they all got away. And I didn't dare snitch on them."

Claire said, "You wore borrowed sneakers? I didn't know that."

"Did I mention we were poor? All my clothes were hand-me-downs from the neighborhood kids."

Rowena considered this. "Good thing you didn't live in an all girls neighborhood."

"Right. Thank God for small favors. So once I was in juvey, I decided that I didn't want any part of the grown-up version and started to straighten myself out. They had a shrink on staff, and he told me that college was out of the question for me, that a more realistic goal would be McDonald's, or maybe janitorial work. Well, I thought of my dad and said to myself, no effin' way. So when I got released, I signed up at Joe Frazier's gym and learned to box. Worked odd jobs there to pay my way."

"I've heard this part," said Claire, standing up. "Keep talking, Joe, I'll get the coffee and dessert. Rowena, sit."

"Yes, Mother."

"Got to be pretty good, made it to the quarter finals of the Golden Gloves. My opponent, though, was a kid whose dad was a big noise at the Philadelphia *Inquirer*, and the newspaper promoted the hell out of the Gloves in the sports columns and with free advertising. I outboxed the kid all three rounds, but he never went down. My trainer was already raising my hand, and we were both jumping up and down, sure I'd be going to the semis. But when the decision came in, the judges and the ref gave the win to the other kid. I never heard such booing from the crowd, they were throwing trash into the ring even; and it was then I decided not to go pro.

"After high school, I joined the Navy and boxed there. Ironically, having caused injuries to a lot of guys, I served as a medical corpsman, where I got to patch them up. I got my discharge, let Uncle Sugar pay for my college, worked as an EMT to save for med school, graduated UPenn, and, ta-dah, here I am, forensics boy." A grin broke his face, showcasing his even white teeth. "Guess I shouldn't say *boy*."

"Then Lauren discovered you," said Dale.

"Rediscovered me. That's a story in itself. But right now, I'd rather work my mouth around some of that cheesecake."

After dessert, Claire and Rowena told the men to watch television while they shared some girl talk in the kitchen.

"You're coughing a lot," Claire said. "Not smoking again, are you?"

"Bite your tongue, girl. Look, it's February. Everyone in New England has a cold in February. Load the dishwasher."

"I haven't had so much as a sniffle, since—oops, since that time you'd rather we not talk about."

"When you drank the bitch's blood and became a vamp. You can say it."

"Okay. And you know what else? Do you remember how the first day of my period always knocked me out? Well, I don't have periods anymore since that time."

Rowena thought. "But that means you and Dale will never be able to have kids, right?"

Claire nodded, her expression wistful. "Maybe that's for the best. I mean, considering what we are, what could we expect? A litter of little were-pups? Who want to nurse on blood?"

"Be hell nursing them, wouldn't it?"

"I shudder to think of it."

"So, on another subject entirely, what's the big secret you hinted at over the phone?"

"Tomorrow. We'll send the guys on the History Trail, and then we'll talk."

Both Dale and Joe were history buffs—Dale had taught American history at the middle school level—and neither had been to Boston before, so Saturday presented a golden opportunity for them to immerse themselves in all that the city had to offer: the Old North Church, Faneuil Hall, Old Ironsides, and more. "Not to mention Cheers," added Joe. "When we're done."

Claire and Rowena sat at the kitchen table, coffee mugs before them. The woods and the Charles River, seen through the sliding glass doors to the deck, sparkled with sunlight reflected off the snow and ice. It would go down in the meteorologists' logs as one of the ten best weather days of the year.

"You know we're not the only ones on the Camp David team, right?"

"No, the guy with the boat is, too. And the base commander, of course."

"I mean there are others we don't even know, people above her."

"And you guys are the boots on the ground. Man, you're living a life that Robert Ludlum would've loved to write about."

"I think our friend Joe likes you," said Claire, temporarily changing the subject.

"It's a curse; I'm irresistible. But I cope as best I can."

"I'd remind you that he is a brilliant doctor."

"As is your friend with the boat, right?"

"And he's single."

"As is your friend with the boat, right?"

"I'm not trying to fix you up, you know. With either of them."

"So says the yenta. Okay, girl, you didn't come here to remedy my non-existent love life. What gives?"

Claire explained their involvement in last month's terror event in suburban Washington, and Rowena said she thought they might have figured into the investigation. What she hadn't known, because it was kept from the press, was the email to Pep Boys HQ that read Allahu Akbar.

"This is confidential, you understand."

"Like duh, lady."

"So last Sunday in New Hampshire, a family was murdered, you know about that. Three of them were shot, and all four had their throats ripped out."

"That was a lot closer to home."

Claire said, "And Allahu Akbar was written on the wall in the victims' blood, the press reported that before we could ask them not to." Rowena sipped her coffee and nodded for Claire to continue. "Two acts of terror, five hundred miles away. One well-planned, the other apparently random. Unrelated, right? Except for Allahu Akbar."

"So you're saying that it could be the same person? Or the same terror cell? Or two cells that coordinate attacks?" She thought. "Or maybe a terrorist who commutes? Okay, not funny."

"Or maybe it's a non-Muslim who gets off on murder and who's throwing investigators off his trail with those messages. The Hyattsville attack, we believe, was the work of more than one person, but this one was almost definitely solo."

"All right, very interesting so far, but what does this have to do with me?"

"With us, Ro, with us." Claire took a breath. "See, when we arrived on scene there was some blood on the floor where each family member died. Not much, but some. I'm ashamed to say that in spite of the circumstances, I almost licked my lips." She saw the look in her friend's eyes. "Sorry, inappropriate. But Joe noticed something that made him suspicious, and he called the ME to make sure he'd measured the blood volume in the corpses. He had, and gave Joe the results. Joe estimated the amount of blood needed to write the message on the wall, and the amount left on the floor, and combined it with the volume of blood that the ME found—and when he compared that number to the amount of blood four human bodies normally contain, he came up short. Real short."

"Real short," Rowena repeated. "Oh, shit. Am I getting pale now?" She let the mug slip from her fingers and clatter on the table. Had it been full, coffee would've splashed out. "Because even if it doesn't show on me, I can feel it happening." She held her hands to the side of her head and locked her suddenly teary eyes onto Claire's sympathetic ones.

"Nothing definite yet. Officially an anomaly. But knowing what we've shared, I had to let you know."

Rowena gulped. "So this, this Allahu Akbar guy, he isn't just your garden variety extremist, he's probably a vampire, too? Another Daciana type out there? Thanks for the heads up . . . I think."

"Something else," Claire added. "There were four victims, but there were five table settings. No fingerprints on the extra one, by the way."

"So you're saying this guy sat down with the family, enjoyed a meal, and then had them for dessert?"

"Looks that way."

"God. As if I didn't have nightmares enough already."

Muhammad Al-Jubeir, known to some of his contemporaries centuries ago simply as the Persian, never had nightmares. All his dreams were sweet, and most of them involved torture and death. The Pep Boys attack, his return to terror after nearly fifteen years, had rejuvenated him. He'd nearly forgotten how much pleasure it had been to kill—randomly, not for any ideology, either political or religious, just for the fun, for the pure hell of it. And the family of Bible-thumpers last week was the latest icing on the proverbial cake.

The Persian was a chameleon. He could pass for an Iraqi, an Israeli, an Indian, a Spaniard, and even—as the Hyattsville attack had confirmed—an orthodox Jew. But in origin, he was a pureblood Aryan. A man banished from his native land for his offenses, but too high in social and political station to be executed.

When his travels took him to seventeenth-century England, he'd loved donning the black robes of the witchfinder. Wearing the giant gold crucifix of the faith he privately scorned, he would travel from village to village, where he would hear the accusations of witchcraft: neighbor against neighbor—some with genuine fears, some with grudges to settle, some with covetousness for the accused's land, property, or even spouse. Their motivation never mattered to him. Nor did he particularly believe in witchcraft. What he believed in was his work, and these bumpkins, and the Church whose power they feared, provided him with an abundance of both work and wealth.

There were ways to determine if an accused woman was a witch. She could be locked in a room with a wind-hole and kept there under observation. If a bird flew into the room; if a fly alighted nearby; if a spider spun a web in the corner; that would be evidence the witch had a familiar, through which she could communicate with her infernal master. Heaven help the accused if she had a pet in her home, but most were too impoverished to feed an extra mouth. If the woman were exceedingly ugly, that would indicate the ravages her association with the devil had had on her appearance. Conversely, if she were exceedingly beautiful, she was made so in order to seduce men into the sins of the flesh. If there was enough evidence to warrant a final test, she might be bound and thrown into a pond. If she floated, it meant that the waters of baptism she'd rejected to become a servant of Satan were now rejecting her. If she sank and drowned, well then, she was released from earthly burdens and heaven would welcome her soul.

But this witchfinder's favorite method involved the witch pricker.

Conventional wisdom had it that at some point during a Black Sabbath ceremony, the devil would rise and bestow a kiss on some area of a newly-ordained witch's naked body. At that spot there might form a mole, a callus, a birthmark—or the site might remain invisible. In any case, this area would become numb to pain. Finding the devil's mark on an unblemished woman became the Persian's signature investigative procedure. He used a tool that today would resemble nothing so much as an elongated icepick.

The Persian, who claimed to have studied under Matthew Hopkins, the most feared witchfinder of all, would strip the accused naked in the public square and press the pricker into the woman's flesh. If she cried out, it indicated the devil's mark must be elsewhere. So he'd try again ... and again ... and again. Eventually, weak from loss of blood, her voice hoarse from crying out, she would not respond to another pricking, and the Persian would proclaim he had found the mark.

The march to the gallows, or to the stake, was inevitable.

In one larger village, the Persian found the most compelling case for real witchcraft he'd ever seen. Inhabitants had been disappearing, at nearly regular intervals, and later found drained of blood. They were reported to have suffered punctures, like those made by the witchfinder himself, but made in pairs: closely-spaced marks, on their throats, or perhaps their wrists, or even on the insides of their thighs.

Immediately, he demanded that all women who had reached puberty be summoned before him for inspection. Old women—and wives with possibly vengeful husbands—he dismissed out of hand. Young girls with burly fathers standing beside them he also dismissed. Finally, he was left with a group of young single women, all of whom trembled nearly to the point of fainting.

All except one.

This one was standing still, and her lips appeared to be bordering on a smile. She had a slim figure beneath her peasant smock. Her eyes were large and dark, her hair raven black, and her skin fair, unlike the others, who had been sun-darkened as they worked in their fields. "You," he said, beckoning. "Come here."

She seemed to float toward him and only stopped when she was close, improperly close. "Show me your teeth," he commanded.

She smiled widely. Her teeth were nearly pure white, whereas those of most others were yellow and stained. The teeth were perfectly formed and aligned, another curiosity—but none were sharp enough to cause the wounds the villagers had described. Her breath was sweet, too. A succubus, perhaps? Maybe it was time to begin believing in the devil.

"Take off your clothes," he said in a low voice, his left hand clutching his crucifix, as his right moved toward the hilt of his witch pricker.

The woman didn't make a move. Instead, she whispered, "Are you loath to test me in private, witchfinder? Do you fear your God will not protect you? Are you a coward without those you hold in thrall to stand behind you and cheer you on?"

"Take me to your hut, then," he whispered in response before declaring aloud, "I fear this woman has powers that might prove harmful to those unconsecrated to my divine mission; therefore, I shall test her without witness. Be brave, pray for my continued succor from our Lord, and look for my emergence, with the witch cowed before the might of God."

Once inside the woman's dwelling, she easily slid out of her clothing and stood before the Persian naked, unblushing, unafraid. "You amuse me," she said. "You are, of course, a charlatan of the first order, but I do enjoy your bluster, and the way you project an aura of power. You might one day be useful to me. Now I permit you to stick me, in any spot you wish . . . and observe."

Her inquisitor stood dumbfounded. This wench was actually trying to intimidate him! And . . . she was succeeding!

"Take out your witch pricker," she said again. "Stick me."

As if hypnotized, the Persian stuck the pricker slowly into the crook of her elbow. She placed her opposite hand atop his and pressed the pricker in to its hilt, the tip scraping against the bone of her elbow joint. Still she uttered no cry. Her eyes locked on his and reflected amused condescension rather than fear. He pulled out the tool. Blood bubbled from the wound and trickled down her arm . . . and then the wound closed. Completely. Not a mark showed where the pricker had entered.

His own eyes betrayed his confusion, and—yes—his fear. "What are you?" he whispered.

"Kiss me," she said, shocking him with her sudden lust as she pressed her mouth to his.

The pricker fell to the dirt floor of the hut as the woman locked herself to him, guiding his hands over her body. As he stood dazed, she dropped to her knees and tore down his leggings, leaving him bare from the waist to where the leggings bunched around his boots. She held her hands to his thigh and opened her mouth . . .

But instead of what he'd expected, the woman's mouth opened wider, her lower jaw extending. Fangs swung into place from the roof of her mouth, and they fastened themselves to his inner thigh as he struggled futilely to escape. Soon the feel of their connection became exquisite, intimate, the sound of her slurping strangely sensual. His struggles ceased, and he gave himself over to the woman's desire. Then suddenly, he was lying on the dirt, unable to stand, unable to exert any will of his own. He was her slave, and he was dying.

The woman made a poultice of mud from the dirt floor and water from a pitcher, and applied it to his wounds. Then she picked up the witch pricker, knelt over his face, and jabbed it into her wrist. Her blood spilled into his mouth, and he lapped it up like a thirst-starved dog. His eyes rolled back into his head, and he lost consciousness. When he came to, mere moments later, he discovered that his wrist had healed and that his thigh was clear of any wound marks. A renewed vitality surged through him. And his tongue discovered two items in the roof of his mouth that hadn't been there before.

"You are mine," the woman whispered into his ear. "You will be loyal to me. Now attend to my instructions. I am through with this place and would move on."

The villagers, who had been milling about fretfully outside, soon saw the witchfinder emerge from the woman's hut, one hand in her long black hair as she stumbled next to him, eyes downcast, the witchfinder's crucifix depending from around her neck. "Here is your witch," he declared, his voice grown husky. "She is, further, that most accursed of creatures, the *strigoi*. I have immobilized her with the cross of our Lord, and will take her to London, where I will bring her to trial before the royal court. You are free now, praise God."

47

"Praise God!" they shouted as one, and cheered as the witchfinder's horse-drawn wagon rumbled down the dusty road.

The two traveled for a time without exchanging words. When they reached the city, she bade him stop to let her out.

"What will you do? Where will you go?" he asked.

"I will survive," she answered. "As will you, my friend, for a long, long time."

"Are we to be damned by God for what we have become?"

She laughed. "Who needs God? Who needs heaven? We already have eternal life, here on Earth!"

His tongue played about his newly-formed fangs. The dark-haired beauty smiled and kissed his cheek. "We shall meet again," she said. "Another place, another time." She climbed down from the wagon and looked back at him. "Tell me your name," she said. "Your real name."

He told her. "And what is yours?"

She turned to go, then looked back before disappearing into the crowd. "I am Daciana."

Chapter Six

February flowed into March and April, and every week Rowena called Claire to see if the team was any closer to finding the vampire who'd killed the New Hampshire family. The answer always frustrated her and only made the nightmares worse.

Plus, her cough persisted into the spring weather and Bentley expressed her concern, not for the first time. "Your cold's not gone away, and you're not filling out your clothes the way you used to, either," she said. "Take a day off and go see a doctor, young lady."

Rowena promised she would. But she didn't.

May at Montgomery Blair High School in Silver Spring brought, as it did to most high schools in the country, a severe case of senior-itis. Studies were forgotten, with cramming for exams taking hind teat to preparations for the prom, for the all-night revelries to follow, and the compulsory graduation parties with the fam; when the new graduates would garner congratulations, get their gifts—either in envelopes or parked on the driveway, and after an hour of forced conversation, make the rounds of their friends' parties.

Ahmed Mansoor had circled June 3 on the calendar in the custodians' office. That was the night graduation was scheduled, in the Comcast Center at the University of Maryland. Six hundred seniors would flip their tassels that night, but Ahmed was thinking only of one.

His smoke breaks with Sophie had become a daily occurrence. Lately, he was lighting her cigarettes for her, just as if they were on a date, and the way she looked at him over the flame nearly made him tent his coveralls. The last day before finals, he determined that he would give her a present to remember him by. And if he dared, if she were willing, he'd give her something more personal, something

more intimate, something he'd been wanting to give her
ever since they'd shared their first smoke.

In Solomons Island—a peninsula, really—Jawdan El-
Sayed grumbled as he applied bottom paint to a Hunter
32. *Plug-ugly boat,* he opined, although to the owner's face
he praised its beauty and sailing characteristics. He wasn't
grumbling about the work, though; he was upset about the
phone call from the boss, telling him to make sure he fine-
tuned the Sprinter's engine. He'd reminded him that he and
Ahmed would be taking a road trip this summer, and Jawdan, due to his busy work schedule, would not be included.
Naturally, in keeping with their prior military experiences,
neither of the two accomplices would learn anything more
about the project until they had the need to know.

But Jawdan's contribution would be invaluable when
they reached their target, whatever and wherever it was.
Supplying the van with the weaponry the boss required was
part of his job, and the oversized garage bay in his self-
storage unit held a veritable arsenal. Most of the equipment
was nearly two decades old, but, thanks to his continued
care, it still looked like new . . . and still worked with the
precision of a Swiss watch.

He was breathing more easily these days, although
for the first few weeks in February he'd found himself con-
stantly looking over his shoulder, expecting at any time to
see a man wearing a sheriff's star standing behind him.
Killing the hooker had been an act of necessity, but he
hadn't thought about the ground's being too frozen to hide
her. When the radio announced that the body had been
discovered, so soon, his stomach had dropped. Despite the
care he had devoted to his team's successful, meticulously
planned operations, he stood to get caught for something
so mundane as the murder of a cipher. It didn't seem fair.

Jawdan looked ahead to the summer, when the cruisers would come in. There was never a lack of boaters whose
vessels needed attention. While he worked his repairs, the
occupants of the boat would tool around the area in the
complimentary marina car—to the Calvert Marine Museum,
or the restaurant on the pier, or the tiki bar—leaving him
alone on the boat with certain stray items that he might
liberate. Little things; items stowed in drawers, cabinets, or

below decks that wouldn't be missed until the owner was well under way, and might believe he'd misplaced or already used: a container or two of motor oil, perhaps; a life vest from the store of personal flotation devices; a rigging knife. These would find their way into Jawdan's storage unit. He wouldn't try to resell them; they were strictly for his own private amusement. He displayed them in one corner of the unit, arranged as if inside a trophy case.

Everyone had a flaw of one kind or another, he reasoned. Jawdan's was simply his harmless kleptomania.

As a boy in his home country, the Persian had been a scholar of the highest order, and one of the academic pursuits in which he excelled was the mastery of languages. English was his first, learned at the feet of Sir Robert Shirley, a member of the British Embassy who'd arrived in Persia in 1599 and stayed in country for eight years. The young scholar grew up with one of the sons of Shah Abbas, who with his brothers had his apartment in the shah's harem, guarded by eunuchs, and out of harm's way. This had been a radical—and merciful—alternative to the system in nearby Turkey, where each new sultan would kill his brothers and nephews as a way of ensuring a reign untroubled by familial competition. Sultan Mehmed III, upon winning power in 1595, had murdered all nineteen of his brothers.

Unfortunately, an incident in the harem when he was a virile teenager saw him expelled from court—luckily, with his privates still attached—and from Persia itself. This was considered most merciful, and it was only achieved through the pleadings of his politically-connected father and the shah's son, his lifelong playmate; otherwise, his execution would have been excruciatingly painful and drawn out over many days. Stripped of his wealth, banished from his devoutly religious family, he wandered westward, a pilgrim, adapting to the customs of the countries he visited and picking up their languages. His eventual goal was to reach England, home of Sir Robert, whose tales had intrigued him as a youth. But it wasn't until his forties that he arrived. He found refuge in the Church of England and studied the newly translated Bible of King James I.

He was intrigued by the passage from Exodus which directed, "Thou shalt not suffer a witch to live," the word *witch* being a mistranslation of the Hebrew *chasaph*, or *poisoner*. The king, it was rumored, lived in fear of witches, spells, and other occult manifestations; hence, the translators changed the meaning to keep *Jamie-boy* happy. The Persian, thanks to his linguistic background, noticed the difference immediately, but in it he found the path to a new profession, one which suited his calling: that of witchfinder.

He was forty-four years old when he met the *strigoi* Daciana. He never aged a day after that. And, true to her word, they would meet again. Many times.

But all that had been centuries ago. Today, the Persian, in his latest incarnation as Muhammad Al-Jubeir, was brushing up on his Spanish, in preparation for the *field trip* he would soon be taking with Ahmed Mansoor. Of his two accomplices, the intellectually-challenged Ahmed was the more tolerable, the man most reliable to do the grunt work. Jawdan was more skilled, true, but there was something about him, his kleptomania perhaps, or his innate paranoia, that the Persian had always found disagreeable. Character flaws in others bothered him.

But it was his own character flaw that linked them to him. Years before, they had unexpectedly seen him kill another using his fangs. And after recovering from their initial fear, they had immediately sworn fealty to him, in exchange for his making them immortal like himself. "One day," he promised. "One day, when you are ready."

Rowena's home phone rang at ten o'clock on a bright Saturday morning. "Hope I didn't wake you up," Claire chirped.

"You're so funny, girlfriend. Tell me you've found the creep and run him through a chipper."

"I wish I could. No, the case is cold, and there's been nothing since I first told you. But that's not why I called. Listen, Memorial Day Weekend is coming up in a few weeks. Mark your calendar for Saturday the twenty-third through Monday the twenty-fifth. Dale, Joe, and I will be joining Matthew for a weekend on the water. You're coming, too."

"I am?"

"You am. No arguments, Ro."

"Wasn't about to give you one. I could do with some R and R."

"Good. And here's the other thing. Dale and I are going to pick you up in the Songbird."

"The what?"

"The airplane. I've named it, much to my dear husband's pretended chagrin."

"Uh huh. Like the Golden Goose."

"Now I know what you might say, that Sky King's Songbird was a twin-engine six-place Cessna, and this is a single-engine four-seater; but it's still a Cessna."

"That is not what I was going to say. I was going to ask who was going to be doing the flying."

"Your humble servant, *moi.*"

"Oh well, what have I got to live for anyway?"

"God will get you for that."

"Hey, truth to tell, I've always wanted to take a ride in one of those coffins with wings. So tell me, where do I meet you guys and when?"

Minute Man Airport was an hour's drive northwest from Boston, and Rowena reported promptly at nine, as ordered. The airport was small and charming, with an on-field restaurant, outside of which she met Dale and Claire. Dale checked his watch and nodded his approval. "Favorable winds," he said. "Got us here a few minutes early. Nancy's Air Field Café has good word of mouth. You had breakfast yet?"

"No. I figured with Sky King here driving the plane, I might urp it out." She embraced Claire and gave Dale a brief hug.

"We haven't eaten either, so we'll be taking a chance. But if you're game, I am."

"Screw the both of you," said Claire and led the way into the café.

Forty-five minutes later, filled to the brim with food and with the plane topped off with hundred-octane low lead, Claire performed the preflight inspection as Dale chatted with Rowena. "Ladies," said Dale when they were ready to board, "if you don't mind, I'm going to ride in the back and take a nap."

Claire beamed and opened the right-hand door for Rowena, as Dale entered through the left and climbed into the back. This would be the first time that she was truly the pilot in command, despite her hours logged as such. Except for her solos during flight training, Dale had always been by her side, and she knew that, should trouble occur, he would be there to tell her what to do, or even take over if necessary. His sitting behind her, unable to reach the controls, was a confidence builder par excellence. But she knew he'd be *napping* with his eyes open.

They put on headsets and Claire started the engine, checked the gauges, and turned on the radio. Using the Unicom frequency, she called for a radio check and then announced her intention to taxi to Runway Three.

"Don't mean to interrupt your concentration," said Rowena as the engine revved and the plane began to move, "but I only counted two runways, the paved one and the grassy one."

"That's not the number of runways, that's the runway number. Three stands for thirty degrees. It's the magnetic heading when you're approaching the runway. The opposite end is Two One, which stands for two hundred ten degrees."

"A hundred and eighty in the other direction, right," said Rowena, looking out her window and then to the gauges, wondering what each one meant and how any one person could memorize them all—exactly as Claire had done when Dale took her on her own first ride.

Claire stopped at the run-up area, eased the throttle in while holding the brakes, and performed the magneto check. Returning the throttle back to idle, she checked the instruments and flight controls, explaining each to her passenger as she did, then announced her intention over the radio to depart on Zero Three. After checking for landing traffic, she taxied into position, fed the throttle, and kept the plane on the centerline as speed built up. Somewhere between seventy and eighty miles per hour, Claire eased the yoke back and the plane gracefully left the ground behind.

Rowena gulped as she saw the horizon expand and the greenery of late May reveal itself in an endless panorama. "Holy shit," she whispered. "It's freaking gorgeous." Then she added, "Thank you, God."

Claire grinned as the altimeter needle indicated a thousand feet, and she turned to the southwest and continued to climb. "We're around two hundred miles from our destination, which should put us there in about an hour forty-five; maybe longer, because we're going to show you Manhattan at its prettiest first."

From the back, Dale's voice came through Rowena's headset. "Today's what they call CAVU, ceiling and visibility unlimited, so Claire's going to take advantage and fly down the Hudson River corridor. When we get to Toms River we'll signal Matthew and Joe to drive to the airport and pick us up."

Rowena nodded. "Sure, whatever." Her mouth hung open as she stared at the scenery passing beneath the overhead wing.

They reached the Hudson River north of Manhattan and Claire brought the plane back down to a thousand feet altitude. The George Washington Bridge; Central Park; the Chrysler and Empire State Buildings; Ground Zero; and the Verrazano Bridge filled the windows to Rowena's left. The city seemed to sparkle in the late morning light. Then they were south of the city, the skinny peninsula of Sandy Hook pointing toward them like Cape Cod in miniature. The ocean waves looked like green wrinkles as the plane continued along the shoreline, and then Claire banked right where the wide mouth of the Toms River emptied into Barnegat Bay. A minute later, Claire circled a large white boat in a marina on the southern shore. She circled twice more, wagged the wings, and then continued west until the Robert J. Miller Airpark came into view among the famed New Jersey Pine Barrens.

Claire checked the sectional chart she had clipped to her kneeboard and called to ascertain the active runway. "Runway Six," came the metallic reply. "Winds zero three zero at ten, altimeter two niner point niner two."

"Six equals sixty degrees, right?" asked Rowena.

"You're a quick study," replied Claire. "Now, what's the number on the other end?"

"Um . . ." She ticked off on her fingers. "Two hundred forty degrees. Two Four, right?"

"Bingo. You're a pilot."

"Yeah, like what's that other stuff the guy said?"

"We'll be landing facing sixty degrees, or east-northeast. The wind is from thirty—a quartering crosswind from north-northeast—at ten miles per hour. In other words, no biggie. The altimeter calibration is based on the local barometer setting."

"Sorry I asked. Head, you can stop spinning whenever you're ready."

Claire greased the airplane onto the wide runway and radioed for a tie-down slot. The operator directed her to a spot a short walk from the ops building, and minutes later they disembarked as Claire tied the plane to the tarmac using attach points under the tail and wings. Fifteen minutes later, a blue Honda minivan carrying Matthew Collins and Joe Whitehead pulled into the parking lot, and thirty minutes after that they arrived at the boatyard known as Stump Creek Slipways, where Matthew berthed his live-aboard trawler.

Chapter Seven

At the same time Rowena was being familiarized with Matthew's boat, Montgomery Blair High School senior Sophie Bienkowski and her friends were on their way to Chesapeake Beach for a day's sunbathing and trolling for studs. She was one of six sardined into another girl's compact car, which was filled with blue smoke even before they entered the Capital Beltway. There was a case of beer in a cooler in the trunk, thanks to one of the girls' older brothers, who didn't give two shakes of a dead rat's tail whether his underaged sister got shitfaced or not.

The girls spent the day working on their tans, occasionally dipping their toes into the chilly water of the Bay, and taking turns visiting the cooler, which had been relocated to the front passenger seat. A few hours later they left in two cars, Sophie and another girl having hooked up with two horny young men from Bethesda. They drove them to a tree-shaded dead-end street in an undeveloped housing tract, got them even more drunk, and screwed their brains out. All four agreed it had been a fanfuckingtastic day.

The other four girls now had room in the back seat for the cooler, and they still had a six-pack and two singles left. All eight beers were gone by the time they reached the Beltway. The giggling girls told the driver to gun it up the approach ramp, so they could slip into the traffic without having to slow down and yield. She said that was an outstanding idea and floored the accelerator.

Unfortunately, she sped by the On ramp, so she spun the car with a squeal of tires and in her confusion tore up the Off ramp, where she collided head on with a moving van. The little car's cabin was sheared off at the window line; the girls were decapitated.

Aside from some abrasions from the airbag, the driver of the truck was unhurt.

Ahmed Mansoor, meanwhile, was in a jewelry shop in a strip mall, near the intersection of New Hampshire Avenue and University Boulevard. It was closer than he'd have liked to the former Pep Boys store—the boss had cautioned never to revisit the scene of the crime—but the store had a display in the window that he especially liked. He pointed the proprietor to a certain gold-plated Zippo lighter, examined it closely, pronounced it satisfactory, and asked if it could be engraved.

The jeweler said he had an engraver on site and called her from the back. She told Ahmed that she'd do the engraving in a flowing script, but that he should print the message in block letters so she didn't make any mistakes; there were no refunds on engraved items. She could have it ready for pickup by Wednesday.

Ahmed thanked her and paid for the lighter and the engraving in cash. The jeweler said he'd be all too happy to place the lighter in a beautiful jewelry case and gift-wrap it in exquisite gold paper.

After the door closed behind the Middle Eastern man, the jeweler breathed a sigh of relief, happy to have unloaded that white elephant. "Nobody buys those things anymore," he remarked to the engraver. "Very few people even smoke these days compared to years ago, and those who do buy those damned disposables." He himself, he reflected without any sense of irony, happened to be one of those.

"She's a Kadey-Krogen forty-two-foot trawler yacht," said Matthew Collins as Rowena stared at it from the shore. "She's fifteen feet wide, stands nine feet above the waterline at the bow, and draws around five feet."

It was also the biggest boat in the yard, tied alongside and at the end of a hundred-foot-long wooden pier that jutted into the river perpendicular to the river's shoreline. The others were already on their way to the boat, Joe in the lead, followed by Claire and Dale, carrying their weekend bags. Matthew picked up Rowena's bag, and as they walked down the dock he said, "Bought her from one of the chemists at the plant. He was retiring, and his wife wanted to move back to where they lived before the plant relocated from Cincinnati to Toms River. They bought a place near their son's family in northern Kentucky."

"Not much use for a seagoing yacht in Kentucky, I guess," offered Rowena. She glanced sideways at Matthew as they neared the boat. He was maybe an inch taller than she, sandy hair, fair complected, freckles across his nose, eyes a deep blue. He was trim, not buff like Dale and Joe, and his smile showed perfectly even teeth. *Another British stereotype shattered,* she thought and wondered if he could cook, too.

They climbed aboard the aft deck—Rowena compared it to a back porch—which connected with a walkway to the bow along both sides of the cabin. A ladder to the right side—starboard, she reminded herself—led to the upper deck through a trap door hatch. On that deck, she'd noticed, were an inflatable dinghy and a steering station that she knew was called a flying bridge.

The double doors to the saloon were already open. "You guys raised in a barn?" Matthew called, and he led her inside. The saloon was some eleven feet wide, with a U-shaped galley at the forward end. The flooring was teak and holly parquet, the woodwork polished teak. Past the galley, a narrow three-step stairway led down to a hallway, where the others had gone moments before.

To the left of the stairway, against the port wall, were the three stairs leading up to the pilot house, and it was near them that Matthew placed her bag for the moment. "Cook's tour," he announced. "Galley: all the comforts of home. Twelve-cubic foot refrigerator, twelve-foot freezer, microwave, three-burner range and oven, double stainless sinks. No dishwasher, though; wastes too much water. The porthole above the range is your vent to the outside." He directed her gaze to the saloon. "Sliding glass windows port and starboard, screened to keep out the greenheads and mosquitoes. Yes, the twelve-inch telly between the chairs on the port side has cable, and yes, the boat is air conditioned."

"Really. All the amenities."

"Hot water baseboard heat in the winter, too, put in by the previous owner. Now, let's go below." They walked down the steps into the hallway. "That locker to your left hides a stacking washer and dryer. The next door is to the head; Claire can give you flushing school later. Across the hall, my office, but also a guest stateroom. You can see our

friend Jomo claiming his swing-down bunk, which normally lives against the forward bulkhead. The settee against
the hull will be mine for the weekend."

"And a built-in desk and closet: small but efficient."

"What more would one need?"

They walked the few steps to the end of the hallway
and the master stateroom, which boasted a queen size bed
on the yacht's centerline, and on which reposed Claire and
Dale, arms behind their heads, ankles crossed, contented
grins on their faces.

"Welcome to heaven," Claire said. "There's nothing like
sleeping on a boat to make you relax utterly. You'll see."

Matthew led Rowena back to the saloon and carried
her bag up the steps to the pilot house, where she met the
resident cat, curled up on the watch berth. "Notice the extra
toes?" he asked when Rowena inquired as to its name. "I
just had to name her Digit."

Rowena laughed and extended her arms to the gray
tabby, who came willingly, rubbed her cheek against Ro's
hand, and purred.

"I rescued her from the pound as a kitten. To satisfy
my longing for female companionship. A female who doesn't
talk back."

"Meow, you pig."

"Unfortunately, because of all the wood, I had to have
her declawed. Hated to do it, but I figured given the choice
between losing her claws and losing her life in the gas chamber she'd choose the former. Her litter box is in the shower,
by the way; be careful to take it out before you hop in."

"I'll remember that," said Rowena, stroking the gray
furball now snuggled in her arms.

Rowena looked around the pilot house. Three windows
in front, engine controls and instruments centered in the
command console, along with the ship's wheel. Dutch doors
on the sides, the tops glass with small No Smoking decals
in their lower corners.

"This will be your bedroom for two days," Matthew
said. "Digit sleeps where she wants, so if you feel something
soft and furry nestling into your armpit at night, don't be
alarmed. Now: I'm going to start the engine and prepare to
cast off. Those lubbers below will handle the lines, if I can
get them off their arses long enough."

At Solomons Island Marina in southern Maryland, the holiday weekend brought boaters in droves. Every available slip was occupied, and in the deep, sheltered waters of Back Creek other boats sat at anchor. The weather was severe clear, and Jawdan El-Sayed was severely busy tending to dock lines, seeing that powerboats got fueled, collecting docking fees, and manning the ship's store. He barely had time to grab a smoke out back.

In a couple of weeks, Ahmed would drive down and pick up the panel truck, which Jawdan had not yet serviced for the trip—the trip that he would not be included on. He was still annoyed about that. He knew his job wouldn't let him get away during the summer, but why did the boss have to go then and not wait until later in the fall?

Whatever the trip was about, it promised to make a decent impression, like the Pep Boys store last January ... and the job before, the really big one, ages ago now. For that they had been supplied with all manner of weaponry, much of which still reposed in his storage unit.

The weapon the boss had specified for this mission, in addition to the rifles and handguns and plastic explosives that formed the rest of their arsenal, was a beauty that they'd never had occasion to use. It had been conceived in America just before the end of the First World War and used extensively during the Second: the 3.5-inch rocket launcher, known popularly as the Bazooka. The rockets it fired carried HEAT; that is, high explosive anti-tank warheads. The acronym explained all that needed to be told about the Bazooka's purpose and power. Whatever the boss planned to take out, it would be big and armored, like a tank.

An American-made weapon taking out an American target: it was like getting shot with your own gun.

Chapter Eight

As Claire lay on the padded bench ahead of and attached to the pilot house, with her head resting on Dale's lap, Matthew steered the good ship *Semper Fidelis* toward the mouth of the Toms River from the flying bridge station. He sat on a tall swivel chair bolted to the deck, and Joe and Rowena sat opposite on facing settees. Behind them stood a small mast, which Matthew told them he used for lowering the inflatable dinghy and its five-horsepower outboard.

Rowena remarked about the boat's name. "I had a dog growing up," she said, "and my dad named him Semper Fido."

"Your dad was a Marine, I take it."

"Career. What they call a mustang: began as enlisted, ended as an officer."

"Good for him."

Rowena winked at Joe, the former Navy man. "He said that whenever a sailor called him a sea-going bellhop, his reply was to ask what flavor ice cream was in that Dixie cup on his head."

"Ah, yes," said Joe as he took a swig from his beer can. "The jarheads and the squids. The rivalry goes on, to the end of the world."

Ro turned her attention to Matthew. "I'll bet this boat is a real babe magnet, yes?"

Matthew laughed. "Not really. The babes, as you call them, are not attracted to slowpokes like this. They prefer the speed of the cigarette boats, like that one approaching from the rear."

She heard it before she saw it: a bronze and black fiberglass torpedo, spraying rooster tails in its wake and coming up fast; a long, brightly colored, enclosed hull with a tiny cockpit in the stern. In it sat three people, a balding middle-aged man flanked by two young women. He was clad in a red—oh, say it ain't so, Rowena thought—*Speedo*; whereas the women, half his age if that, wore three-piece swimsuits: two postage stamps and a rubber band. The boat roared by them, and Ro noticed that the top of the man's head was already turning red. The women's long hair streamed behind them, one blond, the other brunette. "Vanilla and chocolate," she said. "I see what you mean."

Matthew joked, "*Semper* here is built for comfort, not speed. I fear that if I were to race another trawler across the river it would be an all day affair. But as I say, and I do say, when one is where one wants to be, what difference does it make how fast one is going?" He added, "Oh, and my lone hundred-forty-five horsepower diesel engine burns only about one gallon of fuel an hour. The boat that just screamed past us burns about fifty gallons of gasoline in the same amount of time."

"We call them hard-on boats," said Joe. "That long hull sticking out is one huge phallic symbol. And you can see what's attracted to them."

"Nice image," Ro replied. "I'll never get it out of my mind, no matter how hard I try."

The Krogen skirted the shoal at the mouth of the river and made for the channel markers in Barnegat Bay. Matthew turned to the south and asked Rowena if she wanted to steer for a while. "Just keep her between the poles with the red and green markers on the top." They switched places, and she saw Matthew and Joe exchange amused glances as she fought to keep the boat from veering from one side to the other.

"Come on!" she commanded, but *Semper* wouldn't obey. "As soon as I get this thing going straight, it moves off course. What's going on, Matthew?"

"Right. No problem. You just have to anticipate the yaw and correct for it before it happens."

"Yeah, easy for you to say. I can see you two laughing at me, by the way."

"You should be looking forward, luv. Joe and I will be your eyes to the side and rear."

"Did you just say you're looking at my rear?"

"Steer the boat, please."

From forward and below, Claire's voice drifted up. "Ro must be at the helm. I never got seasick going from side to side before."

Dale called, "That's okay, Ro. You're doing fine for the first time."

"Thank you," she shouted. "At least there's one gentleman aboard."

Matthew asked Joe to take the wheel when they approached their anchorage, an area on the chart called Tice's Shoal. He scurried down the aft ladder and entered the pilot house, which had two opening portholes aft to the bridge station. "Got it," he called through, and Joe released the wheel as Dale prepared to free the anchor. Once they were in place, Matthew used the electric winch at his station to lower the anchor to the bottom, then put the vessel in reverse to set the hook. When he was satisfied, he shut down the engine and declared the ship secure.

The first thing Rowena noticed was the silence. Yes, there were gulls screeching overhead, and yes, there were chatter and music coming from the hundred or so other boats whose owners were also taking advantage of the long weekend and glorious weather. But the noise seemed far away to her. What she noticed most was the soft slapping of the tiny waves against the hull and the gentle rocking, like a baby's cradle.

Far off the stern was the mainland; closer, off the bow, was the tall dune grass that marked the unspoiled peninsula of Island Beach State Park. The breeze was from the east, a condition that Joe said was fortunate, because if it were from the west it would bring out the carnivorous greenhead flies, in droves. "This vessel would be so covered with those black buggers it would look like boat *au poivre*. And we'd be spending the weekend inside."

Matthew broke out beer, wine, and iced tea, and Joe produced crackers and cheese from the galley. They sat, drank, and nibbled, made small talk, and simply enjoyed the late afternoon spent on the water. Rowena told Claire that she knew now what her friend had meant about how totally relaxing it was on a boat.

"To you birds, yes," said Matthew. "To the captain here, the responsibility weighs heavily upon his shoulders."

Dale and Joe made air violins, and Dale sang, "My heart bleeds for you."

"Bugger off," Matthew said.

After a dinner of shish kabobs from a charcoal-fired grill attached to a fitting near the stern, Claire demanded a serenade from their host. Feigning reluctance, Matthew went below to the hanging locker in the guest stateroom and brought out an acoustic guitar.

Seeing Rowena's puzzled expression, Claire said, "I told you he plays the guitar. We call him Jimmy Buffet Lite."

"Very lite," added Dale. "Pride of the parrotheads and mayor of Margaritaville."

Matthew ignored them. "What would you like to hear?" he asked.

Joe grinned lasciviously and said, "How about 'She Was Only the Captain's Daughter, but She Loved His Dinghy.'"

"Oh no," said Claire. "I know where this is going."

Dale picked up the cue. "How about 'She Was Only the General's Daughter, but She Loved His Privates.'"

Claire shook her head. "Come on, you two, you're corrupting my friend here."

But Rowena brought her up short with, "'She Was Only the Admiral's Daughter, but She Loved His Seamen.'"

"*Et tu, Brute*?" Claire cried.

Matthew said, "Well, since you all seem bent upon a ditty in a lighter vein—oops, perhaps I shouldn't have used the word *vein* in present company." He nodded toward Claire and Dale. "I trust this doesn't mean I need to sleep with one eye open tonight."

Dale said, his expression blank, "You do now."

How amazing, Rowena thought, *that everyone seems so comfortable sharing these confined quarters with a pair of werewolves-slash-vampires.*

"A word of explanation for Rowena's benefit," Matthew said. "Back when I first arrived from Jolly Olde England I decided I'd add to the adventure—new culture plus new lifestyle—and try living on a boat. I joined the U.S. Power Squadron and took every course they offered, then enrolled in a liveaboard course offered by a yachting concern in Toms River. It put theory into practice, as we spent a week plying the bay, the ocean, and the inlets. There were two instructors and four of us students, including a then-civilian bloke named Dale Keegan."

"The plot thickens," said Rowena. "That's how you two met."

"And I've regretted it ever since," said Dale.

"Our chief instructor was a crusty old bugger named Calvin Cobb. His life was all about the sea, from working on a commercial fishing trawler as a young man to opening a tackle shop when he got too old or too tired to haul the nets. Running this class was something he did to ease the boredom of retirement."

"Got it."

"Well, Calvin loved to make fun of our ineptitude, so I gave him a taste of his own medicine with this little verse."

He began by strumming the melody of "Puff the Magic Dragon" and then sang, in a pleasant if unremarkable voice:

"Calvin is our captain, a fisherman of old.

He'd owned a bait and tackle shop, and many tales he told.

He taught the art of baiting; it was a skill he knew.

He was a master fisherman, and master baiter too."

Dale said, "Calvin called him 'Peter Pull and Messy' from that point on."

Rowena decided she liked this guy. "So when you failed as a singer and song writer you went into . . . dye chemistry instead?"

"Yes, it's a carnivore-free field. Record producers, I'm told, are sharks. Turning chemicals into colors seemed much safer to me. I happened to be wrong, by the way."

"Come on. Making dye is dangerous? You boil water, you add powder . . ."

"Ah, but what makes up the powder? Lots of hazardous acids and alkalis, including organic solvents. Acid fumes can coat your skin and get into your lungs, but that's the least of it. We have oleum, which is sulfuric acid plus extra sulfur trioxide to make it super-saturated. The added SO_3 ignites with the water vapor in the air and creates sulfuric acid fumes, like those from volcanoes. Breathe it, and say bye-bye to your lungs."

"Well, that's pretty grim."

"It gets better. If you were to bathe in it, it would strip you to your bones faster than a school of piranhas."

"Grimmer still."

"Once I saw a lab tech take a Japanese beetle and drop it into a sample jar of oleum just to see what would happen."

"And what happened?"

"*Pfft*. Just *pfft*. Instant dissolution."

"Not nice."

"And on the other end of the pH scale is fifty percent caustic soda. You might know it as sodium hydroxide. It's opaque white and thick as Karo syrup, and at that strength it too will eat through just about anything. It just takes a longer time. One day in the lab I inadvertently spilled a drop onto my shoe and didn't notice it. At the end of the day my left foot felt cooler than my right. I looked down, and there was a hole in the top of the shoe."

Rowena frowned. "If you're a full time chemist, how do you find time to do . . . you know, the work you do with these other guys?"

"Right. See, Toms River Dyestuffs and Intermediates is owned by a French company. Lots of the chemists and most of the upper management are French nationals, and you know how those Froggies love their vacation time. Well, if they get a month off every year—and that's to start—their American counterparts must get a month off, too. So when duty calls"—he nodded toward the others—"I simply put in for vacation time. I've not taken many vacation days this year," he added. "A lot of my involvement with this crew has been on weekends."

At Claire's insistence, Matthew serenaded them with soft guitar music, sans lyrics—ribald or otherwise. The music seemed to mellow everyone out, and soon Rowena found her eyelids beginning to droop.

Joe announced he was ready to hit the rack, and the others agreed, saying goodnight and repairing to their staterooms, Rowena to her watch berth in the pilothouse, where Digit was waiting for her. She opened the top half of the Dutch doors and looked up. The moon was the slimmest of crescents, and its wan light allowed the stars to shine at their brightest. She delighted in the darkness and the starfretted sky. Then she slid beneath her sheet.

She heard movement below: bare feet padding to the saloon door. Another pair followed. The door opened and closed. Then the hatch in the stern bulkhead swung open, and two bodies slipped from the swim platform into the water.

Rowena left her bunk and noticed two figures swimming silently eastward, toward the shore of the state park. The darkness swallowed them as she stood at the door and held Digit in the crook of her arm. Some fifteen minutes later, from the parkland, she heard howling from a pair of wolves. Somehow, it made her shiver and gave her comfort at the same time.

She climbed back onto her berth and pulled the sheet over her. The cat found her armpit and snuggled in. *Arthur Ford had been right,* she thought: *there's nothing so strange . . .*

She drifted into the most peaceful sleep she'd known in a long time.

They spent the next morning swimming and sunning, and after lunch Matthew hauled the anchor and turned the boat north. Dale and Claire sat on the aft deck, and Joe and Rowena took up yesterday's places on the flying bridge. "Mind if I try steering this thing again?" she asked, and Matthew was pleased to relinquish the helm.

"Keep us between the channel markers," he said, and Rowena gave him a *duh* look. "Sorry; sometimes I tend to state the obvious."

"No, that's all right. I forget that this isn't your toy, it's your home. Listen, I'm still having trouble keeping it— her—straight. Would you mind guiding my movements on the wheel?"

"I'm going below," Joe said. "Getting thirsty."

Matthew stood behind Rowena and placed his hands over hers as they clutched the large stainless steel wheel. As the boat veered left of the course line, Matthew eased the wheel a quarter turn to the right; as it neared the heading, but before reaching it, he turned the wheel back to the left. The boat continued right until it was dead on the magnetic course; then as it began to turn left Matthew gave the wheel another quarter turn right. "You have to anticipate the yaw," he explained. "You learn to educate your hands to the wheel, just as I imagine Claire had to educate her fingers to the yoke in their plane."

"Got it. But don't back off just yet," she said.

They stayed that way, belly to back, hands over hands, for a long time. Finally, Matthew asked Rowena if she were comfortable.

"Very," she replied, wondering if he sensed any ambiguity in her voice. *If I moved my hips back,* she thought, *he'd get a standing lap dance, but . . . what are you doing, Ms. Parr, you brazen slut?*

Then she reflected that this was the first time she'd thought of herself as Ms. Parr rather than Mrs.

The bay carried the slightest chop, and the cloudy sky lowered the temperature enough to raise goose bumps on Rowena's arms. Her sleeveless white blouse, the top two buttons unfastened, fluttered in the northerly breeze. A ponytail poked out the back of her ball cap. Even without makeup she was a beautiful woman, and Matthew appreciated it when she turned her head toward him to talk, revealing a profile that belonged in a museum: Aphrodite cast in bronze.

Once back at and secured to the dock, Joe checked his watch. "Almost five o'clock," he said.

Matthew confirmed the time. "Weeping Willow Bar is now open. Mainly," he amended, "because the Weeping Willow Bar is always open." He turned toward Rowena. "Madam, may I interest you in a draught of our finest malt beverage?"

"But of course. Now, where is this Weeping Willow Bar, and am I dressed appropriately?"

Claire said, "Follow me," and led her across the boatyard to an old wooden picnic table shaded by a weeping willow tree. "Behold: the Weeping Willow Bar."

Matthew emerged from the weathered clapboard building whose upper story served as the marina owner's house and whose first floor housed the chandlery, or ship's store. "The owner keeps a keg on tap," he explained, nodding toward the two filled glasses he carried. "Fifty cents a glass, honor system, just like everything else in the store. We take what materials we need, log them in individual steno pads, and get a bill at the end of the month."

Rowena took the glass and downed the beer in one long chug. "Didn't know how thirsty I was," she said, almost apologetically. "Next round's on me, Matthew."

"Day on the water will do that to you, luv."

She took his glass, empty now as well, back to the store for a refill. *That's such a nice expression the English have,* she thought. *Luv.*

They spent the evening at the Weeping Willow, socializing with the liveaboards and the other boat owners down for the weekend. Someone suggested a co-op dinner, and galleys were cleaned out for potluck. Later, Rowena stood alone at the shoreline, looking across the river at the lights of Island Heights.

"Meditating?" asked Claire, who had silently come up behind her.

"This is heaven, isn't it?"

"Closest thing to it, for a lot of people. Me, I'm just as happy in the air."

"Reminds me, something Matthew said about educating your fingers to the yoke. Do you think—?"

"Of course you can. By the way, I notice your cough's getting better."

"Must be that clean salt air."

They all retired early and rose at dawn. After a hearty breakfast—bacon, sausage, and a deep bowl of eggs scrambled with cheese—Joe hopped in his car to begin the four-hour drive to Thurmont, and Matthew drove the others to the airpark.

"I loved this weekend," Rowena said, as she gave Matthew a carefully chaste hug.

He handed her a business card. On it was a photo of the boat, *MV Semper Fidelis* in bold type above, the boat's documentation number below, and his name and cell phone number below that. "Call me when you're ready for another ride," he said to her.

Claire, overhearing, rolled her eyes to Dale, who put his arm around her and walked her to the plane.

The flight back to Minute Man Airport was highlighted by Claire's letting Rowena take the controls on the right side of the cabin and helping her educate her fingers to the yoke. It was no easier than steering the boat, but it was almost as much fun. On the ground, Dale saw to refueling as the women walked to Rowena's car—her late husband's Mercedes, bought just a few months before Daciana Moceanu killed him—and made their goodbyes. Dale walked over, kissed Rowena on the cheek, and said, "You know, Matthew's a great guy. I'm the one who recruited him for the team."

"Are you implying something?"

"Just saying."

Rowena pushed him away. "Don't you two have someplace you have to be?"

As the Cessna departed Runway Two One, Rowena doubled over beside her car and coughed her lungs out.

Chapter Nine

Over the years, Daciana kept casual track of the Persian. As his maker, she held a psychic connection to him, a bond that would forever link him to her—a bond with which she could beckon him, and of which he was totally unaware. What this bond was, how it worked, and why it worked, she had no idea. Nor did she care. She simply accepted it, as one accepts the vagaries of weather or the vicissitudes of fortune.

After watching her melt into the London crowds, the Persian turned his wagon around and continued his career as a witchfinder. But now he interrogated the more attractive women in private, ostensibly to protect the villagers from their obscenely seductive spells. These women he would prick as before, but when they were too weak even to call out, much less resist him, he would rape them, bite into their necks, and drain them until they died.

He would reappear after each feeding, holding the woman's body, alleging that in an act of contrition the witch had grabbed his dirk and slit her own throat before he could stop her. "She must be purified by fire," he would tell them, and as the flames consumed her body he would lead the villagers in prayers for her soul.

At the very moment of each of the Persian's kills, Daciana, wherever she happened to be, would feel a most pleasant shudder, nearly sexual in its nature.

Daciana herself, meanwhile, befriended a young woman who had come to London to serve in the royal court. She killed her, assumed her identity, and presented herself in the woman's place. She rose in stature, on occasion took secret lovers, and made sure all of them eventually met sudden and accidental deaths. Usually deaths that included a massive loss of blood.

Two centuries later, during the summer of 1888, she reconnected with the Persian in the Whitechapel district of London. He had found work as a longshoreman, as the often violent waterfront area provided the perfect venue for his occasional kills; she was an artist's model living in the city, delighting in visiting art classes and watching the middle-aged men ogle her impotently as they committed her nude form to canvas. She also did private modeling, and if she determined that the artist was free of family and basically a loner, right: the River Thames was the perfect place to dispose of drained bodies.

On 6th August, Daciana visited the studio of Walter Richard Sickert. The artist asked her purpose, and she replied that she was answering an advert in the paper. "What do you know about me?" he asked, in a tone that smacked of incivility.

She was unfazed by his gruffness. "I know that you are twenty-eight years old, that you trained under the American James McNeill Whistler, and that you socialize with luminaries like Irving and Tree, as well as that Irish scoundrel Stoker. Your work is impressionistic and dark. Is that enough?"

"Bah," he said, placing his brush on a table and wiping his hands on an apron. "You know nothing. You are a chorus girl, and I have no use for chorus girls. Other painters can have them. Give me the hags! Now leave."

This was unexpected, and an affront that Daciana could not tolerate. She met the Persian at the docks and suggested that they right the wrong Sickert had done her, tonight. A joint kill, their first ever. After dinner in a local pub, they posted themselves a safe distance from Sickert's studio and waited for him to leave. When he did, they were in for a surprise.

He came out wearing a military uniform.

Intrigued, they followed him into Whitechapel. The night was cold for summer, and fog rolled in from the river. This was, in fact, the coldest and wettest summer in ages, and cloaks and capes were the preferred outerwear against the rain and mist.

Sickert walked into a pub, where he struck up a conversation with an older and very unattractive woman at the bar. "He likes hags," Daciana whispered to the Persian as they took a table near the corner. "But what interests me is why the uniform, when he is not a soldier. What is his game?" Soon the twosome were joined by another woman and another man in uniform. They drank and left together, parting company once they had walked a couple of blocks. The artist and the prostitute found an alley and disappeared. Daciana whispered that they should stand on the street and wait a few moments. They would take him down in the throes of sexual release.

Suddenly they heard a woman's muffled scream, followed by a man's grunts. They'd expected the grunts, but not the scream. Again and again the man grunted, and each grunt was accompanied by a thudding sound and an ever-weakening scream.

When silence returned, the two *strigoi* backed into a doorway until Sickert emerged from the alley and walked off into the fog. Then they entered and saw the woman's body, lying on the ground with multiple slashing stab wounds.

Inspiration struck Daciana. "Let us not be too hasty about killing this man," she said. "He may prove entertaining." They looked down at the poor woman's body, then at each other. It would be a shame to let all that fresh blood go to waste.

The newspaper would list the victim as forty-year-old Martha Tabram, one of London's *unfortunates*—the euphemism for prostitutes—whose husband had expelled her from their home for her habitual and uncontrolled consumption of alcoholic beverages.

The couple decided to keep watch over Sickert, and in the early hours of 31st August their vigil paid off. A woman later identified as forty-four-year-old Mary Ann Nichols, another unattractive unfortunate, was surprised by Sickert on a fiercely stormy night as she staggered, drunk, on a back street. He strangled her unconscious, slit her throat, and savagely mutilated her genitalia. The body was discovered by a constable before Daciana and the Persian could partake of the spoils, but they knew they would have another opportunity in time. It occurred about a week later.

At 5:30 on the morning of 8th September, they watched their target kill Annie Chapman, a woman in her late forties, first strangling her and then slashing her throat as he had done to Nichols. Next, he surprised them by going a grisly step further: as she lay on the ground, he eviscerated her, removing her innards and placing them upon her upper body. The coroner was later shocked at the carnage; but the two people who earlier had observed the artist at work knew they had found a kindred spirit. As such, they decided to let him live.

Three more killings, each more ferocious than the one prior, occurred, the last victim being Mary Jane Kelly on 9th November. By this time, the artist had identified himself in mocking letters to Scotland Yard as Jack the Ripper.

Meanwhile, over the next three years, some dozen more victims succumbed to heinous murders, attributed by many to be the work of the Ripper. A missionary to London's East End at the time wrote, "There was a general panic, a great many excitable people declaring that the Evil One was revisiting the earth."

No one would have suspected that the beautiful artist's model could have had anything to do with those later crimes.

Walter Richard Sickert died peacefully in January of 1942, at the age of eighty-one.

By that time, Daciana and her cohort had found new pursuits and new pleasures in Nazi Germany.

The mood among Montgomery Blair High School's Class of 2009 was somber. Tributes to their four classmates killed in an automobile crash over Memorial Day Weekend adorned the walls, trophy cases, and hastily erected display areas outside. Graduation was but nine days away, and the administration decided it would be appropriate to leave four chairs empty at the ceremony in silent acknowledgment of the students' loss.

"Shit, Monsieur, that coulda been me in that car," exclaimed Sophie Bienkowski as she sneaked another smoke with Ahmed in the custodians' office. "I went with them to the beach."

"Why didn't you drive home with them?"

She took a deep puff. Her cheeks pinched in, making her look like she was sucking pudding through a straw. "Marybeth and I, we met some guys. You know. They drove us to her house, after—"

"After?" As if he didn't know.

She ignored him. "I didn't color my hair today," she went on. "And I went light on the makeup, in honor of them."

Ahmed tried to look supportive while inwardly acknowledging the triviality of her *tribute*. But that was all
right; he wasn't looking for Mother Teresa, after all. "You're
very pretty, even without the makeup," he said. "You have a
natural beauty, you should be aware of that."

"Stop, you're makin' me blush."

"Now remember, you're to see me right here when
school lets out for the last time. I have a little going-away
present for you."

She brightened. "Why, thanks, Monsieur. You sure do
know how to make a girl feel good."

He nodded. He surely did, and in a few days she would
know just how good.

Rowena Parr left the doctor's office, her face set in
stone, and drove home in silence. She parked the car and
pressed the radio's off button, even though the radio hadn't
even been on. She jumped as music blared and pushed
the button again. She walked into her house and headed
straight for the first floor bathroom—not to use the toilet,
but to stare at her reflection in the mirror above the sink.
She picked up the magnifying makeup mirror and studied
her eyes. She put the mirror down and took a drink of water
from the tap. She never drank directly from the tap; there
was a filter on the kitchen faucet. But she wasn't in the
kitchen. And it didn't matter now anyway.

It was only mid-afternoon, but Rowena walked directly
to her bedroom at the top of the stairs and put her purse
on the nightstand. She took out her cell phone, punched
a Maryland area code, shook her head, and canceled it.
She faced the mirror above her dresser and said, "Say it.
Go ahead, say it." She really tried, but she couldn't get the
words out. The first two were hard enough; the third, impossible.

Rowena removed her blouse, unfastened her skirt, and
stood before the mirror in her bra and panties. She reached
behind her and unfastened the bra, letting it fall free. She
examined her breasts in the mirror, stared at them for a
long time. Suddenly her eyes filled with tears. She turned
her back on the mirror and collapsed face down upon the
bed. Tears soaked the pillowcase, and saliva made it slip-
pery.

Over and over, the doctor's voice—so conciliatory, even though she'd said the words so many times to so many other women—ran through her head like an audio loop: "So sorry . . . began in the lungs . . . metastatic . . ."

Rowena cried herself to sleep, but she woke up every hour or two and had to cry herself to sleep all over again.

Pillow talk had become one of their favorite aspects of lovemaking. Following its consummation, always fulfilling in itself, they would cuddle and whisper endearments before drifting into the embrace of sleep, nesting like a pair of spoons.

Tonight, though, was different.

"Something's on your mind . . . besides me," said Dale.

"I'm worried about Rowena."

"How so? She wasn't coughing so much last weekend, compared to February." He knitted his eyebrows. "Come to think of it, she did seem to clear her throat a lot."

"Did you see how she'd lost weight? I mean, she had a beautiful figure to start with, but she doesn't have as much of it as before."

"Her figure, you say. Now that I did notice."

Claire pinched his nipple, causing an *Ouch.* "Notice her figure, or notice her weight loss?"

"She does cut a fine figure," he said, covering his nipples with his hands.

"I think you're a were-pig, you know that?"

He gave her a barnyard grunt, then grew serious. "All right. What are you thinking?"

"I don't know what to think. She quit smoking more than five years ago, when she got pregnant. But maybe—"

"Has she seen a doctor, do you know?"

"I don't know."

"Call her tomorrow. It's not like we've got a busy schedule."

"That's the other thing, the lack of something to do, no leads to pursue," said Claire. "Four months, and we still have no clue as to who did the Pep Boys bombing. Police, FBI, Homeland Security, plus our little team, and no one's the wiser."

"Don't forget the New Hampshire family."

"Uh huh. Again, no traces: no hair, no skin, no DNA to try to match up. It's not like us. Well, like you; I haven't been on the team that long. I hate the thought of having to wait for the next attack before we have a chance at finding out who's responsible."

Dale sat up in bed, all thoughts of sleep banished. "Feel like a run tonight, work off some of that worry? It's a beautiful night."

"A four-legged run?" He nodded. She sat up and kissed him. "I think I'm up for that."

Wednesday, the third of June, was a day off for seniors, at least so far as they were concerned, and the underclassmen basically just sat around and signed each other's yearbooks. Any pretense at a dress code was forgotten, as boys wore shorts and sleeveless T-shirts and girls wore shorter shorts and tank tops. Montgomery Blair High School was officially Hormone Central.

Ahmed Mansoor pulled his car up to the loading dock, but purposely left his gift on the front passenger seat. Then he walked up the steps to his office. He was the only custodian working in this wing of the building today, so privacy was assured.

Right on schedule, Sophie breezed into the boiler room and popped into the office. "Hey, Monsieur, our last smoke together. Let's get wild and have two. What can they do to us? Fire you? Tell me I can't go to graduation?" She fished a cigarette from her purse. "Frankly, I don't give a shit whether I go to graduation or not. My folks don't intend to be there, why should I?"

"They don't care?" he asked as he lit her cigarette and then turned the flame on his own.

"Get this," she said, exhaling. "When I turned eighteen, they kicked me out of the house."

"Really? Why?"

"Eh. They call it tough love or something. Mom probably heard about it on Doctor Phil. That's all she does all day, look at frickin' TV. She said I had to learn respect for her and Dad and respect for their rules, and when I did I could come back."

"So where did you go?" Thinking, *I wish you'd come to me.*

78

She snorted a laugh. "There's lots of friends I can crash with. They tell their parents I'm sleeping over for the night, their parents say whatever, and the next day I crash somewhere else. No biggie. Been doing it for a month now."

"Your parents don't try to get in touch with you?"

She pulled out her cell phone. "They know my number; they just don't call. But I can be just as stubborn as them, know what I mean?"

"I do."

She stubbed out her butt. "So, ready for ciggie number two?"

"Oh, yes," he said. He opened a desk drawer, closed it, slapped his pockets, and made an O with his mouth. "Wait, I remember. I left it in the car."

"My present?"

"It's right down the steps."

They walked together to Mansoor's ten-year-old green Jetta, Sophie grinning in anticipation. He opened the passenger door and presented her with the gift. She unwrapped it and opened the jewelry box. "Oh, Monsieur," she said, drawing the gold-plated Zippo from the box. "It's like yours, but gold."

"Look again."

"Ooh, it's engraved: *To Sophie, from Monsieur*. I love it!" She stared into his eyes. "I don't know what to say."

"Then let me. I have really enjoyed our little meetings, Sophie. You have come to mean a great deal to me."

"Aw, you're sweet," she said and tiptoed up to kiss his cheek. At the last second, he turned his face to hers so their lips met. And before she could recover, he had his arms around her and his tongue in her mouth. She struggled and finally was able to push her face back. "What the fuck?" she nearly shouted. "What're you, some kind of perv?"

He put his hand over her mouth. "Come on, Sophie, you know what you do. I hear the talk in the halls. All I want from you—hey!"

She managed to bite his palm, and as he pulled it back, he hit her with his other hand—a roundhouse fist to the temple. She collapsed like a punctured balloon. *Shit.* He hadn't meant to do that.

Mansoor picked up the dropped lighter and put it in his pocket. Looking around to make sure they hadn't been noticed, he opened his trunk and tossed Sophie inside. "Good thing I came prepared," he muttered, as he took out the bottle of chloroform and a cheesecloth rag.

He walked up the steps, picked up Sophie's purse, made sure she hadn't left anything else behind, and drove away. He had rope in his basement, and lots of rags for her mouth. After securing her—and enjoying her—he would return to the school and finish his duties for the day.

That night, inside the Comcast Center at the University of Maryland, the festiveness of graduation ceremonies was tempered by the vacant seats representing the seniors' fallen classmates. There was another vacant seat, unnoticed by anyone except the students to either side, who weren't surprised that the senior class slut didn't show up. When the Superintendent of Schools called the name of Sophia Anastasia Bienkowski and no one stood, the school board president placed her diploma on the table behind him and the superintendent went on to the next name without missing a beat. Frankly, he was grateful she didn't show up. She'd spent almost as much time in his office as he had over the past four years, and the thought of shaking her hand—not knowing where it had been last—was repugnant.

On Friday, June 5th, a visibly shaken Rowena Parr applied for medical leave. When she told her boss the reason, Bentley hugged her, said if there's anything she and Elliott could do—and meant it—and followed up with questions about treatment. Rowena dodged them.

"I've got a lot to think about," she said. "I'm going to discuss my options with my parents. They deserve to know."

"Of course."

"And I know this will sound like I'm totally exploiting our friendship, but—"

"Take as long as you like. All I ask is that you keep me informed, on a regular basis. Phone calls, emails, carrier pigeon, any and all are acceptable. You know Elliott and I love you, Rowena. We want you well, and not because you're indispensable to Jones Publishing. You're indispensable to us personally. Never forget that."

They hugged for a long time. Then Rowena took a last look at her office, wondering if she'd ever see it again, visited briefly with the other editors and staff, and walked out of the building.

The inflammatory manuscript by Muhammad Al-Jubeir remained in her desk drawer. She had completely forgotten about it.

All that mattered was the fact that she was *so* not ready to die.

Chapter Ten

The Persian had read *Mein Kampf* soon after its publication in 1925, and in the ascendancy of the Austrian buffoon he saw an opportunity to further pursue his sadistic hobbies with both impunity and legitimacy, as he had as a witchfinder under the rule of James I of Britain. He considered both men to be no more than useful idiots.

He began his tenure in the Nazi party with no particular animosity toward the German Jews, just as he'd had none for the innocent villagers accused of witchcraft three centuries before; they were simply a means to an end. But as time went on, and he observed the Jews obediently boarding the boxcars that transported them to their deaths, he developed an antipathy born of disgust that they appeared to offer no resistance to their tormentors. History would later prove him wrong, but history would also prove millions of others, globally, wrong about or blind to the agenda of Adolf Hitler.

It was during Hitler's reign and under his urging that Persia changed its name to Iran, the Persian word for *Aryan*. The Persian was indeed a true Aryan; the Nordic ideal espoused by Hitler was a fraud.

Daciana joined the Persian in Poland at Oswiecim—in German, *Auschwitz*—she as a nurse and he a physician's assistant. Both worked with Josef Mengele, the infamous Angel of Death, one more useful idiot—but one who provided them with as much *Blut* as they desired. The operating tables had channels on the sides like those on a meat cutting board, with a spout at one end that directed the victims' blood into a bucket that one or the other of them was all too happy to volunteer to empty after the day's work was done.

Toward the end of the war, as the Russians advanced upon the camps, the pair slipped away and eventually wound up back in England, where they merged into the crowds of beleaguered Brits and worked on rebuilding and restoring the island kingdom to its pre-war greatness. They were welcomed at Oxford and decided to pursue degrees there, with the goal of achieving professional accreditation as instructors; he in Middle Eastern history, she in bio-medical sciences. They achieved those goals and taught for years, leaving eventually, as their faculty peers began to notice that neither one seemed to age a day from the time when they were students.

When they left university, Daciana and the Persian decided to part company for a while. Although bound by blood, their relationship, both personal and sexual, had grown bland, as it had in the past and would in the future. They would meet again, she promised, and when he asked how she always managed to find him, her answer was always cryptic. Like a cat, she enjoyed teasing him, although unlike a cat, she had no intention to kill him when the game was over.

Because the game would never be over.

She crated her amassed wealth and shipped it to America, which was still undergoing its post-war boom period. It looked to be an exciting place, full of optimism and good will, full of promise for a young and beautiful Ph.D., a place in which to establish herself professionally. She found employment at a succession of colleges and universities and did post-doctoral work in the new field of genetics; and in time she joined the faculty of a small New Hampshire university named Criterion, where a few years later she married a fellow professor and remained relatively faithful.

The Persian, on the other hand, had grown nostalgic for the Middle East. He railed at the prospect of an Israeli state, remembering what he perceived as the Jews' victim mentality during the War years, and joined the anti-Semitic faculty of the University of Basrah in Iraq. He taught history for years, using his classes as propaganda platforms against Jews in general and Israel in particular.

In the mid 1980s, he was noticed by Saddam Hussein when he enthusiastically endorsed the genocidal Al-Anfal campaign that wiped out some two hundred thousand Kurds and other ethnic groups. Saddam took the Persian under his wing, brought him from the university into the ruling party, and as time passed, allowed him to share in the joys of the rape rooms and private torture chambers. He rose in rank and privilege, becoming a trusted advisor to Saddam and mentor to his sons Uday and Qusay. Life was good.

Until their father foolishly decided to invade Kuwait.

There are invasions from without and others from within. Rowena's was the latter: her own cells were attacking her, and as the oncologist explained, with the progress so rapid the outcome was never in doubt. After saying goodbye to Bentley, she drove home and sat at her kitchen table, drinking coffee, staring out the back window at the Charles River, which sparkled in the sunlight that dappled the ground in her tree-shaded backyard. At times like this, she longed for a cigarette to calm her nerves, but it was tobacco that had comprised the vanguard of the invading force, wasn't it? *At this point,* she thought, *what does it matter whether I smoke or not?*

There was no way she was going to discuss her condition with her parents, despite what she had told Bentley, at least not now. They had recently rented an RV and were somewhere in Montana. Every week or so, they'd send an email with photos of them: standing before Mount Rushmore, or the Crazy Horse statue—which, although far from complete, was more to their liking; looking up at Devil's Tower; surveying the battle site at Little Big Horn; watching Old Faithful blow its stack. Today they'd be on their way to Glacier National Park, and Rowena vowed she wouldn't disrupt their vacation on their first month of genuine retirement.

Her father, Marcus Mitchell, had grown up on the mean streets of Southeast Washington. The term *black community* was an oxymoron here, for there was no community, no fellowship, just survival by any means possible. Unlike Jomo Kenyatta Whitehead in Philadelphia, Marcus was never involved in petty theft, never joined a gang; he was a loner. But no one messed with him. Word was, the kid would snap your arm soon as look at you, as evidenced by the damage he'd done to an older *brother*—and how he hated that term—who'd tried to hustle him—only once—for his lunch money.

Marcus grew up with one goal in mind: join the Marines; no, *become* a Marine. Friday nights during the spring and summer would see the young man standing outside the Jewel of Southeast, the Marine Barracks at 8th and I Streets, a city block that included the enlisted barracks, the band's auditorium, officers' quarters, and the home of the Commandant, all bordering a grassy parade ground. Tour buses would let out visitors, who were then escorted by Marines in dress blues to the bleachers on the 8th Street side of the grass, thousands of them filling the stands, to see the weekly two-hour Moonlight Parade.

One day he called the barracks and made a reservation for himself. He dressed in his only suit, the one he'd worn to his high school graduation a few weeks earlier, and hot and humid as the evening was, he endured it proudly. The guys he was coming to see wore dark blue-black jackets with high collars tight to their necks; if they could manage that, he could manage a light jacket and a loose-fitting shirt and tie.

What amazed him most—what amazed most of the six thousand spectators, as a matter of fact—was the Silent Drill Team, who performed an intricate seven-minute drill with no commands ever being issued. The drill culminated with the troops forming a long line facing the crowd, standing at attention as a Marine rifle inspector marched in to face a man near one end of the line. The man unfixed his chrome bayonet, brought the rifle to inspection arms, and flipped it to the inspector, who made the rifle blur around his body before returning it, flipping it from behind his back. As the applause mounted, the inspector marched to the other end of the line and did it again with another Marine. As he marched away, the stands erupted in applause, and Marcus was on his feet.

The rifle inspector was *black*.

One month later Marcus was in Parris Island, and four months after that he was in Viet Nam. The year was 1969, and he was eighteen years old.

The next year he earned a Purple Heart for wounds suffered in combat and a Bronze Star for heroism. With his platoon ambushed in the field, his fire team laid down a base of fire while he radioed for helicopter evac. When the choppers came in, Marcus continued firing to cover the men climbing aboard and then slung the wounded platoon commander over his shoulder and was pulled into the ship last.

"Holy fuck, Mitchell," said one of his fellow grunts. "You got more holes in you than a Swiss cheese." Marcus later said he never realized at the time that he'd been shot.

The wounded platoon commander, Lieutenant Rohr, not only survived, he was awarded his captain's bars while in the hospital and reassigned to an administrative post in Saigon. He asked Battalion HQ for one perk: the recovering Corporal Mitchell to serve as his aide.

Marcus politely requested to be returned to the field, but Rohr said he was too valuable to him. As the captain noted, Mitchell had saved his life; now he was doing what he could to save his. "Sir, I can't be an office pinky," Marcus protested while accepting the post as graciously as he could, "I mean, look at me: pink I'm not."

In Saigon, Marcus, at age twenty, became friendly with a Vietnamese family named Vo, and more particularly with their eighteen-year-old daughter, Kim-Ly. Kim's mother was training her to take over the family's tailoring business; the girl herself, because of her beauty, had been urged by certain elements to become a prostitute, but her own and her family's honor would not be compromised no matter how poor they might be. She and Marcus fell in love, and with Captain Rohr's official endorsement they married. When Marcus rotated back to the States, Kim-Ly came with him. She was three months pregnant with a daughter they would name Rowena, after Marcus's mother.

Marcus was assigned to the division personnel office at Second Marine Division, Camp Lejeune, North Carolina, for the remainder of his enlistment. He then reenlisted for embassy school and was assigned to the American embassy in Berlin. Germany was more welcoming to American servicemen than was America itself at the time, especially to those of mixed ethnicity, so Rowena spent her childhood relatively free from prejudice and discrimination.

What added to her self-confidence was the fact that she was not only daddy's little girl, she was also daddy's little Marine. She could be sweet as sugar or tart as a lemon, and while her mother instilled in her the protocols peculiar to her gender, her father taught her survival skills, making of them a game to keep her entertained while learning.

Kim-Ly found work in a tailor shop and soon garnered fame for her meticulous dedication to detail. In her, Rowena found a role model for women's value in the workplace and their equality to men.

As his tour of duty wound down, Marcus applied for drill instructor school, and the family next found itself in San Diego, where he trained recruits from 1976 through 1978. At the end of that tour, his regimental commander recommended him for warrant officer training, and after earning his bars his first assignment was at Headquarters Marine Corps in Arlington, Virginia, where he ran the personnel office. Also at HQMC was his former boss in Nam, now Colonel Miles Rohr. They renewed their bond and ran the section with expediency and efficiency, earning praise from the higher-ups.

Marcus served twenty years and retired as a chief warrant officer. He and Kim-Ly bought a townhome in Alexandria, where they invested their savings and his pension in a dry cleaning and tailor shop. Marcus worked the back, Kim-Ly the front—and did tailoring between customers— and Rowena, now seventeen, worked the counter after school and on weekends. A year later, she graduated and was accepted for baccalaureate studies at Criterion University in New Hampshire.

Which reminded Rowena, now thirty-seven, that inside her desk drawer at work was a manuscript from a Criterion professor that awaited attention—that is, rejection. She admitted to herself again that she shouldn't have kept it that long. She should have returned it with a form letter immediately. But she couldn't concern herself with that now. There was something else that dominated her every waking minute these days.

A matter of life and death.

But there was a matter of ethics. She phoned Bentley and explained the situation, told her where the MS was sequestered, and suggested that she return it with a rejection letter. Bentley said no, it had been too long in limbo; instead, she would call the professor at the university and speak with him personally. A half hour later, Bentley called back and said she'd been informed that the professor was on his summer break and had just begun a vacation trip to the western states. The secretary would leave a note for him to call Jones Publishing upon his return. Rowena apologized again, and Bentley told her to forget about it and just get well.

Right. Like that is going to happen.

The thought returned: *a matter of life and death.*

She said goodbye and made another call, the one she had prevented herself from making earlier, the one prefaced by a Maryland area code.

"What the hell is this!" screamed Jawdan as Ahmed Mansoor opened the trunk of his Jetta. Visions of the hooker he'd killed in January were still banging around inside his skull—not for the fact that he'd killed her, he'd killed many more before her—but for the fact that someday some tiny clue could bring the law down on his head.

And now here was another hooker, or at least someone who dressed like one, all trussed up and gagged and lying in Ahmed's trunk. She stared at him furiously, coal-black mascara leaving runs down her cheeks and along the sides of her head.

"I didn't know what else to do," admitted Ahmed, and related the story of how Sophie Bienkowski happened to be there.

"Can't keep it in your pants, can you?" said Jawdan, as if he had license to judge. "What am I supposed to do with her while you and the boss traipse across the country on your little field trip?"

"Well, you can fuck her for starters, although she won't give you the satisfaction of so much as a twitch. All she does is lie there like a piece of raw liver, if you know what I mean."

"And then what do I do with her?"

"I don't know. Crab bait?"

The girl made a strangled sound in her throat and struggled against her bonds.

"The answer is no." He hadn't told the others about Connie. No one could know, ever.

They argued, and finally they agreed that Ahmed would begrudgingly take Sophie with him in the Sprinter. They loaded it with the rocket launchers and rockets, along with their standard complement of firearms, C4, Thermite, and detonators, and then handcuffed Sophie to one of the framing ribs that lined the wall of the van opposite the sliding door. On a rack above her, inside a steel cabinet, hung the weapons. On the floor, they placed three air mattresses and a twelve-volt pump. They stripped her naked and moved a chemical toilet beside her. The girl's mortification was complete.

"I gave her this lighter," Ahmed said. "Engraved and everything. But when I tried to kiss her, she called me a pervert. I reminded her of all the guys she'd gone down on, all I wanted was a little piece of that, in appreciation, you know, and she said that if I got that thing near her mouth I'd have a new nickname: Stumpy."

"Very funny."

Ahmed returned the lighter to Sophie's purse and tossed it into the truck. Since Jawdan wouldn't take her off his hands, there was no choice but to let the boss decide what to do with her. And man, would he be pissed.

They met at the Cozy, a modest restaurant/motel complex in Thurmont, Maryland, a place that had one small room off the entrance grandly labeled "The Camp David Museum," containing photos and memorabilia of the President's retreat from the days of FDR to the present. Rowena was shaking as she hugged her friend, and Claire found it difficult to release her from that hug. The smells from the hot buffet mingled with the scent of Rowena's skin. It was something that Claire could detect easily, the stinging scent of fear; and if she granted Ro's request, Ro would be able to detect it in others, too.

Claire suggested that they eat first, and she piled her plate high; Rowena barely lifted a serving spoon on the line. "Figures you'd make us meet at a buffet, the way you eat," said Rowena. "Place doesn't make any money off you, does it?"

"No, but it does off you. You're all profit."

They sat at a small table and Claire began devouring her chicken as Rowena nibbled at her iceberg salad.

"You can come up for air any time you want," said Rowena.

"You're being flip," Claire replied. "I understand that."

"So, where's your infinitely hunkier half today?"

"He's doing a training exercise with a new group of soldiers and Marines up in the woods. Escape and evasion. Survival. It's fun watching the guys eat bugs and salamanders for the first time. Of course, when I took the course, it didn't bother me at all."

"Naturally."

"And not that you asked, but Joe is in D.C. attending a forensics seminar."

"Do they know I'm here, and the reason I'm here?"

Claire put down her fork and looked into Rowena's eyes. "Dale knows. No secrets between us. But no one else. Not Lauren, not Joe, not Matthew. Dale and I talked about it for a long time. Speaking objectively, you could be a threat—unintentional, but a threat nonetheless—to any number of people; to the security of the team; and even to yourself. Remember, originally the team wanted to kill me when they found out what I was. Make that am." She placed her hand over her friend's. "God, Ro, I can't believe this is happening."

"Tell me."

"You do realize that your life will never be the same."

"It'll never be the same either way. As things stand, it's just going to end a lot sooner."

"You've never seen me morph." Rowena nodded. "You're going to have to see me in wolf form, and also with my fangs down. You've got to be sure you want this."

"I don't think you should show me right here," she said with a weak smile, encompassing the room with a gesture. "I've got a cabin next door."

"That'll do. Just try not to wig out when I do it."

Chapter Eleven

The cabin was the third in a line of three, elevated on short pilings, with three steps to the heavy wooden door. The siding was cedar turned gray with age and a few spots of mold. The one-story triplex looked not only like it belonged in the woods, it looked like it was hewn from the woods. Rowena turned the key and opened the door.

It was dark inside, with the window shade down and the muslin curtains drawn. The bed was a double, with a nightstand on one side and a chair on the other. An old dresser, with ill-fitting, sticking drawers and a lace runner across the top, stood beneath the lone window.

"Be it ever so humble," said Rowena as she tossed the key onto the runner, next to her overnight bag.

Claire closed the door and turned the dead bolt before telling Rowena to sit in the chair. She herself sat on the edge of the bed, looking down at her. "Ro, you've got to tell me there's no hope for you from traditional medicine. That your life is measured in months and not years. That you really want to go through with this."

Rowena took a deep breath—and coughed mightily. "Honey, I drove nearly nine hours straight through to get myself here. Every minute of that drive there was nothing else I thought about. Nothing. I used up an entire box of Kleenex; check the floor of the car if you want. It's not that I *want* to go through with this; I *have* to. Sweetie, a long time ago some guy called me a ballsy babe. Well, about dying I'm not so ballsy. I'm scared shitless."

"Then I have to show you what to expect of yourself. Look." She opened her mouth. For a second she looked pensive, as if she were thinking of murmuring an endearment; but then her jaw kept moving down, and her stunning beauty became grotesque as her skin stretched and a pair of needle-sharp fangs swung down from the roof of her mouth.

"Oh my God," Rowena whispered, nearly dumbstruck. "Just like Daciana."

"This is only part of it," said Claire, after her fangs swiveled back up and her jaw returned to normal. "The fangs are always there. They're hollow, and just before you bite, they shoot out a drop or two of an anesthetic that numbs the skin of your victim, so it barely feels the punctures. When the fangs are inside, though, there's definite pressure from them. Can you live with knowing you've got fangs? All the time? Can you live with knowing that you must have the blood of others to keep you alive?"

Her friend gulped. "I'm afraid to ask—where do you get the blood from?"

"Well, I could tell you that we never take human blood, but that would be a lie."

"It would?" Ro's voice was weak.

"Animal blood is what we take mostly, and mostly when we're wolves. It suffices. But on occasion, Joe brings us human blood. He has contacts in the medical community who give him tainted blood. He tells them he's doing postdoc work on AIDS research."

"You drink HIV-contaminated blood?"

"Our bodies assimilate it. We're immune to infection, remember? That's why you called me."

"How . . . how does it taste?"

"Nectar of the gods, and no, I never thought I'd say that, but it's true. Should I go on?"

Rowena nodded, her expression fearful.

Claire began removing her clothes. When she was naked, she stood before Rowena and smiled sadly. "I was hoping you'd never have to see this, Ro. In a way, I'm ashamed. I know that I'm a monster, but—all right, I'm going to go all Forrest Gump on you now—monster is as monster does. You understand." Another nod. "I—that is, Dale and I—can morph completely or partially. I'm going to do a partial first, then segue into a full wolf. Don't be alarmed, I won't hurt you. I'll end up being what Dale and I looked like when we took out Daciana."

Rowena was already trembling when Claire's fingers thickened and her nails grew pointed and black. Fine blond hair sprouted from, and covered, her entire body. Her nose and mouth formed a short muzzle with saliva-coated scimi-

92

tars, different from her vampire's fangs, curving down from above and resting alongside her lower jaw. Her breasts flattened and her nipples were joined by four more, in two neat rows of three each. Her shoulders hunched and her arms rippled with muscle. Her pale blue, nearly gray eyes did not change; they stared into Rowena's coal-dark ones, and she tilted her head to one side, as would an inquisitive dog. She was waiting for a response.

Rowena muttered, "In for a penny . . . go ahead, go all the way."

The wolf woman's head straightened and she lowered herself to the floor as her muzzle extended, her ears grew pointed, and her lower spine extended into a bushy tail. Her hands and feet were paws now, and Rowena thought that she was looking at the most beautiful, most fearsome creature she'd ever seen.

Claire, in her incarnation as Luna the wolf, took a step backward, waiting, allowing Rowena to take her transformation in. "Claire," she said, "if I didn't know who you are and what you are, I'd want to reach out and pet you right about now. But I'm afraid I'd lose my hand."

The wolf advanced and placed her head on Rowena's lap. Slowly, cautiously, her fingers touched the animal's ear and scratched its base. Luna closed her eyes and sighed. With her other hand, Rowena ruffled the fur of the wolf's cheek, and she could have sworn she saw the animal smile. Then Luna backed off, stared for a moment at Rowena, and morphed back into the tall beautiful blonde Rowena had known and loved as a friend for years.

Silently, Claire put her clothes back on and sat on the edge of the bed.

"Well?"

It was a full minute before Rowena answered, a minute in which she was consumed by hacking, with large gouts of sputum, bloody now, falling from her mouth to the tissue she held. "Yes," she said.

"There's more you need to know. If this works, and I expect it to, not only will you never get sick again, but you'll be stronger than you ever thought possible. Your eyesight and hearing will be acute, but your sense of smell will be the strongest of all. Canines *see* through their noses, which is why you see dogs poking their heads outside car windows all the time. They're taking in the sights, as it were."

"Okay, I get that."

"As for your appetite, you'll be feeding the wolf as well as the human. Your food: raw or cooked will make no difference. You'll be partial to red meat, but the human part of you will still crave fruits and vegetables. Good so far?"

Another nod.

"Taste is affected by smell, so everything you eat will taste more intense than ever. And whenever you're in a room where people are smoking, you'll want to gag. Or rip their lungs out, which I wouldn't advise."

"Uh huh."

"And one other thing, unless there's more I've forgotten for the moment. Unless you're physically killed, say decapitated or bled out, or consumed by fire, you'll live forever."

"Claire . . . how long is forever?"

She thought a moment. "Well, at least until the end of the world, when the sun expands into a red giant and turns the Earth and everything on it to a cinder."

"And when can I look forward to that?"

"From what I've read, around five billion years or so."

Rowena gave a sheepish grin and stood. "Only five billion? Gee. Hardly worth making plans then, is it?"

"So it's a go?"

"It's a go."

"Take off your blouse."

"Not getting kinky now, are we?"

"No, you just don't want to get blood on it." Claire stared at her friend, her expression sympathetic. "When you're nervous or scared you crack wise, anyone ever tell you that?"

Rowena took off her blouse and draped it over the chair.

"Now sit on the bed and lean your head to one side. I'd advise you to close your eyes."

To say the boss was pissed when he saw the girl trussed inside the panel truck would be like saying a nuclear bomb was a Fourth of July sparkler. He wanted to shoot Mansoor where he stood; no, he wanted to rip his throat out and drain his body dry. Right now, in front of the girl.

He wished he could kill them both, but he needed Ahmed Mansoor. He and Jawdan El-Sayed were useful to him, at least for now. Eventually he would have to break his promise to them—something that bothered him not at all—to protect his own identity, before moving on. At this moment, he thought he would truly enjoy that.

For now there was this woman—this child—that he had to deal with. Mansoor's problem was always that he thought with his little head instead of the big one. She would need to be disposed of, but where? And when? And how?

The girl was young; she must have family. But Ahmed said her parents had kicked her out of their home, and he further assured him that according to the paper no missing person report had made the news. Muhammad tempered his anger. The girl, he hoped, was just a speed bump, and inside the panel truck he could negotiate it with efficiency. Already, he was formulating a scenario.

The Sprinter was tall, commodious, and without windows behind those in the cab. The girl would travel with them in the back, hidden behind the curtain and muzzled, as she was now. They would overnight in Walmart parking lots, in areas the management always provided for RVs and camper trailers, a smart business move for the retailer. No attention would they call to the van or to themselves.

On the highways, they could remove her gag and release one hand at a time to restore her circulation. They might even take advantage of her sexually, one driving the van while the other had sport with her. It would be amusing, he thought, if she were to try to pull a Patty Hearst and affect Stockholm syndrome behavior. It wouldn't work, of course, but it would be amusing if she tried and actually believed she had won them over. He anticipated her look of surprise when she found out for a certainty, despite her attempt at deception, that she was really about to die.

"For this mission, your name is Manuel," he said to Mansoor. "Mine is Jesus." He smiled as he pronounced it the Hispanic way. "We are Mexicans, legal ones, bound for California, looking for jobs in construction or building maintenance. I speak Spanish, so I will do the talking if anyone questions us." He handed Mansoor a forged driver's license.

They were not going to California at all, but Ahmed didn't need to know that yet.

Rowena returned to consciousness with a thin gold chain around her neck, a five-pointed star depending from it, lying just above her breastbone. It had been Claire's.

"I want to give this to you," said her maker, "as a reminder, both of what you are now and also what you mean to me." She touched the juncture of Rowena's neck and shoulder. "How do you feel?"

Rowena looked down and saw blood that had dried as it flowed down her body. It had come from—where? There was some soreness where neck met shoulder, but no indication of a wound at all. "Something's happening," she replied. "I can feel a change. Like my insides are all carbonated, like club soda."

"Run your tongue across the roof of your mouth."

She did, and her eyes grew large as saucers. "I can feel them."

"And what you feel inside your body, I'd guess, is the destruction of your cancer cells."

Rowena sat silent for a long minute. "Okay. My first thought is that we should share this cure with everyone who has cancer. But—"

"But evil people get cancer, too, don't they? Imagine the numbers of good people who could be killed by bad ones, simply because of one act of kindness."

She lowered her eyes to her lap. "Yeah, I know about that."

"Chin up, sister, it's time to take a walk in the woods."

Claire drove them to Cunningham Falls State Park. She parked the car and they hiked up the mountain until they could see the perimeter fence of Camp David. Normally, Rowena would be out of breath by now. She wasn't even slightly winded. "We'll start slowly," Claire said. "Take a look at that tree limb above your head."

"You mean the one that's ten feet off the ground?"

"That's the one. Jump up and grab it."

"Oh, right."

"Go ahead. I mean it."

Rowena jumped—so high that her hands flew past the limb and she banged her forehead. She fell to the ground, seeing stars.

"That's an official Oops," said Claire as she helped her friend to her feet. "Want to try it again?"

Rowena was stunned, not so much from the blow as from the realization of her newfound strength. This time, she put less effort into it and managed both to reach the limb and climb onto it with the agility of a cat. She looked down at Claire. "Can't catch me," she taunted.

Instantly, Claire was beside her, and they scrambled through the tree like a pair of monkeys. "Tarzan!" Rowena shouted as she leaped from the upper branches of their tree to the next one a dozen feet away. Finally, Claire called her down, and they met again upon terra firma.

"What do you think?"

"I don't know what to think," Rowena said. "I've never felt so . . . so alive. I mean, where's that undead feeling?"

"You're not a zombie."

"Arrrrgh, but I could make a meal of some brains, I could." She laughed.

"Seriously, are you hungry now?"

"Like I could eat a—no, belay that, I like horses."

"Let's get back to the Cozy. I want you to have a good night's sleep before we practice shape shifting."

The next morning, Claire joined Rowena for breakfast: pancakes, eggs sunny side up, sausage, buttermilk biscuits, and coffee. Then they visited another restaurant across town and enjoyed an order of chipped beef on toast, plus a bacon and cheese omelet and more coffee.

They drove back to the Cozy, where Claire told Rowena to sign on for two weeks' lodging. Then she drove her back to Cunningham Falls. "We'll need time, Ro, if you're going to be trained properly to handle your new powers."

"With great power comes great responsibility?"

"Yes, Spidey. Look, after I was turned I realized there was a lot I had to learn—about my abilities, about my animal nature, and about my moral code, which I compromised the hell out of. I couldn't share this with anyone, not you, not Ray Jones, no one. And I had to learn control. I killed some people who weren't particularly nice, but who didn't deserve to die either, and I'll live with that forever."

"I've got it, sweetie, and you're right. At this point, I'll take all the guidance I can get."

"Dale will do some of the training. But again, he and I will be the only ones who know. This is doubly clandestine, Ro, no one can know but us three. I don't mean to be melodramatic, but all our lives might hang in the balance if the higher-ups learn we're doing independent work. That makes us a threat to the team's security, maybe even national security. You have to understand that."

Rowena closed her eyes and absorbed her friend's words. Claire continued: "Dale is especially putting himself at risk by being complicit in this operation. Not to be harsh, but he's doing it strictly for me, not you. And I love him so much for that I can barely stand it."

"I don't know if I should be flattered or offended."

"Don't take it the wrong way. He likes you a lot."

"But there's too much at stake, I get it. And Claire, your putting your job and maybe even your life on the line for me means more than I can ever express. Or repay." She reached forward and took Claire in her arms. Tears filled her eyes.

Moments later, Claire broke the embrace. "All right, recruit, ready to begin your basic training?"

As Rowena Parr was learning the ropes as a shape shifter, eighteen-year-old Sophie Bienkowski was chafing at the ropes that bound her ankles to the Sprinter. Her legs were slightly elevated and spread, so she could not bang her heels against the floor. One hand was cuffed to the frame behind her, and the other was free to position the chemical toilet beneath her and to use the biodegradable toilet tissue. At the moment, she was perched on the edge of one of the three air mattresses, her purse beside her, where Mansoor had tossed it. Sophie was naked, gagged, and totally shit-scared.

Ahead of her, Monsieur and the other guy—officially Manuel and Jesus now, for whatever reason she couldn't guess—were driving leisurely on some Interstate somewhere in the middle of the country. They'd been on the road for three days now. Monsieur was driving, the other guy navigating. In keeping with whatever game they were playing, they wore Mexican-style cowboy hats—sombreros, she thought they were called. Monsieur even wore a string tie, one of those bolo things. Both of them were smoking away, one cig after the other, and she was dying for a cigarette.

Dying? she thought. *Really dumb choice of words, girl.*

Because she was smart enough to know she was really going to die.

Unless . . . could she convince them that she was on their side? That she had taken their cause as her own and wanted to help them any way she could?

Except she had no idea what their fuckin' cause was.

The guy Jesus had left his seat and was making his way toward her. She motioned with her free hand that she'd like to have a smoke, and the old fart nodded and almost smiled. He cautioned her not to shout, as if anyone in another car could hear her anyway, and unfastened the gag. "Thanks," she said and opened her mouth for the cigarette he held. He lit it himself, not trusting her near a flame, and placed it between her lips. She dragged deeply, gratefully.

Maybe they weren't going to kill her, she thought. If they were, why would they waste a smoke on her?

"Where are we?" she asked between puffs.

"Not for you to know," he said. "But I'll tell you anyway."

Oh no, she thought, *they are definitely going to kill me.*

"Because I like you."

All right, maybe not.

"We are in Kansas, approaching Denver, Colorado, but we'll not be stopping there. We'll detour south, to Colorado Springs, pick up another Interstate, and then cut across the state to Durango. I've heard it's very popular as a tourist attraction."

She shook her head. "But we're not tourists," she protested, making sure to use the plural pronoun, including herself in the team.

"No, we're not," he said. "But I've never been to that part of the state, and I'd like to see it before I die."

"Before you die? You're not some kind of suicide bomber, are you?"

Jesus laughed. "Not at all. There is no future in that." He laughed again.

Sophie exhaled the last of her smoke. He held a small ashtray and she stubbed the butt out. "Thanks." *All right,* she thought, *time to put my plan into play.* "You know, sitting like this with my legs up in the air really sucks. If you untie my ankles and take off this handcuff, I could give you a totally awesome fuck."

"Sophie, Sophie, Sophie, I don't need to untie you. I could do you as you are and not worry about your trying something foolish."

"Okay, you're right. But it wouldn't be as much fun now, would it? I mean, with me just lying here and all. Might as well just beat your meat and be done with it."

Jesus seemed to consider. That smirk, though, never left his face. "I think I might take you up on your offer. But if you try anything foolish, I promise to kill you."

"I promise I won't."

She had never put so much effort into the act as she did with Jesus. She moaned and groaned, shoved her tongue as far as she could into his mouth, gave him love bites on the neck and shoulder, ground her hips against his, and three times whimpered that she was coming. It was a bravura performance, but a performance was all it was. Jesus, though, seemed to buy it as genuine. *Score one for the good girl,* she thought. *And Monsieur, up there in the driver's seat—yeah, you—sneaking those glances in the mirror, probably driving with one hand in your lap, eat your fuckin' heart out.*

The next day they pulled into Durango and Jesus decided he liked it. The narrow-gauge steam train that took tourists over the mountains to Silverton could prove an enticing target on their way back. They overnighted at a campground, and bright and early the next day they headed north on the San Juan Skyway.

"Oh, shit, boss," whined Mansoor as they climbed thousands of feet with no end in sight. "I don't like this one bit. There's no shoulder, no guard rails, and there's blind switchbacks, too. The van's too big for this road. And it's a million miles to the bottom."

"Just keep your eyes on the road, my friend, and don't look to the side or the rear. Take your time. There's no one behind us, and even if there were, we're in no hurry. We can't afford to be in a hurry."

The road climbed to an elevation well above ten thousand feet. To the right, the dropoff was sheer and straight down; to the left, across from the double yellow line, the other lane butted up against a wall of rock. Every now and then, a small boulder would be resting in the road where it had fallen, necessitating a swerve around it. Mansoor was sweating, despite the fact that even in June there was snow on the rocks above and below. He couldn't fathom why the boss was so unflappable. *Oh, right,* he reminded himself. *Nothing can kill him.*

"Steady now, you're doing fine," said Jesus as he unfastened his harness and made his way to the back. When they'd left Durango and started up the mountain, he'd removed Sophie's gag and untied her ankles. The manacle on one wrist was all that held her in place. And he was now unlocking it as well.

"Ready for another fuck?" she asked, trying to keep her tone bright.

"I am so ready," he said. "But first, I have a little surprise for you." He lowered his face to Sophie's inner thigh.

"You going down on me? Oh my God, at least let me perfume myself or something."

"That won't be necessary, Sophie," he said, and pressed his face to her thigh.

Her skin didn't feel the punctures, but the flesh beneath understood that something foreign was inside her leg. And when she saw the blood flow into his mouth, she was so petrified she couldn't so much as whimper.

She was growing weaker by the minute and lightheaded as well. *This is something out of a horror movie,* she thought. *There's no such thing as—*

She felt her purse against her arm. And inside the purse was her cell phone!

As Jesus concentrated on his thirst, his face buried in her thigh, she placed one hand on the top of his head, holding it in place and moaning as if she were in a state of rapture. Then with her free hand, she flipped open the phone, and with a thumb well practiced from texting, she speed-dialed her home phone. Her mother picked up almost instantly.

"Sophie? Sophie, where are you, we want you to come home."

Jesus heard the mechanical voice and lifted his head, but Sophie pushed it down as hard as she could. "Mama, mama! I've been kidnapped—by a fuckin' *vampire!* Help me!"

Jesus forced himself up and grinned. Sophie's face was white. Her body was weak beyond lethargy. She knew this was the moment of her death.

"Not so clever," said Jesus, licking his bloody lips. He slid open the side door, letting cold air and road noise in. Immediately outside was a gulf, across which stood jagged peaks dotted with evergreens and spotted with snow. Sophie clutched the phone as if it were a lifeline, tears erupting from her eyes as the vampire rolled her to the edge of the opening and casually heaved her into the abyss. He kicked her purse after her, all evidence of Sophie's having been with them sailing into space.

Plummeting down with her back to the earth, Sophie saw the door slide closed as the slowly moving truck grew smaller and smaller. It felt almost as if she were lying on a cushion of water, watching the truck fly up and away. Her purse seemed to float in the air above her. There was no high-speed elevator or roller coaster feel at all as she fell, and part of her wondered about that.

The phone was still clutched in one hand as her body slammed onto a flat rock, pulverizing every bone, then bounced off and rolled down a rocky slope, until it came to rest beside an intermittent stream fed by gentle snowmelt.

Chapter Twelve

Two wolves—one blond and one sable—ran through the Catoctin Mountain forest. Their prey, a terrified doe, crashed through the brush ahead of them, her eyes frantic. The wolves flanked her to either side, as if herding her, and as she bolted with renewed effort, she suddenly stopped short as she faced a third animal, larger than the other two and with a shaggy light brown coat. Its green eyes mesmerized the doe, and her forelegs collapsed beneath her as she fell to the ground to be set upon by the others. The two females thrust themselves against her hind legs, breaking them between their jaws as the shaggy male went for her throat. In moments, she was dead.

An arrow or a bullet would have been more merciful, but in the wild no animal dies a merciful death. Even the strongest, as it grows old, falls prey to a younger, who itself will one day be killed by its own successor.

The shaggy wolf and the blond female tore the doe apart as the black one studied their moves and learned. Soon the male jerked his head in the black's direction and she joined them in their feast.

A half hour later, two women and a man, blood-spattered and naked, bathed themselves in an icy stream. Then they picked up their clothes where they'd cached them and dressed. No one spoke.

"So," said Claire finally. "Your first kill. How did it feel?"

"I can't describe how it felt. How it still feels," said Rowena.

"Did you enjoy the killing?" asked Dale. "Does it make you want to kill again?"

His eyes and Claire's locked onto Rowena's. A lot depended upon her answer.

"I can honestly answer no to both those questions," she said. "I killed because it was in my nature, my need to survive. Yes, there was a thrill in the chase, but not in the kill itself. I love all animals, so part of me is mourning this beautiful thing we just killed."

"Good," said Dale. "You should do this every now and then, if only to reinforce the fact that meat doesn't grow on a Styrofoam tray inside heat-sealed plastic wrap."

"Understood."

"Rowena," he continued, "it's the middle of June. You've been here two weeks, and you've learned what we have to teach you. We've saved you from a horrible death. But now you have a responsibility to us. I know Claire told you this already, but I've got to reinforce it, for your sake as well as ours. You don't dare share what you are, or what we are, with anyone. You don't hunt where you can be discovered. In fact, it's better that you don't hunt at all, unless it's with Claire and me. We're not asking you this; we're demanding it."

"I understand, and of course I'll comply. Dale, Claire, I'd do anything for you. In fact, I would've done anything for you, even before I got sick. Aside from my parents, you're the closest thing I have to family these days."

Claire hugged her and asked what she planned to tell Bentley when she returned to work.

"I've been thinking about that. How about I tell her that I went to Johns Hopkins in Baltimore for a second opinion, they diagnosed me with something other than cancer, and—"

Dale interrupted: "No. Tell her you visited Claire and me to tell us goodbye, in person, because you knew you didn't have long to live. Because of our government connections, we got you into a testing program at the National Naval Medical Center in Bethesda, where they're working on a drug that targets cancer cells while leaving healthy cells alone. It forms a shell around the cancer cells and starves them until they die and are flushed out of the body in the urine. The drug is in its early experimental stages and not ready yet for FDA review. And that's all you can tell her, because for proprietary reasons you weren't given any more information than that. They never told you the name of the drug, the dosage, anything like that. Tell her, too, that everything you've told her is on the Q.T. This information is officially classified top secret."

"Wow," she said. "That's some story."

Claire laughed. "Took us half the night to concoct."

"And now," Dale said, "you're officially in remission. But you'll have to return to Bethesda regularly for check-ups."

Claire said, "And when you do, instead of Bethesda you'll drive straight to the Cozy, and we'll spend a day or two in the forest, hunting. You'll need that, to satisfy your wolfishness."

"We'll call you when we have some time. Maybe a month, maybe sooner." Dale extended his hand. Rowena took it and drew him to her in a tight hug.

"Thank you so much, thank you both so much. God, I love you two."

"As well you should," he said, a smile crinkling his eyes.

"So go," Claire said after a hug and kiss. "Lauren's on her way back from D.C. tonight, and we don't want you anywhere near this place when she returns."

Late spring and early summer nights at Camp David are special. The air is dry, it carries only the slightest chill, and the stars seem to shine nearly as brightly as they do in winter. Claire and Dale walked hand in hand to Lauren Bachmann's cabin, and on the way they met Joe Whitehead. At the cabin door, they saw Matthew Collins approaching from the parking lot.

"Uh oh, this can't be good," said Joe. "When you're called in all the way from Joisey, that means something big's going down. What gives?"

"No clue," said Matthew. "Just got the call to take a day off and report. And here I am."

"And here we are," said Lauren Bachmann from her open doorway. "Now get inside before the moths carry us all away." As she spoke, a zap came from the electrified grate above and to the side of her door and a huge moth fell to the ground.

"Cor! That thing's big enough to fillet," said Matthew as they hurried inside. "What's up, Commander?"

They took seats and Lauren poured coffee all around. "This could be big," she said without preamble. "There was a kid missing from her graduation exercises at Montgomery Blair High School two weeks or so ago. Just disappeared into thin air. Yesterday, her body shows up in southwestern Colorado."

"Her body," said Joe.

"Details, please," said Claire.

Lauren consulted her notes. "Her name's Sophia Anastasia Bienkowski, and she appears to have been something of a hell raiser. Mom and Dad kicked her out of the house when she turned eighteen, a tough love kind of thing. They told her to call them when she was ready to act like their daughter again, and they refused to call her first."

Joe took a swig from his mug. "I think I can identify. Although Blair's in a pretty high-end neighborhood, right?"

"Silver Spring."

"Well, guess I can't identify all that much."

Lauren went on: "So Sophia crashes at her friends' houses. They tell their parents they're having a sleepover. No grownup knows that Sophie's been banished from her home. Well, she's a no-show at commencement, and her friends start talking. No one's seen her. But no one thinks to file a missing person report either. They figure she's shacking up with one of her many boyfriends."

Claire said, "Sounds like the perfect girlfriend to bring home to meet Mommy."

"Yes," agreed Dale. "Just keep her away from Daddy."

"So how does she get to Colorado?" asked Matthew.

"No one knows. Have you ever heard of the San Juan Skyway?" Head shakes all around. "It's officially Route 550, and its other name is the Million Dollar Highway. Well, kiddies, I drove it once, and I'll tell you, I'd give a million dollars not to drive it again. I only did it to attend a friend's wedding in Ouray, a town at the north end. Now, Ouray is beautiful—it's called America's Switzerland in the brochures—but the road up and over the San Juan Mountains to get there is listed as one of the most dangerous drives in America."

"So you're telling us this girl was driving on the road and went off the cliff?" said Matthew.

"No. There was no car. She was tossed off the cliff, stark naked, with her cell phone in her hand. There was a GPS chip in the phone, and that's how authorities found her."

"So someone kidnapped her and sailed her into space," said Joe.

Lauren cocked an eyebrow. "Perhaps not some *one*; some *thing.*"

"Uh oh," said Matthew. "Check, please." He looked at Dale and Claire. "No offense, mates, but things that go bump in the night aren't exactly my cup of tea." His glib expression concealed the fact that this was more than traditional British understatement.

"A chopper rescue team zeroed in on the body and lifted her out. Her bones were powdered; they said hoisting her body onto the gurney was like trying to lift Jell-O." Lauren took a mouthful of coffee. "They got there pretty quick; the scavengers hadn't taken too much from her. No eyes, of course, they went to the birds first thing. The coroner found only one wound that he couldn't attribute to animals or birds, and that was a pair of very neat puncture marks centered over her femoral artery."

Matthew said, "Which could be . . . a rattlesnake? Please say rattlesnake."

"Well, this is where it got the attention of my handler. It seems that before Sophia died she was able to make a brief call to her mother on her cell. It was her mother who contacted the authorities. Sophie had screamed that she'd been kidnapped by a vampire. A fuckin' vampire, to be precise."

"Famous last words," Joe said.

"The connection was still active when she was tossed over. Sophia's first point of impact was on her back, and she was probably holding the phone in front of her when she hit."

"Bloody awful," Matthew said.

Claire blinked. "Why am I suddenly thinking of the New Hampshire family?"

Dale nodded. "If the girl's killer is a vampire, we have to wonder: are there two of them out there, or does our New Hampshire friend like to travel?"

Joe added, "What are the chances? First, there's the one, Daciana, whom you killed. Then there's the one in New England, and now another one out West. Or at least another attack, if it's the same one." He took a breath. "Silly me. Here I used to think they only lived in comic books and movies."

"But wait," Lauren said. "As the infomercial goes, there's more. Whoever killed this girl tossed her purse over the edge with her, probably to get rid of any trace of her being with him. Assuming it's a him. Anyway, her driver's license confirmed her ID. The purse held her house keys, some paper money and change, cigarettes, and a gold-plated Zippo lighter."

Dale cocked his head. "Engraved? Lots of guys I know engrave theirs."

"Bingo. It says, *To Sophie from Monsieur.*"

Joe said, "Well, guys, looks like we're going to Colorado."

"No, the body's en route to D.C. as we speak." Lauren added, "And you, Dale and Claire, will be paying a visit to Mrs. Bienkowski tomorrow. As a pair of social workers working in conjunction with the police. Find out who this Monsieur character is. There's no indication that he's involved, but we've got to start somewhere."

At the Solomons Island Marina, Jawdan El-Sayed, a.k.a. Jerry, began his workday cleaning the public rest rooms, as usual. Also as usual, he gave them a lick-and-a-promise rather than a thorough scrub and swab. This work was beneath a man with his skills. But someone had to do it, and there were only two more weekends left in the month. The management had hired a cleaning crew for July through October, the marina's busiest months. September and October would see the return of the snowbirds, boaters who spent the summers up north and the winters in Florida. Nice life, if you can get it.

Someone had left a copy of the Washington *Post* on the floor, and Jawdan took it into a stall with him. As he sat and did his business, he thumbed idly through the pages of the Local section. Something caught his eye: a photograph of a young girl with colored streaks in her hair. It looked like it might be a yearbook shot. The girl looked familiar. *Take away that raccoon makeup around her eyes and that black lipstick, and she could be a ringer for—hell, forget ringer. She was that girl. The one that Ahmed had hogtied in his trunk.* Despite the air conditioning, he broke into a sweat as he read the article beneath the photo:

LOCAL GIRL FOUND DEAD IN COLORADO
SILVER SPRING:
The body of a young woman presumed missing since early this month has been found at the bottom of a canyon in Colorado's San Juan Mountains. Sophia Bienkowski, 18, appears to have fallen from a cliff at the edge of a high and narrow mountain road linking the towns of Durango, Silverton, and Ouray. Foul play is suspected.

The tag line read that because the girl might have been a kidnap victim, the FBI had been called in to investigate.

Jawdan's bowels turned to water.

When they reached Price, Utah, Jesus told Manuel to stop at the Staples store. Manuel went in alone and bought five tri-fold poster boards, black markers, and poster paint. At a home center, Jesus bought five steel signposts, wood furring strips, bolts and nuts, a battery-powered drill, an adjustable wrench, and a sledgehammer, while Manuel stayed in the van. They bunked overnight in a small motel on the north side of town and brought the poster board and paints inside with them. Wearing latex gloves so as not to leave prints, they meticulously laid out lettering and painted carefully inside the lines they'd drawn. Jesus checked the paperwork he'd downloaded before leaving New Hampshire, and was satisfied that they were on schedule. This would be a masterwork, and he chuckled as Manuel marveled at the boss's ingenuity.

Before dawn, they drove north on North Carbonville Road, alongside the railroad tracks that led to Helper and beyond. In Helper, they picked up U.S. Route 6 and followed it into Price Canyon, where they pulled over onto a deserted dirt trace and took their signs—bolted to the posts and reinforced with the furring strips—and pounded them into the rocky soil facing the railroad track, so that the lettering could be read from the train.

Jesus had conceived this idea from reading about the old Burma-Shave signs that bordered the highways sixty years and more before. They featured a comic verse spread over four or five signs, followed by the Burma-Shave logo on the last one. They were something every traveler looked forward to seeing, to relieve the monotony of the drive. Three of his favorites were:

Said Farmer Brown / Who's bald on top / I wish I could / Rotate the crop. *Burma-Shave*

The monkey took / One look at Jim / And threw the peanuts / Back at him. *Burma-Shave*

If daisies are / Your fav'rite flower / Keep pushin' up / Those miles per hour. *Burma-Shave*

He especially liked the last one, because it was potentially more grim than jest.

Once his own version of the Burma-Shave signs was in place, Jesus and Manuel returned to the Sprinter and took out the 3.5-inch rocket launcher and three rockets. They put construction helmets on their heads and positioned themselves past the signs.

And waited.

The target was the California Zephyr, heading from Chicago to San Francisco, the train route considered the most beautiful in all of North America. It was filled with tourists this time of year, some from Chicago and points east, others from its intermediate stops en route. The most popular cars, naturally, were the glass-domed observation cars, where passengers could absorb the beauty of the Rockies and Utah's great canyon lands, as they wended their way to San Francisco. But a great many of them would never get to leave their hearts in the City by the Bay; they would leave them instead in Price Canyon, Utah.

"We will not take out the engine," Jesus said. "Maximum damage to human life means we aim for the observation cars. What is especially gratifying is that the people will see the rockets coming at them split seconds before they die."

"And the government will be scouring the area for a terrorist sleeper cell," said Manuel, "but they won't find one. And we, meanwhile, will be on our way home." He looked at Jesus. "Won't we?"

"Yes. But with a slight detour. I saw something when we drove through Durango which interested me."

"You won't tell me what?"

"In time."

"Oh no. Does that mean we have to drive back over those mountains? I swore I'd never do that again."

"I'm afraid it does, my friend. But you did so well the first time, and going south, the cliff wall will be to your right. The dropoff will be eight or ten feet to your left."

"Piece of cake," Manuel said sarcastically. He made to light a cigarette, but Jesus stopped him. "We don't want to leave any butts on the ground that can leave traces of DNA. Not to worry, Manuel. The train is coming soon, and we'll have plenty to keep us occupied."

From their cover of brush, which protected them from being seen from the scarcely-traveled road, they only had to wait a few more minutes before they heard the clack-clack-clack of the approaching train.

Inside the diesel engine's cab, the engineer frowned and said, "What the hell?" as he saw the progression of signs along the right side of the rail bed. He read them as he passed, knowing that his passengers would be reading them, too, seconds later:

You infidels / Are doomed to die / Your body parts / Will fill the sky. *Allahu Akbar*

Then he saw, on the other side of the tracks some fifty yards ahead, two men wearing helmets. One picked up a familiar-looking metal tube. An Army veteran, the engineer recognized the Bazooka. "Shit!" he yelled. "Big air, big air!" And he applied the air brakes to each car in the line. The train shuddered and shrieked, making sparks on the rails, but its forward momentum carried it on. The engineer knew the passengers were being thrown willy-nilly about the cars, and some would sustain injuries, but it couldn't be helped. He had to stop the train, and he had to stop it *now*.

Too late. The slowing train continued, past the men. They were both grinning; the one who had just loaded the rocket waved. The engineer looked behind him and saw the first round blast from the tube. He felt the impact almost before he heard it. The train rocked to one side, then managed to right itself. Another rocket, and a third, and one car tilted too far. It fell onto its side, dragging its neighbors over with it. The screech of metal wheels and metal passenger cars grinding against rails and rocks added to the cacophony, as did the engineer's angry, frightened, and futile scream.

The signs alongside the rail bed had proved prophetic.

Chapter Thirteen

After saying goodbye to Dale and Claire, and intending to visit her old haunts in the D.C. area, Rowena debated driving to Gaithersburg and taking the Metro into town, knowing that the city's traffic would be horrendous. In the end, she opted to drive to the Virginia side of the Potomac and then take the Metro from her hotel to the tourist sites. If you can drive in Boston, she reasoned, you can drive anywhere. Rowena wanted to visit the new World War II Memorial, the Korean War Memorial, and of course the Vietnam Wall—where new names were still being added, as the remains of American combatants were discovered and returned home.

She had been away from Boston for two weeks and needed more time to lend credibility to the cover story that Dale and Claire had concocted, explaining her participation in the NNMC Bethesda experiment and the time needed for the doctors' monitoring of her progress.

The DoubleTree Hotel in Crystal City, near the Pentagon Metro station in Arlington, was her choice of accommodations for a week. She planned to be back at work at Jones Publishing on Monday, July 6th. In the meantime, she placed another call to Bentley Williams, telling her of the ongoing experimental procedure and the researchers' optimistic prognosis. She again impressed upon her boss the need for absolute confidentiality. She was not even to tell her husband Elliott. "If you do, you'll have to kill him. And then I'll have to kill you."

The reason, she reiterated, her voice solemn again, was that if word got out it could raise panic in the pharmaceutical industry, whose cancer treatment drugs could become obsolete overnight. The financial damage to those companies would ripple through the market; stocks would plunge; employee pension plans could suddenly find themselves seriously in the red; and *panic* would be the operative word for a long, long time.

Bentley said she understood. She remembered learning that polio had been the last major disease eradicated, back in the 1950s, and as a result whole medical practices—which had dealt solely with all aspects of infantile paralysis—were suddenly out of work. Since then, no disease had been conquered. "It's more profitable to treat than to cure," she remarked, and Rowena called her a cynic of the worst order. Privately, she wondered if there was a grain of truth in what her boss had said. Also privately, she congratulated herself on the panic-in-the-pharma-industry canard, which she'd made up herself.

The next day was Tuesday, and Rowena took the Metro to Alexandria and her old neighborhood. Her parents' dry cleaning and custom tailor shop was gone, replaced by a small boutique. Thinking of her mother, she remembered that, proud as the diminutive and dainty woman was to be an American citizen, when invective was called for, she could swear a blue streak in her native Vietnamese. Her father was able to pick up some of the words, but to Rowena they were gibberish. And whenever she asked what they meant—and later, when she asked to be taught them—her mother would cut her off with a "Not yours to know."

The townhouse was still there, still in good shape, being watched over by a neighbor during her parents' absence. Quite a difference, Rowena thought, from her father's environs growing up across the river in Southeast Washington. She hated it when blacks, and whites plagued by liberal guilt, called those neighborhoods ghettos in order to garner pity for the poor and disadvantaged. True ghettos, she insisted, were areas where the citizens were captive; where their poverty was enforced by government mandate; where there was virtually no hope of escape. A ghetto was Warsaw in the 1940s, not Southeast, or Harlem, or Joe Whitehead's North Philly of twenty years later. They were simply slums, and if the people who lived there felt powerless to escape; if her bleeding-heart former college classmates wailed about the *prisoners of the ghetto;* she could always hold up her father's example to set them straight. Joe's now, too.

As a book editor, she had an expression for those who diluted the language with purple hyperbole: word perverts.

Late afternoon found Rowena back on the Metro, this time bound for the Iwo Jima Monument in Arlington. She was still in awe of the statue, of the words UNCOMMON VALOR WAS A COMMON VIRTUE engraved on its pedestal. Any one of those men could have been her father, had he been born a generation earlier. The view beyond the statue, of the Potomac River, and of the city of Washington so far away it looked like a museum diorama, still was enough to take her breath away.

Buses with Marine Corps logos on the sides drove up. Troops in black blouses got off two of them, carrying rifles; others in red blouses disembarked from the rest, carrying bugles and drums. All of them wore white trousers, gloves, and white-crowned caps. A crowd of civilians gathered, and Rowena joined them. At the hotel she'd picked up a flyer for the Marine Corps Memorial Ceremony, held every Tuesday during the summer months.

The troops formed up behind the monument, and at precisely six o'clock the Drum and Bugle Corps marched from either side to the parade area in front, and played a series of songs with a martial air as they performed intricate marching drills.

Officers—*my dad could've been one of them,* Rowena thought—marched to the center of the field and called the ceremonial troops forward from the rear of the monument. Once they had lined up facing the crowd, which by now was enormous, the color guard advanced the American and Marine Corps flags, flanked by two riflemen. The sight stirred her, as it did so many others.

The ceremony climaxed with a performance by the Silent Drill Team and a pass in review. Rowena was surprised to find tears in her eyes. When she returned to the hotel, she called the Marine Barracks and reserved a seat for herself at Friday's Moonlight Parade.

At the same time, the Marine standing duty at the Camp David gatehouse was admitting Sergeants First Class Dale Keegan and Claire Delaney, wearing civilian clothes and badges identifying them as members of U.S. Government Social Services, to the compound. They drove to the parking lot and headed for the chow hall, where they met Commander Lauren Bachmann and Joe Whitehead. Matthew Collins had already returned to his civilian job in New Jersey.

Dale began the debriefing over dinner. He told her that they'd met Mrs. Bienkowski, a short, plump, and plain-looking woman in the throes of grief for her daughter and obviously in the dark as to how her naked body had ended up at the bottom of a ravine nearly two thousand miles away.

Claire formed an empathic bond with the woman almost immediately and learned through her tears of Sophie's rejection of all things right and proper; of her parents' attempt at tough love; and of their guilt at kicking her out of the house when she turned eighteen. "Sophia," her mother said, "means wisdom. In the end, I don't think any of us had much of that."

They asked if they could see her daughter's room, which had been untouched since Sophie left. Claire picked up a bottle of perfume and sniffed the scent. She wrinkled her nose. Hardly the fifty dollars an ounce variety; more like two dollars a gallon.

Dale asked her about the lighter, and Mrs. Bienkowski drew a blank.

She directed the faux social workers to a couple of Sophie's friends, and the first one they visited told them that *Monsieur* was the pet name Sophie had given the school's janitor. "They used to sneak smokes together in the boiler room during study hall," the friend said. "Everyone figured the guy had the hots for her, but Sophie dismissed the idea as stupid."

Next stop was the school, where the administration was working through the summer. The principal identified Monsieur as Ahmed Mansoor, one of the day custodians, and gave them his home address, noting that he was on vacation and would be back at work after the July 4 holiday. In the car, Dale called his contact at the FBI, and after procuring a warrant, a team converged on the little house off Piney Branch Road. There was no answer to their knock. Instead of kicking the door in, action-movie style, one of the agents simply picked the lock and they walked inside as if they were invited guests.

The house was what the locals termed a rambler: a small one-story home with a basement. The interior was dusty and unkempt; evidently, after a day of cleaning bathrooms and classrooms, it was too much like work for Mansoor to clean his own house. Dale noticed the smell of tobacco and an overall musty scent, but Claire's nose found something more.

"Sophie was here," she told him. "I can smell her perfume. It's only a trace, but I'd swear this is the same stuff. Very distinctive: eau de compost." She relayed the information to the FBI agent in charge. In the trash, another agent found tissues smudged with lipstick and what looked like eyeliner. It was enough to have the agent in charge set up a stakeout.

When Dale and Claire finished their report, Joe added news of his own, relative to the pair of punctures on the girl's inner thigh. He rushed through a DNA test and found a second strand, not Sophie's. It contained an unknown element, and on a hunch he compared it to the readouts of Claire's and Dale's that he had on file. When he discounted the couple's lupine DNA, he isolated their vampire marker and found it matched Element X.

"Which means there definitely is another bloodsucker out there," said Claire.

"I know what you're thinking," said Joe. "But there was no DNA evidence in the New Hampshire home, other than that of the victims."

"There's another thing," said Lauren. "Just before you got back, we got word of a terror attack on a passenger train in Utah. Let's start connecting some dots, shall we?"

When the Sprinter reentered Colorado, the towering San Juan Mountains were clearly visible despite the vast distance between them and the truck. Manuel was already sweating at the prospect of driving over the pass once again, but luck was with them when they reached Montrose. An eighteen-wheeled oil tanker pulled out in front of them, and he and Jesus both decided that it would be prudent to follow it into Durango.

The vehicles passed through Ridgway and Ouray—bejeweled with flowers of indescribable color and variety, graced with waterfalls flowing from the surrounding cliffs—and began the slow climb up the Million Dollar Highway.

With the view ahead partially obscured by the tanker, Manuel felt a little more at ease; but only a little. At one point, entering a blind turn—they heard the driver's warning horn advising possible oncoming traffic—they saw another eighteen-wheeler rounding the bend. Even Jesus gripped onto the armrest and pressed his feet to the floor of the cab. But the drivers' side mirrors passed within inches of each other, separated only by the distance between the road's twin yellow lines, and they let out breaths they hadn't realized they were holding in.

They followed the tanker down into Silverton and blessed their luck that it didn't stop, but continued up the next rise. When they finally crossed the Animus River on the outskirts of Durango, they were home free. They paused at a railroad crossing to allow the narrow-gauge passenger train they'd seen earlier, drawn by an antique, coal-fired steam engine, to cross the road heading for the depot in Durango. Jesus narrowed his eyes and smiled.

"What's so amusing, boss?" asked Manuel.

"Funny you should ask. There's a hotel at the edge of town. We'll take a room for two nights. And tomorrow, you and I are going to take a little train ride on the Durango-Silverton Railroad."

During the next few days, Rowena visited every Smithsonian museum in town, the Newseum, the Capitol, the Holocaust museum, and of course the war memorials. Her father had told her of guys in his unit who hadn't made it home from Vietnam, and she took paper and pencil and made rubbings of their names from the Wall, which she'd give to him upon his return from vacation. She took note of the wreaths and flowers at the base of the wall and couldn't help but be moved by the sight of a man her father's age touching a name on the Wall and crying unashamedly, as his wife stroked her hand over the back of his stained and ragged military utility jacket.

On Friday the 26th, Rowena took the Metro to Southeast and prepared to be assaulted by the sights and smells of the slum neighborhood in which the Marine Barracks, built in 1801, found itself. She was shocked when she saw the second sign on the post, beneath 8TH STREET SE, that read BARRACKS ROW.

The street was wide—the trolley tracks in the center had long been taken out—and flanked by all manner of upscale shops and eateries. The sidewalks were clean, the curbside free of trash. People of all ethnicities—singles, couples, families—strolled the walk without fear of predators. She had never dreamed of such a vivid example of urban renaissance.

With heightened spirits, she ordered dinner at a local bistro and chose to eat at one of its outdoor tables. Later, she found another restaurant farther down the block and ate another meal. She was getting used to her increased appetite; it was scary at first, but now it simply amused her.

There is nothing so strange...

At the corner of 8th and I, Rowena pulled out her cell phone, and the card Matthew had given her with the photo of *MV Semper Fidelis* on the face. She got an answer immediately.

"Matthew, it's Rowena Parr. It's Friday night, you should be out gallivanting."

"Party here at the boatyard," he said. "Where are you?"

She told him and asked if he'd be amenable to a visitor for Independence Day weekend. Nothing, he said, would make him happier. "We can anchor on the river and enjoy the fireworks from there."

When she hung up, Rowena wondered if there had been a Benny Hill-type double entendre in that last sentence. *Down, girl,* she thought, but couldn't hide a smile.

The Marine Barracks Moonlight Parade was as spectacular as it had been when her parents took her to see it as a child, when the rest of 8th Street and its environs were crime-ridden slums. She made a note to tell her father about the revitalized neighborhood when she saw him again.

There was so much she had to tell her parents—none of which could include her transformation into something neither fully human nor fully animal. She giggled as one thought popped into her mind: *what happens if I ever need to see a dentist?*

After the parade concluded, on a whim Rowena decided to explore her father's old haunts, ostensibly to see if the gentrification had extended past 8th Street. She turned not toward the subway entrance, but instead toward the Naval Weapons Plant at 8th and M. The multi-storied perimeter structure was walled in red brick, like an ancient castle, with the only entry an arched opening at the end of 8th Street, guarded by an armed Marine.

She turned right, walking in the direction of the waterfront at Maine Avenue, her eyes sensitive now to the street lamps, and able to see deeper into the darkness around them. Her ears, too, were keen to pick up the slightest sounds. But she was still caught by surprise when she heard "Hey, sister," from behind her.

They were sitting on the steps of a porch, their dark skin and clothing blending so well with the old row house and the night itself that she had walked by without noticing. There were only two, she noticed as they shuffled toward her, one tall, about six feet four, the other barely her own height, but broader and muscle-bound—from a prison gym, perhaps.

Just keep walking, she told herself. *You were stupid to venture beyond the safe zone; don't compound it now.* But she could feel a surge of adrenaline as their footfalls grew louder. A vagrant breeze brought the pungent scent of sweat from them, and she thought that she probably wouldn't have needed her preternatural senses to detect it.

The pair flanked her, and as they passed beneath a street lamp Rowena saw that the taller, who was wearing a sleeveless black T-shirt, was tattooed over every visible inch of his arms and neck. The blue ink, barely visible against his darker skin, was all swirls and curlicues, peppered with Asian characters that, for all she knew, might've been copied from a restaurant menu. The shorter man wore his hair in an afro, which almost made her laugh. Probably, he thought it made him look taller.

"Yo, so where you headed for, this late at night, ho?" asked the tall one.

Rowena tightened her lips. "Wherever it is, you don't want to go there."

"Ooh," said his friend. "Bitch talks tough."

"Yeah, I'm about to shit a brick," said the other.

"Hey," Afro said, studying Rowena's face as she tried to keep her expression neutral. "Sister's a chink, bro. Look at her eyes."

"Well, ain't that some shit. Hey, I'm wonderin' if it's true what they say about chinks. That their snatch is slanted like their eyes."

"I think we should find out." Afro put his hand on Rowena's bare arm, stopping her. They were between street lamps, the night black as pitch, the neighborhood still.

"Don't . . . go there," she warned. She could feel the change beginning, and as one part of her wanted to hold it in check, another wanted to release it.

But what would happen to my clothes if I morphed, the rational part interceded. *And how would I get back to my hotel with them all torn and bloody, without attracting attention? And what about my commitment to Claire and Dale?*

"Man, bitch has hairy arms," said Afro.

"Prob'ly a real hairy bush, too," said the other with a grin, and Rowena could see gold caps on his teeth.

"Don't . . . do this," she said, her voice turning guttural.

"What chew gon' do, ho?" said the tall one as his hand reached for her throat. "Bite me?"

Reason left her, and Rowena bit down hard on his hand. She felt her teeth, her wolf's teeth, easily pierce the flesh of his palm, grinding through the thin bones and meeting, uppers and lowers, somewhere inside. She shook her head, and part of his palm along with his thumb and the first two fingers of his hand came off in her jaws. She spit them out and turned to the other, whose eyes were all whites, as she spun toward him and gripped his throat with her free hand. Her talons dug deep behind his windpipe—she could feel the tubes of his esophagus and trachea—and she wrapped her fingers tight and yanked hard, opening a gaping hole and rendering Afro unable to scream. He sank to his knees, drowning in his own blood.

The taller one was speechless too, his good hand clutching his maimed one. He saw her face continue to transform and began backing away, but it was no good. She was upon him, pinning his arms to his sides as she overpowered him. Her wolf's jaws opened wide and crushed his head between them. He collapsed to the cracked slate sidewalk.

Rowena spit out his face and buried her snout into his skull. His brain was sweet, and his blood—*ye gods,* she thought, *Claire was right. This was the nectar of the gods.*

Reason returned. She looked around, saw no one, and bolted off, returning to full human form as she ran. When she arrived at the subway platform, barely out of breath, she saw in the light that there were flecks of blood on her blouse and some on her face. The few riders standing on the platform looked, but quickly turned away. She found a rest room and cleaned her face and arms and bloody hands, before emerging again onto the platform.

Rowena was breathing more easily by the time she arrived at her hotel, and she luxuriated in the steam of the shower, washing all traces of blood, grime, and guilt down the drain. But as she dried off, she was struck an almost physical blow to her midsection—as she realized that both her human and lupine DNA would be found in the muggers' wounds when they were autopsied. Commander Bachmann would make the connection to Claire and Dale, and then all hell would break loose. Rowena knew she herself was in danger of being terminated, but that didn't strike her with half the fear she felt for her dearest friend and her husband, who had violated every protocol in saving her life by turning her into . . . into what she was now.

She decided she had to call Claire and confess to what she had done. Self defense or not, she could have used her strength to simply knock the potential rapists unconscious. She was stupid in the first place for wandering about the streets of Southeast D.C. so late at night. What had she been trying to prove? *And, admit it, girl,* she castigated herself, *you were trying to prove something.*

She would call tomorrow morning . . . after breakfast. *The condemned ate a hearty meal,* she thought, as she fought back tears.

Sometime shortly after midnight, two enlisted Marines in neatly-pressed civilian clothes were returning to their barracks after taking dates home to their shared apartment in the Northwest section of the city. They hadn't enough money to pay the cabbie to take them all the way to the barracks, but he did drive them to the intersection of Maine Avenue and M Street. They apologized for not having enough for a tip, and he said it was all right, he'd been in the service, too.

They walked unmolested up M Street, their jarhead haircuts and spit-shined shoes marking them as Marines just as much as if they were wearing their dress blues. Last time someone from the hood tried to mug a Marine, the barracks turned out in force and did some serious damage, and the cops looked the other way.

As the two young men reached the halfway mark of their return hike, they saw some unfamiliar shapes on the sidewalk, two still, two moving. Drawing closer, they heard growling and stopped. Two pit bulls were tearing into the remains of two bodies. One of the bulls growled again, threatening to defend his meal against these intruders, as the other yanked something from the abdomen of the second. Blood was everywhere.

"Couple bangers there, you think?" said one Marine.

"I guess. No loss to the neighborhood, that's for shit sure."

The first flipped open his cell phone. "I'll call the cops."

"Be a shame to put down the dogs, though. That'll happen, y'know."

"So what do you suggest we do?"

"First thing, I'd suggest we cross the street."

On Saturday morning, Rowena, steeling herself to make the phone call to Claire, picked up the Washington *Post* on her way to breakfast. She thumbed idly through the first section until something caught her eye: an article about two Southeast men attacked and killed and partially devoured by runaway pit bulls the night before. The owner of the dogs, who ran an illegal dog-fighting operation, was now in custody, and the animals had been euthanized. The victims were identified by fingerprints on file with the D.C. Police Department, where they had extensive criminal records.

Rowena held her breath. The cause of death appeared to the authorities to be the work of the poor dogs. *An autopsy will probably be performed anyway,* she thought, but she didn't think anyone would be looking for DNA. If so, it meant that traces of wolf and human markers would neither be sought nor found. She looked heavenward, exhaled, and whispered, "Thank you, God."

There was, however, another consideration. She still owed Claire a phone call to confess what had happened. It was a matter of honesty, ethics, and integrity, and both Rowena and Claire shared those qualities. Their friendship was bound by them. But what would happen if she made that call? Claire and Dale would be duty bound to report Rowena's turning, followed by the D.C. incident, to Commander Bachmann, and she would have to report it to her handler. The entire team could be compromised, all because of a life-saving act of sisterly love. Plus . . . the phrase *terminated with extreme prejudice* jumped uninvited to her mind.

She made a decision. Discretion would trump valor. Her friends' futures need not suffer from her own stupid behavior. The die was cast; there would be no phone call.

At that moment, the server came to take her order, and she said, "Thanks, but I've decided to try the buffet."

That same morning, Sergeants Keegan and Delaney joined Commander Bachmann on her morning run around the perimeter. They wore their utility uniforms. Dale and Claire would have preferred running on all fours, but they could never do it inside the camp. The two Marines on roving patrol always drove along the perimeter road that paralleled the fence, and it wouldn't do to have a pair of wolves be seen by them running alongside the base commander—especially as the Marines carried loaded weapons.

This particular run, in addition to its normal exercise benefit, constituted a partial venting of their frustration at the news of the recent attack on the passenger train in Utah: at the huge loss of life; at their impotence in preventing it; at the mockery that attended the posting of the Burma-Shave signs.

The course of their run took them past the guardhouse, where the supernumerary stopped them, snapped a salute, and told the commander that she had an urgent message waiting in her quarters. The three of them beat a path to Lauren's cabin, one room of which contained her unofficial office—the one she reserved for the team's business. A paper rested where it had been spit out of the fax machine, and she picked it up, speed-read it, and read it again, slowly.

"Tell us," Dale said.

"Sit down. I'll fix coffee. This could be a long morning. Sorry to have to ruin your weekend, guys."

They sat in the living room, mugs of coffee on the table between them, and listened as Lauren explained: "Years ago, on the way to my friend's wedding in Ouray, I stopped over for a couple of days in Durango. It's a beautiful little town, a little touristy, but the locals are as friendly and welcoming as can be. It's in the heart of mountain country, and I remember seeing a lot of all wheel drive Jeeps and Subarus there, some so old they were held together by rust, but still running. I decided I liked the place.

"Anyway, one of the main attractions is a narrow-gauge steam railway that takes passengers from Durango to Silverton, past the first hump of the Million Dollar Highway. There are closed cars and open cars, and I sat in the open. By the time the train got to Silverton, hours later, I was covered in soot."

Dale took a gulp of his coffee. "I have a feeling I know where this is going."

"Yesterday, as the train was crossing a trestle built out of the edge of a cliff, a bomb went off somewhere between the engine and the coal tender. They were knocked over the cliff and pulled all the cars with it." She took a long breath. "No survivors."

They sat in silence. Finally Claire said, "Any Allahu Akbar message involved this time?"

Lauren nodded. "An email to the Durango and Silverton Railroad office from a library computer, using Suri Clarke's address and password."

"The woman from the Pep Boys bombing."

"Yes."

Dale growled, then caught himself. Claire looked at him. "Exactly," she said. "I'd love nothing better than to sink my teeth into this guy."

Lauren said, "The perp—or perps—sent the message at exactly the moment the train blew. I'm thinking that he, or they, must have taken the train earlier, probably the day before, and marked the time the train was at that spot on the track. They planted the bomb later, probably overnight, and set a timer."

"So we have a roving terror cell?" said Dale.

"It would appear."

"Unless," Claire added, "it's bogus; remember we mentioned that after the New Hampshire killings? Someone slipping us a red herring to lead suspicion away from himself, or themselves? No terror organization has ever claimed responsibility, after all."

Lauren set her mug down hard. "What a hell of a thing to wake up to."

Manuel and Jesus woke up early that morning, in their hotel at Los Alamos, New Mexico. They'd arrived late Friday, leaving Durango immediately after Jesus had sent the email to the railroad office. Jesus, in particular, was annoyed that they had arrived too late to visit the Los Alamos Museum. He wanted to see the replicas of Fat Man and Little Boy, the bombs which effectively ended the war with Japan. But they couldn't stay another day; he had a plane to catch in Albuquerque.

After Jesus's plane departed for Dulles, with an hour's layover in St. Louis—and wouldn't they have loved to blow up the Arch—Manuel sat in the airport lot with an atlas in his lap. The most direct route home would be to head out on I-40 to Durham, North Carolina, picking up I-85 and then I-95 to Washington. The Beltway would take him to U.S. 50 and Maryland Route 2, which led directly to Solomons Island, where his Jetta awaited in Jawdan's self-storage lot.

But I-40 led through Oklahoma City, and he wanted to avoid that, so he took I-25 north out of Albuquerque to I-70. With some serious driving, he could make Denver by tonight, Topeka tomorrow, Indianapolis on Monday, and Frederick, Maryland, on Tuesday. He'd overnight in Frederick and make the easy drive to Solomons on Wednesday, the first of July.

This was perfect. He could pick up his Jetta, drive home on Thursday, and pop in to D.C. to watch the fireworks on the Fourth. On Monday, he would be back at school to begin the summer's maintenance chores, his vacation over. All was well, he thought, anticipating his next meeting with the boss—when he was sure he would receive his reward for faithful service.

As Manuel headed for Denver, Jesus disembarked at Dulles and checked into the Hyatt in Herndon, Virginia. After securing his room, he headed for the hotel's jogging path, which allowed him to smoke to his heart's content as he strolled. The following day, he was in Atlantic City—

not for the gambling venues, but for the outlying slums, which provided easy pickings for his sanguinary appetite. Muhammad's hostility for blacks was as intense as it was for Jews, and he'd made sure the prostitute he'd chosen to feed him was not only drug-addled, middle-aged, and ugly, but black as well. Jack the Ripper would have approved. But unlike Jack's prey, this woman's murder would raise no alarms.

He drove north to Albany next, and on the last day of June he turned the front door key at his home on the campus of Criterion University in New Hampshire.

Now officially Muhammad Al-Jubeir again, he brewed himself a pot of strong tea and reflected upon his successes. At least in his own mind, they more than made up for his one failure back in 1993: the attempted assassination of President George H. W. Bush on his diplomatic visit to Kuwait to commemorate the allied victory in the Persian Gulf War.

He'd headed a team of seventeen men to coordinate the attack. They planted ninety kilograms of explosives in a Toyota Land Cruiser, along with a remote-controlled detonator and ten other devices, called cube-bombs, hidden in various strategic locations in the vehicle. It would have been a glorious act of vengeance for America's unwanted and unexpected entry into Iraq's attempted annexation of Kuwait.

But something had gone wrong. The Kuwaitis discovered the bombs, arrested his entire team—he was the only one to escape—and exposed the plot as having stemmed from the Iraqi Intelligence Service.

Al-Jubeir returned to Baghdad in disgrace. As an immortal he did not fear death, but he did rail at the humiliation of failure, something he had never known to such a degree. An outraged Saddam was ready to condemn him, but his anger was tempered by Muhammad's prior successes, along with his son Uday's pleas for lenience for his friend—a friendship formed and bonded in the torture and rape rooms. They were two of a kind. Almost.

But Saddam's forgiveness was probationary. He demanded revenge against the United States, and it would be up to Muhammad Al-Jubeir to exact it. To attempt another attack on the President was no longer feasible, but something had to go down, something big. And finally, after much research and deliberation, Muhammad came up with a plan.

Chapter Fourteen

On the morning of Tuesday, June 30, Rowena checked out of the DoubleTree and decided to spend the time between now and when she was due at Stump Creek visiting the Eisenhower home and Civil War cemetery at Gettysburg, the Civil War Museum in Harrisburg, and nearby Hershey, where she would see the famous Kiss-shaped street lamps and maybe get a tour of the chocolate factory.

As she got into the car, she phoned Bentley and informed her that she appeared to be in full remission. The doctors had released her with instructions for periodic returns for follow-ups, and she expected to be back at work on Monday. Her boss said she was happy beyond her power to describe.

Rowena drove up I-70 and got off at Frederick to have lunch. She found a Tex-Mex restaurant named Cacique on North Market Street and parked next to a dirty Sprinter panel truck that she thought might have been white once.

Exiting the restaurant with a lit cigarette in his mouth was an angry-looking man who could have been Hispanic, considering his sombrero and bolo tie. He nodded to her as they drew closer.

"Damn manager kicked me out," he grumbled, the cigarette bobbing up and down as he spoke. "Can't smoke anywhere these days."

Rowena smiled and shook her head as he got into the Sprinter and slammed the door. The engine started with a roar, and when the driver threw it into reverse it nearly jumped backward. *Temper temper,* she thought.

Over a lunch of mesquite-grilled rib-eye steak, very rare, she tried to empathize with the driver of the panel truck. Smokers these days were often considered second-class citizens, at least in their own minds. But one thing gave her pause, now that she thought of it. That man might have looked Hispanic, but his accent, slight as it was, was anything but.

On Wednesday, now heading east from Harrisburg, Rowena learned that the Hershey chocolate factory no longer offered tours, but she was welcome to visit nearby Chocolate World for a Disney-type ride showing how chocolate is produced. She thanked the receptionist, but decided to press on, maybe overnighting in Philly instead.

On that same first day of July, Ahmed Mansoor parked the Sprinter outside the gate of the storage yard in Solomons. Jawdan would be working at the yard, so he called him on his cell. Maybe *Jerry* could cop a few minutes to open the yard, exchange the Sprinter for the Jetta, and let Ahmed get started on his way home to Takoma Park.

He didn't expect what he heard.

Five minutes later, Jawdan pulled up in the marina's half-ton pickup. "Don't go back," he said as he jumped from the cab. "They found the girl."

"What? How?"

Jawdan told him about the GPS in her phone. Also: "I'm only guessing now, but if they found her they probably found the lighter you gave her, and if the cops canvassed the jewelry stores, and if—"

"And if the engraver remembered and talked to them . . . hell, my address was on the sales slip. They could be watching my house right now. Jawdan: what do we do?"

Jawdan took a step back. "What's this *we?*"

"Oh, come on."

"Listen, Ahmed. I was never a part of this. There's no reason to involve me."

"Except my Jetta's in your storage yard."

"Yes, and you've got to get it out of there."

"But if the cops know who I am, they would know what I drive, know the license plate. They'd put an APB out on the car. They could be looking for it right now. In fact, they would have to be." Ahmed was speaking in staccato; he slowed down and took a breath. With shaking fingers, he plucked a cigarette from his shirt pocket and lit it. "All right, let's take a moment."

"I've got to get back to work. You take a moment. Then take the Jetta and go. Somewhere. Anywhere. You were never here. I never saw you, I never even met you." He told Ahmed the four-digit code for the gate.

"What if the boss calls with another job?"

"He wouldn't call so soon. He'd let the trail go cold. It was years between the first job and last January."

"And only a few months between that one and this."

"Don't tell me about this operation. I saw something on the news, but I don't want to know anything. Listen, for all we know the boss isn't even aware yet that they found the girl. He was with you, after all, and you didn't learn about it until now. And something like this probably wouldn't make the New Hampshire papers anyway."

"You think I should tell him?"

"You've got to. And hope he doesn't kill you, because the girl was your fuckup, no one else's." He hopped back in the cab. "Be gone when I get back. And, Ahmed, good luck. I mean it. Allahu Akbar."

"Yeah, right."

Jawdan returned to the marina and performed engine maintenance on a 39-foot Gatsby motorsailer until seven o'clock. It was still daylight when he returned to the storage yard. He now had to strip the weaponry out of the Sprinter and return it to his unit inside the cinderblock building. He leaned out his car window, pressed the numeric code for the gate, and entered the yard. Ahmed would have parked the van just behind the building, next to the back door. Jawdan couldn't wait to unload the thing and secure the area. He found he was shaking.

He swung around the building. The Sprinter wasn't where he'd assumed it would be. Frowning, with an uneasy feeling in his gut, he scanned the yard where the owners of RVs, pop-up trailers, and other campers kept their vehicles.

"NO!" he roared when he saw the Jetta.

"What the hell were you thinking, girl?" Rowena asked herself as she paid the Pennsylvania Turnpike toll at King of Prussia and joined the stop-and-go traffic crawling alongside the Schuylkill River. Joe Whitehead had called it the Sure Kill and jokingly called the city of his birth Filthydelphia. She continued castigating herself. "Philly on Independence Day weekend? Duh!" Rowena shook her head.

"Every hotel in the city has to be booked. Let's hear it for forethought, dummy." *Where has my mind gone to die?*

She decided to press on. It was half past three now, the bridge to Jersey was a half hour or so away, and the state was only about sixty miles wide at that point. How long could it take?

Answer: It could take a lot longer than she thought.

The highway took her direct to the Ben Franklin Bridge to Camden. Windows up, locks down, she cautioned herself as she headed for State Route 70, the road that would take her to the shore. Once on 70, she was grateful to find it a four-lane divided road—clogged with traffic, yes, but it was rush hour after all—that passed through typical suburban sprawl. She checked her watch: just past five. Well, it was a straight shot across the state.

Rowena pulled off the road at an all-you-can-eat buffet restaurant, where she filled her stomach and emptied her bladder. Funny, it was after six, everyone should be home by now, yet traffic was no better.

At a roundabout, the four lanes funneled into two, no divider between them, and a wall of pine trees on either side. The crawling traffic showed no signs of abating. Featureless, the road was: no buildings, no billboards, just trees, trees, and more trees. At least the sun was at her back.

More roundabouts—circles, the signs called them— were all that broke the monotony. She crawled by a car on the shoulder with an overheated engine. She wanted to stop and offer help, but what could she do? Besides eat the driver?

Whoa! Where did that thought come from?

Some cars peeled off at a farther circle—the fourth? the fifth?—where Route 72 led to Long Beach Island. By now it was dark, and Rowena's eyelids were growing heavy. Another circle, and she had reached Lakehurst. *I'll crash in flames if I don't get some sleep soon,* she thought. *The stories say we vamps are supposed to stay up all night and only get tired near sunup. Oh well, another myth shattered.*

She craved caffeine, and thankfully saw the Lakehurst Diner at the circle where Route 37, direct to Toms River, broke off from 70. Fortified again, she was relieved to see that 37 was a multi-lane divided highway. But it was still congested.

Every motel along the road had No Vacancy signs post-ed; Rowena had to drive on, fighting sleep, slapping herself to keep awake. *Why am I doing this?* she asked herself, yet again. By way of answer, she thought of the boat and of Matthew, not necessarily in that order, but if she concen-trated on picturing the boat, she found herself drifting into dreamland. More than once she drove across lanes, to be jolted back by the horn of another car she'd been about to cut off.

The highway crossed the northern end of Toms Riv-er's Main Street, and Rowena turned right, out of the traf-fic flow. The town was all but deserted, but then at eleven o'clock who could be expected to be on the streets? At the south end of town she crossed a small bridge, bore left, and drove along the southern bank of the river. Slowly, because Matthew had warned her of the police in the small com-munities here. Traffic stops provided major income to the towns, he said, and when she'd called a few days before, he advised her to set her cruise control at one mile per hour under the posted 25 miles per hour speed limits. And make sure to come to a complete stop and stay stopped for ten seconds or so at each stop sign before continuing. He'd been ticketed once for not making what the policeman had called a *quality stop.*

She almost passed the huge white mooring buoy that marked the narrow driveway to Stump Creek Slipways. A hundred yards down the drive was the river, with two speed bumps between the road and the dirt parking lot. Rowena doused her headlights in favor of parking lamps, so as not to awaken people sleeping on their boats. The yard was dark and still when she pulled into a visitor's slot.

A maintenance shop across from the Weeping Willow Bar housed a small head, and Rowena took her toilet kit with her to scrub the scum from her teeth. Afterward, she stood on the silent shore and stared at the river. Her en-hanced hearing picked up the gentle lap of ripples as they broke against the sand. In one of the sailboats, someone was snoring. Other than that, peace prevailed. She looked at the long pier that jutted out into the river. Like every other boat, *Semper Fidelis* was dark. She thought about walking out and quietly climbing aboard, but that would violate marine protocol; besides, she didn't want to wake Matthew up.

Hmm. He wasn't expecting me until tomorrow; might he be entertaining someone else tonight? If Rowena just happened to pop in, wouldn't that put a twist in the dear Brit's knickers?

She returned to the car and reclined the seat, settling in for a snooze.

Uh huh. Easier said . . . Here she hadn't been able to hold her eyes open on the road, but now she was so jazzed that she couldn't make herself sleep. *How screwed up is that?*

Ahmed Mansoor was panicked. He drove the Sprinter to Annapolis and found a spot to park on a residential side street overlooking the Severn River. He lit a new cigarette from the stub of the current one. He was a chain smoker all of a sudden, just like the boss. But he had a reason. He needed to calm down. To put it bluntly, he felt fucked.

The police knew who he was, where he lived, and what he drove. So he could never return to Takoma Park and never go back to work at the school. The Jetta? Less of a problem. Why would they need to expand their search all the way to Solomons Island? As long as Jawdan kept it in the lot, between those two campers, it wouldn't be found. There was no obvious connection between him and Jawdan, to lead the police there. All right, so far so good.

He could change his identity; rather, keep the Hispanic ID he'd been using on the last mission. There was money in his pocket, which would last for a while. But he'd need to find some work eventually, and if a prospective employer ran a security check on him . . . no good.

He needed a job that he could work while collecting his pay in cash, under the table. That's when he noticed the landscaping truck drive up and discharge a pair of men who looked like Mexicans. One wheeled a riding mower out of the back, and the other unloaded a gas-fired edger. Yes, he could work for a landscaper. But not here, not anywhere in Maryland.

Maryland. The Sprinter had Maryland tags. Oh, hell, this was getting complicated.

His cell rang. It had rung every hour or so, but when he saw the caller ID register *Jerry,* he refused to answer. This time, it was from *Caller Unknown.* That could only be one person.

"Hello, boss," he said.

"Hello, Ahmed. Is all well?"

"No. All is not well." He explained the situation.

There was a long silence. Then, a voice that betrayed no emotion—which Mansoor knew was the most dangerous voice of all: "Your lust has compromised us."

"I am so sorry, boss. So sorry. I wish there was a way to undo it."

"Where are you?"

"Annapolis. In Maryland."

"I know where Annapolis is." Al-Jubeir paused, as if collecting his thoughts. "All right. Keep your phone on. I shall call you back. Are you in a safe location?"

Ahmed told him where he was.

"Don't stay parked there any longer. Strange vehicles in residential zones arouse suspicion. Drive downtown and park near the water, where you'll look like another summer tourist. Walk around. Look relaxed. Keep the phone with you. Understood?"

"Yes, boss," Ahmed replied in a voice barely above a whisper. The connection broke.

An hour later, the phone rang again. Ahmed looked at the ID and shut the phone off, lest the others at the water-front stare at him and wonder why he wasn't answering. He turned it on again in time to pick up the second call, the one he'd been expecting. "Yes?" he said.

"You will drive to New Hampshire. You will drive slow-ly, within speed limits. You will stay overnight in Walmart parking lots, as we did before. Take back roads and avoid tolls. The holiday weekend is coming up, which is good. The roads will be busy with travelers, and the van will draw no undue attention. Do not arrive in New Hampshire before Tuesday the seventh. By then I will have made arrange-ments. I will call you on the morning of that day. Do you understand?"

Ahmed nodded, then cleared his head and said he did.

"Do not repeat these instructions. I hear people around you, and I don't want any of them to eavesdrop. Wait for my call on Tuesday."

Relieved at having a mission and a direction, Ahmed returned to the Sprinter and drove east on Route 50. He crossed the Chesapeake Bay Bridge onto Kent Island and then onto the mainland. He saw a sign for Route 213, the scenic route that paralleled the heavily traveled U.S. Route 301, and followed the eastern shore of the Bay northward. In less than an hour, he crossed the Chester River and decided to spend the night in Chestertown. Tomorrow he'd continue his slow trek north.

Rowena was awakened by a persistent tapping on the driver's side window. She cracked her eyes open against the sleep dust and saw a jolly-looking man with a bushy gray beard smiling at her. She moved the seat back erect and eased the door open.

"Matthew's friend, right?" the man said. "Paul. We met on Memorial Day weekend, remember? Pot luck at the Weeping Willow?"

"Oh. Hello, Paul," she said. "Of course I remember you." *Barely,* she added to herself. At the time, she had been concentrating on Matthew.

"Got in late, I assume."

"You assume correctly. What time is it, do you know?"

"Around seven." He took a step back, as Rowena turned in the seat and placed her feet on the ground. "Um, no way to put this delicately, but you might want to freshen up a bit before you waltz out on the dock." He nodded toward the workshop.

"My thoughts exactly. I didn't want to disturb Matthew last night, the boat was dark. And if he had company, well—"

Paul laughed. He looked like a cross between Ernest Hemingway and Santa Claus. "Honey, the only company he had was that damned cat of his. All he was talking about the past coupla days was you coming to see him."

"Really?"

Paul grinned. "Get yourself to the head. Matthew gets up early."

"He surely does," said a cheery, British-accented voice from behind him.

"Cheese it, the cops," said Paul.

"Great," said Rowena. "Hell of a way to make an entrance, isn't it?"

Matthew held out his hand and helped Rowena out of the car, said hello, and gave her a chaste hug.

"Oh, geez," said Paul. "I hug my sister like that."

"Get out of here, you blighter," Matthew said, grinning. "Rowena, you should've knocked on the hull when you got here."

"We've been over that," Paul called as he walked toward his sailboat. "And why don't you stop with that blighter bullshit? You're in America now, remember?" He was laughing as he climbed aboard.

"Well, now you've seen my Halloween face," Rowena said, comically screwing up her features. "Still want me on board your yacht?"

"It's my home, and yes. When you're done in the head, come out to the boat. No need to ask permission to come aboard; you've a standing invitation. From both Miss Digit and my humble self." He nodded toward the trunk. "Take from your bag what you need for the head, and give me rest. I'll stow it on board."

When Rowena entered the boat's saloon a half hour later, showered and refreshed and dressed in the shorts and sleeveless top she'd taken from her duffel before Matthew made off with it, she noted that he had already placed her bag in the master stateroom.

The cat, meanwhile, greeted her with a series of body rubs around the ankles. Rowena picked her up and got cheek rubs on the side of her face.

"We'll be anchoring out tonight and tomorrow, so I'll take the pilot house berth," Matthew said as he arranged bacon strips on a ridged microwave tray in the galley.

So much for our sharing the master stateroom, Rowena thought. She cocked an eyebrow and changed the subject. "Nothing sexier than a man in the kitchen."

"The U-shape is very efficient, if small." He put the bacon in the waist-high microwave mounted alongside the wood-faced door of the refrigerator. "Microwaving is neater than frying, it gets the bacon uniformly crispy, and with the little spout there in the corner I can pour off the fat and save it for frying up crab cakes."

"You make your own crab cakes? Oh, my God. I think I'm in love."

Matthew nodded toward the passageway. "Might want to arrange your toiletries in the head and put anything you want hung in the hanging locker—that is, the closet. How many eggs, please?"

"All of them." He blinked. "All right, maybe three."

"And how would you like them?"

"Any way you want to fix them, master chef."

After breakfast, Rowena insisted she take KP duty while Matthew readied the boat for cruising. He disconnected the land-fed electricity, cable television, and water lines, then started the diesel engine and let it warm up as Rowena finished in the galley. He told her how to cast off the lines, draping them over wooden hooks attached to the pilings to allow for easier retrieval upon their return.

Semper Fidelis motored south past Tice's Shoal to the deep water opposite Barnegat Inlet, where Matthew joined a motley fleet of mixed vessels, from rowboats to cabin cruisers. He anchored and shut the engine down. "Let's see if we can catch dinner," he said. "If we're skunked, I've a steak or two in the fridge. We won't starve."

They sat on the teak swim platform aft of the stern and lowered their lines to the bottom. A bucket of squid, a cutting board, and a knife lay between them, and a net occupied the space behind. Their bare feet dangled in the water, and soon Rowena felt tiny taps on her legs.

"Those are spearing," Matthew explained. "They're nibbling at our legs to pick off any dead skin."

"Sounds gross, but it sure feels good. Tickles in fact." She looked into the bucket. "An Italian would say you're wasting good calamari."

"Eye-talians eat sheep heads, too. Brains and all. I'll pass, thank you."

The thought of brains brought Rowena back to the deer she, Dale, and Claire had brought down in the forest behind Camp David. The three of them shared the brain, and as wolves they found it delicious. Then she thought of the human brain she'd sampled in Southeast Washington. Not at all pleasant as a memory, but tastewise? Very pleasant, indeed.

"What are you smiling at?"

"Oh . . . just thinking about those zombie movies," she said. "Claire told me once about a girl she knew in high school. Said if a zombie approached her looking for brains, he'd walk right on by."

"Sounds like Claire."

Rowena sniffed the salt tang in the air, listened to the small waves brush against the boat, saw the red and white Barnegat Lighthouse standing tall on the Long Beach Island side of the inlet. This was a little piece of paradise.

"Claire told me you guys on the team wanted to have her killed when they found out what she was."

"I admit to having a voice in that. Having a werewolf running around killing people would certainly not be good in terms of national security, and as for public panic, well. Kind of like the aliens at Roswell back in the forties. Some information should not be promulgated."

"So there really were aliens?"

"Rowena, if I told you . . ."

"I know, I know. So what changed your mind about killing Claire?"

"Dale, actually. He's a dear friend, he vouched for her, and I trust his judgment."

"And then you found out that he's a werewolf, too. And a vampire to boot."

"They prefer the term *hemophage*—more dignified, you know—and yes, that was quite a shock. And to tell you the truth, when Claire stayed overnight with me last January on her way up to see you, I kind of slept with one eye open."

"Really. You weren't teasing, then, when you said that the last time we were all together?"

"I was teasing them, but I confess that when Claire was here alone, I didn't sleep so soundly as usual. I know she's a friend and would never do me harm. But I do have an irrational fear of . . . well, of things that I have an irrational fear of. Rowena, as a kid in England, I was addicted to horror comics, even though they sometimes scared me silly. There was one story, it was called *The Curse of the Bugala* if I remember correctly, and the last frame showed this dark, scaly, humanoid monster coming out of a coal bin, and he was carrying a guy's severed head in one hand. His other hand had long claws on the fingers, and they were dripping blood.

"Now, here's the thing. I had to bank the coal furnace every night before bedtime. That was one of my chores. Our basement was dank and dark—I think the single light bulb drew about one watt—and I shuddered to think that this monster, the bugala, lived in our coal bin. As I said, scared silly. I trembled each time I baby-stepped inside to get a shovelful of coal, peering into the shadows. And the bin was all shadows."

"Wow. The monster in the dark. Enough to scare any kid, I guess. And it stayed with you all these years."

He sat in silence, looking at the water. "Bloody psycho, you're thinking, right?"

Rowena touched his arm, and he turned to look at her. "Lots of us grew up with monsters under the bed," she said. "Or in the closet. Or in your case, the coal bin."

Matthew looked as if he wanted to say something more, but he changed the subject when he said, "Did you know your rod is twitching?"

"What? Oh, look!"

"Set the hook, but not too hard; you don't want to jerk it out of its mouth."

Rowena's rod curved toward the water as she worked the reel and Matthew stood and reached for the net. Up came a flat fish with a mottled brown back and a white belly. Both eyes were on the brown, sand-colored side.

"Right. That's what we're talking about," Matthew said as he netted the fish. "A lovely doormat fluke, I'd wager about three pounds. Fish dinner tonight." He unhooked the fish and tossed it into another bucket, this one on the aft deck. It thrashed and flopped in the bucket as Digit stood on her hind legs to peer inside.

Rowena was thrilled. It was her first time fishing, and she had actually caught something. Moments later, Matthew caught its twin. "Tide's changing," he noted as he checked his watch. "Good time for fluke fishing."

"I thought they were flounder. Am I wrong?"

"Summer flounder, officially. Winter flatties are smaller, and they don't have the big mouth and teeth that these do. Fluke are fatter, easy to fillet, and the meat is nice and thick. Delicious any way, but I prefer them dipped in beer batter and fried, then sprinkled liberally with malt vinegar and salt."

"Like fish and chips."

"Brilliant. We'll have that tonight."

"I like your accent," Rowena said.

"I like yours, too."

Matthew piloted the trawler north to Tice's Shoal, where he set anchor and prepared dinner. Rowena declared she'd never tasted fish so succulent, and Matthew said it was because it was absolutely fresh. Afterward, they climbed to the boat deck and lay on flotation cushions and stared at the stars. The cat lay on Rowena's belly. Her purring was almost as loud as the boat's engine had been. At least a hundred more boats populated the anchorage, what Matthew referred to as aquatic urban sprawl. But Rowena didn't mind a bit. She couldn't remember when she had felt so blissfully relaxed, and she said so. He surmised that floating on the water must be like floating in the womb.

Rowena retired to the master stateroom, the cat snuggled to her side, with the overhead hatch open to catch the breeze. An anchored boat always turns bow to the wind, so no matter which way it blows there's always a breeze below. Her thoughts returned to—no, remained on—Matthew. In spite of the most conducive elements imaginable, he had not made any amorous advances toward her. She wondered if he might be a closeted gay. Or if there were simply something about her that just didn't click with him. And she remembered what Paul had said to him earlier that day: "I hug my sister like that."

He wouldn't—he couldn't—have suspected that she and Claire were now two of a kind. Could he? She placed the fingers of one hand over the pentacle pendant necklace Claire had given her and let sleep overtake her.

The next morning they motored back to the Toms River and cruised past Stump Creek to a waterside restaurant in the town itself, where they docked and enjoyed lunch. Then they headed east again, anchoring off the country club on the north shore. "This place will be crowded later on," he said. "It's the prime spot to view the fireworks."

The evening's display didn't disappoint. Toms River on one side of the river and Beachwood on the other, in addition to Seaside Heights on the barrier peninsula across the bay, all put on simultaneous shows that provided 360 degrees of pyrotechnic entertainment.

But there were no fireworks on board *Semper Fidelis.* Matthew could not have been more pleasant, more accommodating, but now it was Rowena's turn to display reserve. She thought he might be suffering from veddy propah British dating protocol, whatever that might be, and she acknowledged to herself that they had only known each other for a few days—Memorial Day weekend and now this Independence Day. For some reason, it seemed she'd known him longer.

Tomorrow would be Sunday, and Rowena had to make the long haul to Boston to be back at work the next day. Traffic would be a problem, but there was another problem that she had to confront first. She decided, as she lay alone on the queen size berth, that she would just broach the subject head on and clear the air.

Early next morning, back at Stump Creek, Matthew placed her bag in the trunk and closed it. "Lovely weekend," he said.

"Matthew. We need to talk."

He frowned.

"No, wait. I need to talk. Then you."

"All right."

"I like you; I really like you."

"I like you, too. Very much."

"Romantically? Or more like a sister?" She looked at his face. "You're blushing. Sorry. But I'm old enough not to want to play games."

Matthew lowered his eyes and shuffled a foot on the ground. He looked back up and offered an apologetic smile. "Rowena, the reason I was such a bloody gentleman was because of Joe."

"Joe? As in Whitehead? What about him?"

"Well, when we drove out to the airpark to pick you up last May, he told me that he was quite taken by you, and he believed you might fancy him, too. He said that you had much in common, being of similar ethnicity and all that. Now, all may be fair in love and war, but if your sights were set on Joe, I certainly wouldn't want to make you uncomfortable by . . . you know."

Rowena shook her head. "Matthew, Matthew, Matthew. My late husband was a slice of white bread. And I loved him dearly. That ethnic crap Joe spouted to you is pure 1950s, and I want no part of it. You're telling me that's what was stopping you this weekend? You didn't want to step on Joe's Brazil-nut-looking toes? I can't believe it, you Brits and your manners."

He stared into her face. "My God. What a fool I've been."

"What an opportunity you missed, big boy. Here, let me give you a hint." She planted her palms against the sides of his head and pulled his lips to hers. He hesitated but a moment before locking his arms around her waist and drawing her tight to him.

They heard applause and broke the embrace, looking around.

"That's more like it," Paul called from the deck of his sailboat. "The beast with two backs, as your countryman Willy Shakespeare used to say." More heads popped up from the cockpits and cabins of other vessels in the marina. The applause continued. Someone tinkled a spoon alongside a water glass.

"Oh, what the hell," said Matthew, glancing at their audience. "Come back to the boat," he whispered. "Now."

Rowena gave him a coy look. "What's the magic word?"

"Please!"

Rowena got on the road more than an hour later than she'd planned. As she drove up the entry ramp to the Garden State Parkway, she thanked her lucky stars that Matthew's complete surrender to their lovemaking proved he didn't suspect she was anything other than a hundred percent human. And she vowed to keep it that way. For as long as she absolutely could.

Now all they had to do was work out some kind of weekend scheduling.

Chapter Fifteen

Muhammad Al-Jubeir had booked a room for Ahmed Mansoor, under the name Manuel Delgado, at a small independent motel on the outskirts of town. He chose that particular motel for the parking lot behind it, where the Sprinter could be parked and not be seen from the road. Mansoor arrived on schedule, and they repaired to his room. "Can we smoke in here?" he said.

"No. Outside only. But for now, I want you to explain what happened. Everything, no detail left out."

Mansoor told him, and Al-Jubeir quietly cursed. "This is the classic example of the law of unintended consequences," he said. "You thought it would be so simple. You give her a gift, you expect her to put out for it. She doesn't. Had you left it alone right there, there would have been no problem. But no."

"I am so sorry, boss."

Al-Jubeir said, in his deadly emotionless tone, "You are the shit beneath my shoes."

Mansoor cringed and stared at the floor. Outwardly, he looked contrite; inwardly, he was both fearful and seething. The insult was excessive, intolerable, inexcusable. Ahmed had been a loyal accomplice, a trusted associate. Had he not done as commanded, found respectable yet inconspicuous employment? Remained off the radar? And most of all, kept the boss's unimaginable secret these many years? Mansoor yearned for the day when Muhammad would share the gift with him, turn him into a *strigoi* like himself, make him his equal in all things. Then, Mansoor thought, he could break from the boss, go his own way, and enjoy to the fullest his immortal life.

Muhammad continued: "At the least, I should cut off your balls. That would solve any future problems." He scowled. "Of that nature, at least. But then there's the law

of unintended consequences. Who knows what other problems might result from your indiscretions?"

"None, boss, I promise."

Al-Jubeir shook his head. "What is in the van? Don't
tell me it's another woman."

Mansoor took a breath to steady himself. "Just what's
left from the operation. Some C4, all the Thermite, a few
detonators, the rocket launcher—but no more rockets—
and the rifles and handguns."

"And what do you hear from Jawdan?"

"Nothing. I don't answer his calls."

As if on cue, Mansoor's cell phone rang and Al-Jubeir
grabbed it. Jawdan's voice on the other end was nearly
hysterical. The boss told him to keep his head, told him
that the van would be returned and the Jetta disposed of in
time. And he told him not to call again; if he were needed,
the boss would call him.

"First," he muttered, his expression glowering, "I have
to figure out what to do with you."

At the moment, Mansoor was to stay inside and out of
sight. He could walk down the street to a fast food place for
his meals, but that was it. He was to alternate restaurants
so as not to establish a presence. And he would keep his
cell phone on twenty-four/seven.

The next day, Monday, Al-Jubeir checked in at the
university office and pulled the mail from his cubby. Most
was advertising junk, and he threw it away without a second look. But a pink "While you were out" message slip
did not find its way to the trash. It was from a Bentley Williams of Jones Publishing in Boston, re *Diatribe*. About
time. He punched in the number on the slip, wondering
if Bentley was a man's or a woman's name. The way these
infidel women were infiltrating all levels of the work world,
he wouldn't be surprised if it were the latter. Regardless,
it was obvious that the company was going to publish his
book; otherwise, why bother to call him instead of sending
a rejection slip?

Bentley Williams hung up the phone and addressed
Rowena, who just a moment before had walked into her office. "Well, that went well. I assume you heard my firm but
gentle rejection—"

Rowena acknowledged her boss's sarcasm. "That should have been my call. I'm the bad guy here, not you."

Bentley waved a hand dismissively. "You've been through enough unpleasantness lately. Call it my good deed for the year." She smiled. "That said, you must've heard his reaction."

"I heard an explosion coming through from the other end."

"He was, as you Yanks might say, highly pissed. He said he would be coming in tomorrow to pick up the MS personally. Under no circumstances were we to send it back in the mail."

"Uh oh. This doesn't sound positive."

"So much for good intentions. He says he'll be here sometime around noon." She chuckled. "My advice? Don't offer to take him to lunch."

Rowena laughed. "Listen, if I can survive the big C, I can survive a PO'd professor."

"Would you like me to sit in on the meeting with you?"

"Thanks, no. But I appreciate the offer."

"And may I say, for the thousandth time, how well you look."

"You may. I feel great, too. If my return evaluations prove positive, well, the world could change for the better almost overnight." She added: "Not overnight, of course; there'll be months if not years of testing, but still."

"Want to come by for dinner tonight? Elliott's cooking: chicken en croute; sautéed mixed vegetables; brown rice, all accompanied by a nice Riesling. And when I called him, he said he'd be happy to double the recipe."

"Ooh. Talk about an offer you can't refuse. But, um . . . would you mind asking him to triple the recipe?"

The manuscript was on Rowena's desk when its author was shown into her office. He seemed briefly startled to see a mixed-race woman behind the desk. He looked to be in his mid to late forties: of average height, a little stocky, close-cropped black hair, small and close-set eyes, hawkish nose, and a day's worth of stubble, which was supposedly fashionable these days. Personally, she hated the look. He wore a dark blue suit, white shirt, and red tie—much too heavy for summer wear.

He didn't smile; rather, he bared his teeth in a poor semblance that came off as a sneer. Rowena noted his teeth were yellow, with dark stains between them. She didn't need her enhanced sense of smell to pick up the scent of stale smoke that clung to his clothes. He stank like a filthy ashtray.

"Mr. Al-Jubeir," she said, standing and extending her hand, hoping that he wouldn't take it. He didn't.

"Doctor," he corrected. "Or Professor, if you wish."

"Please sit down . . . Professor."

He took the chair in front of her desk and looked at the manuscript on top of it. When Rowena's first boss, Ray Jones, conducted an interview, he always came out from behind his desk and sat in a chair next to the interviewee. Bentley Williams did the same, and so did Rowena. Usually. But today she wanted the desk between them, and it wasn't just because the smell of smoke made her fight the gag reflex. *If there is truth to the saying that there's nothing like a reformed drunk,* she thought, *there's also nothing like a reformed smoker—especially if said former smoker has the nose of a wolf.* No, something else put her off. A sense of impending threat. She could almost feel the waves of hate he radiated.

"So," he said. "You have decided not to publish my book."

"That's true, Mr.—Professor. Actually, before we go on, I have a question if you don't mind. I'm a graduate of the university where you work, and I know that Criterion has its own university press. Surely you must have submitted your work to Criterion first."

He leaned back in his chair. "You are right. They rejected it out of hand."

"Can you tell me why?"

"They called it both defamatory and inflammatory."

"But you teach there. If your words were unacceptable, I wonder why the university continues to employ you on its staff. Again, if you don't mind my asking."

"Ms. Parr, I am a distinguished professor of Middle Eastern history. What your country's absurd political correctness prohibits me from teaching in my classes, I must commit to writing—in order that those who wish to pursue their studies in this area can learn the truth."

Rowena swallowed and slid the manuscript toward him. "The truth."

"Yes. The truth."

"As you see it?"

"No. As it is. Unvarnished."

"Professor Al-Jubeir, as my employer told you yesterday, Jones Publishing does not find your manuscript acceptable. I'm sorry. But I'm sure there are other publishers who would. Might I suggest—?"

His expression darkened. "I want to speak with your employer."

"Mine is the final word here."

The man's brow lowered. "I drove to Boston to give you one more opportunity to reverse your decision. Sometimes a personal meeting can be more productive. Tell me: did you even read the manuscript?"

"Enough to know that it is filled with hate: hate for Christians and Jews; for Americans and East Asians; for whites and blacks; and for women, especially those who strive to work among men as equals. Have I missed anything?"

He took the manuscript and stood. "We are done here." As he turned, he mumbled words she was not meant to hear. But her hearing, like her sense of smell, was much more acute now.

"Well, well. The N-word and the C-word, both in the same breath. How clever of you."

He turned to confront her, malice radiating from his eyes.

"The truth is neither magnanimous nor mean-spirited. It just is."

"Leave my office." She was almost shaking now. "You have no idea what I'm capable of when I'm angry."

He twisted his mouth into an ugly grin. "And you have no idea what I am capable of. Even when I'm not angry." He turned to leave, and as he walked out, he muttered, "As you'll see."

Rowena squeezed her eyes shut to hold the angry tears back. She tensed her hands and slid them across the desk into her lap. A scraping sound made her open her eyes. She saw scratch marks gouged into her wooden desktop. Looking down, she realized that her fingernails had grown into long black claws.

After the professor left the building, and Rowena's talons became fingernails again, she reapplied her polish, walked into Bentley's office, and told her what had transpired. Bentley called the provost in Criterion and, after explaining what had happened and the professor's not-so-veiled threat, had her call transferred to the administrative offices and repeated the message.

But Professor Al-Jubeir did not return to the campus, where security might question him; instead, he drove to the motel where Ahmed Mansoor was staying, and after midnight they drove to the house he'd been renting and cleared it of all his personal goods, which were minimal, and piled them into the Sprinter. There was plenty of room left over. He slept that night in Mansoor's twin-bedded room after an evening of making plans and violating the no smoking rule, and the two of them left the next day, paying cash for the accommodations.

When the maid entered the room later, she could smell that the occupants had been smoking and told the manager. The manager in turn sent a bill for another day's stay as compensation for being unable to rent the room, because they needed a full day to air it out. The envelope was returned a few days later marked Address Unknown.

Rowena herself passed the first two nights after her confrontation with the professor virtually sleepless. She tossed and turned, senses on the alert in case the creep had followed her home, in case he planned some kind of attack on her person. "As you'll see," he'd said as he walked out, again in an undertone not meant to be heard by human ears.

Those days were busy ones for Muhammad Al-Jubeir and Ahmed Mansoor. They involved surveilling the building that housed Jones Publishing. It was a four-story brick unit on Joy Street, one block west of the State House and Library. What distinguished it from the other buildings to which it was connected was something the original owner, Ray Jones, had ordered done upon assuming title to the building—something Bostonians valued as much as gold:

he had the entire first floor converted into a parking garage for his employees.

This made the terrorists' job particularly easy.

Sometime after midnight, Al-Jubeir and Mansoor drove the Sprinter into the garage and parked in the spot reserved for Bentley Williams, closest to the locked steel entry door. The night before, they had determined that there was no security guard to avoid or kill, another weakness that the complacent executive had failed to correct.

The ceiling was supported by steel I-beams and pillars, perfect for their explosive of choice. Thermite's focused blast made it perfect for building demolition; it bit through steel like a candy bar. Mansoor fastened the explosives to the pillars at roughly the same diagonal angle. The heat generated by the blast would exceed 2500 degrees Celsius, and the pillars would all slide in the same direction, causing collapse. Any automatic sprinkler system left intact would result in a steam explosion. The building would be reduced to rubble in no time.

Once the charges and detonators were in place, the two repaired to the van. This time, Al-Jubeir drove. He stopped at the exit, turned right onto Joy Street, and right again onto Beacon. They followed Beacon to the Back Bay section, where they'd rented a room in an old row house that had been converted to a bed and breakfast. It had been the only room they'd been able to find at short notice, and one look at the peeling wallpaper and the missing tiles in the tub surround, taped over with a length of plastic shower curtain, told them why no one wanted to pay the exorbitant daily rental.

They parked the van in its designated spot in the alley behind the building and slept fitfully until five o'clock the next morning.

That morning, Friday the tenth, Rowena drove to work with her paranoia nearly in check. Matthew was scheduled to drive up in the afternoon to spend the weekend, and she was eager to show him the town . . . among other things. As she pulled into the garage, she passed a dirty white Sprinter van idling across the street. It reminded her of the one she'd seen a week or two before in Frederick, with the Mexican driver who didn't sound Hispanic when he spoke.

Those vans seemed to be ubiquitous these days. She didn't take note of the out-of-state license plate.

When Rowena entered the parking garage, the van pulled away.

Her first stop, as usual, was to say good morning to Bentley, who always arrived early. They customarily drank a cup of coffee together and split a bagel in the boss's office before starting work, a most agreeable way to begin the day. And it was a beautiful day. A cold front had brought rain late the night before, and cleared out a lot of the humidity. It would be a nice night to lie with Matthew on the oversized chaise on her deck and stare at the stars.

Meanwhile, an email was being directed from a public-use computer in the State House library to the offices of Jones Publishing, with a blind copy to the Boston Police Department. It contained two words.

Inside Bentley's office, the computer rang its chime, alerting her that she had a new message. She and Rowena were sitting in front of her desk, so she placed her half-eaten bagel on a napkin on the desktop, swiveled the screen to face them, and clicked the mouse.

"Ro, do you know a Suri Clarke?" asked Bentley.

"Not I," said Rowena. "The subject line is blank. Who-ever she is—"

"This better not contain a virus."

"Maybe you don't want to open it."

"What the hell, I'll take a chance."

She opened the message. It read ALLAHU AKBAR.

Bentley looked at Rowena and shrugged her shoulders.

Rowena stared, numb, for a split second. "Pep Boys," she remembered. "Oh my God. Bentley! We've got to get out of here. Now!"

Bentley frowned and asked why. In full panic mode, Rowena grabbed her astonished boss and pulled her to her feet, just as the Thermite ignited and the building collapsed upon itself, with a rumble followed by a roar.

From where they stood at the corner of Beacon and Joy Streets, Al-Jubeir and Mansoor watched the implosion. As the building collapsed, as a wall of dust and debris burst from the rubble, as tons of brick and concrete formed a jag-

ged red and gray mound where a building once stood, they
knew absolutely that there could be no survivors.

Al-Jubeir lit a cigarette and stared, remembering the
incident of fourteen years before.

This was on a much smaller scale; but for personal
reasons it was many times more satisfying.

"Now you know what I'm capable of, you black bitch."

Fourteen years. The year was 1993, and Muhammad
Al-Jubeir needed to redeem himself. His team had failed
in its assassination attempt on President Bush, and failure was not acceptable in Saddam's regime. He could find
himself walking about minus a nose or ears, sliced off by a
dull serrated blade in one of the medical treatment rooms.
Granted, his appendages would regenerate, but how to explain that? No, better to take the lead on this one and come
up with an initiative that would please the country's ruth-
less and omnipotent leader.

If you can't cut off the head of your enemy, disable it by
amputating its limbs.

The Persian's plan was ingenious on two fronts: If it
succeeded, he would be a hero in Saddam's eyes; if it failed,
there would be an ocean between them, and America was a
large country in which to hide.

His team of about a dozen ex-Republican Guards-
men entered the United States in the fall of 1994, seeking
asylum as refugees from the Iraqi regime. They converged
in Oklahoma City, where their contacts knew of a certain
Palestinian expatriate who owned a hundred or so low-
rent apartments that were financed by anonymous Middle
Eastern concerns. The plan was for the Palestinian to hire
them as handymen, for his substandard flats were always
in need of repair—and very seldom got what they needed.
As most of his tenants were in America illegally, they knew
they couldn't complain to the authorities.

The Iraqi team couldn't be bothered giving the buildings the repairs they needed: they were barely qualified to
slop paint on the walls. That was not their purpose.

There was a building in the heart of town that con-
tained offices of the Social Security Administration, the
Drug Enforcement Administration, the Bureau of Alcohol,
Tobacco, and Firearms, and recruiting offices for the Army

and the Marine Corps. It also contained a daycare center for employees' children. Perfect. The more collateral damage, the better.

It was known as the Alfred P. Murrah Federal Building, and it would be their target.

After several meetings in a bar, Al-Jubeir recruited a disgruntled Army veteran named Timothy McVeigh, and soon a Kansas farmer named Terry Nichols joined the plot. Nichols, whose wife was a Filipino mail-order bride, subsequently took many trips to the Philippines—most of them without her, but some with Jawdan El-Sayed—to attend bomb-making training from Al Qaeda explosives experts. He returned to the States a master of the craft.

On April 19, 1995, Muhammad Al-Jubeir's team, Timothy McVeigh, and Terry Nichols made history. But only the Americans were captured and charged.

By that time, the team had long dispersed. Some relocated to Boston and were employed at Logan Airport on September 11, 2001. Others returned to Iraq, to be hailed as avenging heroes. But three decided they not only liked the freedoms the Great Satan offered, they decided they also liked the idea of indiscriminate killing. One was the bomb expert and ace mechanic; another was a soldier useful for grunt work; and the third, Muhammad Al-Jubeir, was the acknowledged mastermind, the ideal leader who would coordinate their operations as he had the Murrah attack.

And as a reward for their loyalty and their silence, he had promised to share his gift with them . . . when the time was right.

They dispersed. The mechanic went to southern Maryland and found work at a marina. The other went to a Washington, D.C. suburb and became a high school custodian. The boss went to New Hampshire, where he took a position on the faculty of a small university. They never called each other. That was the responsibility of the boss, who would get in touch when he felt that an opportunity for renewed terror had safely presented itself.

The next time they heard from him was in December of 2008. The terror attacks seven years earlier had driven the country into national paranoia and gave them perfect cover for their deeds, by providing the perfect scapegoats: Al-Qaeda, Hamas, Hezbollah, and other terrorist groups. By then,

Ahmed and Jawdan were in their early forties; their leader's age was measured in centuries, but his appearance had not changed one whit. He promised them: by the end of next year, they would be vampires like him.

Deception was sadism made subtle.

The morning after the Boston explosion, Ahmed Mansoor and Muhammad Al-Jubeir went down the creaking stairs to the kitchen, where their hostess, an obsequious and overweight middle-aged widow named Mrs. Estelle, offered them a breakfast that consisted of a slice of Entenmann's streusel cake and a choice of generic Cheerios or corn flakes with skim milk. The restaurants in town, she'd explained the first morning, had put through a law prohibiting B & B inns from cooking eggs and meat, because they had been bleeding off business from them. Whether she spoke the truth or not, neither of the men was interested; they ate what she put in front of them and watched the twelve-inch television at the end of the table tuned to "Today in New England" on NBC 7.

"Did you gentlemen hear about the explosion yesterday?" the woman asked her only guests. They nodded, sipping the dishwater she called coffee. "Isn't it amazing that one person actually lived through all that?"

Mansoor choked on his coffee; it dribbled out his nose. Al-Jubeir fought to keep calm.

"Oh, here it is now," she said, pointing toward the television and missing Mansoor's nasal display. The screen showed a video from the day before: responders clearing the rubble, carrying out one body after another. Finally, referring to a stretcher whose occupant wasn't covered, a female reporter identified the survivor as Rowena Parr, managing editor of Jones Publishing, found pinned by a beam, but otherwise miraculously uninjured. She said Ms. Parr was currently in Mass General for observation, but latest reports say she is basically unharmed. "At her side this morning is Dr. Matthew Collins, a friend who arrived from New Jersey. He reports that Ms. Parr is emotionally devastated, but otherwise lucid. Doctors expect to discharge her later this morning."

The two men looked dumbly at each other. "Impossible," said Mansoor.

"Yes, isn't it amazing?" chirped the woman as she began clearing the table without offering seconds.

Chapter Sixteen

The white Sprinter pulled into the parking lot of Massachusetts General Hospital, passing by a number of empty slots until the hawk-nosed man in the passenger's seat found a New Jersey license plate. It was attached to a blue Honda minivan. "Find a place to park just beyond that van," he said. "Then we sit and wait."

Inside the hospital, Matthew Collins sat next to Rowena's bed, on a lumpy chair with a split vinyl seat, and wooden arms with the finish worn down. He shifted in his seat and checked his watch. "Three o'clock," he said. "You were supposed to be released before noon." The chair had grown more uncomfortable with every hour.

Rowena sat on the edge of her bed, fully clothed, where she had sat for the past four hours. Her eyes were fixed on him, but they were not focused on anything in the room. Her only acknowledgment of him was her hand in his. Their palms rested against each other, and his thumb gently stroked the back of her hand.

Finally, the doctor and his team arrived. "Ms. Parr, I don't know if you believe in miracles, but I swear to you I'm looking at one right now."

Slowly, she lowered her head.

"You're free to leave. But I'd avoid going out the front door, because it's crowded with reporters and other media types. There are TV vans from all the local and cable news channels waiting to get a glimpse of you and get a comment."

"Bloody rude," mumbled Matthew.

"It is, Dr. Collins, it is. But it's the way things are. I'm sure you have much the same situation in England."

Matthew nodded, thinking of the ubiquitous tabloids.

"However, I'll have the orderly wheel Ms. Parr to a side exit that leads directly to the parking garage. You can pick her up there."

"Thank you."

Without a word, Rowena moved to sit in the wheel-chair. She held Matthew's hand as she was wheeled to the elevator and down to the exit. The clamor of the media in front of the hospital was loud in her sensitive ears, and the smell of medicinal alcohol stung her nose. She gripped his hand tighter. *Bentley is dead,* she thought, fighting back tears. Janice, Edward, Hank, Julie, all her colleagues, and Amy, the new kid who'd just graduated from Criterion wondering what to do with her BA in English, just like Claire years before.

If she hadn't contracted cancer, Rowena wouldn't have contacted Claire, and if she hadn't contacted Claire she wouldn't be alive herself now. Paradoxically, she realized, it was terminal cancer that had saved her life.

The beam that killed Bentley had fallen on Rowena, too, and she could both feel and hear her own bones snap under the shock: ribs, pelvis, clavicle. Had she not carried the vampire's—the hemophage's—healing ability, she would have bled out internally: two ribs had punctured her lung and a third had struck her heart. But her regenerative powers immediately began knitting the bones and restoring her circulation, and Rowena lay beneath the beam, inert, weeping for her friends, waiting to be discovered by rescuers. Once the healing was complete, her enhanced strength allowed her to free herself from the debris, but the emotional damage she suffered held her down more firmly than the beam.

Rowena thought of what that monster Al-Jubeir had said as he stormed out on Tuesday. "As you'll see." Could he actually have been responsible for this carnage? If she knew that for a fact, she would hunt him down and tear him limb from limb. She could see herself doing it, morphing into some mid-stage between woman and wolf, so she could use her hands to break every bone in his body, one by one. Then she would turn fully into wolf form and rip out his guts. Finally, she would grip his head between her jaws. And slowly, agonizingly slowly, squeeze them shut. She longed to scent his fear, to hear his cries for mercy, to hear the crunch of his bones and revel in the final crushing of his skull.

156

Now I know what Claire went through when she was first turned, Rowena thought. *And I'm lucky that when the doctor put the tongue depressor in my mouth he looked down my throat, instead of up at the roof of my mouth.*

The Honda pulled up to the side door, and Rowena realized that she hadn't been aware Matthew had left her. She stood, gave the orderly a weak smile, and let Matthew open the door for her. "Where to?" he asked.

She leaned against him. "Just hold me for a second, please?"

It took a few moments before she could sit up and fasten her seat belt. "Okay," she said. "We're going to go home now."

Behind them, unnoticed by Matthew as being anything that merited suspicion, was a tall white panel truck with Maryland plates. *Long way from home,* he thought and promptly forgot about it, as a still distracted Rowena gave him his driving directions.

Inside the Sprinter, Al-Jubeir remembered seeing a decal on the van's back side window that read TRD&I. It was white with green lettering and meant nothing to him. But the blue and yellow New Jersey plates suddenly struck a chord. "Daciana," he mumbled, without realizing he'd said it aloud.

"What's that?"

"What? Oh, nothing."

"Who's Daci-whatever?"

"Just someone I knew once. Last I'd heard, she'd moved to New Jersey. Don't get too close to that car, now. If it turns onto a side street, stay way behind and see where it stops. Then turn around. I don't want them to see us passing by."

At the moment of the explosion in Oklahoma City, an electric thrill jolted Daciana Moceanu as she stood before her class at Criterion University. What it signified she had no idea, except that it involved a kill of great import performed by her Persian. When class was over and she repaired to the faculty room, her conviction was confirmed by her chattering colleagues. When she learned during the following days about the two Americans arrested, she knew intuitively that they could not have been the only ones involved. Nevertheless, after their arrest the investigation shut down. Right-wing extremists, they were called by the left-wing administration. The same administration responsible for the earlier killings of innocent men, women, and children at the David Koresh compound in Waco, and the family in Ruby Ridge. *My Persian,* she thought, *probably used the memory of those events to turn McVeigh against his government. Clever, clever boy.*

Daciana meditated daily, sending her will into the ether, exploiting the psychic link which bound the Persian to her. She meditated . . . and waited.

From Oklahoma City, Muhammad Al-Jubeir and his two cronies fled south into Dallas. There they separated, Ahmed flying to Washington National, Jawdan to Baltimore-Washington, and Muhammad to Boston. From there he took a bus to Concord, New Hampshire, not because he had a goal in mind, but because it was something that just seemed right at the time.

When he got off the bus—and she refused to tell him how she knew to be there—Daciana was standing at the platform waiting for him. She drove him to the Criterion campus, and when night fell she moved him into her cottage, where they made furious love that lasted nearly until dawn. They also shared each other's blood, making the bond even stronger.

This was in May, 1995. In June, the current term ended, and in July, Daciana arranged an interview for the distinguished professor Muhammad Al-Jubeir with the Middle Eastern History Department. The department head seemed impressed, but he already had a full complement of teachers. Coincidentally, shortly after Dr. Al-Jubeir was placed on the wait list, one of the teachers, an older, unmarried woman, disappeared without a trace. Her belongings were gone, too, resulting in speculation that the lonely spinster had simply burned out and left without even saying goodbye. In September, the department had a replacement professor on staff.

Five years later, the bloom was once again fading from the rose, and Daciana and Muhammad agreed to cool off their relationship yet one more time, vowing to reconnect at a later date. They remained colleagues, but as they worked in different disciplines and departments they rarely saw each other. Daciana began dating Professor Gabriel Zeklos, and in 2001 they wed in a private ceremony off campus. Daciana's maid of honor was her graduate assistant; Gabe's best man was his lifelong friend Radu—Ray—Jones, president, CEO, and founder of Jones Publishing Company, an independent press with its sole office in Boston.

Then, in a relatively short time, Gabe was murdered, torn apart by a wild animal; Daciana took up with Mr. Jones; he died, apparently of a heart attack; and she disappeared from Muhammad's life without a word of goodbye. When he checked with the administration, he was told she had accepted a position with Monmouth University in New Jersey. This was not an issue. She had left him without notice before, and they had always found each other again.

When she was ready, they would reconnect. He was sure of it.

Meanwhile, he had plans to make, places to go, people to kill.

"Matthew, tomorrow I have to visit Elliott Tavender, he's Bentley's husband. He phoned to say there's going to be a reception at the house."

"I'd like to go with you, if you don't mind."

"Thank you. Bentley donated her corneas to the eye bank and her body to Harvard Med School. The funeral will be a memorial service, no casket, no flowers. Just a lot of love."

They sat in Rowena's kitchen, after a dinner Matthew had prepared from the food she had laid in for the weekend. Had she been cognizant of anything other than Friday's events, she would have acknowledged that his cooking was easily the equal of her own, once again shattering the myth that the English can't cook. Now they drank mug after mug of strong tea.

"I'll make it up to you, promise. After the service for Bentley and the funerals of the others." She took another mouthful. "I just realized, I don't have a job anymore."

"Do you need any—?"

"Money? You're such a love, Matthew. No, in fact if I manage my investments wisely, I'll never have to work again, thanks to my inheritance from Mr. Jones. I stayed at Jones Pub because I liked my job and I adored my new boss—" Her voice cracked. "I'm sorry."

Matthew shook his head. "May I make a suggestion?"

"Sure. Suggest away."

"You have a lovely home, but I think you should get away from it for awhile. What do you think?"

"You wouldn't be talking about a boat ride, perhaps?"

"Something a bit more extensive, actually. Listen, luv. I might have mentioned to you that my full-time employer has been getting some flak from environmentalists lately. Rumor has it Greenpeace might be getting involved. It could get ugly. Whether anything happens or not, I still have three weeks' vacation left, and if you think you can stand my company for that amount of time, I'd love for you to join me. The Chesapeake Bay provides some brilliant cruising grounds."

Rowena left her chair and sat on Matthew's lap. She embraced him and kissed him chastely on the lips. "I also just realized I don't have a car anymore either. Is there public transportation to the elegant Weeping Willow Bar in beautiful downtown Stump Creek, New Jersey?"

He smiled. "There happens to be a bus station in Toms River, but I'd suggest private transportation."

"I just told you—"

"Rowena, I'm not going to leave you by yourself. Not now. While you were being examined by the doctors I phoned in for emergency leave. When all this is over, when you're ready, we'll drive down together."

She looked as if she were about to cry.

"By the way, I'll happily sleep on the couch or in another room, if you'd like; I don't want—"

"No. Me, stay with me. Please, Matthew. I need someone to hold me." She kissed his cheek. "I need you to hold me; just hold me, nothing more. Make me feel safe."

The incongruity of that statement never occurred to her.

The doorbell rang. Before she could get up from his lap, it rang again. Twice.

"I'll get it," said Matthew. "If that's the media, I'll do what I can to shoo them away." He left the kitchen and opened the front door. Three figures stood outside, their faces limned by the porch light. They looked startled to see him, but he had been expecting them for hours. "Claire. Dale. Joe. Won't you come in?"

They sat around the kitchen table and related the news from Camp David, flashing back to the moment Lauren informed them of the latest attack.

"Allahu Akbar. The Boston PD got a blind copy of the message that went out to Jones Pub. That's five messages, five attacks—including the New Hampshire family—in six months. Obviously from the same source." Lauren Bachmann looked from one operative to the other. "And this time, it's personal. How your friend survived that building collapse, Claire, I'll never know, but maybe she can provide some input."

It was Friday evening, just hours after the collapse of Jones Publishing, and the lovely weather that graced Boston had passed by the Catoctin Mountains. The air was muggy, and the breeze, faint as it was, didn't cool anything; it just moved the moisture. The air conditioning unit in Lauren's cabin struggled to keep the temperature inside tolerable.

"We'll take the Cessna to Massachusetts tomorrow," offered Dale.

When Joe objected, preferring commercial transportation for its speed, it was Claire who corrected him—at the same time she hoped she didn't sound like a know-it-all. "From Frederick to Minute Man Airport is about four hundred miles. That's a little more than three hours in the Songbird. Add to that a half hour from here to the airport at Frederick and another half hour to preflight the plane, and you've got four. We'll arrange for a rental car at Minute Man before we leave here, and it's another hour's drive to Boston. All told, five hours."

"Right, and commercial from BWI to Boston Logan is an hour." Joe furrowed his brow. "Oh, wait, I see where this is going."

It was true: a 130-mph piston-engine prop plane would put them at their destination at about the same time as a 400-mph jet, when one considered the hour's drive to Baltimore, the shuttle time from the long-term parking lot, the early check-in, the one-hour-plus flight time, and the negotiating of Boston traffic from Logan to center city.

Lauren said, "If you leave at daybreak, you can get there by noon, talk to the authorities, and do your snooping at the site. After you've gathered your information, you can visit Rowena, either at the hospital or at home. I was on the horn to Mass General on an official line, and when I finally got someone to talk to me, he said Rowena was doing great, and unless tests found something out of the ordinary, she was scheduled to be released by noon."

Claire and Dale kept their expressions blank.

"Make sure you guys get a good night's sleep. And don't let Rowena know you're coming; she might say something about her arriving friends that she shouldn't, especially if she's not coherent."

Later that night, alone in their cottage, Dale and Claire admitted to each other their individual anxiety: about what the doctors might find; about Rowena's lucidity or lack of it; and whether or not she would be able to control her physical appearance.

"I guess we'll find out tomorrow," Claire said. "Oh, and honey, you're flying the plane."

In Boston, Claire nearly cried when she saw the wreckage of the home of Jones Publishing; the home of her first full-time job; the home of so many memories. It was good that Ray was already dead; seeing this would have killed him for sure. She mourned the death of Bentley Williams, too. What little contact they'd enjoyed before Claire had left was filled with mutual respect and even affection. She vowed to make a side trip with Dale and Matthew to Abercrombie's to pick up conservative suits for Bentley's funeral. Joe would have returned to David by then, on a jet from Logan to BWI.

Matthew had phoned the team before leaving Toms River for Boston, so they knew to expect him. What they didn't expect was the sleeping arrangement. Joe mentally cursed his luck as the couple bade their friends good night, hands clasped, and headed for the master bedroom. Well, if he couldn't command Rowena's affections, at least he was happy that she'd latched onto Matthew.

Sunday morning, as they sat in the kitchen over bagels and coffee, Dale debriefed Rowena and learned that the Allahu Akbar message had been the last thing she'd seen before the building imploded. And then Rowena started, almost tipping her chair backward.

"What is it?" asked Dale.

She told them the story of her meeting with Muhammad Al-Jubeir, of his hateful manuscript, of his overt contempt for her, and most emphatically of his threat upon leaving her office. "If he's the one responsible for this, if he's the one who sent the Allahu Akbar message, then doesn't it make sense that he's behind the other attacks—as well as being a vampire?"

Dale began making associations. There was the high school girl whose last words were that she was kidnaped by a vampire. And the family in New Hampshire that had been killed on a Sunday afternoon last winter, whose combined blood volume came up short. And, of course, the Pep Boys attack that initiated this entire sequence.

Rowena told him that when Bentley had called Criterion's administration office to set up an appointment with the professor, she'd been told that he had recently left for a vacation out West. "Does that mean anything to you?"

Claire explained to Rowena about the train attacks in Utah and Colorado, and the Allahu Akbar messages there.

"I guess it does," Rowena said, shaking her head.

The next day would be Monday, and Dale, Matthew, and Joe would drive up to New Hampshire to visit the university, speak with the administration, and—if he was there—confront the professor himself. Claire would stay in Boston to keep Rowena company.

Meanwhile, Rowena, Matthew and Claire would pay a bereavement call on Elliott Tavender. Matthew would drive.

The Tavender living room was filled with flowers, friends, and relatives when Rowena, Claire, and Matthew arrived. The women finally got to meet the widowed Mr. Williams—Bentley's father—and her brother Aston and his family. Elliott tried to keep a stiff upper lip, but at times when he thought no one was looking he would retreat to a corner and his shoulders would shake as he covered his eyes. Anyone who noticed allowed him his space.

Some of Elliott's high school students arrived—in small groups, as if they were hesitant to come alone—and offered awkward, but sincere condolences. Because it was summertime, many of them wore colorful shorts and pullover tops, which made them as conspicuous as piñatas. Still, he welcomed them, shook their hands, accepted hugs from the girls, and didn't bother to wipe their lipstick from his cheeks.

Claire sought out Emma and Benjamin, the Tavenders' housekeeper and chef. They had filled those roles for Ray Jones before his death, and now served the Tavender household, thanks to Rowena's recommendation. The elderly couple seemed as distraught as the rest of the family. They wrapped their arms around Claire, who consoled them as well as she could.

"Rowena," said Bentley's father, when the small group of friends had a moment with him. "My daughter found a true friend in you, I want you to know that."

She assured him Bentley's feelings were reciprocated.

"I only wish that my other son Royce were here to pay respects to his sister. You knew him, if only briefly. Tell me, what were your impressions of him?"

Now I have to lie, thought Rowena sadly. Royce had become interim CEO during a couple of months when Bentley was out with a jeopardized pregnancy, one which ended badly. "He took his responsibilities as temporary CEO very seriously, sir." *He had wanted to turn the company into a porn distributor.* "He was always making full use of his time." *Surfing Internet porn sites and making deals with producers.* "I can't say I really knew him all that well beyond that." *No one, in fact, wanted to.*

"He never made it to that winter conference on leadership in Chicago that I'd enrolled him in."

"No, sir. He just seemed to disappear." He disappeared, all right. Not to Chicago, but to the Bahamas, where Claire tracked him down and fed what was left of him to the fishes.

"And you, Matthew. Do I detect a Northman's accent? York, say?"

"Very good, Mr. Williams. Bradford. I studied at Leeds."

"Really. Your major?"

"Color chemistry. After graduation, I accepted a position with a dyestuff manufacturer in America. Young man's yearning for adventure, and all that."

"Are you an American citizen, then?"

"I am now, sir. Proud to be, as they say. But always with emotional ties to the homeland."

"You have family there?"

"No, not anymore. Like Rowena here, I'm an only child. My parents were killed in a motoring accident shortly before I graduated." He looked suddenly contrite. "I'm sorry, sir. This is neither the time nor the place to bring more death into the conversation."

The family patriarch placed his hand on Matthew's shoulder. "You've a lovely lady in Rowena," he said, mercifully changing the subject. "I wish you both well. And you as well, Claire. Now, if you'll excuse me." He continued circulating among the guests.

"You never told me that. About your parents," said Rowena. "I want you to tell me everything there is to know about you while we're cruising."

"You're saying it's official? That you'll join me on the boat for three weeks?"

She held his upper arm and drew him close. "It's official. But three weeks might not be long enough."

On Monday, Matthew drove the men to New Hampshire and the campus of Criterion University, leaving Claire with Rowena. For many moments, they simply stared at each other. Finally, Rowena asked if Claire could use another breakfast, and they turned to frying more bacon and scrambling more eggs to satisfy their wolf-driven appetites.

The awkward silence over, Claire acknowledged that Rowena might as well know everything that the team had been working on, and she detailed every event from Pep Boys to the present. She also reinforced one other fact: "I just violated every law in the book by telling you this. Even though there is no written law and there isn't even a book. But you get the point."

Rowena said she did.

"And on the subject of our turning you: Lauren still doesn't know. Joe doesn't know. And we don't intend to tell them. Now you tell me, does Matthew know?"

Rowena shook her head. "I wouldn't tell him even if I could. He tries to make light of it, but I think the poor guy is haunted by some kind of childhood trauma. He cares very much for you and Dale, but when he found out about your dual identities, well, let's just say his relationship with Dale is secure, but he still isn't a hundred percent sure about you—even though he wants to be."

"I picked that up from him. So if you want to keep your relationship . . ."

"He'll never know. I can't let him."

"Have you ever found yourself slipping up?"

She hated herself for holding back what she'd done to those two in D.C. "Only once, when that scum professor called me what he did. My fingers grew claws. Good thing he'd gone beforehand. If he'd stuck around, I might have gone for his throat." She saw Claire's expression. "No, not really, sweetie."

"How do the doctors explain your surviving the building collapse?"

"The best my attending physician can come up with is God's will. He's a devout Catholic, he told me."

"Well, let's let that be the official reason, agreed?"

"No argument here."

The men called to say they'd be back in time for dinner, and when they arrived, a pair of standing rib roasts was waiting for them. What they didn't know was that prior to their return Claire and Ro had staved off their appetites with a pair of nearly raw hamburgers each, and that Claire had cached a couple of sandwiches in their room for Dale to eat after they went to bed.

Matthew and Joe performed KP duties afterward, as the others repaired to the deck. That left Dale to brief Claire and Ro on their day. Upon learning from the secretary that the professor wasn't answering his phone, they asked for access to his files and his home. Their FBI identification badges—actual ID, not forged, but with pseudonyms that only the upper echelon of the Bureau would recognize—gave them entrée to his house, which the secretary had told them he rented furnished.

Aside from the furniture and some food in the pantry and refrigerator, the house was empty. No personal effects were left to be found. Matthew nearly filled a memory card with photos taken of fingerprints inside the house, and Joe had collection tubes containing samples taken from the professor's kitchen and bathroom: a swab with saliva from a drinking glass; body hair found in the bed; pubic hair from the toilet rim. Forensics, he acknowledged to himself for the nth time, wasn't so glamorous as certain television programs portrayed it.

Back at the college administrative offices, Dale asked if there were anyone Dr. Al-Jubeir might have told about his leaving, and the secretary said no, he was pretty much a loner. "His closest associate on campus was a Professor Moceanu, and she left Criterion a few years ago to teach in New Jersey. Her husband was killed in an animal attack, and she felt she couldn't stay here any longer. Too many memories, you know."

Sitting on Rowena's deck, Dale and the women shared a look. They had memories, too.

"Now we report to Lauren," Dale said, as the other men were finishing up the dishes and cleaning the kitchen.

"What then?" asked Rowena.

"She reports to her handler higher up and awaits orders. Do we hunt the professor down clandestinely, or do we put his mug on *America's Most Wanted?* Those are the extremes, and I have no idea what she'll be told to do. Ours is not to question why, et cetera."

Joe and Matthew joined them on the deck. Matthew sat on the chaise next to Rowena. Joe took a director's chair. "I just made a reservation to fly out tomorrow," he said. "Can't wait to get these samples analyzed, see if the DNA matches what we found in the high school girl's wounds." He turned to Dale. "Can you and Claire take my duffel back to David for me? I'm using my hard-shell sample case as a carry-on."

Rowena asked if that might prove troublesome with the TSA screeners at Logan. "Seeing those tubes in the X-ray machines and all."

"That's okay. I've got a Homeland Security ID, too."

"You guys think of everything. Speaking of, Elliott Tavender called while you guys were out. The funeral services for all the Jones employees will be held on Friday. We'll go to Bentley's, and we'll visit the others as schedules permit. It's going to be a long day, Dale."

Dale acknowledged her and turned to Matthew. "Claire and I will fly out after the services. What about you?"

Claire answered: "Matthew told me earlier; I forgot to mention it, sorry. He and Ro will drive back to Jersey together. Ro needs a break, and the boat will be the perfect place for it. They're going to cruise the Chesapeake for a few weeks." She winked at Ro and said, "Best thing in the world for you, sweetie."

Boats, Joe thought. *Babe magnets no matter how big and how slow.*

None of the men noticed the Honda had been followed almost to the Criterion campus by two men in a white panel truck. As soon as Muhammad realized where it was headed, he directed Ahmed to turn around and return to Boston. They would endure a few more days of Mrs. Estelle's dismal accommodations, her factory-made coffee cake and bland cereal, and her insipid conversation, and spend their days observing the bitch's house, waiting for the minivan to leave. Then they would go inside and kill her properly.

On Friday, they parked at the end of the street as usual and watched two men and two women wearing suits get into the van. They followed it to an infidel church and knew there was no need to monitor them anymore today.

The next morning, they packed their gear into the Sprinter as they did every day, just in case, and today it paid off. They saw the taller couple leave the house, get into a nondescript sedan, and drive off. That left two still inside. An hour later, a slim, sandy-haired man exited and loaded duffels and a small suitcase into the back of the minivan. Then he returned inside, and when he reemerged he had their target in tow. The woman locked her front door and slid into the passenger seat of the van.

Ahmed followed the van onto the Interstate, until it became obvious it wasn't going back to Boston. "What now?" he asked.

"Follow," said Muhammad, fuming all the more, now that he was fully implicated thanks to Ahmed's lust for a high school teeny-bopper. *Ripples in a pond,* he thought bitterly. Butterfly effect. This guy was a loser, and he thought of how pleasant it would be when he had no further need of Ahmed.

"What about paying our bill for the room?" asked Ahmed.

"Fuck the bill. Fuck that woman."

"Boss, I wouldn't fuck her with your dick." He added, "But if I were you, I'd suck the blood out of her before we left, just for spite."

"Shut up and drive," Muhammad said, looking again at the blue minivan's yellow and black license plate. "We're going to New Jersey."

Chapter Seventeen

They followed the blue Honda across Connecticut, down into Brooklyn, across the Verrazano Bridge and Staten Island, and onto the Garden State Parkway South. The minivan got off at the Beachwood exit and drove down U.S. Route 9, making a left at Pine Beach and then a right at an overhead blinker. The Sprinter remained at least a tenth of a mile behind, no problem with visibility; the road paralleled the river and was straight as a line on graph paper.

Pine Beach was a municipality of only one square mile, so it wasn't long before their prey tooled into Bayville and made a left onto a narrow driveway. The Sprinter drove by, noting the large white mooring buoy alongside the road with painted lettering that read STUMP CREEK SLIPWAYS. The men took the next left onto a residential road that wound around a small peninsula jutting into the river. They stopped at a small public beach occupied by some teens, and a few children with their mothers. Muhammad looked directly across to the boatyard; Ahmed's gaze lingered a few seconds on the mothers. After a few moments, they saw the man and woman walking out onto a long dock.

"Look at the size of that boat," Ahmed said. "It's huge."

"They're carrying duffel bags," Muhammad added. "Obviously staying aboard overnight."

"If the boat keeps rockin'," Ahmed began with a smirk.

"Shut your hole!" Muhammad hissed. "Your libido is what got us into this mess in the first place. Listen. That woman knows who I am. You saw those people, whoever they were, visiting her over the weekend. You saw them looking for me at the university. For the first time in my life I'm the one who's being hunted, instead of the other way around. Because of you, I am a marked man . . . simply because of your lust for that little high school snatch."

Ahmed grumbled, "I told you I'm sorry, a thousand times. What more can I do?"

"Never mind. We'll wait until tonight and slit their throats as they sleep."

The man and woman returned to the van empty handed and drove away. The Sprinter followed them to a Shop-Rite supermarket on the highway, and an hour later followed them back to the boatyard, driving past and assuming their observation position at the beach. The couple carried their groceries onto the boat. No need to observe them further today, no need to invite questions from curious neighborhood residents. Two men in a van, public beach with children, some of them unattended; no, not a good thing at all.

"I'll drive now," Muhammad ordered, and he headed south on the highway until they found a run-down motel with a vacancy sign, run by a Middle Eastern couple just as surly as themselves. "We'll stay here until midnight. Then we'll drive to the boatyard and do what has to be done."

Midnight arrived. The two men had spent some of the time honing their long knives to a razor-keen edge. Their plan was simple: they would park on the narrow shoulder by the entrance of the yard, walk down the long drive to the dock, and slip aboard the boat. Once their work was done, they would return to their motel and then decide what their next move would be. Muhammad, running his thumbnail across his knife's edge, thought he might send Ahmed to meet Allah as soon as the operation was complete. In fact, whoever discovered the dead couple might find a third corpse on the boat.

They made it to the boatyard by one o'clock, parked on the narrow shoulder, and walked down the asphalt driveway across the stone parking area in total darkness. Their sneakers barely made a sound on the packed gravel as they made their way to the dock. Halfway out on the pier, they stopped and stared, thinking the lack of light was playing tricks on them. But it was not.

The boat was gone.

The next day, Muhammad—dressed in a pale blue polo shirt embroidered with the West Marine logo, a pair of new khaki shorts, and boat shoes, no socks—drove a rented sedan down the driveway at Stump Creek Slipways and parked next to Matthew's minivan. He got out, holding a pair of fishing rods and reels, and walked around the boatyard, as if looking for someone. The first person he saw was a tall, bearded man in a stained T-shirt and wrinkled shorts walking out of the shop. He walked to a sailboat docked in a protected pond that fed into a creek—obviously Stump Creek—and then emptied into the river. The gray-haired man stopped and smiled inquisitively, tipping his ball cap back on his head.

"Help you?"

Muhammad smiled back. "Yes, please. I'm looking for Mister—mister—the man who owns the Honda over there. I've drawn a blank on his name, sorry."

"Matthew Collins?"

"That's him. He paid for these rods and reels a week ago, but we were out of stock. They just came in this morning, and I remember he said he'd be cruising soon, so I wanted to deliver them before he took off. But I don't see his boat."

The man extended his hand and grinned through his beard. "Paul."

"Moe," said Muhammad, taking his hand.

"Nice to see dedicated customer service. Rare anymore. But you're too late, my friend. Matthew and his girlfriend booked out late yesterday afternoon."

Muhammad looked at the fishing gear in his hand. "I'm sorry to have missed him. Can you tell me when he'll be back?"

"Sure," Paul said. "He left a copy of his float plan with me. Wait a minute." He climbed aboard his sailboat and returned with a slip of paper. Muhammad had meanwhile replaced the fishing gear in the car. "Okay, here's what it looks like." He traced each notation with his finger. "Tonight they should be in Atlantic City, Farley Marina; next day, Cape May. Friday they'll head up Delaware Bay to the Ches-Del Canal, cross into the northern Chesapeake, and anchor overnight. They plan to cruise the Bay for a week or so and then head home. Back sometime around the middle of August. Not too shabby, huh?"

"Indeed. Can you tell me where in the Bay they plan to be?"

"Not going to drive down and give him the rods, are you? That's *really* customer service."

Muhammad laughed with him. "No, just being envious."

Paul scratched his head. "Let's see. Matthew usually visits Annapolis, Saint Michaels, and Solomons when he cruises."

"Ah. Solomons."

"You know it?"

"No, but I know someone who lives there."

"Lucky bastard. Deep water, lots of places to explore. Barnegat Bay here, so shallow you could walk across at low tide. But you know that."

"Solomons does have deep water, that's what my friend says." Muhammad sighed. "Well, I tried. Would you do me a favor and tell him when he returns that his order is in at West Marine?"

"Will do. Now, if you'll excuse me, I've got a hatch cover to varnish."

They shook hands and Muhammad drove back to West Marine, located on the highway east of Toms River. He brought the fishing gear to the return counter, collected his cash, and drove to the car rental agency, where Ahmed waited in the Sprinter. He filled Ahmed in on what he'd learned.

"What now?" asked his partner.

"Give me your phone. And assure me that Jawdan isn't on speed dial."

"Of course not." He gave Muhammad the number.

"This is Jerry," answered Jawdan. He was standing inside the office, picking up a new work order from the receptionist, a pretty young lady with strawberry blonde hair kept in a ponytail, a kewpie-doll smile, and a modest but certainly adequate figure. Plus a wedding ring, which made her off limits. When he heard the voice on the other end, he almost jumped.

"Everything okay?" asked the girl.

"Oh, yes, fine. Thanks, Cassie. No, everything's fine."

He walked outside and stood where he wouldn't be overheard.

"Listen to me, Jawdan," said the caller. "You said you wanted to be included in our latest operation; well, now you may get your chance. There's a big white boat that just might be visiting your marina in a week or so."

"Um, boss, you've got to be more specific than that. Lots of big white boats come in here."

Muhammad sighed. "This one is a power boat and will have a white man and a black woman aboard. Does that make it easier?"

"What's the boat's name?"

"As if that weren't enough. All right, I didn't see the name. The bow was pointing toward the land. It's got a very tall bow, not low."

"Where's the boat registered?"

"Registered? How would I know that? It's coming from Toms River, New Jersey."

"Okay, large white power boat, Toms River, mixed-race couple, that should do it. What do you want me to do if it pulls in?"

"I want you to kill them."

The Krogen motored south down the Inland Waterway, wending its way through the shallow channel behind Long Beach Island, and then weaving around and about dozens of sedge islands before arriving at the marina in Atlantic City. Matthew and Rowena spent the day soaking up sun on the bridge station, grateful that the greenheads were kept away by the easterly breeze. Matthew had radioed ahead to reserve dock space, and once secured and hooked up to electricity and water dockside, they showered, dressed, and strolled to a waterside casino. They avoided the slots and other enticements, ate at a buffet, enjoyed a show, and returned to the boat late, where Digit welcomed them with rubs and purrs.

The next day, Matthew took the boat out the Atlantic City Inlet into calm seas and allowed Rowena to pilot it to the inlet at Cape May, at the southern tip of the state. They anchored in the harbor, where it took Matthew many attempts to set the hook securely in the muddy bottom. Rowena cooked dinner. The moon was in its first quarter, and they lay on the boat deck and stared at it for a long time. Then they went below and made slow and leisurely love.

Rowena found that when they were intimate she could scent her lover's pheromones. That was wonderfully affirming. But she could also, when their bodies were together as one, sense the pulsing of the blood beneath the skin of his neck. And that was disturbing.

Matthew had set the alarm early, waking them just at dawn. "Long day coming up," he advised, added that swimsuits were the uniform of the day, and had Rowena use the deck wash hose to free the mud from the anchor chain and the hook itself, as he operated the electric winch from inside the pilothouse. They headed west through the Cape May Canal to Delaware Bay, then turned north. "At eight knots, it takes forever to get to the Canal," he advised. "The tide will be with us part of the way and against us the rest. That's how long it takes."

The day had dawned bright, the sky was cloudless, and the visibility was unimpaired. In the distance, they saw a container ship motoring down bay toward the open ocean. Matthew gave Rowena the helm, and she took it, on condition that he stand behind her and cover her hands with his. After a few moments of calm intimacy, she tilted her backside against his frontside, turned her head toward him, and said, "Lap dance, mister?"

"My, aren't we frisky today?" he said.

"You said it would be a long haul, we need to do something to pass the time, yes?"

"Indeed. But it might be awkward as is. If you'll excuse me a moment." He left her, leaving a trail of pheromones, and climbed down the ladderway. A minute passed, and Rowena felt some resistance to the corrections she was applying to the wheel. Matthew returned, and without a word he positioned flotation cushions on the deck. He looked up at Rowena and grinned. "Autopilot," he informed her.

"This thing has an autopilot? Why didn't you tell me sooner? No, never mind." She stripped off her bikini and grabbed for his trunks, then looked from side to side. "Nope. No one here but us seagulls."

Later, spent and lying beneath Matthew on the slick cushions, Rowena looked up and frowned. "Hey. There are planes up there, like the kind Claire and Dale fly. You won't believe this, but they're circling us!"

Matthew laughed. "Not to worry, luv, they're not peeping Toms, they're fish spotters, working with the netters. Look, see them?"

They stood up, the sun drying the perspiration from their bodies—"We'll soap up later, at the anchorage," he told her—and saw the commercial trawlers, their wakes describing huge circles as they drew in their nets. Rowena divided her attention between the boats and the planes, a coordinated symphony between sky and sea.

"I'm going below to the pilothouse and disengage the autopilot. Come with me, and I'll teach you all I know about True Virgins Make Dull Companions."

Rowena grinned wolfishly. "No argument from me there."

"We might want to put our bathing suits back on first."

"Party pooper."

In the pilothouse, they watched the bow waves from a giant tanker as it steamed past. "Hold on tight," advised Matthew as the first wave hit. The bow pitched way up, then crashed down into the wave's trough. Then came the second and third before the water quieted again.

"Not a good time to be threading a needle," Rowena observed.

Matthew called her attention to the navigation chart resting on top of what would be the dashboard in a car: a flat platform stretching from the three side-by-side windshields to the wheel, and from bulkhead to bulkhead. "Note the pencil line I've drawn along the channel to the Chesapeake-Delaware Canal. Do you see the degrees I've marked on the course line?" She nodded. "Now look at the true course noted on the chart."

"They don't match up," Rowena said.

"Right. True Virgins Make Dull Companions. It's a mnemonic for TVMDC."

"And you're going to tell me what that means."

"Right. And I'd advise you to wipe that beautiful little smirk off your gorgeous face, because if something happens to me while we're cruising, you might need to know this information."

She gave him a salute. "Aye aye, captain, sir. Okay, I'll get serious."

"Our course is based upon true north, not magnetic. That's the T." She nodded. "But you know that the magnetic pole is different from true, right? Right. So depending upon your latitude, the compass will show a variation from true north. That's the V. You add or subtract the variation, depending upon your latitude. That information is in the chart key, and when you figure that in, you have your magnetic heading. That's the M."

"Got it."

"But we're not done yet. There's the D to consider, that's deviation. There are electronics in the cockpit, and they can affect the accuracy of the compass by a degree or more, and that's the reason for this little card beside the compass binnacle. Notice that in our case it's zero for all cardinal points, but if we replace any electronics, that could change. Anyway, when you figure in the deviation, you get the compass course to steer by, the C. TVMDC: True Virgins Make Dull Companions."

"I like the way you think."

"But you do understand."

"I do, really. It's why you marked the course line with the heading we'll follow on the compass, not the true heading."

"Brilliant. Now here on the chart is where the canal will let us out into the Elk River, which is at the north end of the Chesapeake Bay. I'd like you to plot a course from the Elk to the Bohemia River."

"Okay, but why don't we just stay between the channel markers?"

"What if the channel's been changed since the chart was printed? It happens. And if there's a dogleg or something, you'll have to know which way to turn the boat to keep between those markers." To her frown, he responded, "And it's good practice."

"I'm thinking Mr. Miyagi in *The Karate Kid.*"

Matthew had Rowena plot course lines from the Bohemia River to Worton Creek, then across the Bay to Annapolis, and by the time she was done they'd reached the mouth of the Chesapeake-Delaware Canal, a major shipping lane for vessels coming north from Norfolk and those heading south from Philadelphia. An hour later they were in the Elk River on a southerly course, and soon after that Matthew turned them into the wide mouth of the Bohemia. They motored on until he declared they had reached their anchorage for the night, near some half dozen other boats, both power and sail. The hook set firm at first try.

Holding a bar of soap, a washcloth, and a pair of towels, Matthew opened the stern gate and stepped onto the
teak swim platform. "This is why swimsuits are the uniform
of the day," he said, and dropped into the river, leaving the
bathing supplies on the platform. Rowena slid in after him,
and they swam some laps around the boat, eager for the
exercise.

Have to be careful not to outpace him, she thought,
holding her enhanced strength and endurance in check.
When they finished swimming and rested, holding onto the
swim platform, Rowena pretended to be as short of breath
as Matthew.

"Now for the soap," he said, and the two lathered each
other up. "The sun's getting low, and no one's anchored aft
of us," he observed.

"Say no more," Rowena added, and their suits joined
the towels on the swim platform. They soaped each other
again, liberally and intimately, and she drew herself toward
Matthew. He hesitated.

"There's the matter of that little foil packet," he said
apologetically.

"You won't need it," Rowena said. "Should've told you
earlier. I'm, um, not capable of having children anymore.
Please don't ask; let's just indulge ourselves in the moment.
This is the closest we'll ever come to making love in near-
weightless conditions."

That night, they spread flotation cushions on the boat
deck and lay still, letting the breeze play over their bodies.
To the west across the river lay the peninsula of Elk Neck,
and farther off, sheets of silent lightning lit the sky like special effects in a Steven Spielberg movie. Rowena's sleep was
dreamless and undisturbed, the most restful she'd had in
recent memory.

Jawdan El-Sayed was suffering through his third sleepless night since the phone call from the boss. It wasn't that
he minded killing so much, but he didn't like the thought
that he was charged to execute a pair of murders that could
be traced back to him and him alone. He still worried that
someone would link him to the murder of the slut from Parole, and if the authorities did, they'd search his condo and
find the key to his storage bay. They would search it next,

and then he would be in the deepest of shit, so deep, in fact, that he could never climb out.

Why am I even involved with all this? he wondered. But the answer was obvious. He wanted the promise of eternal life here on earth. The promise that only the boss could deliver on. But once that was done, once he had been turned, then all bets were off.

Ahmed might be implicated if they found his Jetta on the lot and compared its VIN to the one on his vehicle registration—which they'd have on their watch list for sure because of Mansoor's high school twat. But they still wouldn't be able to find him; he was driving the Sprinter now. And question him as they might, Jawdan's honest answer would be that he didn't know where the man was. In fact, he'd deny having known Ahmed Mansoor at all. What was the man's Jetta doing in the storage lot? Damned if he knew. His defense would be to play upon the authorities' political correctness: *That man and I have Middle Eastern names. Does that make me guilty by association?*

As he finally drifted off into a restless slumber, he was thinking of ways to kill the couple without being caught, while hoping against hope that Solomons Island would not, not, not be one of the stops on their summertime cruise.

Chapter Eighteen

Muhammad Al-Jubeir was thirsty.

He told Ahmed, who had picked up a summer cold, to stay in the motel while he reconnoitered the area for temporary jobs. They would need to keep busy for the next few weeks, until—that is, *if*—the boat returned to its dock on the Toms River. *If* Jawdan hadn't completed his assignment. Or *if* the couple hadn't docked at Solomons at all. He would also make regular trips to the library's public computers, where he would check on any news from Maryland's Chesapeake Bay area—especially any news about the murder of a couple of visiting boaters.

Early in the afternoon, he stopped at a 7-Eleven to pick up a copy of the Asbury Park *Press*. The lead story was about the possible Greenpeace occupation of the Toms River Dyestuff and Intermediate plant as a protest against pollution. The article quoted a spokesman for the company as saying the group would better spend its time chasing after more serious polluters, like those in the paper and pharmaceutical industries. TRD&I processed its industrial waste into harmless liquids—and the company produced a photograph of its waste-processing manager actually drinking some of it from a beaker. Or so the caption stated.

What interested Muhammad more than the story, however, was the fact that a TRD&I decal was on the window of the man Collins's minivan. He immediately drove west on Route 37 to the plant entrance. The road ended at a guard house, and beyond that stood the plant: three rows of buildings—two three-story factories flanking a row of single- and two-story buildings down the center, a water tower atop giant steel legs in the middle of the complex. Three parking lots were inside the gate, one serving each row of buildings.

At the guardhouse, he picked up two applications for employment and drove to a supermarket's parking lot to examine them. From a suitcase he produced a series of driver's licenses and social security numbers and a pair of résumés he knew would suffice. Later, he would return to the motel, where the proprietors, he knew, would be happy to rent their room on a long-term basis. Even though it was summer at the New Jersey shore, the Vacancy sign never came down.

He phoned Ahmed's number and told him about the job applications, then said he was going to be out late, and that he would bring him some food upon his return. Ahmed said he didn't think he could keep anything down anyway, which was what Muhammad had hoped to hear. His next stop was a big box home center, where he picked up some necessities for what he had planned for later that evening.

He ate dinner at a local pub near the highway called the Office Lounge, and then drove east across the bridge to Seaside Heights. He parked in a lot at the southern end of the boardwalk, fed quarters to the hungry parking meter, and strolled the boards. What he saw both disgusted and intrigued him.

There was a notable lack of middle-aged and elderly people, and very few families with young children—mostly a slew of twenty-something punks and their slutty companions. Some of the little girls he did see looked like they were trying to emulate their older counterparts. One wore a T-shirt on which was emblazoned, "Not With You, I Don't!" She could not have been older than ten. Her parents, an unattractive, obese couple somewhere in their late thirties, seemed okay with her sartorial choice.

That shirt was mild, compared to what he saw on the post-pubescent girls. One particularly busty one wore a T-shirt with a large pear silk-screened over each breast. Above them were the words, "Nothing better than" and below them, in larger lettering, "a good pear." Her male companion wore a shirt whose front read, "How can you tell if a girl is ticklish?" On the back, it read, "Give her a test tickle." His arms, calves, and neck were festooned with tattoos, and his girlfriend had so many piercings she looked like she was clad in body armor.

Lights from the booths, noise from the arcades, the staccato tick-tick-ticks from the wheels of chance, and the smells, from cotton candy to greasy sausage sandwiches, all combined to form a mélange of orchestrated confusion.

In the darkness to his right, Muhammad could see the sandy beach and the white coils of surf. Its rumble was low, drowned out by the noise of the crowds, the vendors' canned and discordant music, and so-called attractions to his left.

Actually, Muhammad was looking for an attraction he knew he should be able to find easily, and as the evening wore on, she actually found him as he sat in an outdoor bar, drinking beer and smoking. She sat on the empty stool next to him and asked for a light. Soon they had negotiated a price, and he told her that they would be leaving separately; that she would walk to the parking lot at the south end; and that he would be inside the tall white panel truck. She shrugged her shoulders—what the hell, the price was more than agreeable—and five minutes after he left, she paid for her drink with the cash he'd left her and sauntered south on the boardwalk.

Upon arriving at the Sprinter, Muhammad put more quarters into the meter, before entering the van and inflating the air mattress he'd spread on the floor. He opened the front door at the girl's knock and ushered her inside, locking it behind her.

"We're going to do it here?" she asked.

"I hope you don't mind," he said.

"No, whatever." She looked around. "No windows at least; that's good, right?"

"It's very good."

"No kissy-kissy, you understand? Just a straight fuck, and make sure you're wearing a rubber, that's the deal."

"I understand perfectly," he said.

"You want to show me the money?"

He produced a wad of bills and rolled three Benjamins off. He handed them to her, and she put them into her purse.

"Geez," she said. "If I knew you were that loaded I'd have asked for more."

"Depending upon how well you perform, you may get more than you bargained for," he said.

"You want a BJ, too, maybe? Still have to use a rubber, though."

"Let's see what develops . . . is it Flora?"

"No, it's Dora. Like the explorer."

"Oh. Then why don't you start exploring? And let me do some exploring of my own?"

They went about their business slowly, Muhammad thinking about his vampire lover Daciana as his hands roved over Dora's now nude body, Dora thinking of how she might coax more money from that roll in the pocket of the pants that now lay near them. She took the condom he'd provided and applied it to his erection, giving him the BJ she'd suggested, and then rolling onto her back to allow him entry to her body. She ground her hips against his and grunted as his hands groped her breasts and his lips gravitated from her cheek to the side of her neck.

She barely felt the punctures. But when his mouth locked onto her neck Dora knew that something was seriously wrong. She tried to pull her head aside, but couldn't. Meanwhile, the man's hips were rising and falling, rising and falling, driving himself into her, pinning her to the mattress.

His thrusts grew faster, stronger, more intense, and she realized he was about to come. His mouth pressed harder against her neck, and she could feel a burning sensation where his teeth were pressing, his jaws squeezing tighter and tighter.

Suddenly his thrusting ended in one mighty jolt, and he tightened his buttocks as he stiffened his back and jerked his head upright, tearing Dora's throat out as her eyes bugged and her mouth gaped in a silent scream. The man looked down at her, breathing hard, and she saw bits of her own pink flesh hanging from his teeth, her own blood dripping down his serpent's fangs. His head plunged again to her open neck, and Dora soon stopped struggling and stared at the ceiling of the van, listening helplessly to his slurping and sucking, until the light left her eyes.

Afterward, Muhammad dismembered the girl and put her body parts along with the industrial rags he'd bought—to sop up what blood remained—into leaf collection bags. He put the last of the soiled rags and the new hacksaw into the same bag that contained Dora's big-haired head and hands. The razor-edged knife he'd used was the one he'd intended to use on the black woman. He wiped it clean and kept it. The bags he distributed into dumpsters behind the businesses that lined Route 37. He then changed into a set of shorts and a plain T-shirt and visited an all night Laundromat, where he washed the clothes he'd been wearing earlier.

Shortly after midnight, he stopped back at the Office Lounge for a beer and ordered a small pizza to go. When he returned to the motel, Ahmed was asleep. Muhammad woke him, but he said his stomach wouldn't let him eat a thing. The boss ate the whole pie himself before turning in for the night.

Rowena stared up at the twin bridges that spanned the Bay from Annapolis to Kent Island. The sun made them glisten silver, and the vehicles on them looked like Matchbook models. She told Matthew about her confrontation with Muhammad Al-Jubeir and the hateful epithet he'd called her. "My dad always told me that name calling is the name-caller's problem, not the person's being called the name. I've always believed that. But when this hate-spewing slug called me that, I saw red. I couldn't even repeat it until just now. I don't know why I even did."

They passed under the bridges and heard the road noise from above reverberating off the water below. The Severn River and Annapolis Harbor came into view on their right, the Naval Academy occupying the end of a rounded peninsula studded with sailboats.

"Maybe it's cathartic," Matthew said. "Maybe you're clearing it out of your head, and maybe you're comfortable enough now to share it with me."

She looked up at him from the side settee next to the bridge steering station and stroked his leg from his knee to his shorts. "I think you're right. I couldn't be more comfortable than I am at this moment." She gave his thigh a squeeze. "Thank you, Matthew."

"Thank you, luv. I think as far as relationships go, being comfortable with each other is the prime criterion for an enduring . . . what am I saying? I'm British, I'm supposed to be aloof in these matters."

Rowena laughed and stood up. She turned his head toward hers. "Kiss me, you aloof fool. That's an order, Captain."

"Aye aye, Admiral," he managed to get out before her lips pressed against his and drowned out whatever else he might have been planning to say.

They anchored *Semper Fidelis* in Annapolis Harbor and radioed the water taxi for a ride into town. The capital city of Maryland was filled with nautical shops, chain clothing emporiums, a huge liquor store, and restaurants galore. They enjoyed a midday dinner at a rooftop eatery and gazed out over the harbor, at the myriad boats anchored there, at the Naval Academy grounds, and especially at Ego Alley, the wide, man-made lagoon which jutted into the town itself, where yachts were tied up as if on display and where, Matthew explained, the Christmas Parade of Boats was held.

"On a certain Saturday night in December, people dress up their boats in lights like parade floats and motor up and down Ego Alley to garner the oohs and aahs of the spectators. I drove down from Camp David to see it once, along with Dale and Joe—this was before Claire—and we were suitably impressed. Did you know that Joe had been nominated for the Naval Academy, but turned it down?"

"I did not."

"He was a corpsman at the Navy Yard in Washington, down the street from the Marine Barracks, and he blew the whistle on a doctor, a Naval officer, mind you, who had been pilfering certain drugs from the dispensary. Our mutual friend Lauren Bachmann was the security officer at the time, and she told Joe to keep watch on him and report everything to her. Joe rigged up a hidden camera and recorded the man in the act. The doctor tried to have him court martialed, but then-Lieutenant Bachmann put the kibosh on that. She's the one who wanted to commend him for Annapolis, as you might have guessed. He forbade her from contacting his congressman to get the process going."

"Why did he refuse?"

"He'd decided that he'd had enough and would be leaving the Navy at the end of his enlistment. But they'd kept in touch throughout his medical training afterwards, and when she was assigned to Camp David and her superiors were forming up the covert investigative unit, she acknowledged his skill and integrity and recruited him for the team. He was the first, in fact."

"Good for her. And good for him. I like Joe." She sipped her goblet of ice water. "Not the way I like you, of course."

"I'm happy to hear that."

"I'll bet you are."

They left the restaurant and continued their stroll, walking up the hill to the historic State House and back to the harbor before boarding the water taxi that returned them to the boat.

"Are those jellyfish in the water down there?" Rowena asked once they were back aboard. "They are, aren't they? I just noticed them. They're huge."

"They're called sea nettles, and they're so prolific that one could almost bounce across the Bay on their humpy backs. Those tentacles trailing behind them pack quite a sting, too," he said. "Those are things you don't read about in the tourist brochures."

"Why didn't we see nettles in the Bohemia River?"

"That's fresh water," Matthew explained. "It's why I wanted you to experience the joys of off-boat bathing there, rather than here."

She thought back two days. "And there were joys, were there not?"

"Stop, woman, you're making me blush."

She kissed him again.

"We'll stay in the harbor tonight," he declared. "No need to power up the generator. We'll use the battery to power the lights when it gets dark. If we need lights."

The air was damp, and after a cold supper they sat on a doublewide canvas-webbed chaise on the aft deck and watched the sun set. Rowena wrapped an arm around Matthew, snuggled her head at the juncture of his neck and shoulder, and closed her eyes. Her senses picked up the rhythm of his heart, the pulsing in his arteries. She swallowed saliva, suddenly ashamed of herself for what she was thinking—and for what she was hiding from him.

"Right," he said. "I don't mean to bring this up again if it bothers you, but I can't get it out of my mind, what that cur called you just because you rejected his book for publication."

Rowena shrugged. "It's okay."

"Growing up, the product of a mixed-race marriage—"

"Neither one white, remember."

"Right, neither one white, you must have had some prejudices to deal with growing up."

"Only when we came back to America from Germany, but I remembered what my dad told me and knew that the name-callers were mental midgets, and if I took offense it was my own fault for legitimizing their bigotry. He didn't use those exact words, but you get the point."

"That's very perceptive of your father."

She grinned. "And I remembered what my dad taught me about self defense, which meant that if anyone got too much in my face, I could kick their ass."

"Did you? Kick any ass?"

"Oh, yeah. Lots." She kissed him on the cheek. "Tell you a story. Dad had been assigned to Headquarters Marine Corps in D.C. for his last hitch, where he became reacquainted with the lieutenant whose life he'd saved in Nam. The guy was a colonel now. He invited my dad to the Officers' Club for a drink after hours, and he insisted that Mom join them . . ."

It was against protocol for a full bird colonel to socialize with lesser-ranked officers, and that included warrant officers, who lived in the twilight zone between enlisted and officer ranks. But when Colonel Rohr welcomed CWO-4 Marcus Mitchell, the man to whom he owed his life, to HQMC, he shitcanned protocol and insisted that Gunner and Mrs. Mitchell meet him in the O Club after duty hours.

One of the cliques at the bar was a gaggle of second lieutenants fresh out of Quantico, drinking shots and recounting their days in Officer Candidate School. The most vocal of them was a Mississippian named Wills, five foot eight, dirty blond hair, lowering brow over close-set blue eyes, cocky as a barnyard rooster and nearly as loud. The senior officers, being gentlemen, ignored him and his boot buddies.

Rohr and Mitchell had just finished their first gin and tonic when the door opened and Kim-Ly Mitchell walked in, fresh from work. She stood inside the door, scanning the uniformed men for her husband, and when she saw him and recognized Colonel Rohr, a big smile spread across her face. It had been Rohr, after all, who had set in motion the life she was leading now as a wife, mother, and American citizen.

Then Second Lieutenant Wills had to open his mouth.

He took one look at Kim-Ly, grunted, and crowed to his buddies, "Who's the slope?"

The next thing he knew, a huge black hand was wrapped around his throat, propelling him against the nearest wall and lifting him six inches above the floor, putting him eye to eye with the most fearsome Marine he'd ever seen.

The black man's voice was low, with a hint of the rasp that carried over from his years on the drill field, and that made his tone all the more intense. "That's my wife, you little shitbird, and if I hear you say one more disrespectful word, I promise I will shove your balls so far up your lily-white ass you'll look like you've got three Adam's apples."

The room fell silent, and Wills looked around at the officers gawking at them. Then he saw the bars on his assailant's collar and managed to croak, "Mister, consider yourself on report for assaulting a senior officer." Then, compounding his ignorance, he mumbled, "No spook puts his hands on me and gets away with it."

Marcus squeezed tighter; the man's face turned red.

Then Colonel Rohr touched Chief Warrant Officer Mitchell on the shoulder, a sign to let Wills down. He did, and Kim-Ly walked to her husband and rested a cautionary hand on his upper arm.

Wills gagged, coughed, and tried to pull himself together before the colonel, expecting him to call the MPs and have his assailant removed in manacles. He nodded to the senior officer and affected a pose before him as if to say, "Well?"

Instead of doing what the lieutenant expected, Colonel Rohr said, "Don't you stand at attention when facing a colonel, lieutenant?"

Wills snapped to. "Yes, sir!"

"Good. Now listen to me, you little puke. This man is twice the man and twice the Marine that you will ever be. He is a decorated Viet Nam veteran. He was proving himself in the jungles when you were still bouncing around inside your father's nut sac waiting to be shot off. He is no spook, and his wife is no slope. But you, little man, are filthy white trash. You wouldn't make a pimple on Mister Mitchell's ass. Do you read me, Butter Bars?"

"Y-y-yes, sir."

"Now understand, any report of misconduct always comes across my desk. And if I see *any* report from you about this, I will see to it that the most senior appointment you will ever get is officer of the shithouse. Am I clear? Do you have any questions?"

"Sir, no questions, sir. Would the colonel like me to apologize to the warrant officer and his wife?"

"No. Because I know you wouldn't mean it. You're not qualified to be in the same room with this gentleman and his lady. Do you get my drift?"

"Yes, sir. I'll leave, sir."

"Before you do, lieutenant: If you see Chief Warrant Officer Mitchell outdoors, it is you who will initiate the hand salute, and you who will say good morning, good afternoon, or good evening *sir* to him. And you will hold your salute until he deigns to return it."

"Aye aye, sir," Wills chirped, did an about face, and marched out of the club, never to return. His buddies didn't follow him, but they remained quiet the rest of the evening— or at least until after the colonel and his party had left.

"It was Mom told me that story a few days after it happened, not Dad," Rowena concluded. "We had a huge laugh about it. When Dad came home that night, I told him I'd met this really nice officer at the PX that afternoon, and he'd asked me to dinner. His name was Second Lieutenant Wills. You should've seen how big his eyes got. Then I 'fessed up, and the three of us laughed so hard we had tears in our eyes."

Both of them were laughing now, so hard that Matthew suggested they go inside and below, so they wouldn't disturb the people in the other boats nearby. "Sound carries over the water, you know."

The next day, Saturday the first of August, the weather threatened to turn bad.

"Red sky at morning," quoted Matthew and listened intently to the VHF radio. "NOAA says there's a chance of afternoon thunderstorms accompanied by strong winds."

"Should we be worried?" asked Rowena. "Maybe we should stay anchored here?"

"No, we'll press on. The Krogen is an ocean-going vessel, luv. She's taken Chesapeake storms before. We'll rock and roll, but she'll see us through all right. Digit won't like it, but she's lived through days like this as well. If memory serves, I'll probably have some pee puddles to wipe up later, but that's okay."

"Long as they're not from me. This is where I get my sea legs, right?"

"You already have them. I noticed how unsteady you were yesterday when we were walking ashore."

"I was. And I didn't have anything to drink, either."

"But aboard ship you feel steady again."

"I do. Isn't that weird?"

"Aye, matey, ye're a swashbuckler now fer sure," he growled. "Now report to the foredeck and prepare to haul anchor."

The storm struck as they were abeam Calvert Cliffs, just north of where the Patuxent River emptied into the Chesapeake Bay. Radar painted it as coming in fast, and suddenly the bay became a maelstrom of black clouds, lightning, thunder, and giant foamy waves that pounded the boat's forward port quarter. Matthew steered from the pilothouse, peering through the three windshields as the wipers tried their best to sweep away the pelting rain and the salt water that crashed over the bow and splashed against the glass. Belowdecks, Rowena could hear a series of plaintive meows, and her heart went out to the terrified cat.

For fifteen minutes that seemed like many more, they crested waves and wallowed in the troughs, and then they heard the mayday call. It was on the emergency frequency and directed to the nearest Coast Guard station.

The vessel in distress was an older thirty-foot sailboat named *Daddy's Dolly*. Souls aboard were a married couple and their ten-year-old son. The captain had left the mainsail up too long, and a sudden gust caught the sail, heeled the boat over so its rail was underwater along with the sail, and the weakened wooden mast snapped when the boat tried to right itself. The boat had taken on enough water to flood belowdecks, and it was foundering broadside to the waves. Soon it would be swamped and under water.

The owner gave the coordinates over his now-intermittent radio, and Matthew told Rowena that it was about a tenth of a mile ahead of them. She got the binoculars and spotted the distressed craft almost immediately. "It's out there to the left," she said, and Matthew steered toward it. When they got to within a hundred yards, they saw that the gunwale and the water were nearly at the same level.

Matthew radioed the craft, but there was no answer. The man was hauling in the dinghy that had been trailing behind the boat on a long line, which Matthew called the painter. All three were wearing PFDs, or personal flotation devices—life vests to lubbers like Rowena.

"They need to get into the dink and power over here," Matthew said, his voice almost lost in the roar of the wind, rain, and thunder, his face lit by flashes of lightning. "I'll bring the boat to, while you man the stern and help them aboard."

Immediately, Rowena dropped the three steps to the saloon level and stepped out into the storm. "Put on your PFD!" he shouted, but she was outside already, the normally sheltering overhead boat deck useless at protecting her from the horizontal needles of rain.

Rowena saw the father load his wife and son into the dinghy, saw them stagger and the dink wobble before they sat down, saw the man leap into the stern and pull the rope on the outboard motor. He gunned it toward the Krogen, but got no more than ten feet away from his own boat before the dink was yanked short and whipped around. In his panic, he had forgotten to unhook the painter, and as the boat jerked into its sudden 180-degree turn, the boy fell out.

Before she could think, Rowena dived into the raging sea and began swimming toward the boy, fearing mostly that he would get mangled by the outboard's propeller. She could hear the mother's screams and the father's panicked cursing as he staggered to the bow and fumbled at releasing the painter.

Rowena realized that with her metamorph's strength she was swimming like an Olympian toward the boy, who was screaming and flailing at the water. *It's the nettles,* she thought; *they're stinging him.* But she knew they wouldn't sting her, because she knew from Claire that all animals regarded metamorphs as alphas and didn't—*Ow! What the hell! Pinpricks of pain were lancing into her! Her flesh was on fire! This couldn't be!*

But she had to keep swimming, and as the boy's father unhitched the dinghy, she shouted at him to get to the trawler; she would bring their boy in.

Matthew put the boat on autopilot to keep a heading and ran to the stern, where he threw a life preserver on the end of a line to the couple in the dink and pulled them to the boat. They climbed aboard the swim platform and onto the aft deck and watched Rowena sidestroke toward them with their son under one of her arms in the cross-chest carry. When they got on board, the two were covered in welts.

Matthew shepherded them all inside and got blankets to wrap around them. Then he went to the galley and immediately made a paste of meat tenderizer and water and applied it to the boy, as Rowena smeared her own wounds. "This'll take the poison out," he explained to the parents. "The poison's mostly protein, and the meat tenderizer will break it down. Every galley should have some." He whispered to Rowena, "I'll have some words with you later. Meanwhile, I've business in the pilothouse."

The couple introduced themselves to Rowena as Mark and Dolly Howard, their son as Brad, their appreciation as boundless. They also noted that the storm seemed to be passing, and minutes later the sky was turning blue again. Rowena heard radio chatter from the pilothouse, and Matthew called them all up to join him as a Coast Guard cutter appeared off their bow.

"I've told them you're safe and sound, and instead of trying to take you aboard in these seas, they'll attach a line to your boat and tow it to the Coast Guard station. We'll follow them in. They can debrief you there and see that you're provided for."

"Thank you so much," said Dolly, "and thank you, Rowena, for what you did for Brad. You are a real hero."

Rowena smiled dismissively and sneaked a peek under her blanket. She saw no trace of where the nettles had stung her. And she didn't feel one hint of pain. *Thank you, Claire,* she thought. Young Brad, however, still looked and felt miserable.

The Krogen made a sudden turn to port, knocking them all off balance.

"Bloody hell?" said Matthew, fighting to turn the wheel that was itself fighting back. Looking up, he flipped a switch in the overhead console and control returned. "Damned autopilot went," he said, smiling at his new passengers. "Great way to cap off the day, hey?"

They waited until the cutter had secured the nearly submerged *Daddy's Dolly* in tow and followed it into the mouth of the Patuxent River and the protected waters of Back Creek. Dolly hugged her son and rocked him from side to side, cooing softly in his ear, as Mark began contemplating the paperwork he'd be filling out for the Coast Guard and, more importantly, for his insurance company.

When the boats were docked, addresses exchanged— "We have to send you a token of our appreciation," said Dolly—and goodbyes said, Rowena sheepishly looked at Matthew as he fended off the dock and headed toward the mouth of the creek. His facial expression was grim. "I'm sorry, I acted on impulse back there; I wasn't thinking."

"No, you weren't. And you scared the bejeezus out of me when you dived into the water. Don't ever pull a stunt like that again."

"But I did save a boy's life, didn't I?"

"You were wonderful, all right? I'm proud of you, I really am. But all I could think of while you were saving that boy's life was that you might drown yourself out there."

"Would you believe I was on my high school swim team?"

"Not the same thing, luv. How do you feel, nettle-wise?"

"You know, not that bad. And getting better. That meat tenderizer surely does the trick."

They approached a series of T-shaped wooden docks and Matthew radioed the harbormaster for permission to tie up for a day or two. "Home sweet home, at least for a while, until I get this autopilot fixed," said Matthew.

"And where are we, exactly?"

"One of my favorite stops on the Bay," he said. "Welcome to Solomons Island."

Chapter Nineteen

Jawdan El-Sayed left work early that afternoon, unaware of the drama playing out on the Bay, as there had been unusually light business that weekend and the sudden squall made outdoor activities impossible. He drove north on Route 2/4 and turned left to visit his self-storage unit on Creston Lane. His condo, a 1500-square foot unit on Schooner Loop, was just across the highway. It stood within walking distance of the northern terminus of Back Creek, the deep body of water that bordered the Solomons peninsula on the east. He opened the garage door to his unit and walked inside. He turned on the twin-tube fluorescent lamp, with which he'd replaced the inadequate incandescent that came with the place, closed the door behind him, and sat before his trophies and the cache of armaments, and smoked.

It had been a week since the boss's call, and the boat hadn't shown up. Perhaps, he hoped, the targets had devoted their cruising to the Eastern Shore—Oxford and Saint Michaels were popular with tourists—and wouldn't show up at Solomons after all.

But if they did . . . the boss had said to kill them. That's it: kill them. No how, where, when, or why; he was leaving the details up to Jawdan. He should have accepted that assignment as a compliment to his efficiency, his ability to think through contingencies and act accordingly. But he didn't quite see it that way.

If the couple arrived, and they anchored the boat in Back Creek, he'd either have to row out there in the dead of night or wait for them to come ashore and find a way to ambush them there. But in the summertime, Solomons was like a little city, filled with tourists from Baltimore and D.C., and vacationing boaters from all over who owned townhomes on the creek and docked their vessels there. The boss had no idea what he would be up against.

Plus, he had to show up for work six days a week. *Hel-lo. Did the boss even think of that?*

Also plus, the boss didn't know about that hooker he'd killed on the way back from the Pep Boys hit. So far as he knew, no one was any the wiser, no one connected him to her death. But that's not to say no one ever would.

For a terrorist, Jawdan was behaving irrationally. Maybe he'd lived in America too long, gotten too soft. Fourteen years between Oklahoma City and Pep Boys? That was enough to take the edge off anyone.

What if he decided not to take on the job? Cited the risk and just said no? What would that mean to Muhammad, the mastermind of their little cadre, the man favored by Saddam—Saddam, dead nearly three years now, may Allah have mercy on his soul?

Still, he owed Muhammad his loyalty. And Muhammad had promised him a gift for that loyalty, a gift that Jawdan hoped to claim, very soon. He ran his tongue over the roof of his mouth. It would not be long, he hoped, before a pair of fangs nested there. Frankly, he wasn't all that interested in drinking blood, but who wouldn't accept that condition in exchange for eternal life? No one wanted to die.

Another thought popped into his head: *If the couple did pull in, and he pretended he hadn't had the opportunity to kill them? Which could very well be true, by the way. If he confessed to that, what would the boss do to Jawdan in retribution?*

Maybe, just maybe, he could tell Muhammad that they hadn't visited Solomons at all. *Would he believe him?*

The boss had a knack for telling when someone was lying to him.

There was that Iraqi soldier in Oklahoma City, pretending to be a maintenance worker like the rest of them, who had raped a woman he'd picked up in a bar. This went against all their orders to keep a low profile, to avoid calling attention to themselves. He denied his involvement to Muhammad, but somehow Muhammad saw through the lie; this was the man he and Ahmed had seen drained of his blood to the point of unconsciousness by their commander. The man ended up in the back of Timothy McVeigh's Ryder truck. Gagged, trussed up like a turkey, anchored to the explosives, helpless but still very much alive. Until 9:02 local time on the morning of April 19, 1995.

No, it would not be a good idea to lie to the boss.

Better to hope that the boat didn't show.

Rowena stood beside Matthew in the marina office as he signed them in. The receptionist read the boat's name and documentation number and said, "*Semper Fidelis*, Toms River, New Jersey. You were here last summer, weren't you?"

"Good memory," he replied.

"I always remember the cute guys," she said, with a wink at Rowena. "You gave me a little moonlight serenade with your guitar."

"And your future husband, you might have thought to add," Matthew said, beginning to blush.

The manager walked over and said to Rowena, "Cassie loves to bust guys' chops, especially when they're with their wives or girlfriends."

"Maybe I'll have to bust hers later," Rowena said, winking back. "What's her husband's name, where does he live, and when does he get home from work?"

"Ouch! *Touché*, woman, I yield. You've bettered me on the field of dishonor."

Rowena smiled back at her. "I think we've found a friend, Matthew."

"We need a friend right about now," he said. "Autopilot's out. I don't know if it's something repairable or if the whole thing needs replacement."

"Well," Cassie said, that twinkle in her eye, "we'll do everything we can to see that the answer is the most expensive option out there."

Matthew nodded, a pseudo-sour expression on his face.

"I'll get Jerry to look at it tomorrow." She tossed Matthew a set of keys. "My Toyota's out front. Take your lady out to dinner."

Rowena looked puzzled. "You're giving us the keys to your car? On trust?"

Cassie grinned. "Why not? I have the keys to your boat."

"Fair enough."

"And I'll call Mike and have him meet us around eight. Have your guitar tuned up, there, Mr. McCartney. The better you sing, the lower your dock fees."

Later, after a fine meal at the restaurant on the pier that stretched out over the Patuxent River, and after the moonlight serenade Cassie had coerced out of Matthew—not that he'd objected all that much—Rowena and he returned to the boat, gave Digit her evening cat treat, and prepared for bed. The doors were closed, the windows and ports open, and the hatch above their bed propped up. Screens prevented the intrusion of mosquitoes but welcomed the evening breeze.

"God—and I mean that reverently—this is wonderful," Rowena said as they cuddled on the queen size bed. "It's a whole different world out here. Nice guitar playing, by the way. Kids would hate your selections, but for fogeys like us they were perfect. I know Cassie and Mike enjoyed them. She hugged him so tight they looked like conjoined twins."

"Newlyweds," Matthew said. "Last summer they were engaged, and you should've seen them then. You'd need a crowbar to separate them. But they're cute."

"Are we cute?"

He rolled onto his side and turned her face to his. "Darling, we are cuter than cute."

As they made love, Rowena reflected that Matthew had never called her darling before.

On Sunday morning, Rowena asked if Matthew would mind going to church. Not at all, he'd replied, and they drove Cassie's Camry to the Solomons United Methodist Church. Returning an hour later, she explained that her pastor back in Boston used to tease her by asking where she worshiped between Easters. But since the horror that had attached itself to Daciana Moceanu, she tended to go more regularly. "After all the deaths, both then and recently, of people I love—rather, loved—it gives me comfort."

"Understood."

"And after this past week or so, when all the world seems so bright and fair, well, I think I just want to thank someone—besides you, of course." She nodded toward the sky. "I almost feel reborn."

In her private thoughts, she acknowledged that she had, in fact, been reborn: by Claire, in the lodge at the base of the Catoctin Mountains. Were it not for that transformation, she would surely have died, either in a hospital bed or in the collapse of Jones Publishing.

There were days, there were nights, when she'd had to fight the urge to transform into a wolf, to run free, to hunt. And there were other times when she longed for the taste of blood, when a barely-rare steak was hardly enough to slake her thirst.

Then there was the matter of Matthew. Thanks to his childhood phobia—and she wondered if there was more to it than the bogeyman story he'd shared—he was still not a hundred percent comfortable with Claire; how would he react if he knew that she and Rowena were more kin than friends? They were bonded in a way that no mortal could understand. If the relationship with Matthew intensified, and it definitely seemed to be heading in that direction, would his knowing what she was drive him away? Another man might find it thrilling to cohabit with a woman whom he knew had a dangerous side, but Matthew was not one of those.

Would he consent to being turned himself?

"Three pennies for your thoughts," Matthew interrupted her reverie. "I assume they're worth more than two cents."

"Oh, nothing, just reflecting on silver linings." She leaned against his shoulder. "And you."

When they returned the car keys, they saw Cassie talking with a dark-haired man in coveralls. She saw them and smiled.

"There they are," she said. "Matthew, Ro, this is Jerry. He's going to take a look at your autopilot."

For the briefest of moments, the man's eyes seemed to pop. Then he looked again at the work order and saw the description of the boat and its hailing port; whereupon he took a halting breath and nodded his head once. Acknowledging them, or the job? He didn't offer to shake hands.

Rowena and Matthew led the mechanic to the boat. They entered through the pilothouse door, and before he began working, Jerry pulled out a cigarette.

"Please," Rowena said, pointing to the decals on the Dutch door windows, "no smoking inside."

He grumbled and put the cigarette back into the pack, then began disconnecting the autopilot, his eyes darting to the man and woman when he thought they weren't looking. He opened the case and shook his head. "I'm going to have to take it to the shop," he said. Then he started as he felt something brush against his ankle. Looking down, he gave a reflexive kick, and Digit caromed off the door.

"Hey!" Matthew shouted. "What the hell! It's only a cat, for God's sake!"

"Sorry, I *hate* cats," Jerry seethed. "It surprised me is all."

Rowena picked up the cat, who seemed fine, and cuddled her. "Why don't you just take the autopilot to the shop?"

"Yeah. Why don't I do that?"

They watched him leave. Matthew turned to Rowena, who still held Digit to her breast. The cat was none the worse for wear; she purred like a small motorboat. "What was that you were saying about silver linings?"

"Uh huh. I noticed inside the office that there's a Wi-Fi connection. Mind if I borrow your laptop?"

"Course not. Anything specific in mind?"

"Yes. I want to do some research on those sea nettles."

"How're you feeling, by the way? I don't mean to seem insensitive, but there were no welts on your body last night, so I figured—"

"Never occurred to me. There were other things on my mind at the time, there, Romeo."

"Right. The computer's in the starboard stateroom. While you do your research, I'll get some bait and put the crab trap over the side."

"Now that sounds like a plan."

"That's why I get the big bucks."

Once connected, Rowena went to the ask.com Website and posed one simple question: Do jellyfish have brains? The answer came back no. *That figures,* she said to herself. *For animals to recognize an alpha, they have to have some kind of brain. Universal alpha my ass, Claire.* The boat tipped briefly, as Matthew climbed back aboard with a frozen mossbunker to put in the crab trap. Rowena closed the laptop and went on deck, where she saw him use a wire to fasten the fish, cut in three sections to expose the guts, to the floor of the crab trap. The trap itself was a box formed by what looked like thicker-gauge chicken wire. When it was lowered to the bottom of the creek, the slack line would allow two sides, hinged at the bottom, to drop open and let hungry crabs inside. Pulling up the trap would close the doors, and once inside the boat, the crabs would scramble out and into a waiting bucket. Once a few were harvested, Matthew would boil them in a large pot along with a healthy dose of Old Bay seasoning. Later, their meat could be picked and stored in the reefer.

"Once we've got enough meat, I'll make you some of my famous crab cakes," Matthew said, as he lowered the trap and tied the line to the stanchion at the stern corner that supported the starboard end of the boat deck above them. "Mostly crab meat, with an egg and a smidge of bread crumbs to hold it together, a touch of red pepper, and then comes the secret: fry it in bacon fat. Sprinkle on some lemon and salt—no tartar sauce, that's an abomination—and savor it slowly."

"My mouth is watering already. You can wipe the spittle from my chin if you'd like."

"There's no spittle there at all, but maybe I should look closer." He kissed her.

Rowena said, "How far are we from Camp David, Matthew?"

"Oh, let's see. I'd say around two-and-a-half, three hours. Were you thinking of calling Claire? When I bought the bait, Cassie told me that the illustrious Jerry had already pronounced the autopilot burned beyond repair. Salt air is no friend to electronics, you know. Tomorrow they'll order a new one, so we'll be here for a few more days. How does that sit with you?"

"It sits beautifully, as if you didn't know."

"So call her. Hell, invite the whole crew, we've got the room on board."

As Matthew dropped belowdecks to the engine room, Rowena sat on a deck chair, propped her bare feet on the teak-capped rail, and made the call. It took one ring for Claire to pick up. "Guess where I am right now?" Rowena asked.

"Hmm. That's a tough one. I'd say you were somewhere on the Chesapeake Bay with Matthew."

"Whoa! How did you know?"

She could hear Claire laugh on the other end. "Because Matthew already told us you'd be cruising with him for a couple of weeks. You were there, Ro, remember?"

"Oh, duh. Things were a little confused then, if you remember. All right, can you tell me exactly where I am, smartass?"

From a hundred thirty miles away, Claire hesitated before replying, "You're not on the Bay, you're on a river that leads to the Bay. Not the Potomac, north of it. That would be the Patuxent?"

"My God, how did you do that? Wait. Matthew called you again when we docked."

Claire hesitated. "No, actually he didn't. And I don't know how I knew that. I mean how could I, but it just seemed to be the right answer. This could be getting Twilight Zone-ish, Ro."

"All right, Rod Serling aside, tell me the reason for my call."

"To say hello? It's been a while."

"Aha. No. To invite you and Dale and Joe down for a couple of days' R and R. The Commander, too, if she's got the time off."

"Sounds great, Ro. Lauren's down in D.C. meeting with her superiors, spook stuff I guess, but the rest of us are ready for some free time. I'll check with the others and get back to you in a skosh."

Two minutes later, she was on the line again. "Dale brought me back to reality. We can't leave until Lauren gets back, and we don't know when that'll be. A day or two, maybe more." Claire promised to call as soon as she knew something. Then: "How are you doing? You know what I mean, and it's not about you and Matthew."

Rowena laughed. "You sound cryptic. I'm doing fine."

"Ro?"

"Hey, I just got a mental flash. You know how the mafia has what they call made men? I'm thinking I'm a made man, too, of sorts. Does that make you my capo? Or more like my mother, even though you're younger? What I'm trying to say, is this your maternal instinct coming out?"

There was a pause on the other end. "Ro, I'm responsible . . ."

"Sweetie, you saved my life, twice now by my count; I'm
the one who's responsible, to you. And I haven't betrayed
that responsibility." She chuckled. "Yet."

Finding work at the Toms River Dyestuff and Intermediates plant basically gave the two Mideastern men something to do to relieve the boredom of simply waiting around
for their targets' cruise to end, if in fact it did end back at
Stump Creek. The personnel director had told them they
were welcome to sign on as chemical operators, men who
staffed the factory floor and actually produced the intermediates and dyes. Operators were the backbone of the production wing, the director said, which was his euphemistic
way of disguising the fact that operators were the lowest of
the grunts, the shit shovelers.

The company produced two types of dyes, azo and vat,
the personnel man explained. Vat dyes were applied to car-
pet and drapery fabrics and to upholstery, where color fast-
ness was imperative; azo dyes were less fade resistant and
were used to color the yarns used in shirts and other clothing that wore out usually before the color had a chance to
fade. At one time, almost half of America's azo dyes were
produced at TRD&I; now the industry, like so many others,
was moving to China, but the company's French owners
were doing everything they could to keep the Toms River
operation profitable. If only the Greenpeace threat didn't
come to fruition . . .

Meanwhile, it was business as usual, and that included the upcoming two-week shutdown of the azo manufacturing plant in order for maintenance crews to service the
equipment and recalibrate the kettles. This was when the
chemical operators and lab technicians would take man-
datory vacation time, leaving only a skeleton crew behind.
Morris and *Alfred,* who as new hires were not entitled to
vacation time—even the French had their limits—would be
assigned to clean and calibrate the three-thousand-gallon
vats in which the intermediates and dyes were made.

The azo building itself looked from above like a three-
story letter E: a factory in each right-facing arm connected
by laboratories and wide passages between. Intermediates

were made in the first two factories and forklifted across the connecting passages to the third, to be made into the final dyes. The labs handled production quality control, and the dyes were sent to another building for analysis—where batches were either accepted or rejected by the color chemists.

Morris and Alfred were given a tour of the plant by the foreman. The first floor looked as if giant cook pots with rounded bottoms were suspended from the ceiling: these were the lower portions of the huge kettles and their heating jackets. The second floor was where the domed lids came through, each with an agitator rod down the center, various pipes feeding into it, and a large circular opening near the red brick floor where solid chemicals were shoveled inside. The openings were manhole sized, with hinged lids that were fastened down with nuts and bolts. A giant wrench hung next to each kettle with which to tighten the nuts.

The factory was in full operation, and the noise was jet engine loud. The air smelled of ammonia now, but that would change depending upon what reagent was in use at any particular time. Chemical operators in blue coveralls and steel-toed high-top shoes stood by their kettles and monitored temperatures or attended to other duties. Men driving forklift trucks carried pallets of dry chemicals or drums of liquid to various kettles, where the operators signed for them and added them to their kettles, in accordance with written *recipes* clad in clear plastic sheet protectors. Cookbook chemistry, the foreman said it was.

The new men were taken to a kettle that was temporarily empty.

"Every kettle has a water line," explained the foreman. Then he pointed out a long length of narrow wood next to the kettle, at the top of which was painted a number that corresponded to the one on the kettle. "This is how we measure. You'll add a thousand pounds volume of water at a time, according to that gauge next to the valve, then lower the dipstick to the bottom, take it out, and mark where the water comes to."

"Is that accurate enough?" asked Morris.

"That's what we have the labs for. At certain stages, we sample the product and send it to the lab. The technicians

will tell us if we have to make any adjustments in volume
or raw materials. And we do a lot of that," he added. "That's
one reason we recalibrate the kettles every shutdown period."

"What are these other pipes for?" Alfred asked.

The foreman raised a cautionary hand. "Whatever you
do, don't open those other valves. See the labels next to
them?" Each had a plate engraved with what the line was
for: 20° Bé Muriatic Acid, Sulfuric Acid, Oleum, Ammonium
Hydroxide, 50% Caustic Soda. "That's all bad shit, gentlemen, especially the oleum and caustic. Get a drop of oleum
on you and it'll burn right into your skin faster'n you can
wash it off. Caustic will take more time, but it's thicker than
motor oil and harder to get off. Mix the two together, and
you've got instant boom. As in your ass is grass. Got it?"

They nodded.

"Good. Let's go up to the third floor."

The top floor contained the filter presses, where the
slurry from the second floor was piped to have the liquid
sucked out of the solids. Samples of the solids, or cakes,
were then sent to the lab for purity analysis, and the product itself was then shoveled out of the filters and taken to
the next factory, the middle arm of the E. "You don't have
to worry about any of this," the foreman explained, "but it
doesn't hurt to know about it. It's why the calibration of
the kettles is so important. Nothing that comes out of here
is a hundred percent pure, and it's the percent purity that
figures into how much of our intermediate is added to the
intermediate they make from it next door. Got it?"

"Got it."

Later, as Alfred drove them back to the motel, Morris
said, "I'm intrigued by those other chemicals."

"What do you mean?"

"Just thinking. Saddam would have loved to get his
hands on this stuff."

The crab trap yielded a half dozen giant blue-claws the
first day. Rowena cringed when Matthew dumped them into
the pot of boiling water and heard them scrabbling to get
out. "Remember," he said. "Before you think this is cruel,
these same crabs would happily eat you given the oppor-

tunity. And whether you were alive or dead would make no difference to them."

"That's encouraging," she replied and wondered if crabs had brains.

Once the crabs' shells had turned from dark green to red, Matthew poured out the water, let them cool on newspaper, and wrapped them for the refrigerator. "Another day or so, and we'll have enough for crab cakes. Ever pick crabs, luv?"

"Never. And I can't say I'm looking forward to it."

"Looking forward to eating them, though, right?"

"Yes. And by the way, Cassie told me they have a supplier in Annapolis who can get a new autopilot down here tomorrow. Our new best friend Jerry can install it, and if Claire calls to say the gang from the Hill can't make it down to visit, we can be on our way. Although, in a way I hate to leave this place."

"Understood. There are a lot of restaurants we've not hit yet."

"It's more than that, and you know it."

They decided to walk to dinner. It was a beautiful, breezy evening, daylight beginning to fade around eight o'clock, and they linked hands as they strolled to the river and the next eatery on their list.

"Crab cakes tomorrow?" Rowena asked.

"We'll see what the trap presents us with, won't we? Where do you put all that food you eat? And never seem to gain an ounce?"

"Trade secret," she answered with a wink and a squeeze.

The next day they visited the Calvert Marine Museum and Drum Point Lighthouse, an easy walk from the marina. When they returned, the autopilot hadn't yet been installed. Cassie told them the supplier was sorry and promised tomorrow for sure. The trap contained only one crab, nibbling on the spare remnants of the mossbunker. Matthew bought another fish and wired it to the floor of the trap before lowering it over the side. "Tomorrow," he promised.

Tomorrow came, and Cassie told them that the driver was on his way with the autopilot. She tossed them her keys and told them to explore the area, which both Matthew and Rowena thought was a splendid idea. They took the bridge west to the mainland and drove south to St. Marys City, Maryland's first capital.

"Maryland was a Catholic colony," Matthew said. "Mary . . . Land, the land of the Virgin Mary."

"Never thought about it that way," said Rowena.

"And when the Protestants took over in the late 1600s, they moved the capital to Annapolis, which was named in honor of Princess Anne. An Anglican."

"You do know your history, Matthew. I'm impressed."

"Don't be," he said. "I read it yesterday in one of those brochures in the office."

When they returned to the marina it was late afternoon, and they tossed Cassie her keys. "Filled the tank," Matthew said.

"You'd better have," she said. "Your autopilot's in, by the way."

Back aboard the boat, they saw that while the new unit had been installed, Jerry hadn't bothered wiping his dirty fingerprints off the face.

"Not what I'd have expected," said Matthew. "Good mechanics always clean up after themselves."

"Probably spooked by Digit," Rowena said. "How dopey do you have to be to be freaked by a little cat?"

"Where is she, by the way?" asked Matthew. He psss-psss-ed a few times and decided she must be hiding below. "Probably didn't want to be kicked again."

Rowena wrinkled her nose. "He was smoking in here. Do you smell that?"

"I do now. I'll tell the manager about it. Meanwhile, I'll go below and check to see if she's in her litter box. She likes her privacy, you know."

"I'll haul up our next batch of crabs. Can't wait to eat those famous crab cakes you've been bragging about."

They separated and Rowena went to the stern to pull up the trap. The empty basket waited by her feet. "It's heavy," she said to herself. "Should be some real peacherinos in there." She pulled in the line and saw the top of the wire cage. Through the green water she could see the dark backs of at least three giant crabs. "Yes!" she said. She pulled up the trap and frowned as she held it ready to discharge them into the basket.

"Oh my God," she said as she saw what lay beneath the crabs. "Oh. My. God. No! NO!"

Matthew walked outside. "Couldn't find her anywhere," he said—and stopped short.

Automatically, Claire let one side of the trap down and the crabs slid into the basket.

Matthew's knees grew weak as he stared in disbelief at the parcel of gray fur they'd left behind, splotched with red, and picked apart by the crabs' powerful claws.

Before Rowena could say anything, Matthew ran down the dock and into the office. As he did, he saw an old Taurus station wagon leaving the lot. The driver looked sideways at him. He had a cigarette in his mouth.

"Cassie," he said when he burst through the door. "Your keys, please, it's an emergency. Rowena will fill you in." As she tossed him the car keys, he turned and almost bowled Rowena over as she ran into the office. "Stay here," he commanded. Before she could respond, he was out the door.

Rowena stood there, between the door and the counter, not knowing which way to turn. In those seconds of indecision, she heard the Camry's engine start and saw Matthew peel off in pursuit of the gray wagon.

"What the hell?" asked Cassie. "What's wrong?"

Rowena told her. The color left her face.

"I didn't know you had a cat aboard. Jerry hates cats. But I never thought he could—"

"Cassie, what can we do? I don't know what Matthew intends to do once he catches him, and I don't know who would win if they got into a fight either, but that sonofabitch Jerry—"

"You're sure it was him? I mean, really sure?"

"I could smell the cigarette smoke inside the pilot house. There are No Smoking decals on the windows, but he ignored them once before."

"Jerry's the only one here who still smokes," Cassie said. She picked up the phone. "I'm calling Mike."

"Why?"

"One minute." Cassie hit a button on her cell. The phone was answered on the first ring. Quickly, she explained the situation, acknowledged a reply, and disconnected. She put the phone back on her desk and walked to the counter, where she took one of Rowena's hands in hers. "It'll be all right," she said, staring into the woman's dark eyes. "See, between us girls, Mike's always been a little paranoid about my lending my car out to anyone who comes in, so he installed a homing device so he'd know where it was in case it didn't come back."

Rowena stammered, "How did . . . why . . . ?"

"Relax. You never asked, so I never told you. My hubby's the Calvert County sheriff. He's on his way from Prince Frederick as we speak."

Chapter Twenty

Jawdan El-Sayed sped north on Route 2/4, making sure that Cassie's Toyota was in his rear view mirror. He turned into his condo complex across from the self storage facility, parked in front of his unit, and ran inside, leaving the front door slightly ajar and standing to the side. When the door opened, he would be standing behind it. In his hand was the Louisville Slugger he'd pinched from the hanging locker of a boat that had left early this morning.

He heard Cassie's car pull in next to his and the engine shut down. The door opened and slammed. Footfalls. His front door flew open and Matthew ran inside and stopped—and Jawdan swung the baseball bat, connecting with the side of the intruder's head. The thunk was satisfying. Collins dropped like an anchor.

After closing and locking his front door, Jawdan wrapped the man's mouth in duct tape and then used more to pin his arms to his sides. Then he drew Matthew's legs up behind him and taped his ankles to the back of his thighs.

A feeble consciousness returned, and Matthew looked up to see the boat mechanic standing over him, gloating, a baseball bat in his hand. His legs were cramped, and his head felt like there was thunder booming inside.

"Good," said the Iraqi. "How do you like my little, pardon the expression, cat and mouse game, huh?" He laughed. "Tomorrow you'll be crab bait, you high and mighty English prick. And so will your snooty black whore."

Sweat beaded Matthew's forehead and stung his eyes. He blinked and squinted.

"Aw, don't cry, baby," taunted Jawdan. "I'm going to store you in a safe place for the night, and later I'll collect your girlfriend and have her join you. You'll watch each other die tomorrow. Slowly, in my storage unit, on a heavy plastic drop cloth. I'll want to see the expressions on your faces when I dismember you bit by bit, in plain sight of each other." He added, "It's something I heard went on in Saddam's torture rooms." He laughed. "And you American pussies made such a big deal over waterboarding. You don't know what torture is. Well, as of tomorrow, you will learn." He raised the baseball bat. "I'll give you a tiny taste now. As your American umpires say, 'Play ball!'"

Mike DeMaira's siren screamed as the cruiser raced south, the sheriff keeping one eye on the road, the other on the portable nav screen. He pulled up at the self storage unit in Solomons and stormed into the office, surprising the attendant.

Together, they entered the yard and found his wife's Toyota, parked near an old green Jetta. Mike looked inside and saw the car was empty and the doors locked. He pulled his own set of keys from his pocket, put on a set of nitrile gloves, and unlocked it. He made sure not to touch the wheel or anything else on the driver's side—except the trunk release. The lid popped, and he lifted it. What he saw inside made him cringe. "Ho. Ly. Christ," he said.

"He's pretty well beaten up," Mike cautioned Rowena as they walked into the emergency room of the Calvert County hospital. "Be prepared for that." He had told Cassie and Rowena during their drive up that he'd gone to Jerry's condo, found it locked with the lights out, and his car missing. He'd get a warrant first thing in the morning and search the unit. "Meanwhile," he said, "Once we see Matthew, I'll drive you two back to the self storage lot. Cassie, I'll drive you home in the Vic; Rowena, you can take the extra keys and drive the Camry back to the marina. Unless you'd rather bunk in our spare room for the night."

Rowena assured him that she'd be fine on the boat and thanked them both for everything they'd done. Then they met the doctor, a diminutive young woman in her late twenties with bright blue eyes and blonde hair that reminded Rowena of the Tenniel illustrations for *Alice in Wonderland*.

"We're about to assign Mr. Collins to a room. He has a concussion and some broken ribs; luckily, none of them pierced a vital organ. He won't win a beauty contest any time soon, but he'll be fine. Are you ready to see him?"

Cassie and Mike stood just behind Rowena as she said yes. The doctor drew aside the curtain around Matthew's bed.

Matthew peered through swollen eyelids as Rowena approached and took hold of the hand that didn't have an IV taped to it. His head was wrapped, his face discolored, his lower lip split and stitched. He tried to smile, but it hurt.

"Don't cry, luv," he managed to say as her tears fell onto his face. "As you Yanks say, you should see the other guy."

At around midnight, Jawdan found what he was looking for: a dinghy tied to a private dock on Back Creek. He knew better than to drive back to the marina; his days there, he knew, were over. But he believed the boss would see him through this. After all, he still had value, in the form of his skill with mechanics, firearms, and explosives, and he still had a virtual armory secreted inside his self-storage unit, which no one at work knew he rented. Once he'd killed the two targets, he would contact the boss through Ahmed. He'd tell him mission accomplished first to soften the blow, then describe his situation. He'd need a new identity and a new address. And if the boss balked, Jawdan could always claim that he was just following orders.

He climbed silently into the tiny boat, laid the baseball bat on the deck, placed the oars in the locks, and untied the painter that lashed it to the piling. He rowed toward the marina, barely breaking a sweat in the warm night air. He came to the tall bow of the forty-two-footer first, tied port side to the dock, and pulled up alongside the starboard stern quarter. He tied the painter to the swim platform support and stealthily climbed aboard, his bat in one hand. The big boat barely rocked. He didn't open the swim hatch at the stern, choosing instead to climb over and step silently onto the deck.

The door to the saloon wasn't locked; *how naïve could people be?* He entered, eased the door closed behind him, and stole forward to the stairs leading to the passageway below. He passed the head on the left and the guest stateroom on the right and made directly for the master stateroom in the bow. There she was, visible under a white sheet. Being careful of the low overhead, he would have to deliver a sidearm blow, but it would be enough. He brought the bat around his right shoulder, took a breath ...

And felt the bat torn from his grasp from behind. An arm encircled his neck and thumped his butt onto the passageway sole. A thumb knuckle pressed up against his carotid artery as his arms thrashed. He felt a soft cheek against his own stubbled one. The woman's other hand pushed the thumb harder into his neck. He began to feel lightheaded. His struggles grew weaker.

The woman whispered: "Oldest trick in the book, asshole. Did you think I wouldn't be waiting for you? You walked right by me in the starboard stateroom." She took a breath.

He felt the skin of her cheek change, as if she were actually smiling.

"My father taught me this maneuver, you little prick. I'm cutting off the blood flow to your brain. A few more seconds and you'll be unconscious. But I'm not going to let you die. Oh, no. Not yet." Jawdan gulped.

He felt consciousness ebbing, and the woman released her pressure.

"I want you to look at me," she said and turned his head to the side.

When he heard the growl and saw what it was that faced him, his eyes rolled back into his head and he fainted.

When he came to, Jawdan found himself in the engine room below the saloon's teak-and-holly parquet sole. He lay on a drop cloth on the flat section of deck that joined the sloping fiberglass hull. He was naked, trussed with nylon line and gagged with a rag that smelled faintly of diesel fuel. The woman squatted between him and the engine. She looked normal, not like the beast that had confronted him above. *Must've been a hallucination,* he thought. But this wasn't. He couldn't move; she'd tied him securely.

"I learned a lot about knot tying on this cruise," she said calmly. "From the man you nearly killed tonight—and who's resting in the hospital now. And I learned a lot about you when I saw what you did to his helpless little cat. But you know what? Karma can be a bitch sometimes."

With a gesture, the woman directed his attention to a box by her side.

"See this?" she said. "Sheriff DeMaira—you know, Cassie's husband?—drove me back to the storage yard and gave me the keys to her car. He took her home in the cruiser and said he'd bring her to work tomorrow. He and his deputies will be scanning the area, looking for you. But you know what, Jerry me boy? They're not going to find you. Ever."

He whimpered behind the gag.

"After they left me alone, I called some friends of ours, Matthew's and mine, and they told me they'll be joining us here first thing tomorrow. But tomorrow is something you'll never get to see. You have no tomorrows, Jerry. You're going to meet Allah tonight. And I hope those seventy-two virgins he has waiting for you are all pissed-off nuns with machetes."

His eyes rolled back again, and she slapped his face hard enough to make his cheek redden and swell. "Let me explain why I'm so angry, Jerry. It's about more than my boyfriend and his cat. See, I was happily married once upon a time, with a little baby boy, a job I loved, and friends I loved even more than the job. Life was wonderful. But then someone killed my baby, and then my husband, and nearly killed my friends and me. One woman was responsible for all that. She was a monster, and I mean that literally. She's gone now. But then another monster blew up the building I worked in, killing all my associates. But you know what? I survived the explosion. Want to know why? Because I'm a monster now, too."

Jawdan squirmed. *What's this bitch talking about?* If he could only get the gag out, he might be able to bargain. There was no doubt in his mind that he knew who that last monster was; after all, he had supplied the Thermite. If he identified him for her, maybe she would let him live, let him go. But the gag was tied to his head with another rag; pushing against it with his tongue was useless. He jerked his head up, thrusting his chin forward, and made pleading sounds behind the gag; surely, she'd know he wanted to say something.

But she ignored him.

"After the sheriff and Cassie left me with the car," she continued, her voice soft and calm, "I drove to the hardware store in the shopping plaza. You know, the one near your storage unit? Yes, of course you do. And I bought these heavy-duty plastic bags for your body parts."

Body parts? He nearly soiled his shorts.

"Ah, I see you're looking around. What for? Oh, wait, I know. You're looking for long knives, maybe even hacksaws for your bones, right? Not necessary, Jerry, old chum. See, I'm going to tear you apart with my own hands. And teeth." A whimper came from behind the gag.

"You know one thing that separates man from beast, Jerry? I'll tell you. Poor Digit—that's name of the helpless little cat you killed—didn't know what you were going to do to her until you actually did it. The only actual suffering she did was when you stuck the knife into her before lashing her to the crab trap. But you're suffering now, aren't you, just from the *anticipation* of your suffering to come? Oh, yes you are. You know I'm going to kill you. And do it with extreme prejudice—and pain. Lots and lots of pain. See, that's the difference between man and beast. I love knowing that, knowing that you're suffering, even though I haven't even begun yet."

She smiled at him, as he imagined a mongoose might regard a cobra.

"Ordinarily I would despise what I'm about to do to you, and maybe tomorrow I'll even hate myself for it. But that won't matter to you. It won't matter to you at all. Because, as I said, tomorrow . . ." Her smile, so beautiful, so sweet, so lethal, unnerved him.

Tears streamed from Jawdan's eyes, flowed down his cheeks, and were absorbed by the rags that bound his mouth.

The woman opened the box and withdrew a large dark plastic bag. She opened it wide and placed it alongside him. "You know," she said, "maybe I should take off my clothes. I don't want your blood staining them, after all." She kicked off her boat shoes, took off her shirt and shorts, and then stripped off her bra and panties.

One part of Jawdan's brain acknowledged how beautiful she was; another how fearful.

"Let's see now, where do we begin?"

She looked up and down his body, stopping her gaze at his groin.

Oh no! he thought, and she laughed.

"Not yet," she said. "Not yet. We'll start small." She laughed and flicked his flaccid penis with the back of her fingers. "Speaking of small. Those poor virgins, doomed to an eternity of frustration." She slid her fingers down his legs and bent his toes up . . . and up . . . and up . . . until the bones popped out of their joints. "Ten little piggies," she said as Jawdan lifted his head and banged it down, twisting it in agony from side to side.

"You know something, Jerry? I have a lot of reasons for wanting to hurt you. The first is for the way you hurt Matthew." She wiggled his big toe forward and back, making him weep. "The second reason is for what you did to a defenseless little kitty." She wiggled the other big toe. Jawdan swiveled his head on his neck, tears flowing. "The third reason is that you defied our express wishes by smoking inside our boat." She worked his other toes back and forth, and he screamed behind the gag.

"Now Jerry," she said, "I don't know what other bad things you might have done . . . but I'm betting there are a lot more. Am I right?" He rolled his head from side to side: *No!* "Did you ever notice, Jerry, that the human knees only bend in one direction?"

She wouldn't, she couldn't, he thought through delirium. *She couldn't be that strong.*

"I know what you're thinking," she said. "So maybe it's time for a little visual aid, if only to heighten your anticipation. I told you I was a monster, didn't I? These are the last words you will ever hear, so you might want to pay attention. Watch me, Jerry, *watch me.*"

Before his eyes, the woman's body began to change. It was like one of those movie special effects, done with makeup or computers. But this was real. Her body grew a coat of jet-black fur; her breasts flattened against her chest; her nose and chin grew into a short muzzle, and saliva dribbled from the sides of her mouth. Her eyes, though, her eyes didn't change. The creature turned and straddled his thighs, facing his maimed feet, and brought his legs up at a forty-five-degree angle to the deck. Then, holding his ankles, she dropped herself with a thump onto the middle of his thighs. The crack of his knees was like a pair of rifle shots. She slid aside then, and pressed his feet up until they touched his chest. The skin behind his knees stretched and split in a shower of blood.

Rowena Parr, half wolf, half human, looked down at the man's folded form. Part of her wanted to continue, to dislocate each joint and bite through each bone, and she didn't know which part of her that was, the human or the animal. The more probable answer tended to frighten her.

This is enough, she thought, and held the bag's opening under the whimpering man's head. Her hands, more like paws now, pressed against the sides of his jaw, holding him steady. Then she allowed her head to morph fully into that of a slavering wolf. Her jaws opened wide, showing Jawdan the pathway to hell as she encompassed his head and crunched through bone to release his brain.

The next morning a late-model Ford sedan bearing government plates pulled into the marina. Two men, one white and the other black, climbed out, along with a tall blond woman. Before heading to the boat, they entered the office and spoke with the sheriff, who recognized the men from the description his predecessor had left. The black man asked cordially how the former sheriff was enjoying his retirement, and Mike said that he was out on the Bay every good weather day. He said that all the fish feared him: so much that they knew when he was coming and swam away before he could catch them.

The blond woman excused herself and walked down the dock. "Permission to come aboard?" she called, and Rowena came outside, looking disheveled in clothes that looked like they'd been slept in. Except that she looked like she hadn't slept at all.

"Get your skinny white ass aboard, woman," said Rowena, and the two friends hugged.

When Claire felt Rowena's tears on her cheek, she asked what was wrong. They went inside, where Rowena had a pot of strong coffee ready. They sat in the saloon sipping from their mugs and Rowena told her everything.

"Why did this mechanic want to kill you?"

"No idea. He didn't know us from Adam."

"What time did you kill him, approximately?" Claire asked.

"I don't know, maybe around one in the morning. Why?"

"Just curious. Because at around one o'clock I woke up and felt a kind of thrill. Hard to explain."

Rowena was too preoccupied to think of that now. "Claire, part of me loved doing that, and another was—is—disgusted, ashamed. Am I a sadist, is that what I've turned into?"

Claire stared into her friend's eyes. "Ro. I don't think a sadist would feel remorse. We can talk more later. Where's the body?"

Rowena lifted the sole plate across from the galley and they lowered themselves into the engine room. They had to squat in the height-restricted space belowdecks. Four black plastic bags were lined up next to the Krogen's single engine.

"Neat," Claire observed and wrinkled her nose. "Doesn't smell that strong yet, either. Ice?"

Rowena said yes, lots of ice. "After . . . well, after filling the bags, I spent an hour scrubbing, returning everything to shipshape down here. Then I went topside and saw the dinghy Jerry used tied up to the swim platform. I rowed it up the creek and beached it, then hoofed it back here as the sun was coming up."

"Matthew still doesn't know about you." It was a statement, not a question.

"Absolutely not, I told you I wouldn't do it. But it's killing me to keep it from him."

"Not accusing, just confirming. So listen, here's what we do. You look like hell . . ."

"Thank you for that."

"No, listen. You look like hell because you were awake all night, afraid in case this guy Jerry was coming back for you. That's for the record. First thing, we all visit Matthew in the hospital, then coordinate an investigation with the sheriff, who seems like a nice guy."

"He is."

Claire thought. "We're going to need fingerprints to run through our database. I wonder if this creep has a history we should know about."

"I know where his hands are," Rowena said, nodding toward one of the bags.

"That might be tough to explain, a full set of prints from someone who's officially in parts unknown."

Rowena caught herself in a nervous giggle. Claire immediately caught it, and relief entered their laughter. Claire said, "That reminds me, we left this morning before breakfast. You don't think we could . . . no, I guess not." They laughed again, and when Claire's stomach growled they had to hold their hands over their mouths to silence themselves.

"Okay," said Rowena. "I might have an alternate way to go here. The guy installed a new autopilot yesterday, and he didn't clean up after himself. I think I remember seeing at least one of his fingerprints on the face of the unit."

"Excellent." They climbed out of the hold and walked up into the pilothouse. "Yes," Claire said when she saw the unit. "There's one print I can see right off the bat, and there are probably more that we can dust for. So, Ro. Once things quiet down, we'll see if we can give Joe some busy work ashore while Dale joins us in, um, testing the new autopilot, giving it a shakedown cruise for a couple of hours. It's the logical thing to do before you pay the bill, right? We take some weights with us, and once we're safely in deep water we send Jerry to Davy Jones's locker. Let's see, how can we get some cinder blocks on board without arousing suspicion?"

Rowena gave her a weak smile. "Remember when I told you I'd gone shopping before driving back here last night? I bought more than the ice and saw and the contractor bags."

Claire grinned. "You didn't. Girl, you're brilliant."

"Not cinder blocks, though, I didn't think of that. Four fifty-pound sacks of cement mix. They're on the far side of the engine."

When the sheriff's car and the one containing the others arrived at the Calvert County Hospital, Mike DeMaira told them that he'd received two calls while underway: "One from my deputy telling me that he'd found Jerry's station wagon abandoned near Back Creek, and the other from a local resident reporting a stolen dink."

Claire and Rowena looked at each other.

Matthew had been placed in a private room, as the sheriff had requested before leaving the night before, citing the need for confidentiality in an ongoing investigation. Claire kissed Matthew lightly on his discolored cheek, then turned to her friend and said, "Ro, what was it you said about me once? Shot at and missed, shit at and hit?"

"My favorite expression."

"Don't make me laugh," said Matthew, his voice weak. "It hurts."

Dale and Joe shook his hand, gently, and Rowena softly kissed his swollen lips. Then the sheriff interrupted, taking out his notebook.

"Matthew, I'm sorry to have to ask you to go over this now, but can you tell me what happened last night? Then I can leave you with your friends. Cassie sends her best, by the way. Oh, and the mechanic who did this to you is missing, which I'm sure comes as no surprise. His name's not Jerry, by the way. It's Jawdan El-Sayed. He's an Iraqi national. Been working at the marina for more than ten years."

"Really," Dale said. "That's interesting. Would the marina happen to have his fingerprints on file?"

Mike shook his head. "Not likely. But they'll be in his car for sure."

Matthew recounted the events of the night before. "Okay," the sheriff said. "I'll leave you folks alone for now. Thanks, Matthew. Hope you'll be back in the yard serenading us soon."

Dale said, "Mind if we follow you?"

"Hey, no problem. Glad to have you along." He appreciated Dale's courtesy, as he knew the agents' agenda superseded his own.

Rowena said, "You guys go. I think I'll stay here and stand by my man for awhile." Then she added, "Just make sure you come back for me, hear?"

The first stop was the self-storage facility across the highway from Jawdan's condo complex. The two cars pulled into the lot and parked by his storage unit. As the manager wielded his bolt cutter on the combination lock, Dale nudged Joe and nodded toward one of the dust-covered cars: a green Volkswagen Jetta.

Claire saw it, too. "I think we've found Monsieur Mansoor's vehicle," she said. "And if we need more of Jawdan's fingerprints, I'd bet that whatever's inside the storage unit is covered with them."

The lock snapped, and the manager bent down to lift the garage door. Mike stopped him. "If you don't mind, I'd appreciate it if you weren't here when we opened it up."

"Oh, sure, Sheriff. Got it. Confidentiality and all."

"Let me buy a new lock from you before we leave."

"Absolutely."

After the manager left, Claire remarked in an aside to Dale about the currently fashionable overuse of the word *absolutely*. "Ranks up there with *amazing*." Dale replied that she wasn't a book editor anymore, and she smiled at him. "Old habits."

The sheriff lifted the door and daylight flooded the area. "Oh my God," he said. "It's a freakin' arsenal in there."

They walked inside and Joe took out his dusting kit as Dale produced a camera. Claire seemed more curious about the corner display of purloined items than in the cache of armament. "Look," she said. "A guitar. I think it's Matthew's."

Hanging on a small hook by the door was a set of VW keys. Claire took them and walked to the Jetta. They opened it. The car and trunk were empty, but the glove box held the car's registration. "It's Mansoor's," she announced upon returning. She'd also scented Sophie's perfume in the trunk, but decided not to say so in front of the sheriff.

"Can't be a coincidence, the fact that it's here," Dale said. "Sheriff?"

"Name's Mike, please. You're going to assume control now, I know. No need to look all apologetic, I get it. This is obviously a whole lot bigger than a local issue. Just let me know what you need, what I can do for you."

Claire touched his arm. "Ro told me you're a nice guy," she said. "She's right; thanks."

"I'll just go and get a new lock and then I'll be out of your hair." He tore a page from his notebook and handed it to Claire. "This is his address. Can you get into his house without using keys?" She smiled and nodded toward Dale. "Very good."

When he was gone, Joe called Lauren Bachmann's private number and told her where they were and what they'd found. She was silent for almost a minute. "I'm glad Matthew's all right. Do what you do, and take your time getting back."

"That was odd," Joe said as he closed the phone. "I'd have thought she'd be thrilled. Something's up, and she doesn't sound happy about it. And if the mama's not happy, ain't no one happy."

Dale shook his head. "What we're seeing here could be the link we've been looking for. You are thinking what I am, right?"

Joe nodded. "Talk about serendipity."

As Joe got out his laptop and began downloading photos and taking notes, Claire pulled Dale aside and spoke to him in a low voice. He nodded.

"Joe, Rowena told Claire that Matthew wants the new autopilot checked out."

"Go. I'm going to be real busy here, inventory and all. Just don't leave me overnight. And don't forget to take Matthew's guitar back to the boat with you."

The couple drove off and returned late in the afternoon. They picked up Joe and then drove to the hospital to visit Matthew and pick up Rowena.

"Hope you don't mind, old chum," said Dale, "but I took the good ship *Semper Fi* out to the Bay and checked out the new autopilot for you. Works like a champ."

"You didn't hurt my boat, did you, you lubber?" Matthew's voice was still weak, but growing stronger.

"Hey, I didn't forget what Captain Calvin taught us way back when. I do apologize for the hole I put in the hull, though. When I hit the iceberg."

"I'll put the repair on your bill."

"But we do have to stop at a supermarket on the way back. Seems we ate you out of house and home. Boating does make one hungry, you know."

Claire looked at Rowena and cracked a smile that only she saw.

Chapter Twenty-One

A contingent of investigators from the Department of Homeland Security arrived in Solomons Island on Wednesday, August 5th, and summarily dismissed Dale, Joe, and Claire. The action stunned them; whatever happened to carte blanche? When Dale asked what had changed since their last joint investigation—the implosion of Jones Publishing just last month—the leader of the detail suggested he check with Commander Bachmann.

Controlling his tone, Dale said to the leader, "Make sure you take note of the black hat and crepe hair ringlets on that table in the corner. That could be the link we need to the Pep Boys attack." The leader nodded and dismissed him with a casual flick of the wrist, as if he were King Henry VIII dismissing a courtier. Claire saw the look in her husband's eye and grabbed his arm as she propelled him toward their car.

They left the storage yard and drove to the hospital, where Matthew was being readied for discharge. His head was wrapped, making it look like Boris Karloff's in the mummy movie. Rowena was sitting on the bed next to him.

"Hurt?" asked Joe.

"Only when I breathe."

"Don't breathe then."

"Lovely bedside manner you have, there, Doctor Whitehead."

"Seriously, how'd the staff here do?"

"They were great. Seriously."

"Shouldn't your chest be wrapped?" asked Claire.

Joe shook his head. "Used to be the treatment, but not now. Wrappings make it harder to breathe."

Claire looked at Rowena with concern. She had decided to stay with Matthew and had slept the night in a chair. She looked ready to keel over. "We'll drive you back to the boat," she said. "You both will need your rest, and we can give you some TLC, for today at least."

"Have you finished your investigation already? Don't you have to get back to the Hill?"

Dale shook his head. "Trouble in River City," he said. "But Lauren told us to take our time getting back, sends her regards, by the way. Mind if we bunk on the boat overnight?"

"The guys and I will cook," said Claire.

"Throw out the crabs," Matthew told her. "Or put them on ice and take them back to the Hill with you. I don't think I'll ever eat crabs again."

Rowena lowered her head. After what they'd seen in the trap . . .

The moon was full when the couple rose from their long nap, stimulated by the smell of roasting Cornish game hens coming from the galley and vegetables grilling outside.

"We'll be heading up the Bay for home tomorrow," Matthew announced after their late dinner.

"Will you be all right?" Claire asked.

"Hey, girl," Rowena said, "the skipper and I make a great team. He even taught me about how to tie knots and to navigate by the compass; you know, True Virgins Make Dull Companions."

Joe said, "False ones sure don't," and they laughed, even Matthew, who'd temporarily forgotten what laughing did to him—but wouldn't forget again for a while.

After bidding farewell to Matthew and Rowena and watching the stately trawler motor out of the marina, Joe drove the sedan to the self-storage facility and parked outside the gate. Dale spoke with the manager, who affirmed that he was legally bound not to discuss what was going on inside the yard. The Homeland Security people were still in there, and the manager wished they'd leave soon, because none of his other customers could get in while DHS was working.

Next stop was the sheriff's office in Prince Frederick to thank Mike for his help and to advise him of what was going on now. He informed the trio that he'd already been told by the feds to butt out, and that they'd tell him what he needed to know when and if he needed to know it.

"Don't bet your next paycheck on that," Dale grumbled.

Mike DeMaira shook his head. "At least the boat owner got his dinghy back."

"And I can tell you this," said Joe, as disgusted as Dale was with the bureaucracy. "This morning I got a call from our superior. I sent our friend's fingerprints for analysis yesterday, and they match the marks on the throat of the woman who was strangled last January."

"My God," the sheriff said. "My wife was working along-side a murderer."

Claire, added, "Sheriff, I am happy to inform you that you don't have to keep looking for him anymore. You can call off the hunt. And I'm sorry, but that's all we can tell you."

"With respect, Mike," Dale said, "my wife spoke out of turn. Officially, that is. For the record, we know nothing. And not to sound even more melodramatic, but this conversation never took place."

The sheriff gave them a relieved grin. "Anyone asks, I tell them that Homeland Security is handling everything. Damn, I like you guys. And gal." He shook their hands. "Safe trip home . . . wherever that is."

When the team arrived back at Camp David, they found Lauren Bachmann sitting at her desk and smoking. She stubbed the cigarette out as they entered and without a word took the ashtray into the kitchen.

"This isn't good," Joe said. "When our illustrious commander smokes, you know the fertilizer is about to hit the oscillator."

Lauren returned. "Fifteen years since my last one," she said. "Now I'm halfway into my first pack." She sighed. "Just threw out the rest. In the end, they just compound the screwing I'm getting already. And you guys and Matthew as well. By the way, how is he?"

Claire said he was on the mend, good as new soon, and asked what was going on. Lauren told them to sit down.

"When my handler had me meet with him in D.C., I thought it was to share some information that he couldn't give me over the phone or cyberspace. Maybe a break in our prime investigation. Well, it wasn't to be." She shifted in her seat. "Anyone for coffee?"

"It's ninety degrees outside," said Claire. "How about some ice water? Maybe some lemonade?"

"Lemonade, right," she scowled. "How many for ice water?" Three hands went up, and she disappeared into the kitchen again. "Three ice waters, and one coffee for me."

"What gives?" asked Dale as he took a sweating glass.

"We are in danger of being deactivated."

The words hung there for nearly a minute before Joe asked the obvious: "Why?"

"We don't have the need to know," she answered. "That's the official reason my handler told me. He did say the decision to terminate, if it came down, wouldn't come from him. It'd originate from higher up, and I got the impression that it would be from much higher up, if not highest up."

"That high?" asked Claire. "If the team is terminated, well, that word takes on a rather ominous tone as relates to Dale and me."

"I see your point. But any speculation would be just that—speculation. Not productive."

Dale said, "Any indication of when this deactivation might occur, if it happens at all? You said we are *in danger of* being deactivated, not that we *would* be."

"No. He told me he'd let me know. The purpose of the meeting was just to advise me what was going on behind closed doors, and that I might want to prepare you—and myself—for bad news. He didn't want to surprise me."

"Decent of him, I guess," said Claire.

Dale added, "If we'd been able to get the mechanic's cell phone before Homeland Security showed up, we might have been able to check the records of his calls and see where they took us. This guy wasn't a lone terrorist; that much we can figure out from what we found in his storage unit. Dollars to doughnuts, he's one of the Pep Boys crew." He told her about the black hat and ringlets in the storage unit.

After a moment's silence, Joe voiced what they were all thinking: "Well, doesn't this just *suck?*"

At evening chow, the base commander and her team sat at a circular table and pondered their futures. Lauren said, "So, Dale and Claire, if we're disbanded what do you think you'll do with the rest of your lives? Where would you go?"

They looked at each other. Dale said, "Assuming that we're not deemed a threat to the public good? Someplace with woods and mountains, I'd suggest. Agreed?"

Claire nodded.

"I'd probably look for a teaching job again. Love working with the little blighters."

Claire reflected that they would be unable to produce little blighters of their own.

When Dale spoke her name, it jolted her out of her brief reverie.

"Me? I don't know. As I've asked before, what does one do with a B.A. in English? I could go back to editing, I guess. There are small publishing houses all around the country, not just in the major cities. I could become a freelance editor, too, advertise online, do it from home, wherever that might be."

"But you wouldn't become independent star chambers," cautioned Lauren. "I'm right, aren't I?"

They agreed, but in a way that told her that door would never close completely.

"Joe, how about you?"

"Two possibilities, as I see it," he replied. "I could find work as a forensic pathologist in any major city. Maybe I'd go back to Philadelphia, work for the P.D., buy season tickets to the Phillies and Eagles games." He looked at Dale and Claire. "No biggie to you two, sports, right?"

They shrugged, and Lauren mentioned the other possibility.

"Oh right, I could go into private practice, use my M.D. to deal with living people instead of dead ones."

"Would you practice a specialty?" asked Lauren.

He thought a few seconds and replied with mock seriousness, "Yes. I would specialize in diseases of the wealthy."

They looked at him, faces blank.

"What, not even a smile?"

Dale asked Lauren about her tentative plans.

"I've nearly reached retirement age. For the Navy to give me a new assignment for the two years I have left wouldn't make much sense, but then making sense doesn't seem all that important anymore. If we could remain active, and if I could remain here on the Hill, I'd stay for as long as I could be of value."

She paused, a deeper concern making her frown. "Claire, Dale, as for your status, the former POTUS knew you personally, and he knows—and appreciates—what *special qualities* you possess. As I said, I don't have a clue about Renegade or even how high up the chain of command the knowledge extends. My own handler is aware, naturally, but that's as much as I know. That said, if word of your shape-shifting ability trickles up to someone who sees you as a threat, as we all once thought about Claire here, you two might be in serious danger."

"All danger is serious," said Claire before she could bite her tongue. "Sorry, back in editor mode already. But thanks. We'll be on guard." She changed the subject. "So if you do retire, Lauren, what then?"

"Remember when I told you I had to drive to Ouray years ago to attend a girlfriend's wedding?" They nodded. "Well, she married the boy I'd had a serious crush on back in the day. They're divorced now, his wife left him for another guy, and he and I have been reconnecting via email. He lives in Montana these days, Bozeman; his two girls are grown and gone; and he makes his living as a wilderness guide. Hiking, hunting, fishing, you name it. Loves the big sky, and I just might head west and see if I love it, too."

"Matthew doesn't know any of this," observed Claire. "About our potential problem as a team."

"No. Let's just let him recuperate awhile and enjoy the rest of his cruise with your girlfriend. How's that working out, by the way?"

"This is going to sound pretty stupid, considering what we've just been through, considering that Digit's no longer with us, and considering the fact that underneath these bandages and this shirt I'm black and blue and still hurt like hell, but I can't remember when I've been happier," said Matthew.

"Must be the company you keep," Rowena said kissing his cheek before resuming her scan of the buoys from the flying bridge station. They had crossed the Bay and were entering the Tred Avon River, approaching Oxford.

"We'll anchor off the strand for the night, and tomorrow I should be well enough that we can dinghy to shore and stroll the town. There's a beautiful park bordering the river, and the town itself is like a throwback to the mid-twentieth century. Some of the old stores actually have depressions in their wooden floors that are worn down from decades' worth of foot traffic."

"Sounds wonderful. Oh, and by the way, it's been a long time since I've been as happy as I am now, too."

"Must be the company you keep," he parroted.

The next morning, Matthew remarked that he was feeling better by the day, but it was Rowena who rowed the dinghy to shore and back. Oxford was as he'd described it, and they strolled hand in hand, like love-struck teenagers, along the shady, tree-lined streets.

The following day they left the Tred Avon, motored north past Tilghman Island, and into the Miles River bound for St. Michaels. "This is where the abolitionist Frederick Douglass was born," he said, "but its nickname is *The town that fooled the British.*"

"More tourist info from a brochure somewhere?" asked Rowena.

"No, I actually knew this already. Seems my ancestors from across the pond just couldn't catch a break. It was during the War of 1812. You see the hill just beyond the town there?"

She said yes.

"When the British fleet was seen approaching by the local lookouts, the townsfolk knew that the ships couldn't reach town before darkness fell. So they hung lanterns in the trees highest on the hill and made sure every building in town was dark. So when the British warships anchored in the harbor . . ."

"They fired their cannons at the lanterns, thinking they were lights from the windows. But the cannon balls actually flew over the town."

"Clever, eh? And the fleet left that night, so they had no idea that they'd been bamboozled."

"Clever, yeah. What other historical trivia can you tell me about our ports of call?"

"Well, our home port is Toms River, a name the British attributed to an explorer named William Toms. Love my chauvinist ancestors: they couldn't admit to the truth. See, William Toms never explored north of Delaware Bay."

"So rewriting history is nothing new. How'd it get its name, then?"

"From Thomas Luker, a former New Englander who traveled south, assimilated among the local Indians, married the daughter of the chief, and received the river as her dowry. Hence Tom's River, with an apostrophe."

They anchored in the harbor, and Rowena rowed them to the dinghy dock—"I know, Matthew, I could use the outboard, but I need the exercise"—and they climbed the stairs to the deck of the Crab's Claw Restaurant.

"I decided I can eat crabs again," Matthew declared.

With mock seriousness, Rowena said, "Digit would have wanted it that way."

"Moving on."

A server delivered a mound of freshly steamed crabs onto the table before them, and Matthew taught her how to pick them as they sat looking over the harbor.

That evening, stretched out on flotation cushions on the boat deck, enjoying the breeze and contemplating the stars, Matthew mentioned the arsenal the team had found in Jerry's storage unit. "This could be the link that we've been seeking for years," he said.

Rowena turned her head toward his. "What's that?"

"Claire has already filled you in on part of it," Matthew said. He reviewed the Pep Boys attack, followed by the two train attacks out West. Rowena brought in the murder of the New Hampshire family, and he added the murder of the hooker from Parole, the crepe hair under her fingernails, and the fingerprints that matched the man's they'd known as Jerry. Plus the killing of Sophie Bienkowski and the razing of Jones Publishing. *Allahu Akbar* was associated with every incident but Sophie's and the Parole hooker's murders.

"While he was *stroking* me with his baseball bat, Jerry bragged that he is definitely a terrorist. He said there are two others, one of them a custodian at a high school outside Washington, and he's disappeared, too. He figured that since I was going to die anyway, no harm done to their cover. The team found the custodian's car later in the storage lot near Jerry's unit. The third terrorist is still invisible to us now."

"But you have an idea? Because if you don't, I do."

"Great minds, luv. The third terrorist is guy who blew up your building. Revise that: the vampire who blew up your building. With help from the custodian and weapons supplied by Jerry, no doubt."

"So our bungled execution was a vendetta as much as an act of terror. Jerry was probably under orders to kill us. But how did his boss know we'd be visiting Solomons, when even we didn't?"

"That, my darling, is the sixty-four-thousand-dollar question."

Rowena stared at the stars and said nothing for a moment. Then she turned onto her side so she could look at him. "I get the feeling that there's more you're not telling me. Like the link to an incident you've been investigating for years."

Matthew considered. "All right, understand I'm overstepping here. You don't officially have the need to know. But the Oklahoma City bombing back in '95 was the reason our unit was formed in the first place. Authorities assumed, and later became sure, that there was a Middle Eastern connection. Lauren was directed to pursue these people, and it became a priority that trumped all the in-between work—including the investigation of Claire's werewolf murders."

"Killings, please. She's not a murderer."

"You're right, of course. Sorry."

But, thought Rowena, *in point of fact she was. None of her killings—except Daciana's—had been in self-defense. Then again, the people she killed were themselves either killers or otherwise physical or emotional abusers. Saint Peter would not have welcomed any of them through the pearly gates.*

Had Jerry been a murderer, deserving of execution? Yes, there was the woman he picked up in Parole. Plus, he had beaten Matthew to within an inch of his life; and he clearly had meant to kill us both.

According to what they'd told Matthew, Claire and Dale had tracked Jerry down by scent, and when he saw them in lupine form he put a bullet into his own head. They took him to the Bay and sank him in a hundred thirty feet of water, under the pretense of checking out the autopilot.

"So Jerry was involved in Oklahoma City?" asked Rowena. "And the other two as well?"

Matthew took a breath. "I shouldn't have mentioned it, luv; it's still technically classified information."

"You know that I won't say a word. Now, let's go to bed, and I'll try to restrain myself from jumping your broken bones."

Once belowdecks in the master stateroom, Rowena flipped on the bedside lamp and carefully undressed him, wincing at the discolorations on Matthew's torso. The purple was beginning to turn yellow now. She pulled the top sheet back and they lay side-by-side, naked, Matthew's arm around her shoulders and his hand resting softly upon her breast. She snuggled against him and saw his eyes were open, staring at the overhead.

He turned to look at her, their faces inches apart. "There's something else I haven't told you," he said. "Also classified, but in a personal sense."

She propped herself on one elbow and with her free hand stroked his cheek. "I'm listening."

"The monster in the coal bin. Remember that story?"

She said yes.

"I made light of it when I told you, but my fears go deeper than that. It's a phobia, actually. My counselor told me to try laughing at it. Like whistling past the graveyard or something like that. So I made a joke of it at the time I told you."

"Okay. It was a joke, but there's more to it than that."

"You realize, Rowena, that I've never told anyone this, and I mean anyone. You are the first. And you must promise me—"

"Shh," she whispered and touched her lips to his.

Matthew took a breath. "My parents had a dog. A big German shepherd, Rex was his name. They'd raised him from a puppy. When I came along, my mum thought Rex might be jealous of the newcomer to the family, but my dad said nonsense, he'd be my protector. Well, one day when I was maybe one or two, I was on the floor and saw Rex sleeping. This is what my mother told me; I don't remember this part. She said I crawled over and yanked on his tail. He leapt to his feet and grabbed me by the throat."

"My God."

"And this part I do remember, vividly, and I wish I couldn't. I remember his bark and his snarl, and I'll never forget the look in his eyes. There was his breath, too, and the pressure from his teeth. To this day I don't think he was cautioning me; I think he intended to kill me. Which is why today I shy away from large dogs and gravitate toward cats instead."

"What happened with the dog?"

"Mum was in the room, and she clobbered Rex with a vase, shattered it. The dog let go and started growling at her. She picked me up and ran from the room, closing the door to keep him locked away. Next day, Rex was gone."

"Childhood trauma," Rowena said. "It's never gone away, has it?"

"There's more."

"Oh." She traced her fingers alongside his neck, where the big dog's teeth had once gripped him. No wonder he wasn't comfortable last January when Claire slept over.

Matthew continued: "When I was about eight or ten, there was this neighborhood bully, older bloke, who used to taunt us youngsters with tales of how he was going to kill us if we didn't share our lunch money with him." He smiled weakly. "I went hungry a lot those days. So on our walk to school we'd pass this new home under construction. LeRoy would point to the basement floor, which was still dirt, and tell us he was going to bury us there the day before the concrete was to be poured. No one would ever find our bodies. Once the foundation was in, that trick wouldn't work, so instead he said he was going to gag us and tie us up, and then brick us into a wall."

"How utterly Poe-etic."

"Then he said he was going to run us through the buzz saw, whatever that was. Scared the dickens out of us."

Rowena frowned down at him. "But you told me you were addicted to those horror comics, like the one with the monster in the coal bin. Why did you read them if you were so scared?"

"Because horrible as the stories were, in the end the villain always got his comeuppance, usually in a manner more terrible than what he'd inflicted upon his victims. I'd imagine LeRoy as the villain in each story." He paused.

"Eventually, I became so paranoid that my parents sent me for counseling."

"Did it help?"

"On the face of it. But as an adult, I confess that bullies can still intimidate me. As the cliché goes, I'm a lover, not a fighter. I don't know what it would take to make me shed my fears and leap into action without even thinking."

He continued: "You should also know that as a member of the team, when I learned that the woman whose case Dale was investigating a few years ago was a werewolf, I was the first and the loudest to vote for terminating her. Bad call as it turned out, but you can understand."

Rowena smiled as he reflected.

"Today, of course, we have two werewolves on board, and even though I know that they're more protectors than threats, and that neither would attack me—at least on purpose—when I look at Claire and sometimes even at Dale, I can feel Rex's jaws around my throat."

"But you tease them about their wolf natures. I've heard you."

"As I said, whistling past the graveyard, luv." He sighed and turned his head to her. "So, does that make me a wimp, or just a garden variety nut case?"

"It makes you human," she replied. "Thank you for opening up like that, you don't know what it means to me." *And there's the understatement of the year,* she thought. "Now get some sleep. You told me we've got a ways to travel tomorrow."

Rowena turned off the lamp, kissed him, and resumed her place beside him. In moments, Matthew was snoring softly. It took over an hour, however, for Rowena to surrender to sleep.

Chapter Twenty-Two

The next day proved a long one, as they left St. Michaels and motored north along the Eastern Shore: past Annapolis, past the Chester River and Fairlee Creek, finally docking for the night at Worton Creek. Matthew was able, albeit slowly, to climb the stairs up the bluff to the Harbor House Restaurant, where they enjoyed spicy bloody Marys, ice-cold gazpacho, and huge slabs of steak—and pitcher after pitcher of ice water to replace what had evaporated from their bodies during their hours on the flying bridge.

Afterward, they sat on the Krogen's back porch and stared across the harbor at the wooded shoreline, where a great blue heron waded in the marsh looking for fish to spear. They sat for a long time, saying nothing. Finally, Matthew said that this tiny harbor was one of his favorite places on the Bay and added that when he retired he might just want to make Worton Creek his new homeport. He looked at Rowena to gauge her reaction. Her head was drooped forward, eyes closed, her breath steady. He nudged her awake and told her that he wasn't strong enough yet to carry her inside to bed.

In her dreams that night, Rowena relived her killing of Jerry in the engine room of the boat: the pleasure she took in breaking his bones; the crunch of his skull between her wolf's jaws; the yielding softness and rich sweetness of his brain. She saw herself dismembering him and placing his parts in plastic bags; covering them with ice to avoid the stink of decomposition; imagined Claire and Dale disposing of the bags, weighted down with cement, in the deep waters of the Chesapeake Bay. Had they feasted on his remains first? She vowed not to ask.

Rowena awoke and turned her head in the predawn darkness to see Matthew's sweet sleeping face, hear his steady breathing, feel the heat emanating from his healing body. She reflected on what he had confessed to her last night and realized that she was falling in love with him. Which brought with it profound conflict, for which there might not be any resolution.

She slipped out of bed and walked outside, the dew on the teak deck cool against her bare feet. Climbing the three steps to the foredeck, she padded to the pulpit and turned to face aft. The waters of Worton Creek were dark and still, the bluff black against the fading darkness of the sky, the only lights anywhere coming from the two overhead lamps on the fuel dock fifty yards away.

Rowena turned and faced forward again, eyes turned toward the fading stars. The cloudless sky promised a fair day. Her ears picked up the sound of footfalls behind her, a sound no human ear would be able to hear, and she waited. Matthew's arms encircled her waist, his nose nuzzled her neck, his lips kissed her cheek. She leaned against him and felt his desire for her, scented pheromones for the first time since his hospitalization.

But it was too soon. The doctor said it would take perhaps six or seven weeks for his ribs to heal, and she was not about to jeopardize the process.

"Morning, luv," he whispered.

She turned and kissed him, knowing that her sleep breath was as foul as his, but neither seemed to care.

They cruised north, anchored again inside the mouth of the Bohemia River, and Rowena bathed in the fresh water, while Matthew sat on the edge of the swim platform watching her. There was no way he could have joined her: getting into the water wouldn't have presented a problem, but climbing out, even using the three-rung aluminum ladder hinged to the swim platform, would. He took the soap from her when she was done and watched her swim for a few minutes. When she returned and reached for her bikini top and bottom, she saw that Matthew had removed them from the platform and was dangling them from his fingers, well above her reach.

"Give them back, you dirty old man," she said.

"What'll you give me if I do?"

"Anything you want."

"And what'll you give me if I don't?"

"Anything you want."

"That's an offer I can't refuse."

She laughed, climbed onto the platform, grabbed her swimsuit, and put it on. Together, they dangled their legs in the cool water. Matthew chuckled, and Rowena asked what was so funny.

"I'm remembering a few years ago, shortly after Dale and I met on the boating course. It was Independence Day weekend, I'd just bought the boat, and we decided to motor up to Sandy Hook and watch the fireworks over New York Harbor."

"That sounds like fun. Why didn't we do that this year?"

"You'll understand when I tell you. See, when we rounded Sandy Hook Point and headed for the inside anchorage called Horseshoe Cove, we realized that others had the same idea. And when I say others, I mean hundreds of others. The cove was a virtual Times Square on New Year's Eve. Setting the anchor so we wouldn't bump into other boats tested my mettle big time."

"But you did it."

"I did. Afterwards, Dale sprayed us liberally with Deep Woods Off to keep the flies and mosquitoes away, and we sat on the stern hoisting our drinks—beer for me, straight tonic water for him. And we sweated. Now, when I say we sweated, don't assume I mean glowingly; think rivers flowing from our faces and bodies, washing off the Off and clearing pathways for the flies and skeeters."

"Sounds charming."

"Yes. At that point, I was wondering if I'd done the right thing in choosing to live aboard a boat. But that wasn't the worst."

"Do tell," Rowena said.

"All through the cove, people were flushing their heads, and the waste wasn't going into holding tanks either."

"Ew."

"The lazy current brought with it great clouds of umber sludge, drifting from boat to boat. We were floating in a cesspool, and we gave the anchorage a new name: Horseshit Cove."

"Double ew. But why didn't you put the AC on?"

"The generator would have made a racket. Not good etiquette when so many others are trying to sleep."

"Wouldn't have stopped me."

"Right. So I slept that night in the pilothouse, tossing and turning, the heat and humidity doing their best to keep me miserable. Dale slept on the settee in the saloon, not wanting to go below where it was even hotter. And then, sometime around midnight, another powerboat motored in and set the hook nearby. I didn't think much of it until I heard the splash."

"What fell in?"

"Not fell in, jumped in. In the darkness, a man jumped into the water."

"Right into the *umber clouds of sludge?*"

"Indeed. And he shouted, 'Hey Alice, this is great!' He splashed around a bit, and then called at Alice to throw in the soap!"

Rowena laughed hard, tears forming, and Matthew joined her.

"Next morning," he said, "the fourth of July, we weighed anchor and motored across the Raritan Bay to Richmond Harbor Yacht Club on Staten Island, where we picked up a mooring and enjoyed the fireworks over Manhattan from there. On the fifth, it was back to good old Barnegat Bay and the River Toms. Never again have I ventured to Sandy Hook and Horseshit Cove."

"All right, all that talk has got me headed for the head myself," she said and excused herself.

When Rowena came up from below, Matthew had started a fire in the outdoor grill and was rooting around in the refrigerator for dinner fixings. "So," she asked, "where do you go to have your holding tank pumped out? Is there a pumpout station at Stump Creek?" He ignored her and pulled out a pork loin, which he intended to cut into cubes. She waved her hand before his face. "Hello? Anybody home?"

He closed the reefer door and looked sheepishly at her. "I've a, um, slight confession to make," he said.

"You don't. Tell me you use the holding tank to collect your waste. Our waste."

"I wouldn't tell you that, exactly." He saw her accusatory expression. "But I can explain, luv."

"Oh, this'll be good." She squirmed by him, took some peppers and onions from the netting beneath the overhead cabinets, and began slicing them as he diced the pork.

"Simple question: what do the fish do in the water? What do the crabs do in the water? What do the ducks and geese and seagulls do in the water? Answer: they poop."

"But we've been adding to that."

"Rowena, Rowena, Rowena. Yes, we've been adding our waste to the water, but it's minuscule by comparison. But here's the other thing. Say you've got a small boat that doesn't have a head. Marine regulations say you can use a bucket . . . and then you're allowed to dump the contents overboard!"

"What?"

"It gets better. The next morning at Horseshit Cove? As Dale and I watched, we saw a woman in a small sailboat come topside, drop her shorts, hang her butt over the rail, and drop a load into the water."

"Now that's disgusting."

"But legal. That's my point."

"All right, I see the absurdity. But what do you do when you're at Stump Creek? Tell me, not in the river."

"No. I mean, Number One, yes, but you remember the head inside the shop. Well, there are two more, complete with showers and outside entrances, in the back. We use them for the other function, and Paul cleans the heads every week in return for a reduction in his slip fees. But," he added, "fish and fowl still do poop in the river."

"Speaking of foul."

Rowena gathered the sliced veggies and pork and prepared skewers as Matthew went aft to check on the charcoal.

"Almost ready," he called back.

She put the skewered meat and vegetables on a platter and walked outside. "Well," she said, "I've learned something today."

"And what would that be?"

"I've learned that my boyfriend isn't as perfect as I thought."

He smiled. "Well, thank you for that."

"For saying you're not perfect?"

"No, for saying I'm your boyfriend. I like the sound of it."

She cupped his cheeks between her palms and kissed him, long and lingering. "I could easily fall in love with you, Matthew Collins," she said.

"Well, I wish you'd hurry up about it. I'd long ago fallen in love with you."

At the end of every day's solitary and tedious work at the plant, calibrating one kettle after another, Ahmed would drive the Sprinter east on Route 37 in the direction of Seaside Heights. When they reached Island Heights, a small municipality along the north shore of the river, he would turn right onto River Avenue and park at the public gazebo and pier. It was directly across the Toms River from Stump Creek Slipways on the southern shore.

Usually, he and Muhammad would get out of the truck and walk along the bulkheaded boardwalk, passing by fishermen casting for snappers—bluefish weighing less than a pound—and by crabbers, occasionally by a young couple or an older one, each pair holding hands. The men would pretend to be interested in the tiny sailing boats—more like bathtubs with sails—in which children were honing their skills for weekend races; or in the larger vessels that would cruise the river for the pleasure of watching the shoreline drift by; or in the more serious anglers in outboard-powered skiffs, anchored near their favorite fishing holes. But what they were really looking for was a white-hulled trawler yacht tied to a dock at Stump Creek.

On Thursday, August 13, Ahmed asked a question that had been on his mind since they'd left Boston. He ticked off on his fingers the terror operations they'd accomplished this year: Pep Boys; the passenger train in Utah; the tourist train in Colorado; and the razing of the publisher's building in Boston. He knew nothing about Muhammad's murdering the family in New Hampshire; or the black prostitute in Atlantic City; or the more recent killing of the hooker at Seaside Heights. *Why,* he wondered, *is the boss so dead set on killing just one target, the woman who worked in the publishing house?* Mass murder was more their style.

And there was the other nagging question: when would the boss turn him into a vampire like himself?

Muhammad pointed to a bench by the bulkhead and they sat, lighting cigarettes. He took a deep drag and blew out a stream of smoke. "To review, we've not heard from Jawdan since the day he called you to alert us that the targets had in fact docked in Solomons." Ahmed nodded. "Which probably means that he failed to kill them; otherwise, he would have called with the good news. If he took the coward's way out, and is now on the run, you and I will have to find him and deal with him."

Ahmed swallowed at the euphemism.

The boss continued: "If he tried and failed, he might be in jail as we speak. Worse, he could break under interrogation—especially if he is treated as an enemy combatant. You understand. And even worse, if the authorities are involved, they would have found our weapons cache in his storage unit."

"And my car in the lot," groaned Ahmed.

"So after dealing with Jawdan, we'd have to go to ground again until the manhunt cooled. Worse, our ability to commit further operations would be limited to what we have in the Sprinter, as neither of us would dare return to Solomons."

Ahmed nodded.

"And then there's the other possibility: that the targets themselves either killed or captured him, which now that I think of it, is highly unlikely. As far as our line of work is concerned, those two are amateurs. Whatever Jawdan's status—on the run, in jail, killed or captured—we can no longer be associated with him. He is a threat to our anonymity."

What was left unsaid was that he felt the same about Mansoor. After they disposed of the primary target and her boyfriend, he would have to dispose of Ahmed, too. Nothing personal.

No, very personal.

"I understand what you're saying," said Mansoor. "But you haven't answered my question."

Muhammad finished his cigarette and lit another from its tip. "I'm getting to it. Ahmed, we are long divorced from the Republican Guard; Saddam is dead; we never were affiliated with al-Qaeda; and we were never linked to Hamas, or Hezbollah, or any other terror group. We are free-lancers, guerrilla fighters, bound to no cause but terror itself. We laid low for fourteen long years after Oklahoma City, establishing ourselves as legitimate and productive citizens. Above suspicion. Loyal and hard working. Biding our time until ready to reactivate."

"All of which I understand. Go on."

"The Pep Boys attack was picture perfect, right down to getting the password on the woman's email. I felt good about that. After we separated, I tried logging into her account from various public sources and found that it was still active. This could be important."

"Her husband didn't think to close it?"

"That's one possibility. The other is that some agency told him to keep it open, so they might track our whereabouts. Whenever I found her password was still alive, I logged out and sent nothing. When we blew up the train in Colorado, our message told the authorities that we had moved our base of operations out West. The Burma-Shave signs in Utah also suggested a link to us, although no email was involved. The next attack was in Boston, which means we were back East again. Confusing, yes? Look at it from the Americans' point of view. Are we one cell, or are we part of a network, all using the same email account to send our messages? Also, that message not only lays the blame on some unnamed and totally innocent Islamic terror cell—if I may use the word *innocent* in this context—but it also taunts law enforcement for their own ineptitude. Did you know, Ahmed, that Jack the Ripper used to do the same thing to Scotland Yard's detectives? He even sent them half a kidney from one of his victims, with a note that he'd eaten the other half and found it quite tasty."

Ahmed shuddered. "A regular Hannibal Lechter."

"Please. Jack the Ripper was real."

"Again, returning to the woman . . ."

"Yes, the woman. Finally, the woman. To boil it down, she offended me. Spoke to me as if I were beneath her. Dared even to threaten me. A woman, a black woman at that, speaking condescendingly. To me. Yes, I chose the publisher's building to destroy because that is where she worked. Which means we combined a terror attack with the settling of a personal score. How she survived the attack I don't know, but I do know that she will not survive the next one."

Ahmed said, "What do you have planned for her this time? In case we can't sneak aboard the boat while they're asleep?"

"I don't have a specific plan in mind beyond that. But I think if the opportunity presents itself, I just might make her watch me torture her lover to death first. For entertainment's sake."

"Well, I think you might want to start thinking about your plan now." Ahmed pointed to the river, where a large, slow-moving trawler yacht motored toward her riverfront dock at Stump Creek Slipways.

Chapter Twenty-Three

Rowena tied the Krogen to the pilings, and after the boat was secure, Matthew cut the engine and generator. She hopped onto the dock and waited for him to appear on deck. The sudden silence, following the twelve hours of engine clatter that had accompanied them on their run from Cape May, seemed absolute. Matthew, still tender, climbed gingerly from the boat onto the dock and didn't let false machismo get in the way of accepting Rowena's helping hand. They walked down the dock and headed for the car to make a grocery run. On the way, Matthew saw that *Perfect Partner* wasn't in her slip and learned from a fellow liveaboard that Paul and Cindy were sailing around their usual haunt, Block Island, and were expected back sometime this weekend.

Rowena glanced at Paul's empty slip and said that he would look more at home in Key West rather than an island off the coast of New England. "He entered a Hemingway lookalike contest a few years ago," Matthew mentioned, "but he didn't even place. Now if anyone says he looks like Papa, he just grumbles and says, 'I ain't your goddam papa.'"

Matthew turned the key in the minivan, and the Honda started without hesitation. Before she climbed in, Rowena turned for another look at *Semper Fidelis*, floating tall and proud at the end of the dock. She would be scrubbing her down tomorrow, good old-fashioned brush and bucket work, and Matthew would be standing by with the hose to wash off the suds. She refused to let him do the scut work, citing his healing ribs, and he put on a pretend pout.

"Madam," he said, affecting an even broader accent, "Might I remind you that I am the captain of this vessel?"

To which she replied that in case he'd forgotten, she was the fleet admiral, and he'd better watch his *P*s and *Q*s. Then she kissed him on the cheek.

The first time Rowena had laid eyes on the Krogen, back on Memorial Day weekend, she'd thought it a most ungainly looking vessel. It reminded her of the commercial fishing or shrimping trawlers she'd seen in photos of the fleet plying the Gulf coast. But once aboard, she took one look at the parquet floor, the precision-milled wood joinery, and the exquisite trim, and she remarked to herself that living aboard must be like living inside a finely crafted piece of furniture. Now, having actually been aboard her for nearly three weeks, she knew without a whisker of doubt what had attracted Matthew to the craft; and she also knew that she could easily adjust to such a life herself.

"Come on, I thought you were hungry," Matthew called from the van, and Rowena took one last look at the Krogen before turning and hopping into the passenger seat.

She didn't notice the white Sprinter parked a half mile across the river in Island Heights.

The next morning they went to a local delicatessen for breakfast, what Matthew called the Jersey Shore sandwich: Taylor pork roll—"It has to be Taylor's"—American cheese, and a broken-yolk fried egg on a hard roll. "Beats a McMuffin every time," declared Rowena as she ordered another from the pleased counterman. As they walked out of the deli Matthew's cell phone rang, and when he put it back in his pocket he announced that their friends had just touched down at Miller Airpark.

A half hour later, Claire, Dale, and Joe piled into the van, with Joe occupying the third row. "Well," he drawled, "look like I be in de back o' de bus agin."

Matthew turned around and told him to consider himself royalty, whereupon Dale called over his shoulder, "Yassah, Miss Daisy, where y'all be wantin' to go to today, Miss Daisy?"

"Y'all kin go straight to hay-ell," came the voice from the back.

They returned to the boat yard, and Rowena explained that she had a boat to clean. "We thought you guys wouldn't be coming in until later," she explained, whereupon Claire told her she would have company with the scrubbing, and the boys could join them for a wash party "if they so desire." Dale and Joe looked at each other, gave a what-the-hell shrug, and turned to as Matthew attached a hose to the dock's water line, fitted a nozzle, and stood by ready to rinse.

Across the river, two men trained binoculars on the boat.

"Five of them, all told," observed Ahmed. "Look like the same ones we saw with her in Boston. Probably spending the weekend, yes?"

Muhammad nodded, letting his own binoculars down to his chest, depending from a thin leather strap around his neck. "The man works at the plant," he said, referencing the TRD&I decal on the van's left rear window. "He'll probably be back at work on Monday. We can look him up during our lunch break."

"Then what?"

"Then we'll see."

Late in the afternoon, Paul and Cindy returned, dropped sail, and motored *Perfect Partner* to her slip, just as Matthew was firing up coals in the grill next to the Weeping Willow Bar. "No place like home!" Paul roared from the foredeck. "What's for dinner?"

"We've got steak and potatoes," Dale called back. "You have any vegetables?"

"Tons. And dessert, too: Cindy's cinnamon rolls."

"Then Cindy is welcome to join us," said Matthew. "As for you, the jury's out."

"I've got gin."

"Right, the jury just came back. You're in."

Impromptu pot luck dinners at the Weeping Willow amounted to a bonding ritual among the liveaboards and the weekend boaters who kept their vessels at Stump Creek: an extended family gathering for those who considered themselves family by choice. As the sun lowered over the trees, Cindy suggested to Matthew that this was a perfect evening for some guitar music. As he stood up, Paul told him to wait, he'd walk with him.

"I've made up a song," he announced as they walked toward the boat. "Now all I need's the music."

"That's not a song then," Matthew said. "It's a lyric."

"Okay, then you make up the music, and we'll share in the royalties."

"I've a feeling this is going to be good. As in bad."

They got to the boat, and Matthew asked Paul to climb aboard and get his guitar for him. "Had a little accident," he explained. "Fell down and broke a couple ribs."

"Matthew, Matthew, Matthew," Paul said. "Fell down, my ass." He glanced back at the folks sitting around the picnic table. "That must be some woman you've got there."

"Just get the guitar, would you?"

Back at the picnic table, Paul said to the others, "My song is a tribute to Stump Creek. It only has one verse so far, and my no-talent friend here doesn't have music for it yet. So, with your permission, I'll recite it."

"Fasten your seat belts," said Cindy as Paul let loose:

> *Under the Weeping Willow tree*
> *The village idiot sat.*
> *To amuse himself*
> *He abused himself,*
> *And caught what came out in his hat.*

Paper plates and napkins were lofted at his head, along with a volley of jovial invective. He ducked and called them all unappreciative cretins. Then he said he'd have to check his dictionary to find out what the hell *cretin* means.

Matthew strummed a chord and suggested that this little ditty might be more acceptable in present company:

> *There once was a couple named Kelly,*
> *Who walked around belly to belly.*
> *For in their great haste*
> *They used aeroplane paste*
> *Instead of petroleum jelly.*

This was greeted with laughter and applause.

"How come you don't get trash thrown at you, but I do?" demanded Paul.

"Class wins out," replied Matthew as Rowena grinned and shook her head.

"I heard my dad sing a limerick like that when he was in the Marines," she said, and nodded to Matthew. "Actually, I overheard it. Same chord, professor, if you please. And I apologize in advance for my flat voice."

246

"Ain't nothing flat about you, doll," Paul remarked, as Cindy swatted his shoulder.

"I'll take that as a compliment," said Rowena and sang:

There once was a man from Bel Air,
Making love to his wife on the stair.
On the forty-first stroke,
The bannister broke,
And he finished the job in mid-air.

She got a standing ovation and bowed to her adoring fans.

Paul said, "I know one about a man from Nantucket," but he was shouted down and threatened with more trash.

When they all retired some hours later, Rowena acknowledged to herself that she felt more at home in Matthew's 500-square-foot boat than she did in her 3500-square-foot house in Boston. And the camaraderie displayed by her friends and Matthew's fellow boaters gave her a sense of belonging at least equal to, if not more intense, than anything she'd known in Boston.

Saturday dawned brilliant, not a cloud to be seen, the air crisp—a CAVU day, Claire proclaimed. "Beautiful day for flightseeing. How about it, kids?"

Matthew and Rowena quickly said yes; Dale and Joe said they'd prefer to take in a day at the beach. Matthew drove the crew to the deli for another Jersey Shore sandwich—two each for Rowena, Claire, and Dale—and then ferried them to Seaside Heights, where Joe and Dale got out. From there he drove west through the pines to Miller Airpark, where Claire preflighted the Cessna, put Rowena in front and Matthew in back, and took off on Runway Six, bound for Barnegat Bay.

They did a three-sixty at a thousand feet altitude around Stump Creek and wiggled the wings to Paul and Cindy, who they saw waving to them below. Then it was on to the boardwalk and beach at Seaside Heights on the barrier peninsula, already crowded with bathers. Not a chance of spotting Joe or Dale among them.

Claire flew another circle around the boardwalk, then flew south over Island Beach State Park, where she directed her passengers' attention to Tice's Shoal, site of their Me-

morial Day weekend aboard the Krogen. Less than a minute later they were circling the red and white lighthouse at
Barnegat Inlet. Matthew pointed out the different colors in
the water, and Rowena understood that they represented
different depths; in some areas, the water was so low they
could see gaggles of seagulls—wading.

"Can you show us the plant?" asked Matthew, and
Claire turned to a northwest heading, flying past the Oys-
ter Creek Nuclear Generating Station, bound for Route 37
westbound from Toms River. In the distance they saw the
Naval Air Station at Lakehurst, site of the 1937 *Hindenburg*
disaster. Its huge dirigible hangars were the most promi-
nent features, looking like giant white Quonset huts erected on the flatland beside the long, long runways.

Between the base and the town of Toms River itself,
carved out of a pine forest and bordering a narrow branch
of the river, stood the Toms River Dyestuff and Intermediates plant. As Claire circled it, Matthew pointed out the
three rows of buildings: vat dyes to the east and azo to the
west, with administrative offices, the cafeteria, various labs,
and the giant water tower in the center row.

Next, Claire followed the path of the tributary through
the woods until it led them to Toms River—both the town
and the river itself. She made a series of wide three-sixties
around the town before heading back to the airport, flying
over a sprawling senior citizens' development before arriving at Miller's airspace.

On the ground once more, they headed back to Bayville,
where Matthew suggested that they stop at the Shop-Rite
for cold cuts. They picked up ample quantities of deli meat,
cheese, and salads, then went to the bakery department for
bagels, rye bread, and hard rolls. In an inspired moment,
Matthew excused himself and disappeared, returning from
the dairy counter at the far end of the store with a three-
pound loaf of Taylor Pork Roll.

They returned to the boat and feasted, feeling no pity
at all for Joe and Dale, who would have to make do with
boardwalk food for their lunch. At five o'clock, they picked
them up at the south end parking lot and returned to the
boat yard for dinner and an evening's cruise on the river.

Sunday morning, after a homemade Jersey Shore
sandwich on bagels crusted with salt, Dale told Matthew

to give Lauren a call. It was up to her to tell him about the possible break-up of the team. "Nothing urgent, but call her when you get a chance. Now, how about a ride to the airpark?"

They made their goodbyes inside the ops building, and thirty minutes later Matthew and Rowena watched the Cessna take off on Runway Two Four and disappear into the southwestern sky.

Matthew started the Honda's engine and the air conditioning came on full blast. He didn't put the car in gear; instead, he shifted in his seat, trying not to wince, in order to face Rowena. "Right. You asked earlier about Oklahoma City," he began. "I know you still have questions, and thank you for not pressing me." Rowena said that she didn't want to compromise his position any more than he already had. He continued: "Intel sources confirm the number of Middle Eastern operatives who've returned to Iraq. They're targets of our clandestine forces there, and the success or failure of our counterparts in Iraq doesn't fall into our need to know. Of the terrorists who remained in America, the U.S. has, uh, *accounted* for all but three."

She understood.

"These three, and you know who they are, and *what* one of them is, assimilated into society and laid low. Now the cell is active again, just two of them now, led by the third terrorist."

"But Saddam's dead now."

"Three years come December."

"So why pop up now, when there's no reason to reactivate? Saddam's not pulling their strings anymore."

"Right. That's the salient question here."

Rowena asked why the Iraqi connection wasn't common knowledge.

"The FBI knows, and the CIA and Secret Service of course. Certain members of Congress do as well, and one even promised a full investigation. But it was quelled at the highest levels of power."

"But that's insane. This is a case where the public has the right to know."

"Insane, perhaps, but expedient."

"But since 9/11, we've got thousands of troops in harm's way, and there are still a lot of folks at home who believe we're only there so we can have dibs on Iraqi oil, which is ridiculous. Wouldn't the Oklahoma City connection help to justify our presence?"

"Think of the time period, luv. It was 1995. We'd polished off the first Gulf War, having conquered the supposedly elite Iraqi forces in record time. An assassination attempt against the President had been foiled. Saddam was humiliated on a global scale. America was on a high."

"I know. I was a junior editor at Jones then, first year out of college."

"Now, consider this. What would have happened to that national high if it were revealed that despite our military superiority, we were nevertheless absolutely vulnerable to the most heinous acts of terror here at home? By the very dictator we thought we'd defeated three years earlier?"

"But wouldn't that be another reason we had to know?"

"Let's assume you're right, and I'm not saying you're not. But there would be certain—repercussions."

She thought for a minute. "But the truth—"

"Doesn't always set one free. A consequence of revealing the truth to the American people would have the tendency to return us to war with Iraq—six years before the World Trade Center attacks. The administration would have seen itself presiding over a nation warring not only abroad again, but possibly internally, as it was during Vietnam. The administration didn't want to start another conflict and suffer the unintended consequences: more lost lives, immense financial costs, and lack of popular support. They had American scapegoats already. Singling them out was, as I mentioned, expedient. And politically, it gave the administration rhetorical ammunition to use against the right political wing, which had objected loudly and long to the left's bungling of Waco and Ruby Ridge. And finally," he added, "1996 was an election year."

"You can't be serious, Matthew."

"Once again, I am only speculating, luv."

"But the others in the unit? Does Lauren know—?"

"She can only speculate on the reasons, like the rest of us. I know the news is disappointing, if not downright distressing. You look upset. I'm sorry."

"Distressed, disappointed, deflated. Politics sucks, doesn't it?"

Matthew backed the van out of its parking slot and headed to the boatyard. As they drove through the pines, he engaged in more speculation.

"How do you think Jerry knew we'd be coming? Answer: he couldn't. But he could be alerted to our possible arrival. How so? His boss could have done that, perhaps. But how would he know?"

Rowena picked up the thread. "Because he and the janitor followed us from Boston? They tracked us to the boat? And when they saw we were gone—"

"They sent a *just in case* message to Jerry."

"And if so, they could be still in the area, waiting for us to come back so they can finish the job that he botched."

"That would not be good, luv."

Upon disembarking back at the boatyard, Matthew phoned Commander Bachmann and told her their theory. Then he listened as she gave him instructions and also advised about the threat of the team's deactivation. When he hung up, Matthew said, "Orders from the top, endorsed by yours truly: You're to go with me when I return to work tomorrow. We're not to be out of each other's sight until this is resolved."

"Happy to comply, Captain," she said, kissing him on the cheek.

"I'm serious. Tomorrow morning the team will be flying back here and renting a car at the airport. We're close, luv, dangerously so. By the way," he added, "the commander tells me that our unit is in danger of being disbanded. More politics, I'd imagine."

Rowena caught her breath and let it out. "For a second there I thought you said *dismembered*. Sorry. Go on." She shuddered, as images of what she'd done to Jerry returned.

"Oh, nothing. She just made me aware that it could happen." He looked nervous, and Rowena tilted her head to the side, studying his face. "Oh, all right, I'll just come out with it. You've nothing left in Boston but bad memories, so far as I know, and if you've nothing positive to tie you to the city, would you consider relocating to the beautiful New Jersey shore?"

By way of answer, she tangled her fingers in his hair, brought his face to hers, and kissed him long and hard.

Then she excused herself and gestured toward one of the two heads in back of the shop.

Running through her mind as he walked alongside her was the problem that had plagued her since she realized how deep her feelings ran toward Matthew. He had to know. He couldn't commit to her without acknowledging what she was, and more importantly *why* she was. And why she deceived him still, whereas he had revealed to her everything painful about himself.

As they approached the pair of heads, they saw one of the doors was open. Paul emerged, with a mop in one hand, a bucket in the other, and a newspaper under his arm. "All ready for you, mateys," he chimed. Rowena greeted him and went inside, closing the door behind her. "Here," said Paul, handing the paper to Matthew. "Somebody left this on the back of the shitter. Seems like those wascally Gweenpeace folks are screwing with your company big time."

Matthew read the headline: TR Pipeline Blocked; Production at Plant Ceases. "What is wrong with these people?" he complained. "They're killing the goose that lays the golden eggs. Thirty years or so, this area was in an economic drought. Then TRD&I moved in, and boom, two thousand new, good-paying jobs appeared. Local economy boomed. Now . . ."

Paul nodded; he knew the rest of the story. Local activists had begun complaining that the company was discharging manufacturing waste into the tributary that fed the river and the bay, and that it was another egregious example of big business polluting the local environment. Never mind that the effluent had been processed so thoroughly the water it was more pure than the stream it was being fed into. But the company, in a show of good faith, built an underground pipeline from the plant that stretched six miles to the ocean, and another three thousand feet beyond the shoreline. The last thousand feet consisted of perforated pipe, to disperse the effluent over a wide area.

True, there were times when the outflow was too much for the pipeline to handle, which necessitated an occasional midnight dump into the stream, but no swimmers subsequently emerged from the river looking like Easter eggs.

The article in the newspaper said that Greenpeace activists had sent a team of divers down to plug up the perforations in the pipeline, effectively shutting down plant operations. All production employees were advised not to report to work until the matter was resolved.

"On a happier note," Paul said, "I forgot to tell you, but your fishing gear came in at West Marine."

Matthew frowned. "Beg pardon?"

"Guy came by the day after you left, carrying a couple rods and reels. Said you'd ordered them a week or so before and they just came in. He was actually trying to catch you before you took off. Damn fine customer service, I'd say. Color me a fan of West Marine."

Matthew shook his head. "Yes . . . except that I didn't order any rods and reels. I've got a full complement of fishing gear on board."

"Huh. Well, all I know is that he was wearing a West Marine shirt and said he was looking for the guy who drove the Honda minivan. Stumbled over trying to remember your name."

"The shirt: was it the same one West sells in the store? With the name and company logo?"

Paul tilted his ball cap back. "Yeah, I guess. Why?"

"Just wondering. Um, you didn't happen to tell him where we were going, did you?"

"Matter of fact, I did. We were making conversation, and he asked how long you'd be gone. I showed him your float plan in fact."

"Did you happen to mention Solomons Island?"

"Yeah, now that I think of it. That's right, he said he knows someone who works there." Paul frowned. "Buddy, you don't look so well all of a sudden. Something wrong?"

Matthew said, "Can you describe the man?"

"Well, let's see, about five nine or ten, stocky but not fat—"

"Ethnicity? Did he look like a foreigner to you?"

Paul considered. "Funny you ask. He reminded me a little of those Indians who run the 7-Eleven downtown, but his features weren't that, whaddyacallit, I don't know. His eyes weren't big like theirs, you know? And his nose was more like a beak." He snapped his fingers. "He looked more like he'd be at home riding a camel than driving a car. Yeah. No offense to my favorite limey, but it's hard to find many Americans in America anymore."

Paul inquired about Matthew's injured ribs, thinking his change of complexion might reflect the damage done to them. Matthew told him they were still giving him some discomfort, and Paul repeated his remark about his girlfriend's being some kind of woman. "We're both lucky guys," he said, with a wink, as he left to return the bucket and mop to their place inside the shop.

Rowena finished using the head and Matthew walked her back to the boat. He told her what Paul had told him about the visitor, the man allegedly from West Marine—who was definitely not from West Marine—who had been at the yard looking for him.

She turned to face him, her hands gripping his upper arms. "He is here, isn't he?"

Once aboard the boat, Matthew opened the hatch to the anchor chain locker and pulled out a leather rifle case. He opened it, withdrew a carbine, and then a box of armor-piercing rounds. "Militarily speaking, this is a semi-automatic, gas-operated, .30-caliber shoulder weapon, model M-1. Also known as a Garand. Your dad might be familiar with it, unless it was phased out before his time."

Rowena said, "At close range, you might prefer a pistol."

"Like this?" He pulled out of another bag a Colt .45-caliber semi-automatic, M1911.

"So it looks like we're standing guard tonight."

"Choose your weapon."

"I'll take the .45. Daddy taught me how to shoot."

"I'll take the watch berth in the pilot house. I don't expect unwanted company, but as the Boy Scouts say. . ."

Rowena knew that if Al-Jubeir took a round, even Matthew's entire clip of eight, he'd just keep coming. So if the vampire did show up, she'd have to deliver a round to the brain. She also knew that a .45 round made a small hole going in and a big one going out, and she hoped that would be enough. Her main fear was if she had to morph in front of Matthew in order to save him. The materializing of his childhood terrors could crush him.

Chapter Twenty-four

The couple slept sitting up, nerves attuned to the slightest rocking of the boat, which could indicate someone was boarding. They awoke, unrested, to early morning fog. Rowena fixed breakfast as Matthew stowed the weapons, shaved, and put on his work clothes for the first time in weeks: khaki-colored slacks, short-sleeved blue shirt and tie, lightweight navy blazer. Her own attire was more casual—cream-colored slacks and a sleeveless turquoise blouse—ironed the night before as she awaited a possible midnight visit.

As they ate, Matthew's phone rang. It was Dale, saying that the weather at Miller was below minimums, but should improve in a couple of hours. The team would fly in as soon as they could. Matthew told him that if he and Rowena weren't in the dye lab, where he worked, they would be in one of the three azo factory buildings. They would be empty, thanks to the summer shutdown, and available for giving Rowena a tour of the facilities.

They were waved through the front gate and passed the two workers' lots. The vat dye parking area should have been full, but no cars were there, thanks to the recent directive to stay home until further notice. Matthew wondered how the union would react to the forced shutdown, salary-wise. The azo lot was also empty, save for a sprinkling of cars, a minivan, and a white Sprinter. As they pulled into the management lot, they were met by the foreman of the azo buildings, a burly, white-haired gent in gray work shirt and trousers.

The foreman greeted them and informed Matthew that there was nothing going on today, and that he was heading for a day on the ocean with his fishing buddy. "Only people in the plant are the guys calibrating the kettles and a few instrument mechanics. They don't need me to watch 'em.

Labs are unlocked, if you want to show your lady friend around."

Matthew looked about warily, as if expecting attackers to spring from behind every perfectly-landscaped tree and bush on the grounds. His unease began to rub off on Rowena. The fog obscured the top of the water tower in the center of the complex, but it appeared to be lifting even as they watched. The effect, though, was unsettling, reminding Matthew of the fogs on the English moors.

Rowena said, "No way Al-Jubeir and Mansoor could get into the plant, is there?"

"No," Matthew replied, "not without a TRD&I decal on their car window. I'm being silly." He took her arm. "Come on, let's enjoy a Take Your Honey to Work day."

Once they entered the air-conditioned dye lab, Matthew took off his jacket and loosened his tie. He introduced Rowena to three fellow chemists who were basically sitting around doing nothing. All the samples had been tested, and no more would be coming in until the pipeline was unclogged and production resumed. He showed Rowena a series of cards with skeins of yarn threaded through holes at the bottom. Each skein was the same color, with the one on the left labeled as the standard by which the others would be judged. Four other skeins were looped through the other holes, each labeled with a different batch number. In the one Matthew held for her inspection, three skeins were labeled OK in black pencil, and the fourth was labeled with a red X. Rowena's eyes couldn't tell the difference.

Matthew directed her to the bank of windows on one side of the lab. "Truest light is from the north at nine in the morning," he told her, and she couldn't tell if he were joking or not. He held the skein card up to the windows, and Rowena strained her eyes to make out the tiniest difference in the red-marked yarn. She shook her head.

"This is what you do all day," she said.

"No, but it's part of what I do. Guess you're not impressed."

"Hey, you read dye quality, and when I was working I read manuscript quality. Not so different." She winked and said in a voice meant to be overheard, "So, Daddy, what else can you show me about where you work?" The other chemists laughed, and Matthew rolled his eyes.

After they drank some much-needed coffee with the others, Matthew walked Rowena out of the building to the silent azo manufacturing facility. "Notice the E shape of the building. The three arms are the factory floors, and the connectors in between are the labs. I'll take you to one of the labs first."

An elevator brought them to the empty second floor lab, where Matthew took two pairs of safety glasses from a drawer and handed one to Rowena. The lab had three rows of benches, with work areas on either side, and an elevated shelf in the center of each. Suspended from the high shelf were lines for water, gas, and pressurized air. On top of the shelf stood bottles of reagents, among them hydrochloric acid and fifty percent caustic soda. The bottles were covered in thin white film. "Fumes from the HCl," Matthew said. "I'm sure these bottles were cleaned before the shutdown, but the fumes can eat their way around the rubber bungs."

"I'm wondering what the technicians' lungs look like," Rowena said.

At either end of the lab were more benches, these in an alcove with a vertically sliding glass shield. "The fume hoods," said Matthew. "When you're working with oleum, or ammonium hydroxide, or chlorine gas, whatever, you do it in there."

"The nastiest of the nasty," said Rowena. "What are these rolling chests on the floor?"

"They're for crushed ice. When you're analyzing production samples from the factory, you need to keep the reaction cold to prevent decomposition, so you add ice to the solution when you titrate it. Come on, I'll show you where the ice comes from."

He took her to the third floor, to the passageway directly above the lab, where a huge open cart on wheels sat beneath a chute that hung from the ceiling. "The ice house is above us. It draws water from the stream and freezes it into cubes."

"An industrial-strength ice maker," Rowena observed.

"You pull on this chain, and ice comes down." Matthew demonstrated, and, with a rumble, a cascade of ice roared down the chute and crashed into the cart. He wheeled it to a heavy steel crusher bolted to the floor and scooped some cubes into the hopper. The crusher turned on automatically, and chips, nearly as fine as those carnival vendors used in making flavored snowballs, spewed out the bottom—where the ice chest from the lab would normally be—onto the red brick floor. "You wouldn't want to eat this ice, though," Matthew cautioned. "The river water's untreated. Come on, I'll show you the plant."

They walked to the center arm of the factory, where the filter presses stood, and then took the stairs to the second floor, where the tops of the kettles were embedded, their undersides hanging below. Matthew pointed out the agitator shafts, the pipelines that fed various liquids into the vats, the manholes for feeding solids, and the giant wrenches used to bolt the covers down. The factory's two side walls and the end wall were awning-windowed, providing some measure of ventilation.

"When the plant's operating," Matthew said, "the noise is so loud and the stink is so strong you'd have to wonder what manner of man would choose to work here. But they do. Everyone's issued a respirator mask and a set of earplugs along with their safety glasses and steel-toed shoes, but almost no one uses them."

"Is the plant on both ends the same as this one?" Rowena asked.

"Carbon copies, luv. Care to see one?"

"Not really."

"All right then."

They glanced out the windows and noticed that the top of the water tower was fully visible now and the sky was clear. From above they heard a thwack-thwack-thwack sound that signaled a helicopter, and as they watched, a bright green and white chopper descended to just above the tower. From the open hatch, men with large bundles rappelled down to the catwalk that surrounded the giant tub.

"What the hell?" said Matthew.

"I can guess," replied Rowena.

As they watched, the helicopter lifted away and the men unpacked their bundles. Great sheets of canvas came out, which they attached together and draped over the railing. They tied it to the rail with rope threaded through metal grommets. It was a sign that read, simply, POLLUTER.

"This is going to be interesting," Matthew remarked. "I think they're setting up tents or something up there. We're being occupied."

"Maybe we should hop over to the end plant after all," Rowena said. "It's closer; we'll be able to see more."

They walked past the second floor lab and onto the other factory floor, where a couple of chemical operators in dark blue coveralls were calibrating kettles at the far end near the windows. One of them pulled out a long dipstick and the other marked it. Then they put the stick on the floor, lit cigarettes, and crossed the few paces between the kettle and the windows.

Casually, Matthew and Rowena strolled toward the windows, where the men stood looking out at the activity on the tower. They stopped behind them, and Matthew remarked to their backs that the day was becoming curiouser and curiouser.

The men turned around.

For a moment, the four people froze, as if in tableau.

Rowena's attention was first piqued at the sight of Ahmed Mansoor—where had she seen him before?—and then fixed onto the hateful face of Muhammad Al-Jubeir. "You," she said, her voice a hiss.

Muhammad's eyes widened, and his upper lip lifted in a sneer. "Well, look who's here," he said, and she could hear the poison in his voice.

Matthew said, "Rowena?"

"He's the one, the last terrorist," she said. "The vampire."

From their pockets, the two men each drew a pistol.

"How do they know you're a vampire?" asked Ahmed, turning to Muhammad.

Acting purely on impulse and adrenaline, Matthew rushed at Ahmed, grabbing his pistol hand and twisting his wrist. A split second later, Rowena leaped at Muhammad, who pressed the pistol's muzzle against Rowena's chest and pulled the trigger. The blow knocked her into the air and flat on her back, driving the wind from her lungs.

Matthew was no match for Ahmed in strength. Struggling through his lingering chest pain, he managed to wrest the pistol from him, but lost his own grip. The weapon clattered onto the brick floor and skittered away. The two men grappled, each seeking a grip on the other's throat, and Matthew forced his opponent against a liquid reagent pipe that fed the nearest kettle. Ahmed's arm reached back and found the three-foot-long lug wrench. He yanked it from its hook and slammed it against Matthew's ribs. Matthew screamed as he felt bones crunch, and he tumbled to the floor. His face was contorted with the pain, and his eyes were beginning to water.

Ahmed raised the wrench over his head, intending to crush Matthew's skull. But his legs were yanked out from beneath him as Rowena scissored them between her own legs, and he fell. Rowena was on top of him in an instant, her fingernails grown into claws, when another bullet slammed into her back. She shuddered and turned her head, her face contorted in rage.

"You prick!" she cried. "That's the *second* time you shot me! Do you know how much that *burns?*"

Rowena raked the side of Ahmed's face, slashing through his cheek, exposing his teeth and gums behind the fleshy red-bordered flaps. She jumped to her feet and faced her other assailant. Muhammad, stunned, took two steps backward, then fled. Ahmed stumbled to his feet and followed him. Rowena turned toward Matthew, lying gasping on the floor. She knelt beside him, her fury temporarily replaced with fear . . . and something deeper.

"Don't let them get away," he whispered, his voice the rasp of a file against metal. "Complete the mission. You're the only one who can do it now." He took a painful breath. "I'll be right here when you get back. I'm fine. Really. Now go!"

Rowena stood and looked around, saw no trace of her assailants, but then stilled herself and called her wolf senses into play. From the far end of the floor, she could just hear two sets of footfalls, growing fainter. Her nose also picked up the lingering scents of sweat and tobacco. She ran, her speed more than a match for theirs.

Matthew, flat on his back, turned his head so his cheek rested against the floor and watched Rowena give chase. He acknowledged her preternatural speed and noted the bullet near his face that had passed through her back and out just below her collarbone. He turned his head in the other direction and saw the terrorist's other bullet lying on the floor in a small puddle of blood. Either it had gone straight through, or her body had pushed the slug out as it healed. He fought an image of the devastation she had wreaked on his attacker's face. Mere fingernails could not have done that kind of damage. He saw the pistol that rested nearby and understood why she didn't think to take it with her: Rowena was a weapon unto herself. Tears rolled from his eyes and down his temple, where they collected in the hollow of his ear. He took a deep breath—Lord, it hurt—and a slow-moving stream of blood began to flow from the side of his mouth, where it glistened against the dull redness of the bricks.

Rowena found her quarry on the third floor, running past the filter boxes to the wing connecting the factories. She first overtook Ahmed, whose ruined face was ashen where it wasn't red. One of her hands latched onto his throat and spun him around, and the other gripped his crotch. She lifted him effortlessly and carried him to the ice crusher as Muhammad looked on from a distance, backing toward a flight of stairs.

Ahmed looked over his shoulder, saw what was coming, and suddenly began shrieking, his ripped cheek fluttering and blowing blood. Rowena held him up, as if pondering whether to spare him or not. Ahmed cried and and begged her no, eyes bulging, tears raining down his face.

"I guess we'll need your fingerprints and dental records for a positive ID," she said, her voice suddenly cold and deathly calm. "So it looks like you'll have to go in feet first."

"Mercy! Have mercy!" he cried as his bladder released, darkening his coveralls.

"Mercy? Mercy? You piss-ant prick, I've got your mercy! Like the mercy I showed to your scumbag buddy Jerry. The one who beat up my boyfriend—the one I ripped apart." Mansoor shook his head and wept. "Now *you* take a turn beating up my boyfriend. Guess what that means!"

She slid Ahmed's feet into the hopper. The grinder's blades started whirling, the noise shattering the silence. The steel toes of his shoes proved no obstacle to the crusher, and the blades shredded them as easily as they did the leather. Rowena tilted him upright and watched his arms windmill as his body made its slow descent into the hopper. She looked without regret at what sprayed out the bottom.

Ahmed's soprano shrieks nearly overpowered the basso sound of the grinder; then there was just the grinder itself. With Ahmed's upper torso the only part of him still intact above the hopper, Rowena hit the emergency shutoff switch. His head was tilted back with his mouth agape, collecting falling drops of water that had condensed on the floor of the ice house high above.

The wide passageway was silent. Muhammad Al-Jubeir was gone. Rowena stood still, calming herself, forcing the adrenaline to release its hold on her nerves. The foreman they'd met in the parking lot had told them that there were instrument mechanics at work somewhere in the buildings, but they were probably occupied watching the Greenpeace protestors on the water tower. There was nothing to be heard . . . but there was something to be smelled.

Rowena's nose twitched, and she picked up the familiar scent of tobacco. She turned her head from side to side, and where she found the scent was strongest she began to run. The trail led her to the stairway and down to the hallway with its open doors to the laboratory and the chemists' offices. The scent was strong now. She turned into the first doorway and spotted the terrorist crouching at the far side of the lab, trying to hide behind the end of a workbench. He had his pistol in his hand, and it was pointed at her.

"You dumb piece of shit," she said, standing with her hands on her hips. "Haven't you learned anything by now?"

Muhammad slowly lowered the pistol and stood. "You're right," he said. "You've shown me what you are, and now I know how you survived the explosion at your work. Tell me: did Daciana turn you, too?"

Rowena was brought up short. "Daciana? Daciana Moceanu?"

He snorted a laugh. "She turned me as well, centuries ago." His tone suggested that they might have something in common, that they might even be colleagues of a sort.

Her response quelled the notion. "Well, I hope you're not sitting by the phone waiting for her call, because the bitch is dead. No, she's not the one who turned me; in fact, she nearly killed me. But some friends of mine took her out, and then I helped them do to her what I just did to your buddy upstairs. With great pleasure, I might add. Both times."

"Daciana . . . destroyed?"

"Destroyed," came a male voice from behind her.

Rowena recognized the voice and didn't even turn around. "About time you guys got here. Listen, Matthew's lying on the second floor of the factory next door. The end unit, closest to the water tower. He's broken a couple of ribs, but he says he's all right—"

"Joe's with him now," said Claire, who had entered through the doorway at the opposite end of the lab.

Muhammad turned his head to see a tall, strikingly beautiful blonde staring at him. The same one he had seen in Boston and at the boatyard. Blocking his only escape route.

Dale placed a hand on Rowena's shoulder and stood beside her, eyes fixed on the man once referred to as the Persian. "Our terrorist, I presume."

Muhammad wasn't sure if the soldier type with the crew-cut hair was talking to him or the woman. He kept silent, eyes darting to his left, where the blonde stood statue still, her facial expression undecipherable.

Dale said, "Oke City, 1995, right?" No response. "I'm talking to you." His voice was soft, but his eyes were not. Muhammad nodded slowly. "You were the mastermind?"

Who are these people? Do they know who—what—they are dealing with? He, Muhammad Al-Jubeir, was an immortal. He could slash their throats and consume them . . . if he could convince the black one to join forces with him. Then he could deal with her later. She might even supply him some sport first.

The blond woman spoke: "The gentleman asked you a question. You might want to give him an answer. Waiting makes him angry."

"Are . . . would you be the *friends* who destroyed Daciana?"

"We would be they," said the blonde. "Would you like to experience how we did it? If not, then answer the man's question. Were you the person who planned the Oklahoma City bombing? It's important that you tell the truth."

Muhammad looked from one face to the others. They might have overpowered his lover, simply through force of numbers. The vampire's strength lay in its power to seduce and surprise. "Might I suggest . . . an alliance?" he said. His voice, for the first time that he could remember, was unsteady.

"I won't ask you again," said the man, his voice threatening now.

"All right, yes, for what it is worth I planned the attack, right down to finding an American to take responsibility. That part wasn't easy, let me assure you. I canvassed many bars, met and spoke with scores of disgruntled men, until I found Timothy. His anger against his government was profound; he was perfect. And it was I who sent Terry to Indonesia to learn bomb making." He paused, remembering. "With both men, it was necessary to give them an irresistible incentive. So I revealed my true self to them and promised to give them immortality in return for their cooperation. I regularly drank small amounts of their blood and told them that after their death they would resurrect as vampires. Nonsense, of course, I never shared my own blood with them. But they had heard enough stories and seen enough movies to make them believe it."

"Which is why," Dale said, "that McVeigh went stoically to his execution."

"Also why," Al-Jubeir said, "to this day Terry sits in a cell anticipating his own death and rebirth." He smirked, confidence returning. "Back to the subject, our direction from Saddam was to leave none of his fingerprints on the Oklahoma City operation. He didn't want to precipitate another American invasion, you see."

Rowena said, "So you got away with it. Why didn't you just go back to Iraq? Why did you stay in America? And why did you decide to reactivate after all those years of being safely underground?"

"You are obviously young and recently turned. So much is new to you. But I tell you, when one has been alive for centuries, one looks forward to finding new and interesting ways . . . to amuse oneself."

"Daciana's words exactly," Claire said. "Before we killed her." She held up her cell phone and pointed it at Muhammad. "Smile for the birdie," she said, and snapped a series of photos. "Huh. Your friend upstairs didn't smile either, but at least he had an excuse." She turned to Dale. "Do we need to take back any more proof that we found him?"

"No." He removed a small recorder from his pocket and checked a digital readout. One of the fingers on the hand he had placed on Rowena's shoulder wore a ring that was in fact a wireless microphone. "We have all we need."

Dale turned Rowena to face him. "He's all yours. We'll see you on the factory floor. Matthew's in good hands, but you might not want to take too long."

Claire said to Dale, "What about the guy in the ice crusher?"

"Accidents happen. People play with things they shouldn't. Bloody shame, wouldn't you say?"

They left Rowena facing the clearly confused Muhammad. He had to admit that despite her ethnicity and his deep prejudice, she was a strikingly beautiful woman, and seeing her face and clothes spattered with blood made her look even more appealing. *But why would they leave her alone with me? One on one, she was outmatched.*

What was the woman doing now? Why was she taking off her clothes?

He watched her strip and stand stark naked before him, her clothes draped over a lab bench, her only attire her safety glasses and the gold chain around her neck, a gossamer-thin chain with a star-shaped ornament at the bottom. As he watched, she reached for a pegboard beside the fume hood and pulled down a length of Nalgene tubing.

"You seek to bind me?" Muhammad asked, some of the taunt returning to his voice. "With that?"

"Watch me," Rowena said, and as his face registered shock at what he was seeing, seeing for the first time in all the centuries of his existence, the woman put her safety glasses on the lab bench and morphed fully into the form of a jet black wolf. She pounced upon him before he could resist and clamped her jaws around his right upper arm. She crunched down hard, and his bone splintered. He shouted out his pain, and cried again when she did the same to his left arm. Her weight drove him to the floor. She slavered over him as he lay on the cold tiles, her breath heating his face. But his death would not come so fast, so easy. The part of her that was still human thought of Bentley, of the staff at Jones Publishing, all dead because of him; thought of Matthew, whom Al-Jubeir would have killed in his blind quest to destroy her; Matthew, whom she saw as a man she would gladly marry, if he'd have her, knowing what she was.

She would have to tell him everything, beginning with the fact that she would not be alive today had she not sought out Claire and begged to be turned. She would ask, no, beg his forgiveness for not having been up front with him. She would tell him she would do anything to restore his trust.

Her thoughts went to the bombed-out Murrah Building: of the nearly two hundred victims of that bombing; of the scores of innocent children—like her own child, destroyed by the vilest of creatures: the same one who had turned this monster, this trembling and totally vulnerable vampire whose face was now slick with the drool from her own jaws. She drew her black lips back and snarled, exposing yellow, tusk-like fangs. Muhammad whimpered like a terrified baby, too petrified to struggle.

Rowena returned to human form, and before Muhammad could register relief she tied his broken arms behind him. She kneeled over him and looked down at his contorted face. His jaw opened and his fangs fell into place. She grinned and exposed her own fangs before retracting them. "Surprise," she said. "I've one-upped you. And I've also bitten through both your humerus bones—which I doubt you find very humorous at all." She laughed without mirth. "Ah, good to know I'm still the consummate wordsmith. Muhammad, my pet—oh, I'm sorry, *professor*—we know you expect your arms to heal and then you'll be able to break the tubing. But I don't think you'll have the time. You may consider my voice to be the voice of all of your victims, crying for vengeance. By the way, it pleases me no end to tell you I not only killed your friend upstairs but also your buddy Jerry, from the marina. Slowly, too. I had more time then. And while he was still alive, I crushed his skull, and sucked out his brain." She grinned sardonically. "Tastes like chicken."

Rowena wasn't done. She put her bloody clothes back on, lifted the terrorist without effort, and slung him over her shoulder. She took the stairs to the second floor of the middle factory and looked at the labeling on the lines to different kettles. She found the one she wanted, dropped

Muhammad to the floor, and with the lug wrench began unscrewing the nuts to the hinged manhole cover.

As she lifted the lid, she heard movement behind her. The vampire was on his feet, his arms struggling against the tubing that bound him. He threw himself against her, knocking her back against the kettle's rim. She drove a foot into his crotch, and as he doubled forward, she pushed him headfirst into the opening. As his body thumped against the liner and slid to the bottom of the kettle, she called down, "Just like Hansel and Gretel, yes? Goodbye, you wicked witch sonofabitch."

Able to use only his feet, Muhammad attempted to scramble up the smooth side of the kettle as Rowena turned the spigot that opened the line labeled OLEUM. She heard his screams as the fuming acid flowed into the kettle, splashed onto him, burned through his coveralls, and began corroding his lower legs. The fumes made the air unbreathable, attacking the vampire's lungs, turning the moisture within into sulfuric acid. The oleum ate through his boots, and Muhammad Al-Jubeir began decomposing, the flesh of his feet first, and then the bones, until he had no feet left and fell backwards into the growing puddle. His horrific screams echoed inside the kettle's walls. They would have sounded pitiful, were there pity left in his avenger to be had.

Rowena kept the line open, standing aside to avoid inhaling the fumes that escaped, until shortly after the vampire's screams were stilled. Then she closed the lid and screwed the nuts back onto their lugs. "Help me, I'm melting," she mimicked when she was done, amused that she had just combined two children's stories into one happy ending.

Suddenly: "Matthew!" she cried, and bolted from the middle factory and ran to the end one, where she had left Matthew lying on the floor. She arrived to find Dale and Claire standing by him and Joe kneeling by his side, bending over him. Matthew's eyes were closed. Blood from his mouth lay in a puddle around his head. All eyes turned toward Rowena.

"He's almost gone," Joe said, and Rowena dropped to her knees beside him. She leaned over Matthew, her tears falling onto his face. He took a halting breath and gasped at the pain.

Rowena turned briefly to face Joe, and he shook his head, mouthing the words, "I'm sorry."

Matthew's fingers closed around Rowena's wrist, and his eyes struggled open into slits. He licked his lips and took another agonizing breath. With tears pooling and his voice a rattle, he croaked, "Thank you for not telling me."

Then he closed his eyes and his fingers loosed their grip.

"No!" Rowena sobbed, and then turned her head up to Claire and Dale. Their expressions were deliberately impassive, but their eyes bored into hers. Without uttering a word, they told her that she was about to make the most profound decision of her life.

Epilogue: Rowena Parr

Two years have passed since that day, and here I sit in my home office in Boston, typing, recalling loving memories of my associates at Jones Publishing as well as those I've cared for the most, all of whom were brutally taken from me. My dearest friends of the past few years are scattered to the winds now, and—but I'm getting ahead of myself.

At the Toms River plant that day, Dale had the foresight to purge the kettle of oleum and what was left, if anything, of the last terrorist. It went to the effluent treatment facility and from there was discharged, as a solution carrying a pH of 7.0 or thereabouts, into the stream that fed the river. Muhammad Al-Jubeir had been neutralized—in every way.

Subsequent to the Greenpeace occupation, the French company that owned the plant, citing *the ungrateful Americans*—and galled, if you'll pardon the pun—by the distasteful discovery of half a body in the ice crusher and its attendant rather unpleasant publicity—closed up shop and moved its facility to China.

Joe was now officially in on my being a metamorph—how could he not be—but all agreed that, much as they detested deception, it would be best to keep that knowledge from Lauren, for security reasons—both theirs and my own. Shortly after he, Dale, and Claire returned to Camp David with their official report—more on that later—she reinforced the information that those *upstairs* had been pleased with the discovery and termination of the final three Oklahoma City terrorists. They were also pleased to close the book on what they were calling the Allahu Akbar terror attacks of 2009. Lauren hoped that the news would give her and the unit a measure of job security.

It was not to be.

The ties with the FBI and Homeland Security, and the other agencies with whom the team had enjoyed a professional rapport, were unraveling fast, and the team began anticipating the inevitable.

This past year, Osama bin Laden and Anwar Al-Awlaki were killed, and the powers that be made it official: the unit was now superfluous. No one was more furious than Lauren Bachmann—who had summarily been promoted to captain, the equivalent of full bird colonel in the other services—and reassigned as an aide to the Chief of Naval Operations in Washington. To her, this was a double affront, as she hated politics, and working for the CNO would be all politics all the time.

Between leaving her own duty station and reporting to the new one, she took leave to see her former crush, the hunting and fishing guide in Bozeman, Montana, and from what I'm told things are progressing smoothly and very promisingly. She's just put in for her retirement from the Navy.

My dear friends Claire and Dale Keegan have also moved to Bozeman. Dale teaches at the local middle school and moonlights evenings, teaching history at Montana State, and Claire has hooked up with Lauren's boyfriend's wilderness guide outfit. She's earned her instrument rating and commercial pilot's license and flies clients from Gallatin Field into the bush for fishing, hunting, and camping excursions. She's so beautiful that the company wanted to put her photograph on all its advertising brochures, but she told them not a chance. Her only contribution to the sales effort would be to rewrite the company's amateurish ad copy. Claire still works hard at not correcting other people's grammar when they speak, but it hasn't been easy for her. I'm smiling as I write this.

I don't need to tell you how Dale and Claire spend their free time. There's lots of room and lots of game in Big Sky country.

Lauren herself will move to Bozeman as soon as her retirement papers go through.

Jomo Kenyatta White, the unit's forensics specialist, has returned to Philadelphia, and he keeps in touch now and then. Since the passing of Joe Frazier this year, he's affiliated himself with the boxer's gym and attends all the prizefights as ring physician. He also joined a family medical practice, and reports he's busier—and happier—than he's ever been. He recently married one of his associates, and they're looking forward to a little *family practice* of their own. He doesn't miss his under-the-radar government work at all. And he doesn't call his hometown Filthydelphia anymore.

I think back to that horrific day on the factory floor, and the enormity of what I did still occasionally wakes me up at night. All of Matthew's childhood traumas had become manifested in me, the woman he had grown to love; but with his dying breath, he had acknowledged me as a counterfeit. As a monster.

I desperately wanted to save him. But to do that I would have to turn him into a monster like myself. I was suddenly ashamed of who—of what—I was.

Claire and Dale's expressionless faces made it clear that the *do it or don't* decision would be mine alone. Poor Joe had no idea what was transpiring.

If I did do what I so desperately wanted, Matthew would live forever, and probably hate me every minute.

If I didn't, he would surely die.

Could I live with myself if I let Matthew go?

Even though by saving him I could ultimately lose him?

But I had already been widowed once; and I had suffered my dear sweet baby's being torn from me. Both of them destroyed by the real monster, the one named Daciana Moceanu.

And now I stood to lose yet one more love, due to the machinations of another, an abomination turned by Daciana herself.

The mind works at the speed of light. All these thoughts tumbled through my mind in a nanosecond, and as his heart gave one last, barely perceptible pulse, I lowered my fangs and plunged them into the side of Matthew's neck.

It turned out as I'd feared.

While he was still unconscious, we spirited Matthew's body to the van, weaving through the factory building to avoid being seen. When we got to the van, we placed him in the back and I drove to Stump Creek with Claire riding shotgun and the guys following us in the rental car.

Paul and Cindy were both at work, and the yard was empty. We washed Matthew down in the shower, and Dale and Joe carried him to the boat and laid him on the master berth as I took a long, meditative shower, until Claire came back from the boat with a fresh set of clothes.

Matthew knew what had happened the moment he opened his eyes and looked into mine. "No," he said. That was it. His voice was flat, his expression cold.

The others leaned their backs to the bulkhead, bodies tensed and ready to act if needed.

My eyes began to tear for the second time that day. "Matthew," I whispered.

"What have you done to me?"

"Matthew, you didn't deserve to die. I couldn't let you."

His lips parted, and I could see his tongue exploring the roof of his mouth.

"I'm like ... like you, now, aren't I? And Dale and Claire? You've turned me into something I've feared and loathed all my life."

I nodded.

"Did you do it for me ... or for yourself?"

"Both," I admitted.

"I hate you," he muttered.

My shoulders shook and tears spilled onto his face.

"But I love you, too."

Privately, I took heart from Arthur Ford's words: *There is nothing so strange ...*

When Dale, Claire, and Joe returned to Camp David without Matthew, they told Lauren that he was resigning from the team and would send a formal letter when he was on his feet again. They told her he had been grievously injured in the killing of the terrorists and, in his words, enough was enough.

Meanwhile, after the plant moved its operation to China, Matthew was officially out of a job. We spent the fall months in the Pine Barrens, where I trained him as Claire had trained me. There were plenty of small game and deer to hunt together, and once he overcame his initial distaste of killing—and that, fellow Anglophiles, would be classic British understatement—he adapted. When the weather turned to fall, I suggested we pilot *Semper Fidelis* to a marina in Boston, put it on a cradle for the winter, and settle in to my home for a long winter's nap.

Paul drove Matthew's van to Boston, and Cindy followed in her Bug. They stayed with us for a weekend and wouldn't leave before extracting a promise from us to motor over to Block Island and spend a week with them on their next summer vacation. Which we did.

We're considering taking *Semper Fi* on what boaters call The Loop in the spring: down the Inland Waterway, around Florida, up the Mississippi, across a couple of Great Lakes, down the Erie Canal to the Hudson River, and once past New York Harbor swing north to Boston—*without* stopping for an overnight at Horseshit Cove.

Neither of us has a job, but neither of us is destitute either. Plus, we're in the prime of health—another Brit understatement. Technically, I'm thirty-nine years old, but I was two years younger when Claire made me immortal, and I'll never be a day older; I'll always look like a woman in her prime.

And Matthew will always look like the hunk he is.

We've visited Claire and Dale in Bozeman and found we really like the area. They even suggested that we move out there and grow not-older together. But then, there's Ray Jones's house, my home now, with its priceless H. Hargrove paintings and library of first editions, not to mention my own office, festooned with framed photographs of Matthew and me and the boat, and little Digit, and the good folks at Solomons Island, and Paul and Cindy at Stump Creek Slipways.

Could I move all that? The physical stuff, yes; all the good memories? That might be harder.

But then, there are bad memories too.

Writing is cathartic, and it tends to give one perspective. I have to admit that Daciana Moceanu and Muhammad Al-Jubeir did have one thing right: when one is immortal, one looks to find new ways to amuse oneself. For our purposes, I'd change *amuse* to *fulfill*. In positive ways, of course. Why not do it all?

After all, we have all the time in the world.

Boston, Massachusetts
New Year's Day, 2012

Author's Note

Readers with an interest in 19th-century artist Walter Richard Sickert are invited to read Patricia Cornwell's *Portrait of a Killer: Jack the Ripper—Case Closed* (Putnam, 2002).

The Middle Eastern link to the Oklahoma City Bombing has been compellingly documented, after nine years of investigation, by reporter Jayna Davis in her book *The Third Terrorist* (WND Books, 2004).

The story of Claire Delaney, which details how she herself became a metamorph and formed a lasting bond with Rowena Parr, is told in *The Pentacle Pendant* (JournalStone, 2011).

TURN THE PAGE FOR A PREVIEW OF *HEMOPHAGE*
The new paranormal thriller by Stephen M. DeBock

Hemophage
by Stephen M. DeBock

Hilton Harrisburg Hotel
Harrisburg, Pennsylvania
Saturday night

"So you're in town for what, a convention? A conference?" The young woman sitting at the bar waited for an answer as she sipped a gin and tonic. Her smile was open and inviting, which indicated to the man that she could be either a high-priced escort or a woman alone looking for companionship. Whichever, it made no difference to him, and she surely did look fine.

"Neither, lovely lady," he said. "My colleague and I were at a business conference in New York, and we decided to take a detour on our way back home to Charleston."

"I could tell when you said hello that you were from the South," she teased. "You do know that *damn* and *Yankee* are two words, right?"

He shook his head and grinned. "Someday you Yankees will learn how to talk right. I'm Bobby Justis, by the way." He held out his hand and she took it. Her hand was warm, which he wouldn't have expected, as it had been wrapped around the icy glass. "And?" he said, waiting. "You are—?"

"Naomi. Just Naomi, no last name if you please. I know, mysterious and melodramatic, but bear with me for now." Her chestnut-brown eyes, a perfect match color-wise for her loose, below-the-shoulder-length hair, stared into his watery blue ones over the lip of her glass. "Now answer me this. Unless my geography's way off, Charleston's a straight run down the coast from New York. What made you take a dogleg to central Pennsylvania?"

"Well, Miss Naomi, Jason and I are Civil War re-enactors back home, and we've decided to come by to pay our respects to the Southern dead."

"In Harrisburg? The War didn't actually get this far north, did it?"

"Matter of fact, no. Biggest recruit depot for you Yankees was here, though. Camp Curtin, it was called." The woman raised her eyebrows, as if to say she hadn't known that. Bobby continued: "The Confederate forces came close, though, but they were waylaid a bit south of here, a little town called Gettysburg. Maybe you've heard of it?"

She picked up on his banter. "Gettysburg. Wasn't that where President Lincoln kept a summer home?"

He tilted his head and frowned. "What are you talking about?"

"Oh, come on, Bobby, your being a Civil War buff and all, you must be aware that the President had an address in Gettysburg?" She winked.

He laughed, perhaps a little too loudly and long, but the woman seemed to appreciate it. She lowered her eyes and lifted them again as she leaned forward and spoke in a confidential tone. "I'm just passing through myself. Traveling with my son. He's upstairs, sound asleep I assume; the hotel has a sitter keeping him company. And—all right, I don't want to tell you my last name because I'm running away—not from the police, an abusive husband. I won't tell you where I'm running from, and I won't tell you where I'm running to. I hope you can understand, and I'm sorry if you can't."

"Don't be sorry," said Bobby. "It's all right." He paused. "You know, most abused women are afraid to leave their husbands, leastways that's what I'm told."

"You're not wrong. But after the third beating I wised up. Rather than going to the police, I contacted . . . someone . . . to make some false ID cards for me. Then one day while my husband was at work I emptied our joint bank accounts, bought a used car, and hit the road."

"Wow. That's ballsy. So how old's your boy?"

She took a breath before answering. "He's four."

He ordered another drink for each of them, and after more conversation, during which he took pains to make himself sound empathetic, Bobby placed his hand over

Naomi's as she rested it on the bar. She didn't draw it away; instead, she looked into his eyes and nodded.

"I have to check up on my little man," she said. "But I'd like to continue our discussion. My suite's on the top floor. Two bedrooms," she added. "Why don't you bring something bubbly for us to drink. Just give me a half hour alone to get freshened up, okay, Bobby?"

When the woman opened her door exactly thirty minutes later, Bobby saw she was wearing a hotel bathrobe, open just enough to reveal something filmy and white beneath. Her feet were bare, and her makeup had been skillfully reapplied. Her breath smelled of peppermint. Bobby's face was flush as he walked inside, carrying a bottle and two flutes.

"Champagne, as the lady requested," he said.

Naomi placed the bottle in a freshly-filled ice bucket and whispered, "Be very quiet, my son's asleep in the other room."

She took his hand and led him into her bedroom, where she had turned down the covers to expose crisp cotton sheets. "Why don't you strip down and climb into bed, and while you're doing that I'll take care of the bubbly."

Bobby was fumbling with his tie as she glided out of the room.

Lying between the sheets and grinning at the tent he'd formed halfway down, Bobby heard the pop of the cork, and moments later the woman entered carrying two filled flutes. She offered him one and they toasted, draining their glasses. A few moments later, he was unconscious, his tent collapsed.

Naomi wiped her flute clean of prints and any DNA traces at the lip. She pulled back the top sheet and considered Bobby's pudgy body as he lay spread-eagled in the center of the bed. She knelt next to him and lowered her face toward the inside of his thigh.

She opened her mouth. Her lower jaw extended downward, and downward, farther than a normal human jawbone would allow. From the roof of her mouth, a pair of curved fangs swung down, like those of a pit viper, and she pressed them against his flesh. Blood flowed freely into her mouth, and she sucked it in, barely missing a drop. It was blissful, this blood, better than any poor animal's, better than the drug-addled derelicts she'd drained during her relocation from her New Jersey home to the Harrisburg area, known to locals as Pennsyltucky. She drank and drank, growing nearly drunk on the blood.

She grew aware of company when a tiny hand tapped her on the shoulder.

"Don't be a pig, Mom," said a child's voice. "You're not the only one dying of thirst here."

"Sorry," she said with resignation as she lifted the boy onto the bed. "Don't take too much, now," she admonished. "We don't want to kill him."

"Duh. Look who's talking," he said, looking down at the punctures in Bobby's thigh. He shook his head at the man's limp phallus. "When are you going to learn to go for the throat like they do in the movies, or at least the wrist?" he demanded. "It makes me skeev, sucking so close to a guy's willie, I told you that how many times."

"And as I've told you before, how many times over how many years—"

"I know, I know. Now let me be for awhile."

The little boy closed his eyes as he lowered his lips to the man's thigh. He kept them closed as he drank.

Next morning, Bobby awoke in the bed, fully dressed except for his shoes, and suffering a splitting headache. He sat up slowly and swung his legs over the edge of the bed. He noted a few spots of blood on the sheets and wondered if the woman had been having her period. *Wait a minute,* he thought. *What the hell's going on here? What happened last night?*

Looking about, he saw that all trace of the woman's presence in the room was gone. He stood ... and nearly fell over. "Whoa, vertigo," he said. "What's up with that?" He stumbled shakily into the sitting room and from there to the second bedroom, where the baby would be. Nothing. "Well, good morning and goodbye," he muttered, feeling every bit the fool. He shuffled back to the bedroom and put on his shoes, visited the bathroom and splashed water on his face, then left, noting the Do Not Disturb sign on the doorknob in the hall.

In the first floor restaurant known as Raspberries, Bob-by saw his colleague alone at a table, working on a stack of pancakes. He walked unsteadily toward him and braced himself on the table as he fell into a seat opposite. He shook his head as if to clear it. "Morning, Jason," he mumbled.

"What happened to you?" Jason asked. "You're white as a sheet."

Bobby scratched an itch on the inside of his thigh. "See, I met this woman at the bar last night."

"Uh huh."

"Beautiful she was. And she invited me up to her room."

"Well, good for you. But you might want to keep your voice down. Some folks at the other tables are looking."

Others, in fact, were looking, in particular one slim, very attractive brunette dressed in a long-sleeved light gray blouse and black slacks, who stared with coal-colored eyes over the rim of a coffee cup. A hint of a smile played about her lips. Her companion, a burly Mediterranean type sport-ing a day's growth of stubble and greased, slicked back hair, studied Bobby from the corners of his hooded eyes. Appearance-wise, they made an unlikely-looking couple.

"Oops, sorry." Bobby leaned forward, bracing himself on his elbows. He shook his head again and blinked his eyes before continuing. "I'm tellin' you, she was hotter'n my granddaddy's pit barbecue."

Jason grinned. "And that's hot."

"Thing is, though, nothin' happened. At least I don't think it did." He scratched the itch in his thigh and sat back in his chair as the waitress took his order for juice, coffee, three eggs over easy, ham, grits, and a buttered biscuit. Plus a couple aspirin and a tall glass of water. "Thing is," he said when they were alone again, "last thing I remember we were drinking champagne, and—oh, shit. She drugged me, didn't she?"

"Checked your wallet lately, young stud?"

"Oh no." Bobby reached into his pocket, pulled out his wallet, and sighed in relief. "Well, my credit cards are all there," he said with a grin. "Uh. Wait a minute. Wait. A. Minute."

"What's up?"

Bobby was staring into the bill compartment. "Son of a bitch."

"Don't tell me."

"I had six hundred-dollar bills in my wallet when we checked in. There's only one there now."

Jason chuckled. "Hey, at least she left you something. Damn white of her, you ask me, Bobby boy."

The water and aspirin arrived, and Bobby gulped the pills down. "My stomach's empty, my head's empty, and now my wallet's empty too," he moaned. "I am so screwed." He paused. "Jason, after breakfast I'm going back to our room, pack my suitcase, and we're going to blow this place. I never want to see this damn Yankee town again."

The dark-haired woman sitting with her swarthy companion nearby paid their bill. They walked out of the room, she sparing a sideways glance at the two men as they left.

Declan Mulligan, principal of Derry Township High School in Hershey, arrived in his office early every morning to devote an hour or so of uninterrupted time to reading the Harrisburg *Patriot-News*. Mulligan was fifty-two, happily married, with two children in college. Refusing to become jaded after two decades in administration, he still genuinely cared for the students in his charge and deeply respected the staff who guided their learning.

Mulligan sat at his desk, Monday's newspaper spread before him, and shook his head sadly at the story under the banner headline. Harrisburg, like most cities, had its share of crime, but this one was particularly heinous.

Movement in the hall caught his eye. He looked up and saw the guidance counselor walk down the hall on the way to her office. She glanced in, smiled, and said good morning as she passed. Mulligan thought highly of the relatively new counselor. She was not only well credentialed; she was also doubtless the object of many a schoolboy's adolescent fantasies. He surmised that she was one reason so many boys joined the drama club, where she would assist the director—Dr. Mulligan himself—with rehearsals. A single mother, if she couldn't find a sitter she would often bring her preschool-age son to rehearsals with her. The little boy had an uncanny manner about him that charmed the girls, many of whom said they wished they could take him home with them.

The lady's attractiveness brought her no preferential treatment from the principal. Their professional relationship was strictly that. As after-school drama club advisors, however, they were more like siblings. There was never a breath of scandal about their friendship, nor was there any reason for one.

Declan Mulligan stood, newspaper in hand, and walked to the counselor's office. Auditions for *The King and I* were to begin today after school, and he wanted to confirm that she would be available. She said of course she would.

Then she noticed the headline on the folded newspaper in his hand. "What's that about?" she asked. He passed her the paper and she spread it out on her desk.

It could have been a scene from a horror film, the article began. *But this was worse, because it was real. Jason McElroy and Bobby Justis, both 35, of Charleston, South Carolina, were found dead yesterday in their room at the Hilton Hotel here. Their throats had been slashed and their bodies drained of blood...*

The young woman stopped reading. She placed her palms over the article and looked straight ahead, her expression blank. The color began draining from her face.

Mulligan leaned forward and stared into her suddenly vacant eyes. "Good God, Naomi, what is it? You look like you've seen a ghost."

About the Author

Stephen M. DeBock is a Marine Corps veteran who served in the Presidential Honor Guard during the Eisenhower and Kennedy administrations. A private pilot and former liveaboard boater, his non-fiction has appeared in *American Heritage, AOPA Pilot Online,* and *Living Aboard* magazines. He wrote the text for a coffee-table book titled *The Art of H. Hargrove* and writes the artist's quarterly fan newsletter.

His novel, *The Pentacle Pendant,* in which a contemporary werewolf becomes a one-woman star chamber, is currently available in hard cover, eBook, and trade paperback. Two of his e-publications from Gypsy Shadow have been listed among the top horror stories of their respective years.

Stephen and his wife Joy live in Hershey, Pennsylvania.

FACEBOOK
https://www.facebook.com/pages/Stephen-M-DeBock/295034173887998

CPSIA information can be obtained
at www.ICGtesting.com
Printed in the USA
BVOW03s1429150917
494969BV00001B/2/P